"I WAS BORN OF THAT NEAR CATASTROPHE."

"I haven't forgotten. And that is the single mitigating factor in this entire sordid equation. And the reason I agreed to make the effort."

"But you did not succeed?"

"In convincing her to abandon her quest to destroy herself? No."

"You told her she would die."

"I did."

"And she didn't believe you?"

"She's mortal. It's not as if it was a question of *if*, only *when*. But I will admit that I wouldn't have minded seeing her die better. I would have spared her the pain of being forced to turn against her own kind in favor of a peaceful passing, years hence, surrounded by all those who loved her. But it's not as if that would have changed anything. You're so young, darling. When you've got a few more billion years under your belt, you'll realize that the extra time seeing reason might have granted her will still pass in the blink of one of your precious eyes. That's one of many reasons it's best to avoid becoming too attached to these creatures."

STAR TREK VOYAGER®
THE ETERNAL TIDE

KIRSTEN BEYER

Based on *Star Trek*®
created by Gene Roddenberry
and
Star Trek: Voyager
created by Rick Berman & Michael Piller
& Jeri Taylor

POCKET BOOKS
New York   London   Toronto   Sydney   New Delhi

Pocket Books
A Division of Simon & Schuster, Inc.
1230 Avenue of the Americas
New York, NY 10020

This book is a work of fiction. Names, characters, places, and incidents either are products of the author's imagination or are used fictitiously. Any resemblance to actual events or locales or persons, living or dead, is entirely coincidental.

™, ® and © 2012 by CBS Studios Inc. STAR TREK and related marks are trademarks of CBS Studios Inc. All Rights Reserved.

This book is published by Pocket Books, a division of Simon & Schuster, Inc., under exclusive license from CBS Studios Inc.

All rights reserved, including the right to reproduce this book or portions thereof in any form whatsoever. For information, address Pocket Books Subsidiary Rights Department, 1230 Avenue of the Americas, New York, NY 10020.

"Calmly We Walk Through This April's Day" by Delmore Schwartz, from *Selected Poems,* copyright © 1959 by Delmore Schwartz. Reprinted by permission of New Directions Publishing Corp.

First Pocket Books paperback edition September 2012

POCKET and colophon are registered trademarks of Simon & Schuster, Inc.

For information about special discounts for bulk purchases, please contact Simon & Schuster Special Sales at 1-866-506-1949 or business@simonandschuster.com.

The Simon & Schuster Speakers Bureau can bring authors to your live event. For more information or to book an event, contact the Simon & Schuster Speakers Bureau at 1-866-248-3049 or visit our website at www.simonspeakers.com.

Manufactured in the United States of America

10 9 8 7 6 5

ISBN 978-1-4516-6818-6
ISBN 978-1-4516-7324-1 (ebook)

For Heather Jarman . . .

This is long overdue.

What am I now that I was then?
May memory restore again and again
The smallest color of the smallest day:
Time is the school in which we learn,
Time is the fire in which we burn.

—Delmore Schwartz

HISTORIAN'S NOTE

Portions of *The Eternal Tide* take place outside normal time as we experience it. The rest takes place immediately following the events of *Star Trek Voyager: Children of the Storm*, August and September 2381.

Just go with it.

Prologue

"Her death is a fixed point in time."

"I don't understand."

"Me neither."

"Q!"

"Spare me the attitude. I'm just telling you what I know."

"But that's impossible."

"I know."

"No individual human's death can possibly be a fixed point in time."

"Not usually."

"Q was very specific about that in his Beyond Temporal Mechanics course."

"I still can't believe you stuck it out in that sanctimonious windbag's course for the entire term. Did you even get a passing grade?"

"I passed with distinction, thank you very much. And those of us who weren't the first and only child born of two Q and created specifically to save the Continuum didn't have much of a choice in our course requirements."

"You were born of two Q."

"They had given up being Q before they had me."

"A minor point, I would have thought, considering how you turned out."

"Don't think I didn't ask my adviser when I found out *you* didn't even have to audit Beyond Temporal Mechanics. Q insisted that my dubious parentage actually made it mandatory that I complete several prerequisites most Q don't even have to endure."

"Poor Q."

"Don't call me that."

"It's your name."

"The rest of them can call me what they like but when it's just you and me . . ."

"Fine. Poor *Amanda*."

"Thank you, *Junior*."

"Don't ever . . . oh, never mind. I thought you would understand, but obviously . . ."

"No, I'm really curious. Her death is a fixed point in time. Meaning what?"

"In every conceivable timeline where she exists, she dies at roughly the same moment."

"Under the same circumstances?"

"For the most part."

"That sounds ominous."

"I know. There's actually a timeline where the evolved cube never makes it to the Alpha Quadrant and in that one she slips getting out of her bathtub and accidentally drowns."

"Now you're just teasing me."

"I'm not. It's like the multiverse has it in for her in a way I was always taught wasn't possible."

"Fixed points in time are big things, not small ones. They don't correlate to any individual mortal being's existence. All of the major worldwide wars on any planet, for example. Massive interstellar conflicts. The flashpoint in any given timeline may be slightly different, but with or without any individual's actions or lack thereof, fixed points in time occur anyway. They are part of the larger fabric of space-time, the culmination of energies and events that transcend what we normally think of as cause and effect."

"Thank you for the refresher course, but the concept is pretty much right there in the name: *fixed point in time*."

"What I'm saying is, there has never been an individual

mortal's death, let alone a *human's* death, that qualified as a fixed point in time."

"And yet, hers is."

"Wow."

"And it gets worse."

"How?"

"I'm pretty sure it wasn't always this way."

"But if it wasn't always this way, then that would mean there was a timeline where she didn't die, and if that was the case, you couldn't call her death a fixed point in time."

"What I'm saying is that *now* her death is a fixed point in time, but for most of my existence, I don't think that was the case."

"And how could you possibly know that?"

"I don't. It's just . . . a feeling."

"Did you ask your father about this?"

"Many times."

"And?"

"And he told me to leave it alone. Sometimes things happen for reasons that are beyond our control and we are required to accept them."

"Your *father* said that."

"I know. Doesn't exactly sound like him, does it?"

"Your father? The Q who was kicked out of the Continuum for grossly abusing his powers how many times?"

"Yeah, but they always ask him to come back, don't they?"

"Wait . . . we're Q, aren't we? The last time I checked we weren't *required* to accept anything. That's part of the whole omnipotent thing, isn't it?"

"He assured me that to intervene in any way in a fixed point in time such as this would inject so much chaos into the multiverse that even the entire Continuum might not be able to contain it."

"Wow."

"I know."

"So, what are you going to do about it?"

"I don't know. But I have to find out exactly how this happened, how this one human's death became so incredibly important to the multiverse that it essentially broke its own rules to bring her death about."

"You're doing it again."

"Doing what?"

"Anthropomorphizing the multiverse, something that cannot, by its very nature, be understood in such limited terms."

"Yeah, I had to take Beyond Existential Constructs too, but I didn't find the argument terribly compelling then and I'm even less convinced now. If anything, her death is concrete evidence that sometimes the multiverse can be incredibly petty and small-minded."

"Why are you taking this so personally?"

"She's my godmother."

"You've met her all of twice."

"She deserved better."

"I agree. But there's nothing you can do. Where would you even look for evidence of a reality that by your own argument can't exist?"

"I don't know."

"Oh, my gosh."

"What?"

"It couldn't possibly . . ."

"What?"

"Hang on."

"Amanda? Amanda! Q!" *Where did she go?*

Chapter One

VOYAGER

Captain Afsarah Eden couldn't tear her eyes away from the viewscreen. *Voyager* moved at maximum warp, the deck below Eden's boots thrumming with the engines' strain as stars stretched themselves out in the illusory image that defined this particular version of warp flight.

Eden and her crew were fleeing certain death. And with each second that passed, oblivion was gaining on them. The ship could not maintain its current velocity indefinitely, nor could it safely form a slipstream tunnel to increase its odds of outrunning destruction.

Part of Eden knew that by running, they were only prolonging the inevitable. In some cold, lonely corner of her heart, she had already accepted her own death. But the duty that had bound her to Starfleet and sustained her through the most difficult times of her life demanded that she make this attempt on behalf of those she led.

The temptation, *no,* the desperate longing she felt to order the ship to come about was becoming more difficult to ignore. Did she need to see the beast, to name it before it devoured them? Was it some absurd definition of honor that called on her to stand her ground, even in the face of annihilation?

Or was it simply the fact that she was tired of running? This monster had already taken too much from her. There was no longer any true victory to be claimed here. She was not fleeing a predator that might grow weary of its chase. She was attempting to outrun something that had all but stripped away every last shred of her own identity. She was incapable of resisting or defying it. It would have her. And given enough time, it might actually bring her to accept that its version of Afsarah Eden was truer than the one she had constructed in fifty-plus years of life.

She belonged to this darkness, and as that certainty struck her with the force of a roaring wave, she began to lose her bearings. Her head grew inexplicably light and her knees buckled. Eden reached her right arm back to steady herself against the command chair in which she knew she would never again sit.

Her eyes briefly registered another person standing beside her, and the motion meant to reorient her became a graceless stagger as she unconsciously rebelled against the sight her mind refused to accept.

I'm dead already.

She had to be.

Eden willed the vision to clear, but the longer she stared open-mouthed at the figure next to her, the more that figure seemed to coalesce and solidify.

"Impossible," Eden whispered.

Beside her, Admiral Kathryn Janeway's stone-cold eyes held Eden's with a painful mixture of determined despair.

"This is a dream," Eden said, willing her voice to hold steady even as her senses scrambled for an escape route.

"Feels more like a nightmare to me," Kathryn replied.

The mess hall was all but deserted this close to the middle of gamma shift. Most of the crew members who had signed off a few hours earlier had already eaten, and those looking to get a jump on their day prior to the start of alpha shift wouldn't start straggling in for another hour at least.

Still, Captain Chakotay didn't look up from his padd until the individual who had entered moments earlier made her way toward him and stood silently for a few seconds behind the chair across from his.

"I thought you were planning to turn in early for a really good night's sleep," the weary voice of the fleet commander greeted him.

"And I thought the wee hours were the only ones that ever found you sleeping," he replied convivially as Captain Eden pulled out the chair and sat restlessly.

"Do you mind?" she asked once the deed was already done.

"Of course not," he replied sincerely. "I'm not going to finish this letter tonight anyway," he added, stifling a yawn as he pushed the padd aside and sipped from a cup of tea that had grown cold an hour ago.

"It's unusual to find you at a loss for words," Eden said lightly as she rubbed her eyes.

A faint smile traipsed across Chakotay's lips as he replied, "Is that a good thing?"

"So far I'd say, absolutely," Eden said more seriously.

A few months earlier, before the fleet had crossed paths with the Children of the Storm, Chakotay would have been hard-pressed to imagine himself engaged in such easy banter with Eden. Though she was a distinguished officer and an able leader, he'd found it difficult to warm to her, probably in no small part due to the fact that Starfleet Command had seen fit to assign her to *Voyager*'s center seat when the fleet had first launched and he was still deemed unfit for duty. Once Eden had assumed command of the fleet and officially requested that Chakotay resume his former place as *Voyager*'s captain, she had continued to maintain an aloof distance from those she led.

Recent, near disastrous events, however, had begun to bridge the distance between them, as they were forced to stretch the boundaries of the formal command structure and work together to find solutions to a vast array of challenges, including the loss of one of the nine ships that had originally begun the journey, the almost total loss of a second, and the capture of a third by the Children. Eden had also recently seen fit to share some of her personal history with him, including her mysterious origins, and he'd finally begun to see her not just as his commanding officer, but as an individual: complex, devoted to duty, but painfully alone. Now, he found that he had no compunction in returning her confidence and was actually grateful for the opportunity to share a little of his own current burden.

"It's my sister, Sekaya," he sighed.

Eden's eyes left his as she searched her memory. "She's not Starfleet, is she?"

"No. She has accepted civilian assignments from time to time, but where I've seen the possibility of working for positive change from within Starfleet, she's always been skeptical."

Eden nodded. "Your people's experiences with the Cardassians probably had something to do with that."

"For starters," Chakotay agreed.

Suddenly Eden's eyes widened. "She thought your resignation was going to be permanent, didn't she?"

"She wasn't the only one," Chakotay chuckled. "Of course I wrote to her the moment I reassumed command of *Voyager*, but

I didn't get her response until we regrouped with the rest of the fleet last week."

"She's not happy," Eden rightly surmised.

"No."

What began as a slight pause was threatening to stretch into a lull when Chakotay added, "I don't blame her. She never saw what Kathryn's death did to me, but we have enough mutual friends that word got back to her anyway. Her relief at my resignation was comforting at the time, but I'm finding it harder now to explain my certainty that as much as leaving the service, even briefly, was absolutely necessary, returning *now* is the best choice I could possibly make."

"Do you doubt your choice?"

"Not at all," Chakotay replied firmly. "I know I haven't 'taken a step back or retreated from a better future.'"

Eden's eyes narrowed. "She doesn't mince words, does she?"

"It runs in the family." Chakotay grinned knowingly. "But beyond assuring her that she's wrong, and without actually being able to see her and explain myself in person, I don't know how to convince her. The more I think about it, the more I realize that my choice has more to do with instinct or . . . a feeling I trust but can't really name. I've made peace with my past."

Eden shook her head and smiled mirthlessly. "That makes one of us."

Setting his own concerns aside, Chakotay took a moment to study Eden. Tension knotted her brow and lifted her shoulders. Her black, almond-shaped eyes were uncharacteristically uncertain.

"So, why aren't you sleeping tonight, Afsarah?" he asked kindly.

She sat back in her chair and took a long sip of whatever warm beverage she'd replicated before joining him. "It's nothing."

"I doubt that."

He was pleased to see her countenance soften just enough to let a little light back into her eyes.

"For the last few weeks, I've been having this recurring dream."

"Really?" he asked, genuinely intrigued. Though he was no expert in dream analysis, it, like all manner of subconscious exploration, had been a subject of deep inquiry throughout his life. His curiosity was grounded in his people's unquestioning acceptance of a spiritual realm that coexisted with reality and could be entered willingly with enough practice. But this belief was rare among Starfleet officers—so rigorously grounded in reason, logic, and science.

Eden took another sip before going on. "I'm alone on the bridge. At least at first."

Chakotay kept his expression neutral as he nodded for her to continue.

"We're moving at high warp away from something terrible. We need to go faster, but we can't. I'm absolutely certain the ship is about to be destroyed. And then . . ." Her voice trailed off.

"Then?"

"I shouldn't be bothering you with this."

Chakotay was puzzled by her abrupt retreat. "Then?" he gently coaxed.

Eden studied his face and in a brief instant, Chakotay saw that her concern was not that she would be embarrassed but that somehow she would insult him.

"It's a dream, Afsarah," he said. "I'm the last one who would take anything you say personally."

Eden sighed and dropped her chin in deference to his perceptiveness. Shrugging slightly, she went on, "And then I look to my right and Kathryn Janeway is standing beside me. I know in some ways that should make me feel better. I mean, whom would you rather have beside you in a fight? But the sight of her absolutely terrifies me."

Chakotay lowered his head for a moment to hide the wide smile that erupted on his face at this revelation. Suddenly Eden's discomfort was crystal clear. When he raised his eyes to hers again, he hoped they offered the compassion she deserved.

"It's a captain's nightmare," he said, trying hard to compose himself.

"A what?"

"A captain's nightmare. Most professions have their own version of it. Performers often dream that they're onstage in the middle of a production but don't know any of their lines. Musicians are trying to play a concert but their instruments won't stay in tune. Teachers arrive at their class, begin a lecture, and realize they are stark naked."

The corners of Eden's full lips finally turned upward as he continued.

"And Starfleet captains find themselves facing certain death and the loss of their ships to unconquerable foes," he finished.

"I see." Eden nodded, though not without reservation.

"Every captain I've ever known has a version of it," Chakotay insisted.

After a moment, Eden said hesitantly, "And Admiral Janeway's presence?"

Chakotay felt his face fall into more serious lines. "Kathryn is more strongly identified with *Voyager* than any other individual who has ever served her. When you first took command, you were stepping into legendary shoes. I'd have been amazed if you didn't find that daunting, consciously and subconsciously."

"Did you feel that way when you first took command of *Voyager*?" Eden asked.

Chakotay shook his head. "It was different. I was already part of *Voyager*, and at least at first, I felt like I was merely picking up where Kathryn had left off." He considered his next words carefully, then decided this was no time to hold back. "But you've already told me you feel a certain amount of guilt about Kathryn's death; you used to believe that she wouldn't have died if you and Admiral Batiste hadn't pushed so hard to get this mission back to the Delta Quadrant approved. I don't agree. But it sounds to me like you've got some unfinished business you need to find some way to put behind you."

Eden sat somberly for a moment as his words sank in. Finally she said, "I'm sure you're right."

Chakotay sensed that she wasn't convinced, but he knew the

words needed to be said, and might again, several times, before Afsarah actually accepted them.

"Have you given any thought to my other suggestion?" he asked, wondering if her recent choice to share with him what little she knew of her past, as well as her belief that the answers to that mystery might lie in the Delta Quadrant, was partially responsible for increasing her general level of anxiety.

Confusion flashed briefly across Eden's face before the light dawned. "About seeing the Doctor?"

"Yes."

"I don't know."

"Okay," Chakotay replied, unwilling to push too hard.

"It's a perfectly reasonable suggestion," she acknowledged hesitantly. "I've never shared my full history with any medical doctor who has evaluated me because, honestly, I didn't see the need. And you're right that he might be able to discover some physiological clue to my ancestry. I'm just reluctant to waste resources on my personal agenda," she finally admitted. "As I told Hugh, I'm more than content to allow this mystery to unfold in its own time. I don't need to hurry it along."

Chakotay considered her qualms, then said, "I don't see it as wasting resources, and I'm certain neither did the counselor. To seek answers to a question that is clearly troubling you is not to attempt to commandeer the fleet's many tools for your own personal gain. You're not Admiral Batiste, Afsarah. You've lived with this uncertainty your entire life, and in some ways it's as comfortable as an old friend to you. But your reactions to the Staff of Ren and the Mikhal artifact have changed things. I don't see the harm in acknowledging that and using every tool at our disposal to see if we can unearth any other missing pieces of this puzzle, as long as it doesn't interfere with our other duties."

"We do have a busy few weeks ahead of us," Eden said.

"We'll be at New Talax at least two days before *Voyager* sets out again."

Eden's eyebrows pinched together, creasing her brow. "Two days?"

"You haven't forgotten about the reception, have you?"

Eden raised her hands to massage her temples. "Actually, I had."

Chakotay smiled broadly. "I should have warned you earlier, but there's something you need to know about Neelix: he'll use any excuse for a party. And after the last couple of months, I'm not the least bit inclined to disappoint him."

"Nor am I," Eden agreed.

"Which means you have plenty of time to slip over to *Galen* for a physical," he said pointedly.

Eden sat back and crossed her arms, grudgingly admitting defeat. "Apparently I do."

Chapter Two

NEW TALAX

Lieutenant Commander Thomas Eugene Paris was in heaven—if heaven was defined as piloting the sleekest, most sophisticated and responsive craft he'd ever flown.

For several weeks during *Voyager*'s efforts to rescue *Quirinal* and *Demeter* from their encounter with the Children of the Storm, Paris had known in his gut that his wife, Fleet Chief Engineer B'Elanna Torres, was hiding something from him. They'd had issues with full disclosure a few years earlier that had almost left their marriage in tatters, so he was hard-pressed to understand her willingness to be secretive so soon after their lives had returned to something resembling normalcy. He had chosen to trust her—no easy feat—when she'd promised that what she was withholding was a matter of duty. And that trust had been rewarded days earlier when, at a special briefing for the command staff, it had been revealed that part of the fleet's complement, classified until that moment, were two dozen experimental single-pilot ships. The vessels were intended for deployment in close-combat situations, adding to the number of ships at the fleet's disposal with the hope that they would make the difference between the survival of the fleet and the other unthinkable option.

There was no arguing that these vessels were a departure for Starfleet design. An organization that had defined itself by peaceful exploration would seem to have little use for vessels whose primary function was combat. Even the *Delta Flyer*, its successor, and B'Elanna's creation, the *Home Free*, could never be classified as anything other than shuttles: combat capable, but intended for exploration and self-defense. It was not for Tom to say whether or not Starfleet was *right* to experiment with such ships. But you had to be living in the far corner of nowhere to think that after the Borg invasion, every single aspect of defensive and offensive armaments shouldn't be considered and evaluated for its potential use in the event that another apocalyptic force should engage the Federation.

The flight geek in Tom had stopped listening to the well-reasoned thought processes behind the creation of the Tactical Support Flyer, with its ship-mounted phaser banks and torpedo launcher. The moment he had laid eyes on the three-dimensional holographic projection of the vessel that had accompanied Captain Eden's briefing, he saw only a thing of beauty. Though similar in shape to the *Delta Flyer*, it was considerably smaller. The struts were longer, carrying both phaser arrays and torpedo launchers. The tail section was streamlined, as its only means of propulsion was thrusters. Eden had mentioned that there had been discussions of making them warp capable, though these prototypes were not.

The aspect that beckoned to Tom like a lover's whisper in the darkness was the bio-neural–integrated flight control systems. *Voyager* had been the first Starfleet vessel equipped with bio-neural gel packs—small fluidic devices that processed data in a manner more akin to the human nervous system than standard Starfleet processors. The new TS Flyers' systems were designed to sync themselves to the individual pilot. There was no organic link between the ship and pilot—which, frankly, Tom would have found disturbing—but the new flight control yoke that replaced

the standard flight interface allowed the pilot to customize individual control preferences through his fingertips. This was no
steering wheel or clumsy fly-by-light stick. These controls would
allow the pilot to seamlessly fuse his flying style with the ship's
operating controls and respond infinitesimal fractions of a second
more quickly. Tom knew that could make a critical difference in
a combat situation.

Once the briefing was over, Tom knew that he absolutely had
to take one out for a test flight. To his dismay, the ships came
with a special operations force of pilots housed aboard *Achilles*,
where the flyers were stored. They had spent months training on
them in the Alpha Quadrant before the fleet was launched. Tom
had been able to convince Chakotay that it was essential to fleet
operations that he personally shake one of them down, pointing
out that none of the fleet's command officers could consider how
best to apply this new technology without an intimate understanding of its strengths and limitations. Chakotay had favored
Tom with a look that clearly indicated he wasn't buying it, but
nonetheless had convinced Captain Eden that Tom's suggestion
was reasonable, if not completely aboveboard.

And so it was that this glorious afternoon, Tom and three of
the flight specialists, Lieutenants Mischa, Purifoy, and Zabetha,
found themselves darting through the asteroid field that surrounded New Talax. Twelve other pilots had begun the demonstration, flying numerous formations and mock engagements for
the benefit of those attending the special reception *Voyager* was
now holding for the crews of *Voyager, Galen,* and *Demeter,* and
representatives of Neelix's adopted home who would be hosting
some of them for the next several weeks. Once the show was over,
Paris and his fellow pilots had begun a more rigorous test flight,
entering the asteroid field at maximum safe velocities and assess-
ing maneuverability and tactics while coming, in some cases, so
close to the individual flying rocks that Tom could have counted
the individual grains of fine particulate matter that covered the
asteroids' surfaces. As it took absolutely every iota of concentration at Tom's disposal to pilot his vessel, comm chatter was

minimal. Nevertheless, in the distant portions of his consciousness Tom was aware of Purifoy and Zabetha goading one another on to increased velocity, while Mischa punctuated their remarks with brisk reminders to focus.

As Tom executed a maneuver that would take him between two small asteroids with mere hundreds of meters of leeway, Mischa's voice crackled into his ear, *"Cutting it a little close, aren't you, sir?"*

"Isn't that why we're here?" he replied, once he'd cleared the small, closing window, hoping the tension in his voice didn't betray his relief.

The sensation was exhilarating and terrifying, the precise cocktail of emotions most pilots lived for but rarely felt at the helm of a starship. Tom had often complained about the distance between the starship and flight control. The ability to *feel* the ship and its responsiveness as intimately as he felt his own inhalations was something he'd never been able to achieve, although he'd come close to replicating the sensation when flying his own shuttle designs.

Until this moment, Tom had two great loves in his life: his wife, B'Elanna, and his daughter, Miral. No inanimate object could ever replace them. But the TS Flyer that now held him in its snug embrace and seemed to move more in concert with his senses than his thoughts was quickly making its way onto that very short list.

VOYAGER

"Did you see that?" Ensign Aytar Gwyn asked of no one in particular, though Lieutenant Commander B'Elanna Torres, Lieutenant Nancy Conlon of *Voyager*, and Commander Clarissa Glenn of *Galen* were all within earshot and had been chatting amiably with her since the TS Flyers' demonstration had begun. Gwyn was *Voyager*'s alpha-shift conn officer, an eager, spiky blue–haired half-Kriosian woman who had spent the vast majority of the flyers' demonstration with her nose practically embedded in the transparent aluminum windows of *Voyager*'s mess hall. Conlon and Glenn were clearly intrigued by the sleek ships' capabilities, but B'Elanna, who winced internally as Tom completed the maneuver that had given rise to Gwyn's latest outburst, was finding it difficult to hold down her food.

He's going to get himself killed out there, she decided for the thousandth time since the spectacle had begun. *And if he doesn't, I'm going to kill him the minute he sets foot back on this ship.* This certainty calmed her momentarily, but a new wave of nausea struck as Tom's ship disappeared briefly behind a large asteroid. B'Elanna inhaled sharply and didn't release her breath until he once again made an appearance on the asteroid's far side, gracefully pulling up and circling back toward the formation.

It wasn't that she didn't trust her husband's piloting skills, and she would never begrudge him a little fun. B'Elanna knew part of him still lived to fly, and truth be told, she'd known the moment she laid eyes on the TS Flyers that Tom was going to beg, borrow, or steal his way into the cockpit of one. *But does he have to do it in the middle of a damned asteroid field?*

B'Elanna knew intimately what it was to take risks, even unnecessary and supremely stupid ones. And she was the last person in the universe who would ever have asked her husband to be less than he was. But she simply could not bear to watch, given the fact that even a slight misstep on Tom's part could destroy her happiness.

"They really are something," Conlon said, without Gwyn's excitement. *Voyager*'s chief engineer and B'Elanna had grown quite close through their work, and B'Elanna was certain Conlon could sense her discomfort.

"That's one way of putting it," Glenn replied, with considerably more restraint. The lithe, strawberry-blond woman was *Galen*'s commanding officer, and all B'Elanna knew about her was that she was efficient and capable, and seemed friendly enough.

"Problem?" Conlon asked Glenn.

Glenn shrugged off a shiver. "I've seen ships like these before, just never in Starfleet."

"Where?" Conlon asked.

"An unaligned species near Tendara, where I was raised. They used something similar to harass shipping lanes and commandeer supplies when the mood struck them. We called them pirates. In fact, I don't even remember their real name now."

"Just because a tool can be misused isn't the fault of the tool," Conlon suggested.

Glenn stared hard at the engineer, probably weighing whether or not the remark was worth a disagreement in a public setting. She attempted to keep her tone as even as possible. "You're implying that Starfleet would never stray from its ideals and that the officers asked to pilot such vessels are not betraying our stated goals of peaceful exploration, despite the fact that they are operating a tool that has no real use in terms of either peace or exploration?"

A lanky, wide-eyed young commander responded, "Perhaps we should see the uses to which our commanding officers choose to put them before we judge the ethical issues of their existence."

"Well said, Commander Fife," Conlon replied, patting him on the shoulder as she stepped aside to invite him into the conversation.

Fife, that's right, B'Elanna chided herself. He was part of *Demeter*'s command staff, and if scuttlebutt was to be believed, he had been personally responsible for the mutiny aboard his vessel when it was captured by the Children of the Storm. The fact that the *Demeter*'s captain, Commander Liam O'Donnell, had chosen to allow him to retain his position had been cause for considerable grumbling in the weeks following *Demeter*'s rescue. By all appearances, whatever had transpired hadn't chastened him.

B'Elanna didn't mind as in this instance, she actually agreed with him. She'd weighed the moral questions in the days following the revelation of the TS Flyers' existence and had gone so far as to take Captain Eden to task for keeping them classified. When Eden had revealed that the fleet's next mission was a sweep of former Borg space, suddenly B'Elanna found herself more than willing to accept any tool that increased the odds of the fleet's survival. She trusted the officers that commanded the fleet to use the flyers wisely.

But that didn't mean she wanted Tom flying one of them on a regular basis.

"I trust our command staffs," Glenn replied pointedly to Fife. "I just can't help but think this is the result of too many years of sustained conflict. We used to be explorers."

"We still are," B'Elanna finally piped up, grateful for a reason to tear her eyes away from her husband's flying. "But as the only person standing here who's already been to the Delta Quadrant once, I'm telling you, any native species bent on conflict—and there are some—isn't going to think twice about firing at us because of our desire for peaceful exploration and diplomatic exchange. Sometimes there's nothing but force that will get the job done, and the more force we bring to the equation, the better our odds of survival will be."

Conlon studied B'Elanna quizzically for a moment. The two had already discussed the implications of the TS Flyers, and she seemed surprised by B'Elanna's full-throated support.

"I know," B'Elanna said, raising a hand to forestall a rebuke. "I want to live in a universe where decisions like whether or not to open fire on an alien species don't have to be made, too. More importantly, I want my daughter to live in a universe where everyone is content to disagree agreeably with one another without resorting to violence of any kind."

Undoubtedly it was B'Elanna's forehead ridges, evidence of her half-Klingon heritage, that caused Fife's eyebrows to shoot almost to his hairline at this statement, but she continued as if she hadn't noticed.

"But that desire is a work in progress. If we want to see other sentient species embrace the ethical and moral positions of the Federation, the only way to truly do that is to show them, by our example, why it would be in their best interests."

"You're saying we don't change hearts or minds at the end of a torpedo," Fife noted.

"That's been my experience," B'Elanna sighed ruefully, "which is why Starfleet, and the Federation, will always make the peaceful exchange of ideas and information their first priority. The problem comes when you encounter a civilization whose needs or basic nature are incompatible with our ideals. Once in a while, it's going to be us or them. The Borg taught us that."

"The Dominion tried to teach us that too," Conlon observed.

"And when that's the case, better us?" Glenn asked.

As the face of Miral, sleeping peacefully, flashed through B'Elanna's mind, she replied, "Don't you think so?"

"Of course I do," Glenn agreed. "Half of my training is in command, but the other is in medicine. You look at the TS Flyers and take comfort in the extra security they provide. I look at them and see all the new ways they can damage a body that I might be asked to put back together."

"Holy Rings of Betazed," Gwyn enthused from the window. "Did you see that?"

B'Elanna forced herself to hold Glenn's glance rather than turning to see whatever had thrilled the young pilot. *I'm just not going to look anymore,* she decided. It was probably the only way she was going to remain married over the next few hours.

"Well, this certainly brings back memories, doesn't it?" Neelix asked, casting a wide gaze over the festive atmosphere of *Voyager*'s mess hall. Seven of Nine had to agree. Dozens of individuals were engaged in pleasant conversation. Sipping beverages and nibbling on small edibles, they appeared to be enjoying themselves and the TS Flyers demonstration.

During the years Seven had served on *Voyager*—after she had been severed from the Borg Collective—Neelix had become a close friend. A Talaxian—a species originating tens of thousands of light-years from their present position—Neelix had come aboard at the beginning of *Voyager*'s long trek home and had become the ship's morale officer, among many other useful things. As the ship's chef, he had created many gatherings in this very room similar to the present one. Numerous officers in dress uniforms from *Voyager, Galen,* and *Demeter* were in attendance, along with representatives from the leadership of New Talax, most of whom were clad in well-worn tunics in somber earth tones. The only individuals conspicuous by their absence, as best Seven could tell, were Captains Eden and Chakotay, Counselor Hugh Cambridge, and the Doctor, *Voyager's* original EMH, now serving as CMO aboard *Galen*.

"It really does, Neelix," Lieutenant Harry Kim replied with a wide smile.

"I can't tell you how thrilled I was to receive Captain Eden's proposal," Neelix continued, his enthusiasm infectious. "Obviously, having a Starfleet medical vessel and a ship specializing in botanical genetics and production will enhance our little colony's resources tremendously."

"They'll only be here a few weeks, Neelix," Kim noted, trying to temper his friend's optimism. "They're not going to be able to rebuild your facilities in that time."

"Of course not," Neelix agreed readily. "But after your most recent gift of medical supplies, Doctor Hestax is dying to spend as much time with the Doctor and his staff as possible. We've already created several hydroponic facilities," he added in a rough approximation of sheepishness, "but I don't doubt your people will help us find ways to maximize their output."

"I am certain your people will find the next several weeks instructive and productive, Neelix," Seven offered. "Much more so than the rest of us, I believe."

Kim, *Voyager's* security chief and tactical officer, asked Seven, "You think the fleet is wasting its time visiting what used to be Borg space?"

"To look for traces of the Borg or Caeliar, yes," Seven replied definitively.

Kim shrugged. "So why don't you just request shore leave for the next few weeks when *Voyager* heads out tomorrow, Seven?"

Neelix's eyes widened and he appeared ready to second the motion until Seven quickly curbed it. "I have agreed to serve the fleet in whatever capacity Captain Eden sees fit. Her efforts to ensure that the Borg are gone remain a priority. To shirk my responsibilities would be unworthy of the trust she placed in me when she first agreed to allow me to join the fleet."

"You weren't as certain when you first joined the fleet as you are now that the Borg and Caeliar are truly gone," Kim needled her.

"At the time, I had cause to doubt," Seven agreed without rising to his bait. "My efforts since then to better understand the nature of the Caeliar's transformation of the Borg, and its effects on me, have allowed me to remember that experience more clearly than I initially could." The "transformation" Seven referred to was an overwhelming and awe-inspiring event. It had disintegrated the few Borg implants that had remained in her body after she had been severed from the Collective, replacing them with a form of programmable matter—catoms—that Seven was still struggling to understand. To all appearances, she was fully human. However, as far as she knew, she was the only former Borg now containing Caeliar technology in the entire galaxy. "When the Caeliar welcomed the Borg into their gestalt, they did not coerce anyone. But I can think of no Borg, other than myself, who might have had cause to reject their offer. What I now recall of the event includes a certainty that the Caeliar absorbed or neutralized everything that had once been Borg, and they intended to continue their own 'great work' far from the boundaries of our galaxy."

"Fair enough." Kim nodded. "But Starfleet sent us out here to make sure. Assuming you're right, I guess we can all look forward to several boring weeks ahead."

Neelix asked, "Where are the other fleet ships right now?"

"Our two *Vesta*-class ships, the *Quirinal* and *Esquiline,* with their sister science vessels, *Hawking* and *Curie,* have already set course for several distant points in what was formerly Borg territory. Last I heard," Kim said with a nod to Seven, "they hadn't found anything worth writing home about, but you never know when that could change."

I do, Seven thought, but refrained from saying it aloud.

"And with *Voyager, Achilles, Galen,* and *Demeter* here, that leaves one other, correct?" Neelix asked. "Which one am I forgetting?"

Kim's face clouded as Seven replied, "One of the original science vessels, the *Planck,* was destroyed in a recent encounter with an alien species. I have no doubt this was one of the primary reasons Captain Eden elected to keep both *Galen* and *Demeter* out of the fray for this particular exploratory endeavor."

"Well, we're thrilled to have them here," Neelix replied. "And I'm terribly sorry to hear about the loss of *Planck.*" Obviously attempting to move to a lighter topic, Neelix went on, "And what will the incredibly large *Achilles* be up to, while you and the others are chasing down whatever may or may not be left of the Borg?"

"*Achilles* will engage in a predetermined flight pattern, making it accessible to all of the fleet ships should they require its particular capabilities," Harry Kim replied.

"And what are those again?" Neelix asked.

"*Achilles* is another one of our special mission vessels. Apart from housing those incredible new ships," Kim said, referencing the display that was still capturing the attention of many in the hall, "she contains industrial-size replication and storage facilities. Last month they were able to rebuild the *Quirinal* even after it had crash-landed on a planet."

"Amazing," Neelix said, shaking his head. "Is there anything Starfleet can't do?"

"I hope that is a rhetorical question," Seven replied. "As you well know, there are many things beyond Starfleet's current capabilities."

Neelix considered her words, then replied, "I spent almost seven years aboard a Starfleet vessel, and found new wonders in it almost daily. The life I've lived here on New Talax since then, while incredibly gratifying and fulfilling, sometimes makes me long for the days when few miracles seemed out of reach."

"Your people have done extraordinary things," Kim assured Neelix. "To have created a colony inside an asteroid, to have survived as long as you have . . ."

"Thrived," Neelix corrected him gently.

"Of course." Kim nodded. "You shouldn't sell yourselves short. All of our technology would be meaningless without the dedicated people who implement it, and in that regard, I'd stack your colonists up against our crews any day. I hope you don't see our offer of assistance as any sort of suggestion that you aren't more than capable of getting along without us."

"Not at all," Neelix replied. "I see your offer for the gift it is, in a universe that doesn't bestow such things frequently." Turning to Seven, he said, "I haven't seen the Doctor. Will he be joining us?"

"I believe so," Seven replied. "In truth, I cannot account for his absence now. Perhaps a crew member requires his attention."

Neelix nodded knowingly. "I don't doubt for a moment that if he could be here, he would. In the meantime, perhaps you would introduce me to Commander O'Donnell? I imagine he and I will be working quite closely together over the next several weeks."

Seven turned to comply, but as she searched the crowd, she could not locate the captain.

Commander Liam O'Donnell, *Demeter*'s captain in all but rank, had searched diligently throughout the hall for the most inconspicuous spot he could find in which to endure the next hour. Few men hated a party the way he did. Even had the room been filled with the handful of beings in the galaxy who shared his passion and expertise for botanical genetics, he would have found it torturous in the extreme to endure the painful introductions (*No, I haven't heard of you or your research*), awkward attempts at small talk (*The weather? We're on a starship, aren't we?*), or the gentle prods to draw one out about one's own work (*Trust me, you wouldn't understand*). He would have skipped his own wedding reception had his dear and now sadly deceased wife, Alana, not been as good as her word to stand by his side the entire time and deflect any comment or query that went beyond the vaguest of congratulations on the happy event.

O'Donnell was simply not a people person—at least, not in this context. Bring the same people together in a room with a problem to solve and he'd know what to do, what to say. Here, showered, shaved, and dressed in his best uniform, all he wanted was to become invisible.

Directly across from the small alcove at the mess hall's entrance was a low bench attached to the bulkhead. The majority of those entering the room ignored it, casting their eyes toward the crowd, searching for a friendly face or a tray of beverages. Here, Liam made camp, gauging the smallest number of minutes he would have to remain without giving offense to Captain Eden, who had "advised" him to attend.

The commander was almost forced to reconsider his deployment when, six minutes and twenty-eight seconds after he had made himself comfortable, a lean, middle-aged lieutenant, who didn't even appear to realize O'Donnell was there, nervously checked the crowd and darted with apparent relief toward the unoccupied portion of the bench. Only when an earnest crewman appeared before them both and offered them a frothy pink drink did the lieutenant, who had been muttering quietly to himself, notice O'Donnell.

"Oh, I'm so sorry," he began, visibly checking O'Donnell's collar for pips before adding, "Commander."

"As you were, Lieutenant," O'Donnell quickly replied, hoping that would put an end to it.

"Barclay, sir," the lieutenant added, "Reginald Barclay."

This gave O'Donnell pause, not because he had the faintest idea who Barclay was, but because even *he* didn't seem to experience this man's amount of trepidation.

"Liam O'Donnell," he said, taking Barclay's clammy hand and, immediately upon its release, covertly wiping the lieutenant's sweat on his pant leg.

A pause followed, which O'Donnell fervently hoped would continue indefinitely, before Barclay said, "I just don't have time for this."

O'Donnell wasn't a hundred percent certain Barclay was even talking to him. "Please don't feel you need to stay on my account."

Barclay's head turned sharply, and again O'Donnell got the

impression that in the minute that had passed since Barclay had sat, he had forgotten he was not alone.

"No, sir," Barclay began, "I mean, yes, sir."

O'Donnell would gladly have let it go at that.

"What I mean, sir, is that my work right now is of such pressing urgency that this sort of recreational activity is . . . ," Barclay said, and then began to gesticulate nervously as he searched for the right description of the event that was clearly tormenting him almost as much as it was the commander.

O'Donnell realized, to his surprise, that this was perhaps the only thing the lieutenant might have said that would endear him to his benchmate.

"You serve aboard *Voyager*?" O'Donnell asked.

"The *Galen*," Barclay replied. "I'm a holographic design specialist."

O'Donnell nodded, though he knew little and cared less about holographic creation and implementation. After giving it a moment's thought, he found himself genuinely curious as to what momentous problem would so distract Barclay.

"What's the issue?" O'Donnell asked, actually grateful for a conversation that had nothing to do with him.

Barclay's eyes bugged and for a moment he reminded O'Donnell of his first officer, Atlee Fife. "The issue?" Barclay came just short of demanding incredulously. "Meegan, of course."

O'Donnell's stomach fell. If this was a personal or interpersonal issue with another crewman, he might just have to find a phaser and point the business end at his own head before the conversation was over.

"Meegan?" O'Donnell asked.

"You haven't been briefed?" Barclay asked.

O'Donnell didn't think so, but on any given day it could be hard to say which bits of interfleet trivia would actually find a place to stick in his normally very full head.

"Meegan McDonnell," Barclay attempted to clarify. "The hologram I created—well, Doctor Zimmerman and I created— the one that was possessed by one of eight Neyser consciousnesses and departed with one of the fleet's shuttles when Admiral Batiste was making his escape to fluidic space?" he finished.

Now that he mentioned it, the story did ring a bell.

"You're . . ." O'Donnell began.

"Trying to track her movements, of course," Barclay replied, as if it should have been obvious. "Naturally I was thrilled when the shuttle was recovered by Ambassador Neelix and returned to us, but the logs have been corrupted. More than that, I just can't imagine why she would have abandoned the Starfleet shuttle, one of our most advanced, really, for a mining vessel."

"Did she have a choice?" O'Donnell asked.

"Oh, yes." Barclay nodded fervently. "According to Nacona, the representative of the mining consortium whose vessel she stole, she initiated the hostilities between the two ships. She *wanted* that mining vessel, but I can't imagine why. Its systems are outdated, at least comparatively speaking, and its defenses are minimal. It's true that by changing ships, she is now much more difficult to track, but still it seems the rewards pale in comparison."

O'Donnell gave the situation, as he understood it, his consideration. Finally he replied, "Maybe she really needed to dig a hole."

Barclay opened his mouth to reply, but stopped short. He then favored O'Donnell with a look alight with inspiration. Without another word, Barclay rose and immediately left the hall without a backward glance.

O'Donnell sighed and sipped at the sticky-sweet pink beverage, grateful that by his chronometer, he now had eleven fewer minutes to spend in peace before he could follow Barclay's example and make his own retreat.

GALEN

This is impossible.

The Doctor had processed the data before him several times already. After the first round had been completed, he had instigated a discreet diagnostic of his subroutines to run continuously while he repeated the analysis. When the diagnostic confirmed that all of his systems were functioning optimally, he considered contacting Reg and asking that he be taken off line for a deeper diagnostic, but opted not to for the moment. Instead, he completed his evaluation a third time, and then a fourth for good measure.

During his relatively brief though very full existence, he had encountered all manner of odd, illogical, irritating, and incredibly challenging problems. A hologram who had surpassed his initial programming through years of continuous operation, the Doctor contained the collected brilliance of the best medical minds the Federation had produced. He had rarely, however, come across something so unusual that his subroutines could not calculate an explanation for them.

Today, he had been asked to study the genome of the fleet's commanding officer, Captain Afsarah Eden. She had already briefed him on the few details of her past of which she was aware. Eden had been told a pair of eclectic scientists, Carson Tallar and Miles Jobin, had found her on a distant and unnamed planet. Tallar had been a geneticist, among other things. Both had served briefly in Starfleet but had resigned long before they encountered Eden. Every other member of her race had supposedly perished, and Eden's "uncles" had nursed her back to health and unofficially adopted her. She had traveled with them until she was fifteen, leading a vagabond life every child would treasure but few parents would willingly inflict upon their offspring. Eventually, her uncles bowed to her need of a formal education and brought her to Earth. She was enrolled in an elite preparatory school that, combined with her stellar record, guaranteed her admission to Starfleet Academy.

Though Eden had questioned her uncles as a child and later in their infrequent correspondence until their presumed deaths, they had been evasive about her past and her people. All Eden knew for certain was that her uncles, though deeply devoted to her, had lied to her on numerous occasions about their mutual history. The planet they said was her place of origin was an ana- gram of "Jobin's folly." The uncles had insisted they had never served in Starfleet. But Eden discovered that both of them had served in their early twenties. Their service records were unhelpful. A complete analysis of the sparse Federation records of their travels yielded no additional information.

Eden had accepted that this mystery would likely never be solved and had gone about building an enviable career. However, several months earlier, when reviewing *Voyager*'s logs for Project Full Circle, she had come across an image of an artifact discovered on a planet occupied by a loosely affiliated group known as the Mikhal Travelers. That artifact, first seen years ago by Kes, a native of the Delta Quadrant and a former member of *Voyager*'s crew, had appeared to be a rudimentary, beautifully illuminated starscape. Eden had known, without understanding the source of her certainty, that it was a map of a constellation known by her people as Hanara. She had also known that it was part of a larger map, the rest of which might still be at the Mikhal Outpost.

Recently, Eden had experienced a similar "knowing" when she was presented with another object from the Delta Quadrant, a staff given to *Esquiline*'s commanding officer, Captain Parimon Dasht, during a first contact. The writing on the staff had never been translated, until Eden recognized it as a warning not to trespass on her people's ancestral grounds.

Eden had briefed both Captain Chakotay and Counselor Cambridge. At Chakotay's urging, she had requested a full analysis of her genome, hoping that it might reveal more about her origins. According to Eden, every doctor she'd ever had cause to visit had identified her as a very healthy human.

Looking at her genome, the Doctor saw that Eden was human, but she was like no other human who had ever existed. To see the anomaly, you had to look for it. And once you found it, you would doubt your senses rather than the data.

Because the data was impossible.

The Doctor was certain Eden's uncles had lied to her, and likely about more than the name of her home planet or their past connection to Starfleet.

As Captain Eden, Counselor Cambridge, and Captain Chakotay made themselves comfortable in his office, all gazing at him expectantly, the Doctor fretted over how best to present the information. From a purely scientific perspective, it was a fascinating puzzle that might have no solution. He was all too conscious of the fact, however, that this puzzle was also a person with feelings.

"Well, Doctor?" Cambridge interrupted his thoughts, perhaps more anxious than the others to hear the report.

"Before I begin," the Doctor replied, "I would like to give Captain Eden the opportunity to receive my report privately. As with all matters of such a nature, the data we will be discussing is highly personal."

"I appreciate your discretion, Doctor," Eden said with a nervous smile, "but I am waiving my rights to privacy."

"Are you telling us you've found something?" Cambridge asked.

"I have," the Doctor replied evenly. "Though I am at a loss to understand how what I have discovered has come to pass."

Cambridge exchanged a wide, anticipatory smile with Chakotay. For her part, Eden's face was a mask of stoic composure.

"First, Captain Eden is, as has been previously noted, human."

Cambridge's face fell. Apparently he had hoped for something more interesting.

"However, she was not conceived of human parents."

Confusion passed across all three of the faces before him.

"Humans, like many other humanoid species, are created when two specific cells, each containing one half of their genetic material, combine during fertilization and begin to replicate themselves," the Doctor said.

"Yes, we all know where babies come from," Cambridge interjected.

The Doctor chose to go on without objecting to the condescension in Cambridge's tone.

"During normal fertilization, each parent contributes one sexual chromosome, an X from the mother, and either an X or a

Y from the father. Fertilized zygotes that contain two X chromosomes develop as females."

Even Chakotay seemed to be growing inpatient with the Doctor's recitation of basic science.

"In the case of Captain Eden, her two X chromosomes are identical. Understand that only a complete genetic study would have revealed this. It is unusual for anyone with her excellent physical history to undergo such an analysis, and this result would not be obvious in a cursory review of her genome. Had I not seen it for myself, I would have believed it to be an impossible variation."

"I'm sorry, Doctor," Eden interrupted. "If it's impossible, how am I here?"

"I don't know," the Doctor replied. "What I do know is that you were not born in the normal way, nor were you the product of any medical fertilization technique with which I am familiar. Your two X chromosomes are absolutely identical. They were copied by unknown means and resulted in a viable zygote."

"Could she be a clone of some kind?" Cambridge asked.

"No," the Doctor replied. "Even if a female had provided a single X chromosome for this process, there is no way Captain Eden is a clone of that female."

"How do you know?" Chakotay demanded.

"Because several unique base pair sequences indicate that the X chromosome was provided by a male donor," the Doctor replied.

"I don't have a mother?" Eden asked incredulously.

"Not one that contributed to your DNA," the Doctor replied.

The stunned look on the officers' faces didn't stop the Doctor from forging ahead. "But believe it or not, that is not the most interesting part of your genome."

Eden pulled herself up straight in her chair, her eyes almost pleading for the conversation to end.

"What is?" Cambridge asked for all of them.

"I don't believe a normal male provided the chromosome either."

All three exchanged questioning glances, then Chakotay admitted, "Now you've lost me."

"Captain Eden's genome is perfect in a way no process of natural selection could have created."

"I've actually heard this part before," Cambridge said.

Eden shot him a quick glare that silenced him. "What does that mean? I'm somehow genetically engineered?"

"Yes," the Doctor replied, "but beyond any means of which the Federation is currently capable. In your case, it's as if someone, somewhere, had predetermined which selection of genes would be optimal for physical and mental health."

"Optimal?" Chakotay echoed.

"Most genomes are a mess," the Doctor said as patiently as possible. "There are thousands of useless base pair combinations that evolution simply hasn't found a way to purge yet. Your genome," he said directly to Eden, "is not tainted with any useless sequences. Understand, all humans have some minor genetic issues. Most of them are never cause for concern, and those that are can be easily repaired under acceptable Federation procedures. We don't enhance genetic abilities, but we can easily repair damaged DNA to reverse many disease processes. Your genes are like the textbook example of every single optimal gene. Most individuals are blessed with a few hundred of these at a time. You have all of them. It's as if someone, or something, began with half of a male genetic sequence, optimized each of them, and discarded what was unnecessary, then copied the perfect gene sequence to create you."

"That's impossible," Eden said flatly.

Yes, it is, the Doctor refrained from saying aloud.

"There is no technology of which I am aware that could have created you," the Doctor acknowledged. "But the good news is, you should continue to enjoy the excellent health to which, I am sure, you have been accustomed your entire life, and, if nature has its way, you will outlive everyone here, except me."

At this, Cambridge rose and began to pace the small room like a caged animal. Finally he turned to Chakotay, his arms crossed, and said, "How far from the Mikhal Outpost are we right now?"

"Hugh," Eden started to interject.

"How far?" he asked again.

"Thirty thousand light-years, give or take," Chakotay replied. "But it's less than forty light-years from *Voyager*'s next intended destination."

"What are you . . ." Eden began.

"*Achilles* could easily shadow *Voyager* for the next few days, detouring to the outpost so that you and I could take a look at that artifact in person, along with any other secrets the planet might still hold."

"No," Eden said. "I've said it before and I'll say it again. I'm not using our resources for my personal curiosity."

"We left 'curiosity' behind a few minutes ago," Cambridge chided her. "If this doesn't fall under our mandate to seek out new life and new civilizations, I don't know what does."

"There's one more thing," the Doctor almost hesitated to add.

"Terrific," Eden sighed warily.

"I also ran a deep quantum scan, as part of the rest of your normal physical evaluation."

"A what?" Chakotay asked.

"It's something I created out of necessity when my former medical assistant decided to evolve to a higher level of existence."

"You're talking about Kes?" Eden asked.

"During the last few days she was on board, there was no standard test to evaluate the physiological changes she was experiencing. So I invented one."

Chakotay shook his head in admiration. "Of course you did."

"It's not a scan I normally run, but given my initial findings, I thought it might be interesting."

"Was it?" Cambridge asked.

The Doctor turned the computer interface screen on his desk so that they all could see the results. Even for the uninitiated, they were not difficult to read.

"This," the Doctor said, indicating a series of wavy lines at the top of the screen, "is a normal quantum scan. It's yours, Chakotay, in case you were wondering."

Chakotay nodded as the Doctor pointed out the wildly

different lines beneath. "This is Captain Eden's quantum scan. As you can see, there are multiple irregularities."

After a short pause to allow everyone to absorb the information, the Doctor went on, "A normal scan indicates that at a submolecular level, everything is operating within normal chroniton and multiple possible phase levels."

"And what does this deep quantum scan indicate?" Eden asked.

"That there is something different about the way your subatomic particles are aligned. There are no obvious physiological effects that I can perceive, but it's worth noting that this is yet another way in which you are unique," the Doctor finished.

"I feel fine," Eden insisted uncertainly.

"That's almost exactly what Kes said shortly before she lost submolecular cohesion and destabilized, almost destroying the entire ship in the process," the Doctor noted wryly.

"Do you think I could be undergoing something similar?" Eden asked.

"This was your scan today. We have to consider this your baseline. I'd like to continue to scan you regularly over the next several days before attempting to determine the potential significance of these readings."

"I quite agree," Chakotay said, "which is why the good Doctor here should join you on your little expedition."

Eden looked to all three of them, clearly sensing that she was outnumbered. The Doctor looked directly into her eyes and said, "I understand that this is a lot to take in. I can sympathize with your reluctance to attend to personal concerns given the fleet's priorities. But you are unique in a way I have never imagined was possible. Your humanity might be the tip of the iceberg. I do not doubt that your superiors would approve of your choice to investigate this further, especially given how many unknowns we are faced with. As we saw with Kes, things that are predisposed to change can and do change, sometimes with alarming speed, and the more we can learn before that point, the easier it will be to sense if trouble is approaching."

Eden nodded. Finally she said, "Agreed." Turning to her officers, she added, "I will take your suggestions under advisement and give you my answer tomorrow."

"Afsarah . . ." Cambridge began, but she raised a hand to silence him.

"You really think one night to sleep on this is too much to ask?"

"Of course not," Chakotay replied for the group.

With a curt nod, Eden squared her shoulders and left the others to their thoughts.

Chapter Three

Q CONTINUUM

"I tried."

"How hard did you try?"

"Very."

"Mother."

"You understand I detest involving myself with the affairs of humans at all. Every time I have done so, to humor your father, the tedium has been unbearable."

"This is different, Mother. This is important to me, not Father."

"Your father cares, darling. He truly does. He might hide it well, but I am convinced, much as it pains me to say so, that he once felt a particular fondness for this female, as any of us might for a pet not yet housebroken. And even I must acknowledge that her unexpected resourcefulness and talent for original thinking have been of use to us."

"Us?"

"All right, *me*. There, I said it. Are you happy now?"

"She made a decision to allow Q to exercise his right to become mortal and end his existence."

"And for that, or your father's assistance in ending Q's life, I should never have forgiven either of them. She had no business interfering in the internecine affairs of a species so far above her own as to defy imagination. And as I suspected, that action almost brought the Continuum to a fiery end."

"I was born of that near catastrophe."

"I haven't forgotten. And that is the single mitigating factor in this entire sordid equation. And the reason I agreed to make the effort."

"But you did not succeed?"

"In convincing her to abandon her quest to destroy herself? No."

"You told her she would die."

"I did."

"And she didn't believe you?"

"In her defense, our actions are usually incomprehensible to humans. This has resulted in some serious trust issues over the years. Pity, really, that this time I had no hidden agenda."

"You wanted her to die?"

"She's mortal. It wasn't a question of *if*, only *when*. But I will admit that I wouldn't have minded seeing her die better. I would have spared her the pain of being forced to turn against her own kind in favor of a peaceful passing, years hence, surrounded by all those who loved her. But it's not as if that would have changed anything. You're so young, darling. When you've got a few more billion years under your belt, you'll realize that the extra time seeing reason might have granted her will still pass in the blink of one of your precious eyes. That's one of many reasons it's best to avoid becoming too attached to these creatures."

"But . . ."

"And what have we here? The very picture of familial bliss?"

"Hello, Father."

"To what shall I credit this moment's fit of pique?"

"All I said was hello."

"Yes, and five billion plus years into my existence I couldn't possibly be expected to grasp the many layers of contempt present in your tone."

"You should feel free to grasp any damn thing . . ."

"Junior!"

"Mother, how many times have I asked you *never* to call me that?"

"It's all right, my dear. I'll take it from here."

"I've done all I can."

"I'm sure you have."

"I *have*. I sincerely doubt you'll be able to make him see reason, but I suppose the attempt can't hurt."

"Would you two prefer to be alone for this?"

"Not at all. I'm going. I'm sorry, son. I wish I could have done more, but there you have it."

"What was she talking about?"

"You know very well."

"Are you? How? Haven't we? You're still fretting about your godmother's death?"

"I am."

"Son, you have to let this go. I've told you and told you, there is absolutely nothing we can do."

"We're Q. We can do anything we damn well please."

"Yes, and no. Having the power to do something burdens us with ultimate and often frightening responsibilities. Limits have been established to our choices for the benefit of the entire multiverse. You're not the first Q to wrestle with issues like this. But the mistake you would make has been made, and unmade, by your betters countless times already. We understand the big picture here. And you, for all of the progress you've made recently, are still missing it."

"Her death has become a fixed point in time."

"Oh, not this again."

"No other human's death has ever had such significance."

"I grant you that. But surely you must see that this little oddity of the multiverse only compels us further to act with extreme caution. We wouldn't change it even if we could."

"You have personally been responsible for interventions that resulted in saving the lives of other humans you were fond of."

"Because those interventions served a much larger purpose."

"Or so you thought at the time."

"No. *So I knew*. And so I tried to convince the rest of the Continuum. And so I risked the Continuum's wrath time and again. And so I was recently proved very, very right, when Captain Picard . . ."

"We're not talking about Captain Picard. He was *the thing*."

"The One."

"Whatever."

"Not whatever. *The One*."

"You care for Picard. He shudders every time your name is mentioned, let alone any time you make an appearance, and still, you watch over him like he's a member of the family. Aunt Kathy helped you save the Continuum and you don't think that merits special consideration on your part?"

"I don't *care* for Picard. I admire him. He has surprised and amused me many times during our acquaintance. He was worthy of the time and effort expended on his behalf."

"And she isn't?"

"It's not that simple."

"You made her my godmother. You acknowledged then how unique she was. But once she'd served that purpose, you just, what, changed your mind?"

"I'm not happy about this either!"

"You aren't."

"You thought I was?"

"I thought you might be, or didn't really care, or had just moved on to other things. But you do care."

"Of course I do. Kathryn Janeway was exceptional. She will be missed."

"She doesn't have to be."

"She does. You have to see the big picture here."

U.S.S. ENTERPRISE

Q found himself standing on the bridge of a Federation starship. Just before the command chairs, a scene of some emotional distress was occurring. A man, *Captain Picard,* he suddenly realized, was on his knees, holding his head in his hands and rocking back and forth as if trying to contain the great heaves and sobs spilling from his lips. Three other officers, Captain Riker, Captain Dax, and Commander Worf, surrounded him, seemingly intent on shielding this spectacle from the eyes of the rest of the bridge crew.

Of course, few had eyes for their captain at the moment. None seemed able to look anywhere but at the ship's main viewscreen, where a dazzling sight was unfolding. Multiple cube-shaped ships glowed with brilliant light and gradually, as the light became almost blinding, began to alter their configurations. Vast spikes shot forth from every flat surface of the cubes, transforming them into glorious white stars.

Q turned his attention to what was unheard by the others. Picard's wails had been an echo of the pain, confusion, and horror of billions of minds joined in agony. With the ships' rebirths, conjoined voices were released into individual cries of ecstasy. Theirs was a joy so pure, Q almost wanted to join Picard on the deck.

"You see what I mean?"

Q turned to see his father standing beside him. He knew that even had the others been subconsciously aware of their presence there, none could have seen them, nor would they have bothered to look. The two Q were by far the least interesting thing in the room right now.

"This is the Caeliar transformation of the Borg?" Q asked, though he doubted it could be anything else.

"Magnificent, isn't it?"

"That's not a word you just throw around, Father."

"Why cheapen its meaning? Reserve it for moments like this, the ones that truly deserve it. You feel it, don't you?"

"The single-celled organisms in the room *feel* it," Q tossed back.

"Is there a level on which you could possibly argue that this is not an incredibly positive experience?" his father asked gently.

Q considered the question seriously before replying, "No."

"This is part of Kathryn's sacrifice, son. Even to have her live for all eternity, you cannot wish to see this undone."

"No, but why would that be necessary?" Q demanded.

"Allow me to connect the dots," his father replied. "When Kathy chose to alter time—a choice which she did not have to make, and a choice that many might argue was the height of self-ishness, which is something I had never before seen in her—she set a very particular chain of events in motion. There was no turning back once she destroyed the Borg's transwarp hub in the Delta Quadrant. That choice brought the Borg to the Alpha Quadrant hundreds of years before they would have otherwise ventured so far. That was the price for her choice, and as even you well understand by now, when anyone, Q or otherwise, disrupts the larger forces of time, life, and death, there is always a price. She wanted to spare her crew sixteen extra years in the Delta Quadrant. She put the needs of a few of those closest to her ahead of the many. In doing so, she brought the Alpha Quadrant to the brink of annihilation.

"However, by doing what she did, Kathy unknowingly insured that the only species capable of ending the Borg's reign of terror would be present at this moment. Only this precise confluence of events, including the Borg's actions here, the unending and truly perturbing luck of William Riker and his band of merry misfits— sorry, *multispecies crew*—in locating the Caeliar, and the tenacity of another exceptional, once human female, Captain Erika Hernandez, could have resulted in what you have just witnessed. Pull even a single string from this incredibly dense tapestry, including Kathryn's death aboard that cursed evolved cube, and the sheer volume of chaos injected into the multiverse becomes unmanage-able. More importantly, *this* moment never happens.

"The multiverse is an extraordinary place, son. Though at times it seems perverse in its machinations, it bends toward moments such as this, moments when numerous species take great leaps forward in their evolution and are forever altered. The price paid for this, not only by Kathryn but by sixty-three billion other sentient life-forms, was staggering. But it has resulted in a renewed equilibrium throughout the multiverse. It has self-corrected a wanton and egregious lapse made by a handful of humans thousands of years ago. In other words, it was worth it."

Q bowed his head, acknowledging his father's point, then raised it again in defiance. "Fine. Given what the Borg were and would ultimately become without the Caeliar's intervention, you are right. On balance, Kathryn Janeway's death seems a small enough price to pay."

"Why do I sense a 'but' coming on?"

"Let Aunt Kathy die. Allow all of this to come to pass. Don't change anything until once this magnificence is well behind us."

"And?"

"And bring her back now," Q suggested.

"Dear . . . merciful . . . Hrimshee."

Q CONTINUUM

"What?"

"Did I waste all of the resources I expended on your education?"

"Don't bother with the guilt, Father. As you've taught me well, it's a useless means of passing the time."

"So that's what you've learned? But the much more significant lesson, the one that would have been drilled into you in every course you took, still eludes you?"

"It's a stupid rule."

"Never reversing the death of a mortal is a stupid rule?"

"We're not talking about any random mortal. We're talking about my godmother."

"Stop it."

"But—"

"No. Stop it. If I have managed to convince you that preventing her death would have been a mistake, how can you possibly fail to understand the ramifications of bringing the dead back to life?"

"I do."

"You don't, or you wouldn't suggest it. Like everything else you are no doubt contemplating here, it has been done. And in every case, it ended badly, not just for the individual, but for the rest of the multiverse as well. We're omnipotent, Junior, not omniscient. That's why, over time, we've established a handful of limits to our actions that the entire Continuum agrees are absolutely necessary. Rule six is we don't bring the dead back to life. Just because we *can* do a thing doesn't mean we should. There are certain things we must abide by."

"But—"

"No. No buts. Not this time. Let's look at this from another angle. A little further into the future . . ."

. . .

". . . and so, obviously, you see what I mean."

"What?"

"Son?"

"Sorry, I do. Of course, I do. I see it all, now. I'm so sorry."

"I'll admit watching poor President Bacco wrestle with the latest moves the Typhon Pact is making, including the loss of Andor, may cast a pall on the near past, but this sort of instability is common following events of the magnitude of the transformation of the Borg."

"Andor left the Federation?"

"Were you listening to anything the president of the Federation said in that meeting? I, too, find the obvious aging she has undergone in the last few years distracting, but I assure you, she will rally. The woman has spunk. You have to give her that."

"I do. It wasn't a question. Andor left the Federation. It's just shocking, is all. Didn't they start the Federation?"

"They were a founding member, yes. It will all work itself out. Never fear. And it is an unquestionably better fate than they would have suffered had the Borg not been eliminated."

"Of course."

"So, we're done here?"

"Yes. Thank you, Father."

"Kathryn Janeway was extraordinary, son. I knew her better

than you did, and believe me when I tell you that if any of us could have spared her the grisly fate she met, we would have done so."

"I believe you. It's just difficult. I think she's the first mortal I ever really cared about whose death I've lived to witness."

"It does get easier with time, son."

"I'll try and remember that."

When was that? Andor leaving the Federation? Months, maybe a few years from now? President Bacco is still in office so it can't be too far in the future. That means there's even less time than I thought.

But it doesn't make any sense. Why can't I see it? And how much time, exactly, do I have left? Is it me? Am I the emptiness? Or is the emptiness surrounding me?

What is it? Was it something I did? Something I'm going to do?

I can't think like that. I'm a Q. I don't fear the darkness.

Except this one.

What am I supposed to do?

Chapter Four

VOYAGER

"Good morning," Captain Chakotay greeted his senior officers. "Did we enjoy ourselves yesterday?"

"And well into the evening, sir," Lieutenant Harry Kim noted, as amiable nods from Lieutenant Commander Tom Paris and Lieutenants Nancy Conlon, Devi Patel, and Kenth Lasren matched his own.

Chakotay offered his own smile of approval as he noticed the curious gaze Seven shot toward Counselor Cambridge, who kept his eyes firmly glued to the captain's.

"I'm glad to hear it," Chakotay said, "because now it's time to get to work. We have some busy weeks ahead of us." He turned his attention to Seven, who activated the conference room's three-dimensional holographic display at the table's center as he began the briefing.

"This is our next destination. We have a few hours left before all supply and personnel transfers will be complete, and then we'll be departing to what I have entered into the logs as 'Riley's Planet.'"

Though recognition immediately flashed across Paris's and Kim's faces, it was clear that those in the room who had not served during *Voyager*'s first journey through the Delta Quadrant were curious. Although Seven had not yet been aboard, she had been briefed in order to collect the relevant astrometrics data, most of which had been pulled from *Voyager*'s original logs.

"This wasn't Borg space, was it?" Conlon asked.

"No," Chakotay confirmed. "This unnamed world was discovered several months before *Voyager* entered Borg territory."

"Isn't the rest of the fleet exploring known Borg space?" Patel asked, seeming almost offended that the ship was abandoning one of their mission priorities.

"They are," Chakotay replied. "This world was colonized by eighty thousand Borg drones who had been severed from the Collective when their vessel was damaged during an electrokinetic storm. They lived for some time as individuals, before their inability to form a cohesive society led to brutal warfare between a number of factions, some driven by the race of the drones prior to their assimilation."

The captain glanced briefly at his officers to gauge their response and found Seven was watching Cambridge, who had begun gently tapping his fingers together.

"A small group decided that the only way they could end the violence was to restore their 'collective' nature."

"What?" Lasren asked in disbelief.

"They did not intend to rejoin the Borg Collective, Lieutenant," Chakotay assured him. "But they wished to reestablish a neural connection among themselves in hopes that they might restore order."

"But how could they do that?" Conlon inquired.

"They were Borg," Seven offered, as if that was answer enough.

"I don't mean how was it possible anyone would want to return to a collective state, Seven," Conlon replied. "I mean, without their ship, how . . . ?"

"They needed a little help," Paris jumped in, knowing that this part of the briefing would be difficult for Chakotay.

Unwilling to shrink from his duty, the captain went on, "I was in a shuttle that diverted to the planet when we received a distress call. The shuttle was damaged when Ensign Kaplan and I landed and we came under attack immediately. I was saved by a woman I initially thought was human, Riley Frazier. Kaplan was killed." Chakotay paused briefly, struck again by how every death of those under his command still weighed heavily. "It took several days for Riley to admit to me who her people really were and still longer for her to tell me what they intended to do. I was severely injured, and to help me heal, I was briefly linked to a small number of Riley's people. As a result, I recovered from my injuries. I was also able, during the link, to know Riley and the others of the collective as individuals. I saw that their intentions were good, even if I profoundly disagreed with their course of action."

"Did you help them?" Cambridge asked, apparently finally curious about the subject under discussion.

"Not intentionally," Chakotay replied. "*Voyager* found me, and I brought Riley aboard to plead her case to Captain Janeway. Although sympathetic, the captain was unwilling to provide the assistance Riley was requesting."

"In order to restore their collective nature," Seven told Conlon, "they would have had to restore power to a neuroelectric generator, and the only one large enough was located on their original vessel."

"Which was still intact, though dormant," Chakotay added. "It also contained a number of drones thought to be dead, but after closer evaluation were determined to be in a state of hibernation that could be reversed if that generator were again activated."

"Too dangerous to attempt," Conlon realized.

"That was Captain Janeway's assessment." Chakotay nodded.

"However, the brief link I shared with them had unforeseeable residual effects. Once we refused their request, they reestablished the link with me and forced me to carry out their wishes."

Cambridge's eyes widened. "That must have been unpleasant."

"Yes," Chakotay replied as his jaw tightened. "Riley's people reestablished their link with the others on the planet and, immediately after, initiated the cube's self-destruct mechanism to prevent its posing any threat to *Voyager* or the rest of the colonists. They also offered me their gratitude and assurances that this would be a positive new beginning for them."

"Damn, that was big of them," Cambridge observed.

"It was inappropriate for them to restore that link without the agreement of everyone who would have been affected by it," Seven shot back.

"That was the heart of the captain's objection," Chakotay revealed.

"They should never have done it," Seven stated unequivocally.

The room grew silent, uncomfortable with the former Borg's uncharacteristic outburst.

"Did the rest of the Borg ever come back for them?" Patel asked, clearly hoping to move past this difficult subject.

"It's possible." Chakotay nodded. "It's also possible they met with some other fate before that could have happened."

"Either way, they still retained sufficient Borg technology to reestablish their link, which means they would have been absorbed by the Caeliar like the rest of the Borg," Seven stated with great certainty.

"Also possible," Chakotay concurred.

"They might have succeeded in creating a new, somewhat autonomous society," Cambridge interjected, "and been disinclined to abandon it when the Caeliar came calling."

"Doubtful," Seven replied.

"We need to know," Chakotay said definitively. "This was a unique situation, analogous to, though not exactly the same as, Seven's. The Caeliar transformed all of the Borg and former Borg—except Seven, who remained free of the gestalt by choice.

We need to know if that choice was offered to Riley's people, and if so, what their answer was."

"Well, I for one am curious," Kim offered.

"So am I," Chakotay replied. "Now, if there aren't any further questions, let's get to work."

Tom Paris was due on the bridge, but found himself forced to make an unwelcome detour. He and B'Elanna had spent much of the previous evening in a heated discussion of the unwarranted risks she felt he'd taken during the TS Flyers' demonstration. He couldn't blame her, and understood her need to release her tension. Pity was, after the flight he'd returned to *Voyager* with a different means of tension release on his mind and had been shot down.

Tom entered their quarters to find B'Elanna recycling the breakfast dishes as Miral played on the floor with a small set of blocks. His arrival clearly took his wife by surprise.

"What's wrong?" B'Elanna immediately asked.

"Change of plan," he replied, taking her by the hand and pulling her toward their bedroom.

"It's not that I don't appreciate the sentiment," B'Elanna said, "and I've almost completely forgiven you, but I was due in engineering five minutes ago and the Doctor hasn't gotten back to me yet about—"

Tom took her hands in his, shaking his head as he lowered his voice. "We can't leave Miral with the Doctor for this trip."

"Why not?" B'Elanna demanded, her whisper harsh with disappointment.

"He's not going to be aboard *Galen* for the duration. He's got another mission. Chakotay just informed me. Captain Eden, Cambridge, and the Doctor are headed off with *Achilles* somewhere."

B'Elanna stifled a curse as she glanced toward their living area to assure herself that Miral was still busy with her blocks. When she again raised her eyes to Tom's, they held a fair amount of fear.

"It's better this way," he tried to reassure her. "She'll be with us."

"We're going back to Borg space."

"Near Borg space."

"Oh, that's terribly comforting."

"And Seven is absolutely certain we're not going to find anything."

"What if she's wrong?"

Tom shrugged. "We *have* beaten them before."

"Do you think Admiral Janeway was thinking along those lines . . . ?"

"Don't," Tom practically pleaded.

"I'm sorry," B'Elanna replied, clearly chagrined. "I just can't shake this feeling."

"I know," Tom said. They'd already discussed this several times since rumors of the fleet's next mission had begun floating around. B'Elanna had suggested Miral might be safer with the Doctor, rather than aboard *Voyager*. After the trauma they'd endured at the hands of the Warriors of Gre'thor, Tom was amazed B'Elanna was willing to let Miral out of her sight. He'd privately wondered if her choice to keep Miral close on *Achilles,* while repairs were being made to the *Quirinal* several weeks earlier, had more to do with her unspoken fears than the bond developing between Miral and Captain Drafar. Tom was beginning to realize that whatever B'Elanna feared about their latest mission was greater than her need to personally see to her daughter's safety.

"I don't understand this," B'Elanna said, clearly frustrated. "Every time I think about the coming weeks, I get this knot in my stomach."

"I'd be lying if I said I was looking forward to revisiting the Borg's old home," Tom admitted. "We could leave her with Neelix. I'm sure he'd jump at the chance."

"He would," B'Elanna agreed. "And now that Miral's immunizations are up to date, there's no risk, especially with *Galen* still close by."

"So?" Tom asked.

B'Elanna took a deep breath and exhaled slowly. She glanced

again toward Miral, who had just knocked a tower over and let out a small warrior's cry of delight. Finally she said, "No. She comes with us."

"Are you sure?"

"I don't know what's going to happen. I don't know why I feel this way. But part of me thinks that the only thing worse than exposing her to it would be leaving her alone—"

"Don't even think it," Tom insisted, pulling her into a tight hug.

B'Elanna buried her head in his shoulder for a moment, and Tom felt a shudder pass through her.

She's never going to forgive me, Counselor Hugh Cambridge thought as he directed his steps toward the holodeck. He had felt Seven's attempts to make eye contact with him during the morning briefing. He had chosen to appear professionally distant throughout the meeting. But he feared he would not do as well when it came to hiding the enthusiasm he felt for his upcoming mission with Captain Eden, which was about to impinge on the first "personal" time he and Seven had scheduled: breakfast on the holodeck, or the safest possible "first date."

The weeks that had followed *Voyager*'s encounter with the Children of the Storm and their "mother" had been uncharacteristically busy for the counselor. The destruction of one of the fleet's sister ships created a ripple of post-traumatic stress through the survivors, complicated by the diplomatic victory that had been wrenched from the disaster. Cambridge was pleased that the encounter had resulted in quantifiable positive results for the fleet and the Children, but the price had been too many lost lives.

As a ship's counselor, it had been Cambridge's job to listen and to remind his patients that those who accepted a Starfleet commission did so knowing that their service might end in self-sacrifice. He assured them that, in time, they would make peace with the loss.

Personally, Cambridge did not believe that the *Planck*'s crew had died for a higher purpose, despite the final outcome. Their deaths had been pointless. But then, most deaths were. As best Cambridge could tell, the resulting benefits for both sides had more to do with dumb luck and the willful, brilliant arrogance of Commander Liam O'Donnell than any nobility of action displayed by *Voyager* or *Planck*'s crew. But he would take the good and the bad, believing that it was a rare day when good even showed up, let alone bothered to make itself comfortable.

However, the best thing that had happened in recent days—or the worst, depending on how he looked at it—had nothing at all to do with the mission, and everything to do with his former patient, Seven of Nine.

From the moment they had met, Seven had captivated the counselor. She had a similar effect on most people. She was, quite simply, the most compelling, complex combination of intelligence, strength, and innocence he had ever encountered. It also didn't hurt that she was a perfect physical female specimen. Cambridge didn't bother lying to himself that he was interested only in her mind. He also didn't deceive himself that a purely physical relationship with her, like most he had enjoyed throughout his life, could have been an option. He knew that a casual fling would do unspeakable and malicious harm to her, and that he could not countenance.

It had come as a complete surprise several days ago when Seven had marched into his office, kissed him, and announced that she was willing to pursue a more intimate relationship, were he so inclined. His primitive lizard brain had no trouble answering the question. The rest of him was proving a harder sell. Cambridge agreed to test the waters and suggested the most innocuous breakfast date.

When the counselor entered the holodeck, he was surprised to find no program running. Seven stood against a stark black field, lit only by an orange grid of holographic generators.

"Simple," he said, attempting joviality. "Classic. I like it."

Seven faced him with a hard stare. "I did not see the point in wasting the time necessary to create an appropriate romantic environment as I will clearly be dining alone this morning."

That's my girl, Cambridge thought, relieved.

"It's not my fault," he attempted, opening his arms at his sides, palms out, almost inviting her next attack.

"Explain," she requested.

"I only learned late last night that the mission I am about to undertake—"

"You could have contacted me 'late last night.' You might have suspected that I would be concerned when you failed to make an appearance at the reception."

"You must have known that your presence was the only delight that reception would have held for me."

Her face softened a little as she considered accepting the compliment.

"You also could have contacted me this morning, prior to the briefing, or pulled me aside once it was over to advise me of the change in our arrangements."

"Seven, we haven't even had a first date."

"You could have made eye contact with me at the briefing."

Cambridge hazarded a step toward her. "I'm afraid that might do more to arouse suspicion among our comrades. You see, my dear, we've crossed a Rubicon of sorts."

"It was one kiss, Counselor."

"One kiss was more than sufficient to engender thoughts I fear are too plainly read on my face any time I glance at you."

He felt his heart rate quicken and he saw a flush rising in Seven's porcelain cheeks.

"What's the mission?"

"I'm not at liberty to say."

Seven stared through him.

"You're looking forward to it. You're not sorry you're not spending time with me, or you wouldn't be working so hard to convince me otherwise," she stated.

He physically ached to close the few remaining steps between them.

"You're right. I am looking forward to it. But you are also wrong."

"Explain."

Cambridge considered his options: flattery, deception, a plea for compassion. None of them were as tempting as honesty. He realized, with trepidation, that was the most dangerous choice.

"I'm not sure our attempt to explore a more personal relationship is a good idea. It's not something I have a talent for, nor have I met anyone in years that would even tempt me to contemplate it. But I find, much to my dismay, that I am at your mercy. I shouldn't say yes, but I cannot imagine saying no."

After a long pause, Seven took two paces forward, meeting him eye to eye as the warmth radiating from her body assaulted him.

"Enjoy the mission, Counselor," she said calmly, then stepped past him and exited the holodeck.

Her sudden absence chilled him, like a cloud passing over the sun on a warm day. Still, if this was how she took disappointment, their relationship might hold more promise than he'd dared imagine.

I'm doomed, he decided, without a hint of regret.

Eden resisted the urge to pace the deck before the transporter platform. She had made her decision to accept Hugh, Chakotay, and the Doctor's recommendation within an hour of her return to her quarters. She had spent a sleepless night attempting to recall what she could of her travels with her uncles and the few crumbs they'd dropped over the years about her past and how they'd found her.

She'd always had a remarkable memory and a talent for intuiting odd connections between disparate bits of information. Sadly, Eden had learned that these gifts failed her when the subjects had emotional intensity. Her epic blindness to Willem Batiste's deceit was the best example. As she thought of her uncles, Tallar and Jobin, she felt an inability to connect the dots. Swirling among the feelings of anger at their many lies were deeper and infinitely more intense feelings of love and devotion. Of one thing Eden was absolutely certain: they had loved her, and the choices they had made to mislead her could only have come from a desire on their part to keep her safe.

At 0600 hours, she had informed Chakotay of her decision, giving him time to alert the Doctor and Cambridge. The Doctor was already waiting for her in the transporter room when she entered. As ever, Cambridge was pushing punctuality to its maximum safe tolerance level.

The captain turned to admonish Cambridge when she heard the doors swish open, but found Chakotay moving purposefully toward her. He favored the Doctor with a wide smile of greeting before taking quick inventory of her expression.

"You made the right decision," he said without preamble.

"I think you're just looking forward to having this ship all to yourself," she teased.

He pretended to consider the remark. "You might have something there."

As her eyes narrowed into a glare, Chakotay added, "I promise to return *Voyager* to the fleet on schedule without a scratch on her."

"I'll hold you to that." Eden replied.

"It's a gift, Afsarah," Chakotay assured her. "That our current flight plan takes us close enough to the Mikhal Outpost for *Achilles* to detour to it might be taken as a sign."

"A good one?"

"Absolutely. Most of us have to find a way to live with the mysteries of our past, the questions we never thought to ask, roads never traveled. But I'm happy you may find your answers."

"Is your ship's counselor always this rude?" the Doctor interrupted.

Chakotay turned to him with a sigh. "Doctor, you haven't seen the half of it."

"Oh, good," the Doctor replied.

"But he is also vital to this mission's success," Chakotay advised him seriously. "He and Captain Eden are old friends. The counselor was the first person she took into her confidence. That, along with his background in comparative psychological and mythological studies, should reassure you that his presence is more than warranted. I know you will work together constructively."

"I'll try, Captain," the Doctor replied with a very put-upon air.

"Doctor," Chakotay said softly, "I'm asking you this as a friend."

"Understood," the Doctor said, nodding.

For a brief moment, Eden found herself envying the closeness these two shared. Though it was true she had begun to open herself up to the possibilities of real friendships with those she commanded, she knew what she was seeing here was a bond, forged through years of facing the impossible together. The last two people who had created such a space in her heart had been Tallar and Jobin.

As Chakotay grasped the Doctor gently by the arm, careful to avoid the band where his mobile emitter was fastened, the room's doors again opened and Counselor Cambridge lumbered in, carrying a rucksack over his shoulder. He immediately moved past them and took his place on the transporter pad. After a moment of stunned silence he asked, "Well, what are we waiting for?"

Eden watched the Doctor bite back a response before offering Chakotay a wary nod.

"Be good," Chakotay directed toward Cambridge. "That's an order."

To Eden he offered his hand. "I'll see you very soon, Captain," he said warmly.

"With lots of interesting stories to tell, I hope," she replied.

Chapter Five

ERIS

The Department of Temporal Investigation's vault of artifacts on the dwarf planet called Eris was not a place the Q would normally trouble themselves to disturb. The vast majority of devices stored there had long since lost their original utilities for disrupting the timestream, and most of those that hadn't lacked compatible power sources to make them functional. The reason they were stored here, along with backup copies of all of the DTI's temporal records, was so they could never be used for their intended purposes, and to that end, they were well protected.

More important, the Q did not require anything so crude as the vault's contents to travel through time. As Amanda had learned shortly after she had chosen to accept the reality that she was Q, traveling through time was as simple as deciding where she wanted to go. You didn't even have to pack for inclement weather. Although being a Q came with its fair share of challenges, it also came with many extraordinary benefits, and on the whole, Amanda was pleased with her lot.

She had begun experimenting with her time travel abilities as soon as the Continuum had granted her the privilege. While time travel was exhilarating, the fact was, it took . . . well . . . time. When one was effectively immortal, this might not seem like a stumbling block, but Amanda eventually realized that there were moments, such as this one, where time *was* of the essence. The information she required could be gleaned by a number of well-planned excursions, though she had no doubt Junior had already undertaken them. His certainty that Kathryn Janeway's death was a fixed point in time could not have come from a random sampling of various timelines. He would have thoroughly researched his claim before he'd ever dared to make it. Hers was the unenviable task of finding something he'd missed. And that would take time, which she was unwilling to spend.

Thankfully, if she was right, she wouldn't have to. Junior's father—who had been a guide of sorts to her in her early years in the Continuum—had let slip he'd hidden a device in the Eridian vault, believing it to be the last place any self-respecting Q would look and confident that no one in the DTI would ever learn anything about it beyond the massive chroniton readings it emitted. This would make its storage on Eris mandatory, from their point of view, and as their mission was to protect time without altering it, there was no chance they would attempt to use it.

Not that they could. A Q had created it and only a Q could operate it. Q swore it was his design when he first showed it to her. But Amanda had learned, by using it while unsupervised, that it was actually the creation of the Q who had been banished to a comet for bringing disorder to the Continuum. Amanda had only seen that Q in his brief, prerecorded introduction to the device but had decided instantly that she liked him and that whatever "disorder" he'd brought to the Continuum, they probably needed it.

In appearance the device was unremarkable: a small black stone, known as the "prism." When focused by a Q, it had the ability to bend time in such a way as to allow one to witness the events of *any* timeline. Amanda would have to enter the timeline to experience it, but as a pure research tool, the prism was invaluable.

Having assured herself that she was alone and would not be disturbed by Eris security, Amanda stood in the darkened subvault, holding the prism in her hand. One of Q's design quirks required the user to take physical form in order to operate the device. She cleared her being and brought to the forefront of her concentration that which she wanted to see. Turning the prism three times in her palm, she then held it up and peered through it. Within seconds, the scene she sought appeared before her eyes, refracted at an angle through the prism, but easy enough to see.

It was a grisly sight. What had once been Kathryn Janeway had been assimilated by the Borg. The thing that bore her face had lost all traces of its humanity. Amanda hurried the vision along until the cube that had made her its queen was blown to pieces.

It was harder, after witnessing this spectacle, to focus on the next inquiry, but Amanda forced herself to do so. Patiently, methodically, she watched timeline after timeline and soon enough concluded that Junior might be right in his assessment of Janeway's death.

Finally, Amanda was able to focus her intentions enough to demand that the prism show her evidence of a timeline in which Kathryn Janeway still lived—beyond the moment where she died in every other timeline. She held her physical form's breath while she waited, almost certain that the attempt would fail. Gradually, she felt the prism's heat differential rise, and to her amazement, a new scene played out before her.

It was a moment of chaos on the *Voyager*'s bridge. Janeway was leading her crew through a crisis, barking orders and clinging to her command chair as if her life depended on it. Amanda could faintly hear communications from another vessel, and she searched all of space-time to locate its source. By the time she had succeeded in pinpointing its location, the crisis for Janeway and her crew seemed to pass. Relief washed over all of those present, until Janeway received a call over the ship's comm system and hurried from the bridge. The prism allowed Amanda to follow Janeway as she entered the turbolift and ran to sickbay. There the bloody figure of a blond woman, her beauty marred by metallic objects affixed to her face and hand, her flesh scorched, was being gently lifted to a biobed by a distressed man who bore a striking tattoo on his forehead.

Amanda had seen enough. She deactivated the prism and, with a gentle force of will, chose to enter that specific timestream in order to study it more carefully.

Seconds later, to her alarm, she found herself still standing in the vault on Eris. Several additional attempts yielded the same result. Eventually Amanda was forced to accept that for reasons she could not imagine, this timeline was beyond her ability to reach.

This was troubling, because like so many other things Junior had told her recently, that should have been impossible.

Q CONTINUUM

"Where have you been?"

"Somebody woke up on the wrong side of eternity this morning."

"It's rude to just leave in the middle of a conversation, Amanda."

"I'm sorry. I just realized there might be something that could help us, and I wanted to make sure before I said anything more. I didn't want you to get your hopes up, in case . . ."

"Trust me, there's no chance that's going to happen now."

"Q?"

"What did you find?"

"What's wrong with you?"

"Tell me what you found first."

"No."

"Amanda!"

"No. I understand she was your godmother, but your obsession with this goes beyond anything you could possibly feel for her. You don't feel anything that deeply, except your father's displeasure, and that's exactly what you're risking by continuing to pursue this."

"If that's true, why do you waste your time with me?"

"You're Q. Feelings aren't exactly your forte."

"You're Q, too."

"Yes, but I had a life as a human first. Their experience of reality is informed almost entirely by their feelings, and it's a pretty tough thing to unlearn. And you know exactly why I waste my time with you. We're both different. We're the only children of a race that never procreated until we came along. You're the closest thing I've got to a brother, so even when you're annoying the hell out of me, I'm not just going to write you off."

"Well, I hate to break it to you, but you might want to get used to the idea of being an only child."

"That's not even possible."

"You're sure about that?"

"I am."

"I'm not."

"You're going to have to do better than that."

"I'm waiting."

"Fine. For most of my life, I thought I was like every other Q.

I did what I wanted, went where I pleased, explored the multiverse at will, you know the drill."

"I do. And that's not entirely accurate."

"Okay, up until a while back I did all of those things under strict parental supervision, but after I finished my coursework, the Continuum relaxed that rule."

"What changed?"

"I don't know, exactly. But it started fairly recently, a few years ago, maybe by linear calendars."

"What started?"

"This."

. . .

"*WhattheohmywhatIcan'tohwhatwhere . . . ?*"

"Give it a minute."

"Better now?"

"What was that?"

"That's what happens to me every single time I try to access any point in time that is in the near or distant future."

"Did you hear the screaming?"

"Sorry, that was probably me. It's worse now than it was at first. I can't bear more than a few moments of it. You wouldn't believe the trouble I've had trying to hide this from my parents. They're big on the future, always wanting to show me the amazing things that are in store. I used to love it, really. It was fun. And now I can't . . ."

"This is wrong."

"I know. It's like I don't exist there."

"But of course you do. You're Q. Your existence transcends normal space and time. You exist everywhere at once."

"No, Amanda, *you do*. My parents do. The rest of the Continuum does. There's something wrong with me."

"Okay. Let's just be calm about this."

"You be calm. I'm embracing panic as a new state of existence."

"You said it wasn't always this way. It changed recently. Did something happen?"

"It wasn't anything I ate, if that's what you're asking."

"You know it isn't."

"It kind of snuck up on me. I was actually with Kol the first time it happened."

"How is he? I haven't seen him since graduation."

"He doesn't get out much anymore, stays really close to home since his mother came back. And by the way, *really not* the point."

"Sorry."

"At first I thought I might have discovered some new dimension or something. I played with it. And then I started testing it in incredibly small measures to see if I could fix a starting point for it."

"And did you succeed?"

"Within a few days."

"A few days of when?"

"Now."

"Oh."

"I can still go back in time as far as I want. I've studied every timeline there is. I paid particular attention to the multiple lives of anyone I interacted with on a fixed dimensional plane."

"That's how you figured out that Kathryn's death is a fixed point in time."

"I kept coming back to her, like I was drawn to her. It wasn't a choice, more like an instinct. After a while it seemed like there had to be a connection between what the multiverse was doing to her and what it was doing to me."

"The multiverse doesn't act on you, Q. You're beyond it."

"Amanda, that's what I used to think, too. But I'm almost positive now that somehow, something she did, or didn't do, caused this."

"Something she *didn't* do?"

"Aunt Kathy changed time. My dad told me about it a while ago. I've never seen it because by the time I thought to look, it didn't exist anymore, but there used to be a timeline where she didn't get her crew home in seven years. It took a lot longer. As best I can tell now, as long as that timeline existed, I had free rein throughout all space and time. But that timeline collapsed when she made a decision to go back into her own past and, through her interactions with her past self, changed her future. *Voyager* returned to the Alpha Quadrant years ahead of schedule and everyone was happy. But in that same blink of an eye, my existence was altered, and apparently, so was hers. That's when her death became a fixed point across the multiverse. And the worst part is, because that collapsed timeline no longer exists for me to study, I can't even figure out what any of this has to do with me."

"Maybe you can."

"I've tried."

"I don't mean you can experience it, but you should be able to see it. I have."

"What are you talking about?"

"There's this thing on Eris. It's called the prism. Your father showed it to me once. I swear he uses it more than he'd ever let on, but that's another conversation. It's a time refractor. Any Q can use it to see every timeline at any point. I was just there and I saw a timeline where Kathryn Janeway survived beyond the point of her death everywhere else."

"I'm going there now."

"Wait."

"Amanda, I don't have time—"

"Wait! When I found that one timeline, I had the same thought. Not exactly, because I didn't know the specifics of your problem, but I tried to enter that timeline to experience it so I could give you a full report and prove you wrong. But I couldn't do it. I could see it through the prism. But I couldn't go there. Just like you can't go to the future."

"You saw the blackness?"

"I didn't even get that far. I never left Eris."

"That's impossible."

"We seem to be reaching that conclusion with alarming frequency these days, don't we?"

"What did you see through the prism?"

"Kathryn Janeway was on her ship in the Delta Quadrant.

There was some sort of emergency. There were serious injuries to a few people. But the crisis passed and she was still alive."

"That's not much to go on."

"The prism isn't the most sophisticated tool. I did sense, however, that there was another ship involved in what was happening. And I'm pretty sure it still exists."

"What ship?"

"I'm going to find it and take a look."

"I'm going with you."

"No."

"Why not?"

"It's too dangerous."

"What have I got to lose?"

"Q, I don't know and I don't want to know. Maybe this is what causes your problem in the first place, if it's connected at all. But you're staying as far away from it as I can keep you until I understand more."

"It's not your job to protect me, Amanda."

No, it's mine.

"Did you hear that?"

"What?"

"Never mind. Amanda, please take me with you."

"No. I promise I'll come back as soon as I know anything, and then we'll take this to the Continuum."

"No, we won't."

"They might be able to help."

"You think? Because my guess is they're going to look at the only two Q in existence not created at the dawn of time who are suddenly having difficulty traveling in time like any normal Q and decide *we're* the problem."

"You might have a point there."

"Then I'll go to Eris and use that prism thing."

"Wait until I get back. I won't be a second."

"Fine."

"I'll be right back."

"Amanda!"

"Amanda?"

"Amanda . . ."

My poor darling. Why didn't you tell me?

Chapter Six

VOYAGER

"Well, Mister Lasren?" Chakotay asked, wondering if the long-range sensor scans of the tranquil-looking planet on the main viewscreen were really all there was to see.

"Coordinates confirmed, sir," Lasren replied from ops. "It's definitely Riley's Planet."

Chakotay willed his stomach to settle as he awaited the next series of reports. Much as he wanted to know the fate of Riley Frazier and her collective, he'd never been able to dismiss the notion that from the moment they'd first met, he'd been dancing with the devil.

"Scans of the surface from this distance are not going to be entirely accurate, Captain," Lasren continued, "but it appears that the collective has expanded since your last visit."

"Indeed," Chakotay replied softly. A sharp pain shot up along the left side of his spine, evidence of his tension. The thought that Riley's relatively small "cooperative" might have seen fit to add to its numbers was one nightmare scenario that had plagued him since *Voyager* had departed this sector years earlier. There was nothing they could have done about it. A single ship, far from home, wasn't about to wage war on eighty thousand sentient life-forms who only wished to live in their perverse version of peace. And much as it galled Chakotay, *Voyager* had only been able to dispatch warning buoys before departing, advising travelers of the nature of the planet's inhabitants. Still, the captain was truly shocked that things turned out this way.

Once Borg, always Borg, I guess.

Watching Seven grow into her humanity had given Chakotay hope that Riley and the other former Borg might manage to evolve. Now, he wondered if he had ever truly appreciated how unique Seven really was.

"How many inhabitants are you reading, Lieutenant?" Tom Paris asked.

"Over two hundred thousand," Lasren replied.

Chakotay turned, and his eyes met Tom's. The disappointment and trepidation both clearly felt were mirrored back to one another.

"Are we picking up any evidence of Borg technology?" Chakotay asked.

"No, sir," Lasren replied. "There are a number of energy readings, but none that register as Borg."

"Maybe the Caeliar's reach extended here too," Tom said, hopefully.

"Captain, we've got incoming," Harry Kim reported from tactical.

Tom quickly ordered, "Red Alert." Then added, "On-screen."

Under the circumstances, Chakotay wasn't going to fault his first officer for being cautious.

A ship replaced the image of the planet. Its hull shared the dark black coloring of a Borg cube, but that's where any similarity ended. A harsh-looking vessel, configured like a wide, multilevel isosceles triangle, approached. The point and adjacent sides of the widest, forward angle appeared to be the command component of the ship. It comprised the entirety of the vessel's upper level. Its rear section angled back toward the center point, giving it the appearance of a wide V, and was lined with thrusters. Small nacelles were affixed to each of its sides. Beneath this array, a second level was visible, filling in the rest of the "triangle." The rear ends of this level were also equipped with propulsion systems. Weapons arrays were evenly spaced and integrated into the upper and lower levels. It wasn't one-twentieth *Voyager*'s size, but its sharp angles and obvious firepower were intimidating nonetheless.

"Whoever they are, I don't recognize them," Tom offered.

"Neither do I," Chakotay agreed. "What's their distance, Harry?"

"Five hundred thousand kilometers and closing," Kim replied.

"Why are we just picking them up?" Tom asked.

"They appeared, following a visible interphasic disruption," Kim replied tensely. "Looks like they've got a form of cloaking technology."

"Are they alone?" Chakotay asked, clearly troubled by this news.

"Reconfiguring sensors now, Captain," Patel called from the bridge's aft science station.

"What else can you tell me about them, Harry?" Chakotay asked.

"Crew complement is fourteen humanoid life-forms. Their shields and weapons are standard for a ship of their size," Kim reported.

"Open a channel," Chakotay ordered.

"Aye, sir. Channel open," Lasren replied.

"This is Captain Chakotay of the Federation *Starship Voyager*. We are here on an exploratory mission. Please identify yourselves."

A few tense seconds passed before Lasren advised, "Incoming response, audio only."

Following a burst of low static a rough, rasping voice that sounded like it had been run through a few too many computerized compressions replied, "*We are the Tarkons. We claim this part of space as our own.*"

Chakotay tried to keep things friendly, though his gut advised him that wasn't going to last long. "We didn't mean to arrive unannounced, but the last time we were here, this area was unaffiliated."

"*Are you challenging our claim?*" the voice demanded.

"Not at all," Chakotay immediately replied. "We've only come to take a look at the fourth planet in the system. We have no hostile intentions toward you or the planet's occupants, and we'd appreciate the opportunity to proceed in peace."

"*The planet in question is one of our resettlement facilities. You will not proceed,*" the voice answered curtly.

Chakotay looked to Lasren and motioned for him to silence audio. When Lasren had nodded the all-clear, Chakotay said, "Why does the name Tarkon ring a bell?"

"When we were charting the Nekrit Expanse, we were warned by the Mikhal Travelers to avoid Tarkon space," Kim replied.

Tom added, "The Tarkons were known for their propensity and skill in stealing other people's vessels."

The hazy warning Chakotay had been struggling with crystallized. "I remember. It was Zahir who told Tuvok about them, right?"

"We charted a course well clear of their known space," Tom added, "which at the time didn't extend this far."

"So they've been busy," Chakotay said grimly. "Lasren, I need better data on the planet's inhabitants. If our friends are telling the truth, they could have colonized the planet over the objections of Riley's people, or if their acquisition was more recent . . ."

"You mean if the Caeliar absorbed Riley's people?" Tom asked.

"Yes. The Tarkons might have just come along and claimed what was left," Chakotay replied.

"We're going to have to get closer for that," Lasren replied, "unless Seven can assist me."

"Chakotay to Seven of Nine," the captain called over the comm. "Have you been monitoring our communications with the Tarkons?"

"*Yes, Captain. I am in the process of attempting to enhance our long-range scanners for more detailed physiological signatures,*" Seven replied. "*I will require a minimum of fifteen minutes to complete the operation.*"

"Harry, how much damage can those ships do?"

"Once they're in range, which they will be in five minutes, not a lot. We can hold out against one indefinitely. But if there are more of them out there . . ." Kim warned.

"Noted."

"Let's hope this one likes to chat," Tom offered.

"I haven't gotten that impression, but I could be wrong," Chakotay replied, nodding to Lasren to reopen the channel.

Before Chakotay could resume the conversation, the Tarkon vessel's captain—Chakotay assumed—stated briskly, "Starship Voyager, *under article forty-seven, section thirteen of the Tarkon Commercial Charter, you are in violation of our territory, which is considered an act of war. You are ordered to surrender your vessel and prepare your crew for transport to the nearest Tarkon resettlement facility. Hold position and prepare to be boarded.*"

At this, Tom's eyebrows shot up in amusement. "Who do they think they're kidding?" he asked softly enough that only Chakotay could hear him.

"Tarkon ship," Chakotay began as diplomatically as possible, "as I've already indicated, we came here in peace. We were unaware of your claims to this part of space, and now that we've been apprised of it, we will willingly depart without conflict."

"*Your intentions are of no consequence. Prepare to be boarded,*" the voice replied.

"They've cut the channel, Captain," Lasren advised.

"If we allow them to detain us, we will get that closer look we've been hoping for of Riley's Planet. I'm assuming that's the nearest resettlement facility," Tom offered with a healthy dose of sarcasm.

Chakotay weighed his options for a moment. His mandate was to avoid armed conflict except in the most extreme circumstances. While learning the fate of the planet's former "colonists" was a priority, he wasn't sure it rose to the level required for him to initiate hostilities. However, remaining in Tarkon space was going to be construed as starting hostilities, whether *Voyager* fired a single shot or not. His gut told him the Tarkons wouldn't be making such a ridiculous threat if they didn't believe they could back it up. Past reports of the Tarkons certainly gave credence to the possibility.

"Ensign Gwyn, plot a retreat course that takes us on a fairly wide arc toward the planet. Lasren, alert Seven that this is the best look we're going to get, so make it count."

"Captain, if I may?" Gwyn interrupted.

"Ensign?"

"There's something really odd about that ship's propulsion configuration."

"How so?" Tom asked, taking a close look at the readout he was getting from his command chair's data panel.

"The wider, upper array of the vessel has to have full navigational capabilities. The lower array is too small to contain a warp drive. It's actually completely unnecessary, unless . . ."

"Unless?" Chakotay asked as his flight controller's voice trailed off.

"Captain, the Tarkon ship is altering configuration," Kim quickly advised.

How does a single ship alter its configuration? Chakotay wondered as the incredibly disheartening spectacle played itself out on the main viewscreen.

"Helm, evasive maneuvers!" he ordered as what had been a single ship broke apart into five smaller vessels. Four of them had previously been the ship's lower level. Once freed from the wide-angled bar that comprised the upper level, they were revealed as smaller but incredibly maneuverable and well-armed ships. The V section continued its approach, arming its own weapons in the process as its four compatriots moved into a diamond formation, obviously intent on surrounding *Voyager*.

"Four more Tarkon vessels decloaking," Kim's raised voice called from tactical.

Chakotay did the math instantaneously. A moment ago they had been facing one Tarkon ship. Now they were facing twenty-five. Avoiding hostilities now seemed impossible.

Suddenly, bright yellow energy beams erupted from the bellies of each of the four smaller vessels. They were not, however, directed at *Voyager*. Instead, they merged at a central point and as they did so, numerous identical beams formed in concentric circles around the center where the beams initially converged.

The four vessels' approach vector widened, and the net they had cast between them did the same, clearly preparing to engulf *Voyager*.

Chakotay didn't wait to see more. "Helm, get us out of here, maximum warp."

Seven of Nine did not normally find it debilitating to perform her routine functions in astrometrics. She had slept well and consumed an appropriate amount of nutrients to sustain her before beginning her duty shift. Her day's work thus far had consisted of aligning the sensors at her disposal to provide the most detailed analysis available of the planet *Voyager* had come to investigate. Although she firmly believed it was an exercise in futility, she intended to gather as much evidence as possible of the "nothing" she was certain they were about to find.

Although she had been surprised the moment *Voyager* dropped out of warp to discover signs of a much larger population than Riley's colonists could possibly account for, that could not have caused the wave of light-headedness she felt.

She forced herself to focus past it and was soon dividing her attention between Chakotay's conversation with the Tarkon vessel and the redistribution of power required to optimize the astrometric array.

The second wave of dizziness unsteadied her on her feet and caused her gorge to rise. This sensation was followed by a brief, piercing pain above her right eye and at the base of her neck.

Inhaling deeply to clear her vision, she heard Chakotay call to her from the bridge and marshaled all of her resources to answer him and continue the task at hand.

As she waited for the array's realignment and watched the status bar creep incredibly slowly toward operational levels, a third and significantly more intensive wave of disorientation took her knees out from under her.

Seven found herself on the deck, reaching for the edge of the station above her to pull herself to her feet with one hand as she lifted the other to tap her combadge and call for assistance.

As another pain sliced through her head, both her arms dropped and her body tumbled onto the deck. Bright flashes of light forced her eyes closed but continued to penetrate the darkness as she lost consciousness.

Chapter Seven

U.S.S. ACHILLES

Commander Tillum Drafar, Captain of the *Achilles,* entered the transporter room with his final report for Captain Eden. Her team was already assembled, and each carried small equipment packs on their backs. They were quite prepared for a long journey on the surface of the relatively small planet below.

"Good morning Captain, Counselor, Doctor," he greeted each of them officiously before settling his attention on Eden. Though Captain Eden was considered tall for a human female, the top of her head only just reached his shoulders. At two and a half meters high, Drafar was considered of average height for a Lendrin. "I have spoken with the resident administrator, a gentleman who called himself Ghert, and he has cleared your team for transport. He has indicated that you should be mindful of all posted signs and consider yourselves welcome to visit the local tavern in Midrin, which is the closest encampment to the area you will be exploring."

"How thoughtful of him," Eden replied without enthusiasm. Intelligence on the Mikhal indicated that they offered fair terms in trade of information or resources, but by nature were suspicious of strangers and anxious to embellish the truth if it might result in any sort of advantage in negotiations.

"Is it my imagination, or is the outpost a little busier than it was the last time *Voyager* stopped here?" Eden asked briskly.

"Ghert did indicate that traffic around the outpost has increased significantly in the last few months. Apparently," Drafar continued, "reports are continuously flowing in about the lack of activity along the borders of territory formerly known to be held by the Borg. I did not inform Mister Ghert about the Federation's contact with the Caeliar, but did advise him that we had not noted any Borg activity en route to the outpost."

"Good," Eden acknowledged. Soon enough, any space-faring species daring enough to travel near Borg space would likely come to the same conclusion, but the Federation fleet hadn't returned to the Delta Quadrant to "spread the good news," as it were. Rather, they had come to confirm it. If at some point the matter were decisively settled, Starfleet would be apprised and new orders might be issued about releasing the information to any natives the fleet encountered.

"My transporter chief," Drafar indicated the officer behind him, "will ensure that your team can be extracted at a moment's notice, should the need arise. And, if there is anything else you require, you have but to contact me."

"Thank you, Commander," Eden replied with a curt nod.

"Ghert also asked if your team might not prefer to wait until morning in the northern hemisphere before beginning your work. He indicated that the path you intend to study can be treacherous at night."

Eden dismissed his suggestion with a shake of her head. "I appreciate his concern, but we'll be fine, Commander," she replied, joining the others on the transporter padd.

Drafar had to admit, he was curious about the abrupt change in *Achilles'* orders. He had spent several days working with his flight controllers to plot a course that would keep his ship within range of all fleet vessels currently exploring former Borg space so that they could provide backup. While orbiting the Mikhal Outpost at Captain Eden's discretion, *Achilles* was leaving *Quirinal* and *Curie* particularly vulnerable: *Esquiline* and *Hawking* could rendezvous with them hours ahead of *Achilles* should the need arise, but that thought left Darfar uneasy. Captain Eden had not shared the particulars of her mission with him, and as fleet commander that was certainly her prerogative, but he found it distasteful to perform a task without understanding every aspect.

"Safe travels," Drafar said with a nod, then turned to his transporter chief. "Energize." A few moments later, Eden, Cambridge, and the Doctor disappeared in a shimmer of light. After the weeks spent in round-the-clock controlled chaos repairing *Quirinal,* he should have been happy that this mission would provide a brief respite.

Sadly, that was not his nature.

The landing party materialized in a small, circular clearing in a dense forest of what appeared to be evergreen conifer trees. The tall, ancient-looking trees blocked what little light was cast by the three moons orbiting the outpost this night. As they were in a waning gibbous phase, the moons would illuminate the artifact the team had come to investigate—though not as brightly as when they were full—as they had on the night the images of them had been taken by Kes.

Cambridge had not questioned Eden's insistence that they begin their journey at dusk. By day, it was likely that the starscape carved into the rock a few meters up the path ahead would barely be visible. He had wondered at Eden's rather sharp mood. For the present, the Doctor seemed content to keep his own counsel, though the moment they materialized he had taken a small medical tricorder from his pocket and begun a silent scan of Eden.

Captain Eden remained rooted in place for several moments after they had materialized. She took short, measured breaths as she gazed about the clearing, almost as if she expected an attack.

To their left was the beginning of a barely discernible trail. It widened a short distance farther along. A large stone marked its continuation where it turned sharply and curved upward. In several places the clearing was dotted with cones dropped from the trees overhead. They appeared very similar to the familiar Earth pine cone. As ever, it seemed that nature followed certain patterns, even across the vast distances.

"Well, Afsarah?" Cambridge asked, wondering if her physical presence here was having an effect on her.

"Well, what?" she snapped, without so much as glancing toward him.

Cambridge looked first to the Doctor, whose raised eyebrows indicated that he had noted Eden's hostility. He gently closed his tricorder and busied himself pretending to study the trees overhead.

Coward, Cambridge thought ungenerously as he moved to stand directly in front of Eden.

"Something wrong, Captain?" Cambridge asked more gently than was his wont.

Eden finally met his eyes and as she did so, he noted a very uncharacteristic anger glowing there. "I should never have let you talk me into this," she replied quietly.

The counselor felt a faint smile rising to his lips. "That's just fear talking, Afsarah." Even in the pale light of the clearing he could see that she was shaking, though the night was perfectly warm. "You'll need to set that aside for the next several hours."

"I'm seriously considering returning to *Achilles* and ordering them back on their previous course. It doesn't matter how unique my genome is, or where I actually came from. This is a waste of time."

Cambridge had actually expected this. He was about to say as much when the Doctor stepped forward. "Captain, if I may?" he asked, then continued on without waiting for what would surely have been a negative response. "You are right. This is a waste of time. Given the fact that your uncles likely never visited the Delta Quadrant, and certainly did not after you were with them, it is beyond the realm of possibility that this is your home. *But,* you have said that much of the life you spent with them consisted of examining the artifacts of ancient species. It is possible that you responded as you did—to your first sight of the image that is waiting for you just a little ways up this hill—not because it was directly linked to you, but because it represents something significant that your uncles were seeking. If you can't bring yourself to act now on your own behalf, would you consider doing this for them?"

Eden's face lost its stiffness as she considered the Doctor's words. Finally she said, "They lied to me."

"On some level you have always known this to be true, Afsarah," Hugh chided her softly.

"It's one thing to know it," she replied, "and quite another to *know* it."

"For now, you know nothing," the Doctor corrected her. "However, the answer you are seeking, the one that might bring you some semblance of peace, could be here. Surely that's worth the risk that you might be disappointed by whatever we find up there."

"I'm not afraid that I'll be disappointed, Doctor," she replied evenly. "I'm afraid I won't be."

"Whatever this secret is, Afsarah, you can't hide from it," Cambridge insisted.

"I have, for over forty years now. I've pretended I was just like everyone else. The feeling that I had when I first saw that thing, there was hope in it, a little bit of certainty, and that was comforting. But there was also darkness within. And that darkness almost overwhelmed me when I read the writing on the Staff of Ren. Maybe I'm not supposed to find the answer."

"I've seen you through ordeals that were worse than this little hike and I've never known you to react with such intensity," Hugh reminded her. "You must either face whatever this darkness is *now*, or it will most surely come to deal with you later, when you least expect or are prepared for it."

Eden considered this, stepping a few paces past Cambridge, to the base of the path. "Tricorders out, gentlemen," she ordered. "We're only going to have one shot at this, so let's make the most of it."

A series of large rocks that appeared to be part of the natural formation of the hillside dotted the path that rose quite steeply in a few places until they came to the stone they were seeking.

The image Eden had seen was as brilliant as it ever was—a constellation, bright stars varying in sizes, cast throughout a roughly ovoid series of lines. Bending to examine it more closely, she imagined that time would never dim its light nor distort the intricately carved whorls. The small stones seemed to glow with an inner light rather than the reflected brilliance of the moons.

Her initial reaction to the image had been so intense, so visceral, that Eden had expected something similar when she finally gazed upon the stone itself.

She was disappointed.

Its beauty was no surprise—that had been eloquently captured in the image. And beyond her certainty that the constellation depicted was known as Hanara, the stone seemed to hold no deeper mystery.

She studied it silently for a few minutes before turning to Cambridge and the Doctor with a shrug. "I don't get it," she said, disappointed. "It is what it is."

"You said it was *part* of a map," Cambridge attempted to encourage her. "Where is the rest of it? What's missing?"

Eden didn't think, she placed her hand slightly above and to the right of the starscape carved on the stone. "Illiara would be here. And this area belongs to Oskria."

Cambridge stiffened as his eyes widened. "I beg your pardon."

As she realized what had just happened, Eden felt a chill run through her. The same intuitive knowing that had been such fun when she was a little girl had just returned with a vengeance.

"Correct me if I'm wrong, but the stars you are referring to are not in our databases, are they?" the Doctor inquired.

Though her heart began to thump loudly and irregularly in her chest, and some distant voice buried deep inside begged her to stop, Eden found herself replying, "Illiara and Oskria aren't stars. They're galaxies."

"Visible from the same vantage point where one would have seen Hanara?" Cambridge asked.

Afsarah Eden tried to quiet the cacophony now swirling in her head, wondering why at this moment she was remembering her dream of *Voyager* as it fled at maximum warp from its own destruction. Willing the image of her nightmare to recede, she replied, "Yes."

The Doctor again pulled out his tricorder and quickly scanned her. Her heart began to slow and she rubbed her arms vigorously to eliminate the goose bumps that had popped up all over them.

"Interesting," the Doctor noted as he completed his scan.

"How so?" Eden demanded.

"There are some significant fluctuations in your subatomic scan," he replied. "I have no idea what, if anything, that might indicate, but they seem to be receding now."

Cambridge was already making his way a little farther up the hill.

"Where are you going?" she asked.

"Kes's guide indicated that there were more of these along this path—the only known artifacts of the race believed to have first inhabited this planet. If you're right, it's possible they weren't born here, but came here from someplace quite distant."

Eden nodded. Though part of her still wished to refrain from learning anything more, nothing could have kept her now from continuing.

"Shall we?" she gestured to the Doctor, who nodded vigorously. Cambridge was already out of sight, but a few moments later, a rustling of loose stones was followed by a loud curse.

They hurried up the steep, sharply curving path, using the large rocks that now lined it for leverage. Cambridge was standing a few paces down the path in front of another glowing rock face, holding what looked like a large stone in his hand.

"Are you all right?" Eden asked immediately.

"In my haste, I tripped," he admitted with chagrin, preparing to toss the stone before Eden reached out her shaking hand to him.

"Wait," she said, taking it from him and holding it up to the faint moonlight to examine it.

The Doctor obliged her by activating his wrist beacon. "What is it, Captain?" he asked.

Eden's brow furrowed as she studied the stone. It appeared to be the fossilized remains of a honeycomb. It was an odd thing to find in this environment. "I don't know," she replied, but she gently placed the stone in her backpack before joining Cambridge at the second illuminated stone.

"Well?" Cambridge asked, as if confident he already knew the answer.

Eden found it hard to breathe.

"Illiara," she whispered.

"And you thought this was going to be a waste of time," he teased.

Automatically, Eden reached for his hand. Staring at the second, brilliantly illuminated carving, similar in style but completely different from Hanara, she had never felt so alone in her entire life.

Chapter Eight

BETA QUADRANT

Amanda had hoped that her brief expedition to the ship Kathryn Janeway had been in contact with during the moment when she was busy dying in every other conceivable timeline would be a simple thing. As soon as she saw the ship in question, a large shuttle whose name and registration number were not visible, she decided she should have known better. Though she refrained from giving voice to her initial reaction, the thought formed in her consciousness anyway.

That's impossible.

As a Q, Amanda took in the object before her, instantly noting everything about it, down to its subatomic essence. What was visible to her heightened awareness was, quite simply, half of a ship. That half appeared to be perfectly intact and holding position—*No, frozen in position,* she corrected herself—in an otherwise uninteresting area of space, millions of kilometers from any other stellar object.

The impossible part was the other half of the ship, which, as best she could tell, did not exist.

Half of the vessel could not have survived an event that would have so neatly sheared off the other half, which would have contained its propulsion and engineering sections. Therefore, Amanda concluded, somehow the rest of the ship still existed, perhaps in some kindred but alternate dimension or reality. Her first assumption, that the rest of the ship had been pushed slightly out of phase with the visible half, was easy enough to disprove; all possible phases were visible to her if she sought them out. Amanda set about searching the other, less plausible but still conceivable alternative dimensions, folds in space-time, subatomic interspatial phenomena. Every single avenue available to her ended in frustration.

At this point she would normally have called in another Q— Junior, or even his father—to help her see what she was missing. She was Q, but had been so for only a tiny fraction of the time the rest of the Continuum had existed. She was not proud or arrogant enough to assume she should have access to every single facet of her omnipotence. But her last conversation with Junior kept her from asking for help. It was possible that whatever was happening to Junior, and now to her, was a quirk of her birth, and if so, might alter irrevocably her standing within the Continuum and the freedom it granted her.

Deciding she could always call for help later, Amanda opted to take a closer look, willing herself to enter the intact and visible portion of the ship.

She chose not to take solid form, and congratulated herself immediately when, upon boarding the vessel, she discovered that a single human male inhabited it. He looked to be in his eighth decade of life. He was puttering about a small cabin just off the fore operations and flight control compartment. As he searched among a vast collection of padds and personal items, he was engaged in what appeared to be a conversation.

"Of course you wouldn't let it go," he said to the emptiness around him. "Which meant she couldn't either. But I swear it was almost worth it when that rabbit-thing popped up out of the ground . . ." At this, his words trailed off into the good-natured laughter of fond remembrance.

Amanda began to focus her attention elsewhere when he continued, "What?" After a brief pause, "No I didn't. . . . Because she would never have forgiven either of us. And before you say another word, may I remind you that if you had just listened to me . . ."

Amanda strained to discern another presence that could have been supplying the other half of this man's discussion. Soon enough, she satisfied herself that whatever time he had spent in his current condition had left him, at best, marginally competent. Apart from her presence, which he was incapable of perceiving, he was alone, and probably had been for a very long time.

Leaving him to his benign madness, she moved about the rest of the ship quickly, only to discover a barrier. It appeared to be nothing more than an acute absence of everything, as if someone had drawn a large black curtain over a part of the vessel.

Something deep inside her was repulsed by the darkness. Every sense she had told her to flee and consider this particular mystery unsolved.

But the thought of Junior—his terror at what his existence had become and the lengths he was considering going to to set it right—convinced Amanda she could risk no less than he. If she went back now, with only a vague, impossible understanding of what she was witnessing, Junior would immediately return here with her, and for reasons she could not name, that troubled her more than her own well-founded fears.

Releasing those fears and reminding herself of her limitless abilities, Amanda moved closer to the emptiness. Only then did she perceive its power over her. Why had she ever feared it? She belonged to it, and it to her. It was her birthright. It was the most magnificent, perfect energy that had ever existed. All that was Q meant nothing in the face of this brilliance. It quietly demanded surrender of all that she was, and with great eagerness she began to pour herself into its insatiable need.

It swallowed her whole.

Q CONTINUUM

"Why didn't you tell me?"

"Mother?"

"My dear one, you should never have kept something like this from me."

"You were listening, weren't you? You had no right."

"No right? I'm your mother."

"I seem to remember a vast swath of time when you weren't even willing to acknowledge that, let alone help me with anything."

"You were behaving like a . . . never mind. Besides, that was about me and your father, not me and you."

"It sure felt like it was about me!"

"I know, I'm sorry. But that's not why you didn't tell me about this darkness."

"No, it isn't."

"Come with me. We'll go to your father and together we'll—"

"I can't. Q is coming back. I told her I'd wait."

"Who?"

"Q."

"Who?"

"Mother!"

"I'm sorry, I just . . . Darling, there is no Q."

"Of course there is. She was just here. Who did you think I was talking to? You know her. You even like her, which is amazing considering how few individuals there are of which that can be said."

"This is worse than I thought."

"No. *She is* Q. She was Amanda Rogers, born of two Q who left the Continuum to become human and whom the Continuum then executed for reasons I'm still not entirely sure I understand."

"I know the two Q of whom you speak, but they never had a child, dear. You are the only child ever born of the Continuum."

"Mother!"

"Search the Continuum yourself and tell me that I'm wrong."

"This is ridiculous. She's . . ."

. . . but that's impossible.

EVOLVED BORG CUBE

The deed was all but done. Standing amid dozens of drones, the cube's queen stood before a dais surrounded by exposed conduit and cabling. Her face—or what was left of it, with its humanity subsumed to the vessel's will—was a mask of concentrated force. A snarl tinged her lips. She remained perfectly still as Q watched and waited for his moment.

He had witnessed this scene hundreds of times. The only significant battle being waged right now was *not* between the cube, the monstrosities it had birthed, and the desperate Federation fleet currently engaging them, it was within what had been Kathryn Janeway. Buried deep within the creature's mutilated essence, all that was left of his godmother was searching desperately for a chink in the wall that separated her from the Queen's power. She raged ferociously against all that the Queen was and all that she desired. Beyond them, Seven of Nine waited within the embrace of an ancient device to deliver a virus that would destroy the cube. Only Janeway could grant Seven the access she required. Within moments, the Queen's will would falter just long enough for Aunt Kathy and Seven to succeed.

In that moment, Q was certain he could retrieve his godmother, now that even the history of the Q Continuum seemed up for grabs . . .

What could possibly have happened to Amanda?

. . . he saw no choice before him but the unthinkable.

"Why are you torturing yourself needlessly, my darling?" his mother's voice chided him softly.

"This ends now, Mother," he replied. "I don't have a clue about what is happening to me, or what happened to Q. But I know it is connected to all of this, and if I have to face expulsion from the Continuum to find the truth, it will be a small price to pay."

"Stop this!"

"I'm about to."

"You must not do this!"

"I have no choice."

"But I do."

Surprised by her words, Q allowed his concentration to falter, though the cube was seconds from destruction and the absolute end of Kathryn Janeway's life.

"No Q can prevent Kathryn Janeway's death," his mother insisted.

"I know."

"And no Q can bring her back to life once she has died."

"Yes, I know that too," Q replied, wondering if this had all been a ruse to scuttle his opportunity to change this critical split-second in time.

"But there is a moment in every sentient being's existence, a fraction of a second between life and its end, when they remain intact but are no longer bound by the rules of normal space and time."

Q paused to consider her words. She seemed sincere, but he had never heard of such a thing.

"There is?"

"Yes. We've studied it at great length and found it to be one of the more puzzling mysteries of existence. The Continuum has chosen to allow it to remain a mystery, and as Q, I am content that it should ever be thus."

Against his better judgment, Q found his hopes lifting. "A fraction of a second? What use is that to me?"

"To you? None. But to me, it will suffice."

"How?"

"I can extend that moment indefinitely. I can allow you to speak with your godmother without breaking the rules that bind us in this instance. It will be frowned upon, but I will face the Continuum's wrath."

"You'd do that for me?"

"I'm your mother."

"I . . . I don't know what to say."

" 'Thank you' might be appropriate."

"Thank you."

"Return to the Continuum. I will join you shortly. Speak of this to no one."

Q cleared his consciousness of the many new opportunities this revelation presented to him. It would never do to have his mother suspect the use to which he now intended to put her unexpected gift.

"I'll be there as soon as I can," he replied.

"You have some other pressing business to attend to?" his mother demanded incredulously. "Perhaps I did not explain in sufficient detail the risk I'm about to undertake on your behalf."

"You did. And I do understand. But, yes, there is one stop I need to make. It won't take a second."

"You have one second."

"Thank you. Oh, and, Mother?"

"Yes?"

"This time, when you speak with her . . ."

"Yes?"

"Try and be nice."

"I'm always . . . oh, fine. I'll try."

As his mother's concentration shifted to what was left of Kathryn Janeway, Q carefully folded back the fabric of space-time as he departed so that his movements would be undetectable by his mother and the rest of the Continuum, a trick his father had taught him and for which he should really thank him the next time they spoke. At the same time, Q willed himself to the far end of the galaxy.

OCAMPA

The moment he arrived, Q assumed physical form, hoping that the black and red uniform he now wore would stir sympathy—a remembrance of things past.

The view of the planet from the mouth of the small cave nestled in the red rock canyon was actually startling. The last time he'd been here with Kol it had been a wasteland. Now, vast swaths of green, blue, and orange foliage dotted the valley below. He could taste the moisture in the air and feel the thrum of a fragile and varied ecosystem all around him.

Another thing he didn't remember was a precisely placed stone near a small mound of dirt a few meters from the cave's entrance. A name, Lia, was carved in simple block letters on its rough surface.

His mother, Q thought. He'd once heard the sordid tale of Kol's birth over a lengthy game at Fortis when Kol was on one of his losing streaks. The Ocampan female who'd played a part was of no concern to Q now, though Kol had obviously mourned her passing. The Q had come in search of the significantly more powerful being that had contributed to Kol's existence.

A subtle electromagnetic shift heralded her arrival. Though she could easily have communicated with him in her less substantial, noncorporeal form, the power that had disturbed the energy field around him quickly coalesced into the figure of a radiant woman with startling blue eyes. Golden hair hung in loose waves over her shoulders, and despite her diminutive size, no one with any sense would ever mistake her for a young being. She carried the weight of experiences unimaginable inside her, but wore them well.

"Hello, Kes," he said the moment he found his breath.

"Q," she greeted him. The warmth in her voice was genuine, as were the ever-present misgivings. He couldn't blame her. He'd first met her son at a time in their lives when both were determined to remain as far from responsibility as possible, and he had instigated a number of excursions of which she would never have approved. Kol had outgrown such frivolities before Q, but he hoped Kes could see that he had matured since the last time they'd met.

"If you're looking for Kol," Kes began, "he's busy in the southern colonies these days. Almost ten thousand settlers are reclaiming the land there, and he's helping them develop their planting techniques."

"You must be very proud of him," Q acknowledged.

She immediately picked up on the sincerity in his sentiment. "I am," she admitted with a smile whose brilliance could put stars to shame.

"Actually, I came to see you," he finally offered.

"What could *you* need from me?" she asked with genuine curiosity.

He had neither the time nor the inclination to dissemble.

"Someone is going to die, and I believe that has to be changed," he replied simply.

She crossed her arms as a faint shudder passed through her. It was a strangely Ocampan gesture from one who had left such things behind long ago. When her eyes met his again, they were weary.

"You know, as I do, that death is merely a transitional state. The energy of a life force cannot be destroyed, only released into the universe, unhindered by physical form."

"Or consciousness, or sentience, or any of the other organizing principles that give that life force definition," he countered.

"You don't know that. And since neither you nor I will ever experience it, perhaps we shouldn't be so quick to judge it," Kes suggested.

"I'm not judging it. And normally, I wouldn't trouble myself with the fate of a single individual whose impermanence is a foregone conclusion," Q added for good measure.

"You have the power to intervene in any matter/energy transformation process you want to question. I'm sure you also know, as do I, that it is a risky proposition that can produce significant disruptions to the wider tapestry of time and space."

"I do, which is why the Q are forbidden to take such actions."

A faint smile lit her face. "I guess I should have given the Continuum more credit." After a moment Kes went on, "You've obviously grown, Q. But perhaps not as much as I'd hoped, if you're considering something like this."

"We're actually not talking just about my past here," Q corrected her gently. "We're talking about yours, too."

"Mine?"

"The person whose death I mean to delay is Kathryn Janeway's."

He felt the sting of his words wash through Kes as if he had slapped her. Her eyes were aglow with sorrow.

"I'm so sorry," she finally said. "But like so many I have known and loved, her day had to come. And, more than most, all that she was to me will live forever in my essence, and in the part of yours she has touched."

"You have no interest in helping me?" Q asked, careful to keep his tone neutral.

"I'm not even sure that I could," she admitted. "And if I did, I don't think she would thank me for it."

"You understand I'm not talking about the death of a woman who has lived the hundred-plus years normally granted to her species now. I'm not talking about a peaceful passage into a new state of being surrounded by family and friends reaching calm acceptance of the inevitable together.

"I'm talking about a life force of great magnificence cut short by an entity so evil it dismembered every aspect of her being before consigning her to oblivion. It enjoyed making her last moments a living hell. It tortured and mutilated her, turning her into a monster so horrific, no one who saw it will ever remember anything other than that sight when they think of her. It delighted in taking as many of Kathryn's former friends and fellow officers down with her as possible."

Q could feel the distress his words were causing Kes, and he could only hope they would be sufficient.

"Who did this to her?" Kes demanded.

"The Borg."

Tears welled in Kes's eyes, but she did not wipe them away.

"I had no idea," she finally managed.

"You never thought to check in on the woman who had done so much to make the existence you now enjoy possible?"

"I have," she corrected him, "and would have again. I just thought, I always thought there would be time."

"There isn't."

"You intend to stop this from happening?" she asked.

"That would be too much to risk. But there might be another way. I'm certain I can't do what needs to be done alone. I need help," he admitted.

Even in despair, the inner radiance of Kes's life force was almost too brilliant to look upon with physical eyes.

"I don't know," she whispered. "What you described of her death is unthinkable. But to change it could be even worse."

Q's head dropped. If what he had already revealed was not enough to compel the Ocampan to aid him, then nothing would.

He forced his eyes to meet hers. "When you decide, you know where to find me."

Chapter Nine

AXION, NEW ERIGOL

Seven knew this place. The incredibly tall structures, the labyrinth of multilevel walkways connecting them, all surrounding a wide courtyard, had been the setting of her nightmares once the Caeliar had gone. She knew now that it was a Caeliar city, Axion, one of few that had survived an escape attempt by a handful of captured Starfleet personnel. It had been saved—only through the sacrifice of many of its sister cities—by traveling back in time and to a great distance from its original location in what had become the Azure Nebula. Over the ensuing centuries the Caeliar had found a planet, dubbed it New Erigol, and reconstructed what had been destroyed. Then they waited for destiny to catch up with them.

Finding herself at Axion might have been frightening. It was not. Now that it had ceased to hold any power over her whatsoever, it was simply strange.

The city, as she always found it, was eerily silent. Once, tens of thousands of beings had inhabited it. But in her experience, there was only ever one entity that met her here.

Wondering what the Caeliar-human child Annika might now require of her, Seven strolled gingerly to the side of a long rectangular reflecting pool from which the girl traditionally emerged when she wished to torment Seven. Staring into the black of the water, Seven tensed as it began to ripple, steeling herself against any return of the power this child had wielded over her.

She expected the child's hybrid form to greet her. Instead, the water was soon lit by a bright white light that, once resolved, contained a face Seven did not recognize.

The woman appeared to be human, with strong features and short grayish blond hair. Though her image was two-dimensional, she smiled the moment her eyes locked with Seven's.

"Is Chakotay with you?" she asked. "I know he is near."

"To whom am I speaking?" Seven asked, though something in her already knew the answer. Whence this knowledge had come, she could also hazard a fair guess.

"I am Doctor Riley Frazier," the woman replied. "I need your help."

VOYAGER

Chakotay hurried into sickbay to find Seven sitting upright on a biobed, tentatively rubbing the area above her right eye. *Voyager* had beaten a hasty retreat from the Tarkons, who had managed to keep pace with the ship even at maximum warp. After the slipstream drive was engaged, a jump of only two minutes had brought *Voyager* to an area of space far from any star systems and well clear of the Tarkons.

The captain had been considering the wording of a report he was not looking forward to writing when he had received the call from Doctor Sharak, reporting that Seven had collapsed at her station.

Seven greeted Chakotay with troubled eyes and a weary sigh as he entered sickbay.

"What happened?" he asked. Seven had seemed to have gotten past the initial difficulties of her transformation. He couldn't help but worry that he and Counselor Cambridge had misjudged her recent equilibrium.

"Miss Seven fell into a state of unconsciousness brought about by heightened activity in the area of her brain where your former EMH's confidential medical file indicates she possesses something called 'catoms,'" Doctor Sharak, a Tamarian and *Voyager*'s current CMO, replied, clearly struggling to remain composed. Chakotay was surprised by his tone, as he was usually quite cheerful. The doctor continued, "I understand it is Miss Seven's preference to be treated by your former EMH, but any and all data that could affect her ongoing health *must* be kept in her medical file. Miss Seven awoke of her own accord just as I was accessing the information required to treat her condition. She seems fine now, and I am filled with relief that these actions did not pose a threat to her life, but we might not be so fortunate in the future."

Seven explained, "It was my request that the Doctor segregate his ongoing research about my catoms in his personal files. They are a subject of great curiosity to many in the Federation, and until I am certain that I understand their limits and uses, I do not intend to become a guinea pig."

Bafflement spread across Doctor Sharak's face.

"Are these devices that the Caeliar left inside your body capable of altering your physiology to resemble that of a pig?" Sharak asked seriously.

Chakotay bit back a smile. Tamarian syntax was structured around metaphorical allusions, and although Sharak had made monumental strides in his grasp of Federation Standard, there were still times when he struggled with idioms.

"They are not," Seven replied with equal seriousness. "I was referring to the standard scientific practice of experimenting with new technologies upon lower life-forms."

Doctor Sharak's relief was palpable. "Initra at Delmos," he said, nodding.

Although Chakotay was intrigued by the reference, there were more pressing matters at hand.

"I agree, Doctor Sharak, that information vital to Seven's health must be readily accessible. It was an oversight and will be corrected immediately." Turning to Seven, he then asked, "Do you know what caused you to lose consciousness?"

"I was contacted through my catoms by an individual identifying herself as Doctor Riley Frazier," she replied.

Chakotay's pulse began to race as she continued, "She and forty-six other members of her previous collective remain in a hidden location beneath the planet's surface. She sensed my presence, and yours, as soon as we approached the system and is requesting our assistance."

The captain took a deep breath to center himself. "Are you well enough to brief the rest of the staff?"

Seven nodded. "With the doctor's permission, of course."

Somewhat mollified, Sharak smiled, "As long as Miss Seven returns for a full evaluation as soon as her duties allow, I am in agreement."

Chakotay wondered how long Seven, who usually took great care to be appropriately addressed, would allow Doctor Sharak to continue referring to her as "miss." She slid from the biobed and said, "Thank you, Doctor. I will return as soon as possible. If I experience any discomfort in the meantime, I will contact you at once."

Before they left the sickbay, Chakotay called senior officers to the conference room. As soon as the doors closed behind them, the captain turned to Seven with a mischievous grin and asked, "Miss Seven?"

Cocking her head slightly, after a moment's thought, Seven replied, "He intends it as a term of respect. In the absence of a rank it is technically a correct form of address."

"If it doesn't bother you, Miss Seven—" Chakotay teased gently, but she cut him off abruptly.

"Doctor Sharak may use the term as he sees fit. You may not."

Any lingering doubts that Seven had been damaged by the exercise of her catoms vanished. Chakotay was relieved, as the rest of his day had become significantly more complicated.

• • •

A dull ache began to throb at Tom Paris's temples as Seven made her report to the assembled senior staff. He noticed with interest that Chakotay seemed to be sharing a private joke with Seven, while Harry Kim, Kenth Lasren, Devi Patel, and Nancy Conlon listened respectfully. However, B'Elanna followed Seven's words with a look of mingled trepidation and resignation on her face.

"There was not time for lengthy discussion," Seven said, after revealing her communication with Doctor Riley Frazier. "Our contact was terminated quite abruptly, presumably when *Voyager*'s departure from the system created too great a distance between us for our catoms to bridge."

"*Our* catoms?" Kim interrupted.

Seven's eyes narrowed as she turned to him. "Yes. Originally I believed that we would find no traces of the Borg or Caeliar during this mission, but I now must reconsider my position."

Kim accepted her admission graciously with a simple nod. Tom stifled his amazment. He could count on one hand and no fingers the number of times he had ever heard Seven even imply that she had been wrong about anything.

Unruffled, Seven continued, "Obviously, the transformation of my Borg implants into catoms was not a unique event. I do not believe it was common among the Borg who were offered membership in the Caeliar gestalt. Doctor Frazier's circumstances were as unusual as my own. However, without more information from her about her Caeliar experience, I cannot begin to calculate the number of former Borg who might now exist outside the gestalt."

"We know of at least forty-eight," Chakotay interjected, obviously anxious to move things along.

"We have to go back for them, don't we?" Tom asked, not relishing the prospect.

"Riley was Starfleet before she was assimilated," Chakotay began. "Whatever she became, we cannot ignore her call for help. Beyond that, our mission directive is quite explicit: investigate thoroughly any evidence of Borg or Caeliar activity in the quadrant. We're going back."

"The Tarkons' weapons are formidable," Kim offered. "My readings of the energy web indicated that it would have trapped *Voyager,* even with our shields at maximum."

"I was able to detect multiple phase shifts in the area that might have indicated additional cloaked vessels," Patel added.

"We're facing, at minimum, twenty-five ships, between us and the planet," Chakotay noted.

"Yes, sir." The science officer nodded. "Probably more."

"We need to transport forty-seven people from beneath the planet's surface," B'Elanna said. "That will expose us for several minutes to whatever weapons they have, while our shields are down."

"When we return, I might be able to resume my link with Doctor Frazier," Seven advised. "If they are able to move their group closer to the surface, it will cut down the time we are vulnerable."

"For a minimum of six or seven transport cycles," Lasren pointed out.

"Even if we can get close enough for the transport," Kim said, "we're going to take fire, Captain. And we're going to have to return it if we want to get near that planet."

"We could exit the slipstream corridor close enough to the planet to surprise the Tarkons," Tom suggested. "If we can get in and out before they can move into position, it might work."

"Too risky," Conlon countered. "I know Gwyn is good, but if our calculations are off by a fraction, we'll pass right through the planet."

B'Elanna offered her fellow engineer a nod of agreement.

"We need a distraction," Chakotay stated. "Harry, I need a countermeasure for those energy nets and evasive patterns for attacks from multiple vectors. Devi and Kenth, optimize our sensors to detect all threats out there. B'Elanna and Nancy, we need a way to transport forty-seven people simultaneously from the planet because we're only going to get one shot at this."

"And how long do we have to accomplish this miracle?" B'Elanna asked.

"Three hours," Chakotay replied.

"Oh, good," Conlon said. "I was worried we were going to be rushed."

Chapter Ten

ACHILLES

After too brief a respite for Cambridge, during which he had cleaned up after the seven hours they'd spent hiking the rest of the trail and the Doctor had done whatever it was he did when his presence wasn't required, the three regrouped in Eden's guest quarters.

"And where are we?" Cambridge asked as he entered, immediately taking the seat beside Eden on the short sofa that formed almost the entirety of the cabin's seating area. The Doctor had pulled a chair from the small work station, and his padds were laid out before him on a low, oval coffee table. For a ship of *Achilles'* size, it seemed to Cambridge that the designers were positively stingy with the space allocation for crew quarters.

"We are no closer to figuring out what the five artifacts we discovered have in common, beyond the obvious, or where the sixth might be," Eden replied with a sigh. On a small table beside the sofa, she had placed the three items she had taken from the surface: the fossilized honeycomb, a large pine cone, and a beautiful flower that resembled a sunflower. Why these particular items had interested the captain, Cambridge had no idea.

Beyond the Illiara representation, the team had discovered the one depicting Oskria. The final two starscape renderings the trail had held were Betsila and Shrask. All had noted that the distance between artifacts had increased dramatically as they progressed. But none of them could see any significance in the spacing, apart from the fact that as they climbed, the clusters of large rocks grew denser and the hillside steeper.

Eden had been certain that another artifact would be found

several hundred meters beyond Shrask. But the hillside had ended and there was no telling what direction one might need to travel to locate the missing Lazria artifact. Of its existence, Eden had no doubt, but she was unable to determine where it might be found.

When not lost staring at the alien sunflower, Eden studied a padd that contained the images they had seen that night, arranged according to her understanding of them, in a single view. Considering them, Cambridge had to admit that it was a striking and lovely view of stars. However, comparisons with every known star chart in the Federation's database yielded nothing to match them, and even Cambridge was beginning to believe that, tantalizing as this mystery was, it might be impossible to solve. One question plagued him.

Placing his feet on the coffee table and leaning back with his hands clasped behind his head, he asked Eden, "What happens to you when you do what you did on the planet today? You said you've done it ever since you were a little girl. You stare at an object and suddenly, you just know something about it."

Eden continued to study her padd.

"It's nothing I do, or seem capable of calling on at will, if that's what you're asking," she finally replied.

"Whatever it is, it either affects or is affected by your subatomic makeup," the Doctor interjected. "Your scans altered significantly every time you encountered an artifact and were able to designate it."

"She's been doing this since she was a child, so by doing it again today she is no more likely to dissolve into some sort of subatomic goo than she was at any other time," Cambridge said.

Eden rubbed her eyes. "Maybe we should get a good night's sleep and come at this fresh in the morning."

"Of course, Captain," the Doctor said, beginning to collect his padds.

"You still haven't really answered my question, Afsarah," Cambridge said, remaining comfortably in place.

Eden considered him wearily, then replied, "It's hard to explain. It's like, I know the whole story."

"Go on," Cambridge urged gently.

"It's as if I read the information somewhere, or just always knew it, but it doesn't come to the front of my consciousness until I'm looking at the object in question. There are flashes, moments when I think I can hold the entire history of whatever I'm looking at in my mind. I see not just the artifact, but the people who created it, their lives, their deaths, even their intentions, strange as that might sound."

"Strange, I'll grant you, but it's an incredible thing to witness," Cambridge offered. "What was the story of the people who left those carvings?"

"I can't tell you now," she answered. "I might have been able to if you'd asked when I first saw them. The only thing I still hold clearly in my mind now is that these images should be arranged as they are here; that someone, somewhere, saw this when they looked up at the sky. And I know that farther this way," she indicated a point beyond the padd she had picked up and held on her lap, "would be Lazria."

"Is this intended to point you to a planet somewhere on this map that is significant to you, or perhaps to your uncles?"

Eden shook her head. "I don't know, maybe."

"Do you need to see Lazria to know what else might be on this map?" Hugh asked.

"I won't know until I see it and I don't know where to go from here. Without more information, I can't imagine how we would use this map to locate my home planet. I came here, hoping to find it, but I'm beginning to believe that wherever it is, it might just be too far away to ever be reached."

"Sleep on it, Captain," the Doctor gently urged. "You've earned your rest. If there's anything you need during the night, I'll be available." He then stared at Cambridge with eyes that virtually commanded him to get up and leave Eden in peace.

For now, exhausted as he was, Cambridge saw no reason not to humor the hologram.

"See you both bright and early," Cambridge said as he rose from the couch and followed the Doctor out of Eden's quarters.

He hoped nothing else was going to happen tonight, because he had every intention of being unconscious for the next several hours.

Once the Doctor and Cambridge departed, Eden rose from the sofa, almost ready for bed and intent on doing her best to pretend that this day had never happened. In truth, part of her was relieved that she had only learned what she had. The time spent scrabbling among the rocks had been like her adventures with Tallar and Jobin, so much so that she'd felt as if they were walking beside her, instead of the Doctor and the counselor. That had been pleasant. The rest—what it might mean for her or might have meant to her uncles—seemed so far beyond the probability of comprehension that Eden was beginning to believe she could put the entire episode behind her without regret.

The gnawing sense of dread that tinged the edges of each discovery she had made thus far still haunted her. But she was content to leave it on the fringe of her consciousness. Whatever unnamed thing she had feared had obviously not come to pass. Eden wondered if the anxiety that had knotted her stomach when the day began was connected to Tallar and Jobin's fate. To lose them without ever knowing when or how they had died had troubled her deeply. Over time, she had come to a grudging acceptance. However, she had never shaken the feeling that if she had stayed with them rather than pursuing the normal life they'd wanted for her, things might have been different for all of them. This was the one regret that might never leave her. But even if her search for the truth of her past ended here, she decided she could live with that.

Yet, the images on the padd unsettled her. Usually the answers she was seeking came without effort. That this one did not meant it might be beyond her, but an itch in the back of her mind told Eden this was not the case. Instead, it suggested, she was not seeing the nose upon her face.

Eden set the padd aside and turned again to the alien sunflower. It was a beautiful specimen, but usually nature did not so transfix her. She thought back to her days with Jobin and Tallar but could not remember once encountering a similar flower.

Let it go, something in her begged.

The captain started toward the cabin's 'fresher. As soon as she had reached it, she bent low to splash a little warm water on her face, then rose and caught her reflection in the mirror.

"*Perfection,*" Tallar's voice came unbidden from her memory. Suddenly a warm spring day returned to her with breathtaking clarity. She was kneeling over a freshwater pool as Tallar sat next to her, doodling in the dirt with a short stick. "*Let those with eyes to see know such perfection,*" he had said when he saw her staring at her reflection.

She remembered the conversation well, though she hadn't thought of it in decades. The love of both of her uncles had been a fierce, unmovable thing. Like any parents, they had seen more of her strengths than her weaknesses, her beauty rather than her flaws.

This particular day, Tallar had been pointing out to the timid adolescent girl the perfection of her features, at least from a mathematical point of view. That the Doctor's studies of her genome had shown similar, bizarre results now troubled her and tainted the memory.

As with most of the things they did, Tallar had turned the simple compliment into a lesson. For hours after describing how her features were in perfect mathematical proportions, he had gone on to explain the significance of the "divine proportion" or "golden ratio" that for scientists, artists, and architects throughout the galaxy held a special fascination.

The ratio was a simple mathematical expression. Two numbers were said to be in the golden ratio if the ratio of the sum of the quantities to the larger quantity was equal to the ratio of the larger quantity to the smaller one. It was an irrational mathematical constant, something that had never particularly interested Eden, though her awkward younger self enjoyed solid proof that her face was pretty. Tallar had gone on at great length to describe the uses to which many had put the golden ratio:

drawings, buildings, and numerous other artifacts. Because the ratio produced pleasing lines, whether expressed in rectangles, triangles, spirals, or even in physical forms, it occurred with greater frequency in many cultures than other mathematical constructs.

In fact, the golden spiral was sometimes linked with another integer sequence that yielded similar results when constructed in spiral form.

Hurrying back to the sofa, Eden looked again at the honeycomb, pine cone, and sunflower. All of them occurred naturally on Earth, but to find all three in such close proximity on a distant world had alarmed her on a subconscious level.

With trembling fingers she mapped out the precise locations of the starscapes they had discovered that day on the hillside, using topographical data provided by the ship's sensors as a guide. She instructed the computer to calculate the distances between the artifacts and then, the number of large rocks present where the artifacts were discovered.

She knew what she was going to see. Finally, she instructed the computer to extrapolate the point on the surface where the next artifact was likely to be found. It complied in seconds, and Eden felt the blood rushing to her head as it placed the Lazria artifact at the edge of the desert that began just south of the hillside they had already searched.

The math told her unequivocally that the entire hillside was an artificial construct. Decoding it required a detailed aerial view, and advanced calculations, another constant in evolving civilizations.

The honeycomb, the pine cone, and the sunflower were clues. The rock formations surrounding those that the starscapes were carved on and the distances between them were equally important, but only if you knew what you were looking for. Eden sat, taken aback at the depth of planning that had gone into the creation of the puzzle before her.

The mathematical expression in question was common, a Fibonacci sequence, where each integer was the sum of the two that preceded it. It occurred in nature in a variety of instances, including the honeycomb, the pine cone, and the seed head of the sunflower, but was replicated on the hillside in the numbers of rocks upon which the starscapes had been rendered, as well as the relative distances between them. Beginning in the clearing at 0, they followed 1, 1, 2, 3, and 5. The next integer was 8 and that, the computer indicated, was related to a longitude and latitude found bordering the southern desert. The length between integers was not a standard Federation measurement, but it was constant, roughly a quarter of a kilometer. More important, the arrangement of the starscapes on the hill formed a perfect Fibonacci spiral, almost exactly the same shape as a golden spiral.

"Let those with eyes to see," Eden said softly, as the eerie inner silence that foreshadowed her intuitive episodes descended upon her.

Beyond Lazria, Altreen. *Beyond* Altreen, Vesra. *Beyond* Vesra, Unasala. *Beyond* Unasala, Pesh. *Beyond* Pesh, Kehlia. *Beyond* Kehlia, Som.

Though she now knew precisely where all of the markers were, she no longer needed to find them. The end of the journey lay roughly thirty-five kilometers into the southern desert along the arc of a golden spiral.

Som.

The starscapes so diligently rendered on the surface below were not a map that led to a distant planet. They led to something on the planet itself, likely buried somewhere below its surface.

Eden had no idea what *Som* was, but she damned sure wasn't going to wait until night fell again on the southern desert to find out.

Commander Drafar stood on the *Achilles* bridge next to Ensign Rosati's ops station. He knew the harried young woman was doing her best to locate the requested coordinates and that she was frustrated at her inability to complete the task at hand.

The moment the bridge's rear tubolift doors hissed, Drafar turned and his mouth actually fell open. Standing in the door, resting one arm on the frame, stood Counselor Cambridge, clad in a long brown robe tossed over he did not care to know what. The counselor looked terribly put out to have been summoned to the bridge in the middle of his sleep cycle.

"Is it possible I imagined the emergency call I just received?" he asked hopefully.

Drafar didn't know how his fellow officers ran their ships, but if Cambridge had been his responsibility, the counselor would have been assigned several extra duty shifts de-ionizing resistor coils with a microfilament during which to consider proper attire for a Starfleet bridge. As this was not Drafar's privilege, he simply closed his mouth and hoped that the firmness of his gaze communicated his displeasure as he replied briskly, "You did not."

The Doctor hurried past Cambridge onto the bridge and immediately reported, "She is not in her quarters, and her rucksack is missing." Turning to Cambridge, he added, "Nice of you to join us, Counselor. Does the term 'emergency' not carry with it an implied command to move quickly where you're from?"

Cambridge ambled toward the pair, blinking the sleep from his eyes.

"Captain Eden transported to the surface of the planet without advising either of you of her intentions?" Drafar asked.

"She what?" Cambridge demanded, now considerably more alert.

"We just covered that, Counselor," the Doctor interjected. "Try and keep up."

Drafar stepped between them and said, "I have just received an urgent message from *Voyager*. *Achilles* will depart orbit within the next half hour to render aid as requested. When I attempted to advise Captain Eden of this development, I did not receive any response from her quarters, and the ship's computer was unable to locate her. Our logs indicate that two hours ago she transported to the surface without leaving word of her destination or the intended duration of her away mission. I am even more surprised to learn that neither of you seem to be aware of her actions. We can't get a signal from her combadge, and there are no discernible life signs present within a radius of ten kilometers of the transporter coordinates, the maximum distance she could have covered."

Cambridge's eyes again met the Doctor's, this time filled with concern. Drafar could not sense what was communicated between them, but he was satisfied that the counselor was now completely awake and ready to be of assistance.

The Doctor looked back to Drafar and indicated the ops station, asking, "May I?"

"You have some special expertise in sensor configurations of which I am not aware?" Drafar shot back harshly, though he didn't normally allow his emotional response to a situation to color the manner in which he performed his duties.

"In this case, I might," the Doctor said, unperturbed.

"By all means." Drafar nodded to the Doctor, who moved quickly to stand beside the ops console.

"This tricorder contains the parameters of a subatomic scan. If you patch it in, your sensors might help us pinpoint the captain's location," the Doctor advised Rosati.

Ensign Rosati, both perplexed and intrigued, quickly created the new routine. Within moments, she offered Drafar a subtle nod. "We've got her. Captain Eden is three hundred meters below the surface and appears to be continuing downward."

Without another word, Cambridge hurried toward the turbolift.

"Counselor?" Drafar asked of his back.

Cambridge turned back. "Commander?"

"It is customary when having settled upon a plan to advise a starship's commander of your intentions," Drafar observed.

"I'd have thought it was obvious. Go to *Voyager*'s aid. The Doctor and I will go after Captain Eden. Let us know as soon as you're back."

"Take pattern enhancers. You'll need provisions for at least two days to be on the safe side," Drafar advised.

Cambridge nodded wearily as he asked, "We won't be within walking distance of a nearby settlement?"

"Her initial transporter coordinates were over fifty kilometers from the nearest inhabited area," Drafar replied.

"Well, this should be ghastly," Cambridge quipped. "Doctor?"

As the EMH followed the counselor off the bridge, Drafar wondered if the captain would be pleased when they joined her. Eden might have had her reasons, and they might even have been good ones, but that did not mitigate the danger she had placed herself in or the damage she had just done to Drafar's opinion of her and her judgment.

Chapter Eleven

Q CONTINUUM

Kathryn Janeway sensed rather than felt Q's hand free hers as a familiar sight took shape around her: a long deserted stretch of highway beneath a brightly lit, cloudless sky. Just ahead, a small, ramshackle white house in desperate need of paint sat on dry brown dirt dotted with weeds.

The first time Kathryn had experienced this representation of the Q Continuum, there had been others present. A dog had been stretched out on the porch as a woman sat, leafing through a large magazine. Q and the Q she had come to think of as Quinn had also been there, attempting to demonstrate to her the incredible ennui that accompanied immortal existence.

This time, the only individual present was Q's female companion, she of the fiery red hair and acerbic tongue, whom Kathryn might have found considerably more tolerable were it not for her insufferable arrogance.

Q stood on the porch of the house, her long, trim body nicely accentuated by the black and red command uniform she had the unmitigated gall to wear. She gestured impatiently for Kathryn to follow her inside, but something equally powerful stayed her.

This isn't right.

The voice was her own, but Kathryn couldn't place its source.

When she had been alive, she might have called it intuition. Now, whatever she was—and Q had already been annoyingly vague on the topic—there was considerably less distance between her conscious desires and the thoughts and needs of what she used to think of as her subconscious mind. All was one now, which was both good and bad. Good, in that it brought a sense of empowered clarity to her existence she had never before known but often longed for. Bad, in that it made decisions such as this harder than they might have been. For her to do anything, even something as simple as following Q onto the porch of the shack, she must want it with her entire being, and for now, her being was divided on the subject.

"What are you waiting for?" Q demanded, a familiar petulance creeping into her tone.

"Why have you brought me here?"

Q's shoulders dropped, her chin lowered to her chest, and her head moved slowly back and forth. Finally, she bit back what Kathryn sensed were her first three or four retorts and replied simply, "Because Q asked me to."

The thought of seeing the entity that would always, in her mind at least, be Q, the one who had tormented and toyed with Jean-Luc Picard numerous times before adding Kathryn and her crew to his list of diversions, was almost enough to propel her forward. He was a maddening creature, but could be, at least in Kathryn's experience, almost reasonable. His mate, Kathryn didn't trust at all. But the fact that Q had need of her was worth investigating.

This isn't right, part of her asserted again. Kathryn took a moment to search within for the source of discord. It was surprisingly simple to locate. She understood that she was in the Q Continuum, but on some level she knew that she was meant to be elsewhere, and soon. Too far behind her—*she dared not look*—was unspeakable agony. The further she moved from it, the more centered and calm she became. Beyond this moment, however, a peace she could only imagine, a sense of knowing beyond all, willed her toward itself. This great still point was her true destination, and to refuse to throw herself into it now with her whole being felt almost as painful as glancing toward what she had left behind.

The female Q stood, arms crossed and foot tapping impatiently on the porch. Suddenly, Kathryn understood that she was being held here by this Q's power. More important, she knew that she could release the tie that bound her here of her own accord. She had been accustomed to thinking of Q as an entity of power beyond any she could imagine. Only now did she see that, at least in this moment, her own will was a match for any that opposed it.

That's right. Let go, her deeper knowing urged.

Kathryn smiled. Whatever game Q and his mate might have in mind was intriguing, but did not approach the pull of this other unnamed and unknowable force. She had no hand to raise in farewell, but knew that Q would sense the gesture. Her will faltered, however, when another figure stepped out of the shack, saying, "Mother?" He then turned, and the relief in his eyes at seeing Kathryn was so palpable, so overwhelming, that all thought of moving on was instantly banished.

Q, she thought with genuine happiness.

No longer the lanky, awkward adolescent she had known, the man before her had matured into a striking creature. Both his parents were visible in his features, though he still favored his father. Gone was the reckless arrogance he had inherited. The power that was his birthright radiated from him, cascading over Kathryn in warm, golden waves, and she wondered if either of his parents knew what an astonishing being they had created. *Why was all of this so much easier to see without eyes?*

"Hello, Q," Kathryn greeted him with genuine pleasure.

"Aunt Kathy." He smiled, and immediately his warmth overwhelmed Kathryn as he moved quickly toward her, his eyes alight.

"Won't you join me inside?" he asked respectfully. "It's a lot more comfortable."

"All of this is an illusion," Kathryn corrected him gently. "One that is no longer necessary."

Q looked back to his mother, his face clouded by concern.

"She's not wrong." The lady shrugged.

Turning back to her, Q said, "As you wish."

Kathryn heard his mother's voice echoing, "I'll leave you to it, but do hurry things along." Suddenly, the desert landscape was gone, as were all points of reference. Darkness replaced it, but not the dizzying blackness of the void. Instead, Kathryn floated in absolutely calm waters that more easily transmitted thought and sensation than any environment she had ever experienced. It was the freedom of zero-*g* without the environmental suit, the buoyancy of diving without a breathing apparatus, more luxurious than any of the countless warm baths she had taken in her life. If she had a memory of her existence prior to her birth, she might have recognized it as the womb of the universe.

She was alone, but for the presence of her godson. And yet it seemed as she grew more accustomed to her new environment that the potential for life within this place was infinite.

"You are the Q who wished to see me," Kathryn realized. Until this moment she had assumed every reference his mother had made during their encounters prior to and since her death to "Q" was to her husband, rather than her son.

"I am, Aunt Kathy," he replied, the need that flowed from him disturbing the gentleness that enveloped her.

"I would help you if I could," Kathryn said, "though how there is anything I might do for you, that you cannot do well enough for yourself, is difficult to imagine."

"I know," Q offered, "but surely you are beginning to sense that as you exist now, there are many options available to you that were not when you were alive."

Kathryn knew the truth of his words. But she did not understand how the tenuous connection she now felt to both the living universe and the exponentially greater power that still beckoned to her from beyond it would give her any power that could rival a Q.

"This is a moment that every sentient mortal creature experiences," he answered her unspoken question. "It usually occurs for an infinitesimal period immediately following their death."

"How long have I been dead?" Kathryn wanted to know.

"Longer than a fraction of a second," he confirmed. "My mother graciously extended the time normally allowed so that we could speak."

"To what are you speaking?" Kathryn asked.

"All that you ever were, are, and will be," Q explained. "This is you, Aunt Kathy, unbound by the limits of physical reality. Were you to remain like this indefinitely, you might begin to understand what it is to be Q."

"I hope you're not planning to offer me membership in the Continuum," Kathryn said, perturbed.

"No," he reassured her. "That is not within my power."

"There is very little that is not within a Q's power," Kathryn pointed out.

"I would not be allowed to offer it, and I am certain the rest of the Continuum would not agree to it," he clarified.

"Then, why am I here?"

"Something is wrong with me, Aunt Kathy."

"Something that your parents or the rest of the Q cannot fix?" she asked, amazed by the notion.

"I believe so."

Kathryn stretched her senses to their limits and found no trace of deception in him.

"You're afraid of something?" she asked, pinpointing the strongest sensation pouring through him. "What in the universe could a Q fear?"

"The multiverse," he corrected her. "When you lived, you experienced a single thread of reality. But you knew then, and know now, how many additional strands form the entirety of what is."

Kathryn had always hated anything related to temporal mechanics. She found, to her surprise, that in this place, the many facts of time and reality and the way they interacted were less confusing than they had once been.

This isn't . . . The voice of her greater consciousness again attempted to force its urgency upon her.

"Tell me what you fear, and quickly," Kathryn said.

"You won't understand unless I share it with you."

She wasn't sure she understood the distinction. Then, in what might have been a second, or a thousand lifetimes, Kathryn felt the sum total, as well as every individual piece, of this Q's experience of the multiverse descend upon her like a crushing wave. His reality merged into hers, and everything she would have asked, every lesson, every test, every triumph, and every terror became *theirs*.

She experienced her death countless times and in so many various manners that shock had no choice but to give way to numb acceptance. He had visited each of these deaths, witnessed them, and counted them, until nothing but the absolute end of her existence was real. The horror of it submerged beneath the oddness of it. Like him, she found herself puzzling over, and was somewhat insulted by, the seeming insistence of the multiverse that she be erased from all time.

Briefly, she touched the absolute freedom he had once known. She gloried in the truth of what it was to be Q as infinity yawned before her in all of its terrible beauty. She knew the Q, Amanda, who had become a treasured companion and shared his unimaginable confusion as the unknown extinguished her light.

But none of this prepared her for the darkness. She sensed his desire to spare her what he could of its nature, but she opened herself to what he would have hidden from her. Her deaths had been nothing compared to the finality this darkness promised. It was neither more nor less than absence; it was an ending beyond what she sensed awaited her once this had passed. It was a silence so profound, an emptiness so vast, that it threatened to crush her essence beneath its absolute magnitude. In this place, Kathryn had not lived and died countless horrible deaths. Here, neither Kathryn nor Q nor anything they had ever experienced as real had ever been.

Only his strength dragged her clear of the abyss. Even once she had returned safely to the tranquil depths of the Continuum, it took Kathryn time before she could summon the will to unravel where and what she had just been.

"Are you all right, Aunt Kathy?" Q prodded gently.

At this, an incongruous laugh erupted from the center of her being. When it had settled, she replied, "I think I haven't been all right for a very long time, and doubt now that I ever will be again."

"Please don't be angry with me," Q said, and in that instant, he was once again the fragile, awkward boy she had once known and mentored. His concern for her washed around her like a gentle breeze. It gratified her to know that the effort she had expended on his behalf had not been wasted.

"I'm not angry," Kathryn replied. "I understand now the gravity of the threat you perceive, not just to yourself, but to the entire multiverse. I'm glad you felt you could bring this to me, but I confess I'm still at something of a loss to imagine what I might do to help you."

"Would it comfort you to know that I believe you have already done it?"

"I suppose it would, if I understood how that was possible."

"I don't believe it was always this way. The only way you become a key strand in this tangled web is by your own actions, or lack thereof."

Kathryn was struggling to keep up. "You believe that all of this is connected to the choice Admiral Janeway made when she altered time." Suddenly, the entire picture snapped into focus. "You believe that something she encountered, and resolved, prior to turning time inside out was undone by her later actions. The multiverse has now been forced to extreme measures to correct the inherent imbalance her actions created."

"You always were a quick study," he commended her.

This isn't right.

"Be quiet," Kathryn ordered her better angels. Until now they had pleaded the case of her highest self. At this moment, she found them annoying, and was struck by the remembrance of how often this had also been true when she was alive.

"I'm sorry," he apologized.

"I wasn't talking to you," she assured him. "We have more

than one problem before us right now, and the truth is, I'm not certain which is more pressing."

"Shall I complicate things further for you then?" he asked.

The laughter was building again within her. It was sad how limited her appreciation of the absurd used to be.

"I see the truth in what you have shown me, Q," Kathryn said, trying to bring order to what was quickly unraveling into chaos. "I understand that her actions, *my* actions," she was forced to acknowledge, "might have had unforeseen consequences. But there is a part of me that also knows that my role in this is done. Indeed, the multiverse seems quite adamant on that point. And much as I would like to spare you the terror you now confront, I am reminded that to act in any way now in opposition to the forces compelling me to move beyond this might only make things worse."

"That really is the question," he agreed. "And powerful as my mother is, I, too, understand that this artificial prolonging of what should be inevitable cannot continue indefinitely. Allow me to present you with your options."

"I have options?" Kathryn asked, surprised.

"Two."

"Sounds simple enough," she replied, though she doubted "simple" would have anything to do with whatever he was about to propose.

"You can, as you are undoubtedly aware, choose to release yourself from this moment into whatever is beyond mortal life. I don't know what that is, but I also doubt that your sense of it is misguided. It might be beckoning you to oblivion, or to a marvelous plane of existence that the Q are denied by virtue of our immortality."

The thought that she might be going to a place the Q could not know saddened her as much as it comforted her.

"You can leave this problem to the forces already in motion, trusting that whatever is to come for me—and all those still living—will be the best possible outcome. The significance of your death cannot be in doubt. No other mortal's death has stretched across time as yours does. You can decide that this is, as it now should be, for the greater good of all."

"Or?" Kathryn asked.

"Or you can return to your life, certain that you possess within you the power to do what you once did, to prevent this darkness. You beat it once, Aunt Kathy, and I trust you more than the unnamed and random forces of the multiverse to do whatever it is that must be done to beat it again."

"I can return to life? Your mother said that was impossible."

"She was referring to the fact that it is forbidden for a Q to do this for you."

"Then I don't understand."

"It is not, however, forbidden for a Q to show you how to do it for yourself."

Kathryn pondered the question before her more deeply than any she had ever faced.

Finally she asked, "Are you sure there isn't a third option?"

Chapter Twelve

TARKON SENTRY VESSEL *ABRACUS*

"*Opportunity detected,*" the computer's sonorous male voice stated, followed by a series of blips as the "opportunity" was thoroughly scanned.

Senior Acquisitions Executive Culbret immediately activated the display. The scan results appeared, scaled for size, in three dimensions in the dedicated viewing area just beyond the carrier's forward flight control station. The carrier's pilot and four other acquisition specialists focused their attention on the display. The specialists simultaneously fed the salient features of the vessel as well as the estimated value of each of its component parts to the pilots of *Abracus*'s capture ships.

It had been more than eight cycles since Culbret had detected the first opportunity coming within range of his sentry pool: the vessel identifying itself as the Federation *Starship Voyager.* The acquisitions executive still tasted the filth spat from his belly when that ship had escaped his pool, summoning speed as it ran, clearly using subspace alterations the Tarkons had yet to master. The sums lost in its abrupt departure had been staggering. Should news of it reach the Board, he might face demotion—or worse, distribution of all of his current assets among his junior specialists.

The opportunity now before him, a much smaller ship with impressive tactical capabilities, would not be so lucky.

"*Vessel class unknown. Signature match to vessel self-designated as Federation,*" his computer advised. "*Estimated total value of components intact, one thousand nine hundred seventy-six notes, less permanent resettlement costs associated with transfer of the pilot. At scrap, six hundred twenty-three notes.*"

"Did you stray too far from your mother ship?" Culbret asked softly of the lone ship that had just emerged from the edge of the nebula that blanketed seven sectors of Tarkon space, including the fringes of the system that held their newest resettlement planet. His previous scans of Federation *Starship Voyager* had detected smaller craft within the larger ship's holds, but none that matched the specifications of the vessel now before him. *Part of a convoy?* Losing its bearings within the nebula was understandable. The cursed thing played hell with Culbret's sensors as well, but also provided a certain welcome privacy for the Tarkon's work in this newly claimed sector.

The acquisitions executive hoped the vessel—whose course would soon take it out of the system along a similar route Federation *Starship Voyager* had taken while fleeing—was not alone. It was a worthy opportunity and had already transgressed by entering Tarkon space. The vessel's ordnance would be a welcome addition to his assets, and this ship would be no trouble at all to capture. Culbret welcomed the chance to seize more like it, should they be hovering within the outskirts of the nebula.

"Set course to intercept," Culbret ordered, and his pilot immediately altered course.

"Capture ships, prepare to detach."

The single vessel, now so far from its fellows, was a small prize, but one that would at least partially satisfy the hunger left by the earlier loss of Federation *Starship Voyager*. Culbret briefly considered hailing the ship, advising it of its trespass, and giving it a chance to surrender without incident, then opted against giving away *Abracus*'s presence too soon.

Not that it mattered. Within minutes, the ship would be his.

VOYAGER

"The Tarkon vessel has moved into detached formation and is on course to intercept TS Flyer Thirteen," Kim reported from tactical.

Normally, Chakotay would have been able to see this for himself, but the nebula prevented clear visual transmissions, and until *Voyager* cleared it, they were relying on sensor data. Sensors were not functioning optimally within the nebula, but Conlon had devised several methods of compensation.

Commander Drafar had suggested approaching the planet from the fringes of the nebula that surrounded the entire system. The tactic came with its share of difficulties, but it allowed the two larger Starfleet ships to come much closer to the planet than *Voyager*'s initial foray and remain essentially undetected. If all went as planned, the element of surprise might reduce casualties on both sides.

At least Chakotay hoped so.

"*Voyager* to *Achilles*," Chakotay called.

"*Achilles* here," Drafar's deep, resonant voice boomed through the open channel.

"They've taken the bait."

"*Of course they have,*" Drafar replied.

Chakotay stifled a chuckle as he waited for Kim to confirm that the next stage was proceeding as planned. He had heard of Drafar's confidence in himself and his crew. He was learning that the stories paled a bit in comparison to the genuine article.

"Confirming TS Flyers One through Twelve and Fourteen through Twenty-four have cleared the nebula and are moving to intercept the Tarkons," Kim reported.

The captain felt Tom tensing beside him, trying to hold himself motionless. Chakotay knew his first officer wanted to be in one of those TS Flyers.

"The Tarkons are scrambling," Kim reported, unable to keep the satisfaction from his voice.

"Take us to Red Alert," Chakotay ordered. "Helm, prepare to engage, maximum impulse."

"Aye, sir," Gwyn responded. She seemed to be chomping at the bit. "Course and heading confirmed."

"*Achilles* confirms ready as well," Lasren advised from ops.

Chakotay released a breath and was about to give the order to engage, when Kim called out, "Four additional Tarkon vessels have deployed in the area." After a moment more, he added, "They have assumed detached formation."

"Keep a close eye on them, Harry," Chakotay ordered. "The flyers need to hold their own for a few minutes, but if it looks like the Tarkons are getting the better of them, I need to know sooner rather than later."

"Understood, sir," Kim replied firmly.

Having never seen the TS Flyers in action, Chakotay hoped they were up to the task of defending *Voyager* and *Achilles*. Tom had nothing but praise for the pilots and their sleek ships, but this was a type of battle in which Starfleet vessels did not traditionally engage. If they proved unequal to the task, Chakotay would be forced to order *Voyager* and *Achilles* to move in. The mission to rescue Riley's people was a priority, but he would be damned if it came at the cost of twenty-four of Starfleet's pilots.

"Ensign Gwyn, engage," Chakotay ordered. "Ensign Lasren, get us a visual of the fighting as soon as possible."

"Aye, Captain," Lasren replied.

Controlled chaos played out on the main viewscreen. Forty-nine ships moving at high impulse were engaged in a dogfight, illuminating the blackness of space with streaks of weapons fire.

Chakotay had no sense of who might have the upper hand, but as long as the TS Flyers kept the Tarkons busy for another few minutes, the mission had a real chance of succeeding.

The Tarkon vessels were not deploying their energy webs. Traces of bright yellow erupted from their forward weapons arrays, but none seemed to hit their targets. The TS Flyers had been launched from *Achilles* and held their position until the Tarkons had committed themselves to capturing what they believed was a single, helpless ship. Now, the twenty-four vessels were maneuvering in open space, and so far they had intentionally avoided destroying the Tarkons. Their fire had disabled several ships and succeeded in leading the Tarkons away from their resettlement planet. The *Voyager* crew now had the time they needed to execute their equally difficult portion of the task at hand.

"Distance to Riley's Planet?" Chakotay asked as the battle receded from the main viewscreen and the brownish sphere took its place.

"Five minutes to transporter range," Lasren replied.

"B'Elanna?" Chakotay called.

"*We're almost ready,*" the fleet chief engineer's voice replied.

"You have four minutes," Chakotay advised.

"*No problem,*" B'Elanna said, her determination buoying Chakotay's own.

"Captain, two more Tarkon sentries have been disabled."

Chakotay wished he could tell them to keep up the good work.

Suddenly Patel's voice piped up from her station. "Reading three additional interphasic disruptions."

Kim called out, "Three additional, no, fifteen additional Tarkon sentries now engaging."

"Damn," Tom whispered softly.

"An energy net has been established," Kim continued. "TS Flyer Six has been surrounded."

Tom tensed. "That's Purifoy."

"TS Flyers Eleven and Nineteen have gone to his aid," Kim reported. "Two Tarkon vessels destroyed. TS Flyer Six is clear."

"For how long?" Tom muttered.

"Commander Paris," Chakotay said sternly, "what is the status of our sensor link with *Achilles*?" What he thought was, *Focus, Tom.*

Paris did a quick check of his display and said, "The nebula is interfering with the link—a loss of ten to nineteen percent." The slightly chagrined look that accompanied his words made it clear that he understood Chakotay's unspoken command.

"That's what B'Elanna expected, right?" Chakotay asked.

"She was hoping for less than seven percent," Tom replied. "We should have a stable link once *Achilles* moves clear of the nebula."

Chakotay knew the TS Flyers were acquitting themselves well out there, but he didn't think they could hold on for much longer.

"Captain," Kim called out. "Ten of the Tarkon ships have broken off and are in pursuit of *Voyager*. Five TS Flyers are following."

"Lasren?" Chakotay asked.

"Two minutes and forty seconds to transporter range."

"Will the Tarkon vessels overtake us before that?" Chakotay demanded.

"It's going to be close," Kim replied.

Beads of perspiration were forming along Lieutenant Nancy Conlon's forehead as she worked furiously to stabilize the sensor link between *Voyager* and *Achilles*. The engineer expected the current lag to clear as *Achilles* moved closer to the fringes of the nebula, but she knew every second was going to count for the plan to work.

The problems she and B'Elanna had faced in the last few hours had been staggering. *Voyager* did not have enough transporter pads to accommodate forty-seven people at once. But Chakotay had been adamant they would have only one chance. Once they had been advised that *Achilles* would be joining *Voyager*, B'Elanna had stopped referring to Chakotay by numerous colorful Klingon epithets. With *Achilles'* help, she was certain that what had been impossible would be no problem at all.

Commander Drafar had been a hard sell, but he clearly knew B'Elanna well enough not to discount out of hand any suggestion she made. *Achilles* didn't have enough individual transporter pads for forty-seven people either, but B'Elanna believed that their cargo transporters could be modified to safely lock onto Riley's people and collect all of them in one fell swoop. The fact that cargo transporters weren't rated for personnel transport didn't trouble B'Elanna in the least. Conlon had already learned that much of B'Elanna's reputation had a great deal to do with her ability to use whatever was at hand, whether it had been designed to perform the function she required of it or not.

B'Elanna and Drafar had spent the bulk of the last two hours modifying the *Achilles'* transporters and running simulations. The real problem was getting *Achilles* into transporter range, establishing a lock, and dropping their shields without getting blown up by the Tarkons, who no one believed would take kindly to the presence of the Federation ships. In addition, *Achilles* taking the lead would leave the TS Flyers vulnerable for far too long.

It was at this point that Conlon had suggested that *Voyager*'s transporter system could be modified to act as a relay for *Achilles*. Once *Voyager* was in position to establish the sensor lock, the necessary data could be transmitted to *Achilles* through a shielded sensor beam. *Voyager* would not have to drop its shields in order to establish the lock, so it would be less vulnerable to the Tarkons. *Achilles'* systems would then complete the transport, leaving Drafar close enough to the TS Flyers to be able to collect them once transport had been completed.

Conlon would not have made the suggestion had she realized that both *Achilles* and *Voyager* were planning to begin the operation from within a section of the Nekrit Expanse that was a Class 9 nebula. Once both ships were clear of the nebula, the sensor lock could be established, but Conlon had assumed she would have the opportunity to perfect the relay system well before this critical moment. As it was, she was constantly reconfiguring the system on the fly, while *Voyager* evaded the Tarkons.

B'Elanna's focused composure should have been reassuring;

instead, Conlon found it maddening. As she wiped the sweat from her eyes, B'Elanna was working calmly to minimize the width of the annular confinement beams. The subjects being transported were all located several meters below the planet's surface, adding another layer of complication to a plan that was already fraught with possible disasters.

Conlon sneaked a peek at B'Elanna's controls and said with awe, "You could transport a single grain of dust from the surface with that setting."

B'Elanna smiled briefly. "It's a modified skeletal lock," she replied.

"A what?"

"Something I came up with years ago, but solving this has forced me to push it to new limits. It's designed to lock onto specific mineral components when life-sign readings are inconclusive."

"And you're assuming they're going to be?" Conlon asked.

"There are over two hundred thousand people on the western continent. We're looking for forty-seven needles in a haystack, with nothing to distinguish them from the other needles that are walking around on the surface above them," B'Elanna replied. "I'm opting for a level of detail here we wouldn't normally require."

Conlon shook her head and returned her attention to her panel. "And while a thing of beauty, it will all be for nothing if I can't get this sensor lock stable."

B'Elanna shifted her eyes to Conlon's display and said, "Reroute power from these reserves." She indicated two noncritical systems. Conlon did as instructed, and the readings fell to within one percent of optimal.

Both relieved and annoyed for not reaching the same conclusion first, Conlon said, "You know, there are moments working with you when I really don't like you very much."

"You're welcome." B'Elanna smiled, then hailed *Achilles*.

"*Voyager* to *Achilles*. Captain Drafar, thirty seconds to transport. Stand by."

"*Voyager, we will clear the nebula in ten seconds,*" Drafar replied. "*Achilles, standing by.*"

Nothing like cutting it really, really close, Conlon thought.

The next several seconds were a blur for Lieutenant Harry Kim. Once he had locked phasers on the Tarkons, they instantaneously perceived the threat and broke formation. The vessels targeted their forward weapons systems on *Voyager* as their energy nets dispersed.

The ship shuddered, and shields fell by twenty percent during the first barrage.

Harry checked his readings as the sentries regrouped for another attack run. "Ten more Tarkon vessels have broken off pursuit of the TS Flyers and are approaching our position," he alerted the bridge calmly. "Two more direct hits like that and our forward shields will go," he added.

"B'Elanna, what is your status?" Chakotay called.

After a few moments of silence during which Harry was certain he aged a year or two, B'Elanna's voice rang out clearly, "*Transport complete, Captain.*"

Chakotay didn't waste a moment.

"Gwyn, set course to rendezvous with *Achilles* and prepare to go to slipstream velocity. Harry, lay down cover fire."

"Aye, Captain," both replied in near unison.

What followed was one of the most frenetic battle scenarios Harry had ever endured. Phasers were fired under automatic control, since the computer could read and compensate for the speed of the Tarkon ships more quickly. The tactical officer was manually targeting photon torpedoes, focusing on the carrier vessels, but it felt like he was swatting gnats. It didn't matter how many he took out; within seconds, more were taking their place.

Achilles was laying down cover fire, but *Voyager* was taking a beating because it had placed itself between the larger ship and the Tarkons.

Harry had confirmed nineteen of the forty-five Tarkon vessels destroyed when eight more had managed to re-form their energy nets. They were approaching *Voyager* from both fore and aft, and he was forced to conclude that one of them was likely to catch their prey.

"Evasive maneuvers," Chakotay called to Gwyn. "Harry, get the forward ships out of our way."

"*Achilles* reports all TS Flyers aboard," Lasren cut through the chaos as Harry manually targeted the center of the energy web with a photon torpedo spread.

His aim was true, but as *Voyager* moved toward the explosion, it took a pounding that sent shockwaves throughout the ship, in spite of Gwyn's struggles to maneuver through the force. One move Harry had mastered, in the years he had spent as the tactical officer and chief of security, was holding on to the sides of his station when it counted.

"Shields down to ten percent," Harry called as he attempted to get a lock on the Tarkon vessels in pursuit. He might have imagined it, but he thought he sensed a sluggishness in the ship's responsiveness.

"Helm, maximum speed to slipstream jump coordinates," Chakotay ordered. "Is *Achilles* still with us?" he asked of Tom.

"Yes, Captain," the first officer replied.

Harry estimated they'd be clear in the next twenty seconds. The moment *Voyager* engaged its warp drive, the Tarkons directly behind them did the same, but the energy net was no longer pulling *Voyager* toward it.

"All hands, prepare to go to slipstream velocity," Gwyn called from the conn.

Harry continued to deploy torpedoes, until Gwyn had completed her countdown. He had no idea how many Tarkons had lost their lives as the slipstream corridor formed around *Voyager*, cutting off pursuit. What he did know was that the Federation Fleet had just made another enemy in the Delta Quadrant.

When Chakotay finally gave the order to stand down from Red Alert and compile damage reports, the tension of the last few minutes gave way to numbness, followed by almost overwhelming fatigue. They had survived and accomplished their mission. Harry hoped that the forty-seven people who had just transported to *Achilles* were worth the price.

Chapter Thirteen

MIKHAL OUTPOST

The midday sun rode high over the southern desert as the Doctor and Cambridge materialized in what initially appeared to be the middle of nowhere. The Doctor immediately activated his tricorder and within seconds located Captain Eden. She was no longer descending, but was now moving on a more or less horizontal plane.

Before them stood a massive cluster of large rocks. Between the nearest two was a low opening, only recently and haphazardly dug out, presumably by Eden. At the base of the entrance, now partially obscured by the unceasing movement of the sands, was another starscape similar to the ones they had previously discovered.

The Doctor was pointing a medical scanner at Counselor Cambridge. The readings he received produced an audible "Hmmff."

Cambridge stopped clearing the sand from the newly discovered artifact and turned to the Doctor.

"Problem?"

"These readings suggest that we should begin our descent without further ado."

Cambridge's brow furrowed in confusion, which pleased the Doctor no end because the expression was unusual for Cambridge.

"As a photonic being, I could easily follow Captain Eden at a brisk run and likely overtake her in the next hour. Were you inclined to take better care of yourself—and maintain a routine of rigorous exercise, like most Starfleet officers—you might be able to keep pace with me. However, I suspect even a light jog would have you panting for mercy in less than four hundred meters."

"So, what you're saying is that we have at least two hours ahead of us with nothing but the pleasure of each other's company to distract us before we reach the captain?"

"Depending upon how many rest breaks you require, Counselor."

"Amazing," was Cambridge's cryptic response.

Wondering if he was being complimented, the Doctor shrugged and stepped toward the tunnel's entrance. "To what, exactly, are you referring?" he asked.

"There are a number of officers aboard *Voyager* who have spoken to me at some length about the great strides you have made over the years in surpassing your programming. Many of them even find you to be quite a pleasant conversationalist."

The Doctor smiled as humbly as possible. "The officers you speak of are some of my closest friends."

"That must be it," Cambridge replied, "because, frankly, I don't see it."

The Doctor's smile faded. "That's amusing, because many of the same officers have also had kind things to say about you, but as best I can tell, a more pompous, insubordinate, and generally unpleasant officer has never been admitted to Starfleet's ranks."

"You don't get around much, do you?"

"Shall we?" the Doctor asked, gesturing to the entrance.

"After you," Cambridge replied with mock civility.

The first five hundred meters of their journey commenced in silence. Cambridge was more than content to leave well enough alone when the Doctor's wrist beacon suddenly illuminated countless reflective points covering every surface of the tunnel. Clearly the stones were dotted with a luminescent mineral, which made the journey through the darkness quite lovely. But as they continued, Cambridge couldn't shake the sense that they were walking through space, flecked with stars.

The counselor suddenly stopped, pulled out his tricorder, and scanned three hundred and sixty degrees around him. After a few minutes, the device emitted a series of beeps, which halted the Doctor in his tracks. How a hologram could elicit such a perfect rendition of a weary sigh was a marvel. For the moment, Cambridge's hands were shaking as he asked the tricorder to confirm its findings.

"Do you require rest?" the Doctor asked when he had returned to Cambridge's location. "I admit you've gone longer than I expected without complaint, but . . ."

"Be quiet," Cambridge ordered as he moved quickly back up the tunnel a good fifty meters and repeated his scan.

"That's the wrong direction, Counselor."

"Bloody hell, if all you care about is making haste, then by all means do so," Cambridge spat back sharply.

The Doctor seemed to consider the option before slowly retracing his steps and moving to within a few meters of the counselor.

"I take it you believe you have found something significant?" the Doctor asked more patiently.

Cambridge lifted his eyes from the tricorder and played his wrist beacon over the walls again.

"Do the walls and floor of this tunnel remind you of anything, Doctor?" Cambridge asked.

"Other than the walls and floor of every enclosed tunnel like this I've ever traversed?"

"Look again," Cambridge instructed, wondering if the Doctor's programming would include the kind of data his own mind meticulously catalogued. He doubted it.

The Doctor did so, and finally replied, "Now that you mention it, they do bear a resemblance to the artifacts we discovered yesterday. But the sheer volume of the reflective points suggests they are most likely a natural property of the stone through which the tunnel was carved."

"They're not," Cambridge replied, stepping several paces back to where the illuminated surfaces began.

"Would you mind sharing with the rest of the class?" the Doctor asked.

At this, a light laugh stole from Cambridge's mouth. The Doctor could try one's patience, but at least he was able to admit when his knowledge was deficient.

"This area here," Cambridge said, indicating the first illuminated section, "is a precise map of the stars surrounding our current position."

"You mean, this planet?" the Doctor asked, now curious.

Cambridge nodded. Moving farther along the tunnel, he said, "We're heading toward the boundary of the Milky Way, and by this point, we are reaching the closest formations in the outer Cygnus Arm."

The Doctor seemed well and truly flabbergasted. He quickly shone his light down the tunnel and emitted a short gasp. "Counselor, the lights fade here, and there is darkness for several meters."

"That's to be expected, don't you think?" Cambridge replied, now certain of at least one thing. Whoever had placed those artifacts on the surface did so to point the way toward this tunnel, and whatever lay at its end was most likely the key to their identity. "Care to race me to the Sagittarius Dwarf Galaxy?" he asked.

The Doctor didn't bother to reply, but hurried on ahead until once again, the walls and floor glowed with tiny, brilliant lights.

"This tunnel is a map," he finally said.

"Maybe," Cambridge admitted.

"What else could it be?" the Doctor demanded.

"A travelogue," Cambridge replied.

"Left by whom?" the Doctor asked.

Cambridge shrugged. "I don't know, but I'll bet Afsarah does."

Eden sat among the ruins, engulfed in desolate numbness. When she had first entered the tunnel, hours earlier, the anxiety she had held at bay for so long almost overwhelmed her. She had forced herself to take slow, regular breaths as she continued forward, and within minutes reached the first starscape map she recognized. She knew *this* was where a journey had ended. Its beginning waited several kilometers below.

The names of the constellations she passed embedded themselves in her memory. She was walking into history, written thousands of years ago, literally set in stone. The thoughts, feelings, hopes, dreams, and terrors of those who had lived it gathered thick around her like a mist. Beyond the names by which these stars had been called, a reverence for them crept into her consciousness. They had not been merely known by those who had created a permanent record of them here, beneath the desert; they had been loved.

It was not long before the absence of her uncles, Tallar and Jobin, became almost unendurable. Eden had no idea how much of what she now beheld had been searched for by them or known to them, but she did not doubt that this was the place they had been seeking during the years she had traveled with them. The thought that they had been denied the truth revealing itself to her with each step she took was almost too painful to bear.

However, still missing was the catalyst for their search. Eden had always believed that her entrance into her uncles' lives had been a happy accident, and she had not deterred them from their greater quest for knowledge. Only now did she suspect that their work had become more focused after she had joined them.

The captain had long ago abandoned all hope of ever learning more about their quixotic journeys. She'd never given any credence to the idea of fate, or destiny, and the notion that some larger guiding hand played any part in the day-to-day realities of the living had always seemed preposterous.

For the first time in her life, Eden began to doubt her casual acceptance of science and wonder how much of Tallar and Jobin's life had been rooted in some sort of personal faith.

Finally, her journey had ended as the tunnel opened into a cavern so vast, it nearly brought her to her knees. All around her, carved deep into the walls, countless images of the life and death of this place's former inhabitants glowed with an unnatural light. The collective brilliance of it made her wrist beacon unnecessary.

The first atrium—a space just under a hundred meters wide and twenty meters high—was dotted sporadically with carefully wrought obsidian staffs, some still intact, extending from the floor to the ceiling. They were symbolic rather than physical barriers. Anyone able to translate the words etched into them would have known, as she had the moment she had touched the so-called Staff of Ren, that they held a warning not to trespass further. Clearly, over the centuries, others had found their way into the caverns. *Grave robbers,* she thought harshly. All those who had preceded her here had come to plunder. The treasures they had stolen were priceless, but the greater loss was the opportunity to study the unique history revealed beyond the barrier.

Beyond the atrium, the cavern widened considerably, opening at least an additional thirty meters overhead. Eden had no idea how much time she had spent absorbing the life stories of those who had made this place home, when her legs finally gave out beneath her and she crumpled to the floor. The tears she wept for herself—for the lost Anschlasom, and finally, for her uncles—flowed without cease. It wasn't that she had never known pain in her life, but she had never before been a conduit for it. As she began to lose herself in its depths, she ached for its end, even as she understood that "the end" had been the beginning for the travelers who had finally come to rest here.

The captain did not hear the approach of her fellow officers. When Hugh placed a tentative hand on her shoulder, gently speaking her name, Eden turned to face him, expecting to see in his place Osterna, the leader of the doomed Anschlasom, reaching out from beyond death to claim his daughter.

Unable to resist, she had thrown herself into his arms, and eventually the sobs that racked her body began to subside.

It might have been hours later when she woke to find that the counselor and the Doctor had created a small camp. She had been wrapped in a standard-issue emergency blanket. Hugh's uniform jacket had been rolled beneath her head, to lift it from the stone floor.

Every slight movement brought with it a dull and nauseating pain. As soon as she stirred, the Doctor had rushed to her side and placed a cup of warm, slightly bitter liquid to her mouth.

Scanning her thoroughly, he advised her that she needed rest, but was otherwise in reasonable health.

"Thank you," she managed weakly.

Cambridge took up position beside the Doctor and smiled down at her. "You've had quite a day, haven't you?"

Once they had seen to the physical safety and comfort of Eden, Cambridge and the Doctor had taken a few hours to familiarize themselves with the immense cavern. Beyond the entrance atrium, a massive, probably communal space held enough archeological data to keep several generations busy. Using their tricorders, they meticulously mapped the adjacent tunnels and caverns that broke off from the main chamber. They spent considerable time puzzling over the most prominent and unusual artifact in the cavern: a smooth, black surface whose center seemed to be lit from behind by a small white light. It hung in a perfect circle beginning about ten meters from the floor and rising almost to the top of the rear wall. Both agreed that it was not a natural formation—it had clearly been placed there. It had not been carved from the surrounding stone, and their equipment could not identify its molecular structure. It was undeniably beautiful, and equally frightening, as if a large black lake had been frozen and suspended before them.

So awe inspiring was the cavern that all of the petty disputes Cambridge and the Doctor had been engaged in were forgotten. They moved eagerly from one area to the next, calling out to each other as interesting discoveries were made, theorized about the significance of a particular figural representation, and ultimately stared at the black surface together in silence.

Once Eden had awakened again and been thoroughly fortified with food and drink, they settled themselves in a small circle. Any thoughts of chiding her for her recklessness were banished by the enormity of her discovery.

"I am grateful you came after me," Eden said shyly.

"You are our commanding officer—" the Doctor began.

"And our friend," Cambridge interjected for good measure.

Nodding, the Doctor finished, "We could not have done otherwise."

"Nevertheless, thank you," Eden replied.

The captain quickly recounted the mathematical secrets of the various artifacts and their locations and how they led to the discovery of the tunnel.

"Would I be right in assuming that you have found here at least some of the answers you were seeking?" Cambridge ventured.

Eden stared deeply into his eyes, knowing that the truth would be plain upon her face, then said, "You would."

"Was this the home of your people?" the Doctor asked.

Eden shook her head, smiling, and pointed behind her to a large mosaic that depicted several tall figures with four upper arm-like appendages and two legs. A round protrusion above an elongated oval torso might have indicated a head, but it was impossible to tell if the two fine stalks that rose from the top of the head were antennae, eyes, or merely decorative headdresses. "Those were the Anschlasom," she said. "They first came here a little over ten thousand years ago. When they discovered other primitive life-forms on the surface, they built this place and retreated to it, to live out the short time left them in peace and without corrupting the natives. It seems that many space-faring races develop some version of the Prime Directive."

"But they left the map we found above?" Cambridge asked.

Eden nodded.

"If they were so adamant about hiding themselves from the others on this planet, why didn't they leave?" the Doctor inquired. "And why leave the map at all?"

Fresh tears rose to Eden's eyes as she "remembered" the years of debate over that second question. To hold them back, she focused on the first and much easier question to answer. "Their ships were too badly damaged, and this planet lacked the natural resources necessary for them to rebuild." After a moment spent regaining control of her emotions, Eden continued, "They were content to vanish from this part of the universe's history, but they needed to tell their story to themselves. It created a sense of cultural continuity, as all that they had been slowly turned to dust around them."

"The galactic references in the tunnel . . . They were from quite far away, weren't they?" Cambridge asked.

"They were from a galaxy so distant we've never actually seen it. While I cannot confirm this in any factual way, my guess would be that they were among the very first life-forms to attain sentience." As Cambridge and the Doctor studied her, Eden continued, "They had explored and colonized much of their galaxy and had begun to venture farther out. Some headed toward the other galaxies they could perceive, searching for new life-forms. A smaller group set their course toward the void that, as best they could determine, was at the outermost edge of the universe. They wanted to know what, if anything, lay beyond it. They spent thousands of years studying it and testing it. Their technology was astounding—not even the Caeliar's compares. Eventually, their efforts resulted in the revelation of something remarkable: an anomalous fragment within the void unlike anything they had ever seen. They did not create it; rather, they were convinced that it had always been present, though imperceptible to their sensors. But their actions were the first to bring it into contact with what we would call normal space-time."

"Did it happen to look anything like that?" Cambridge asked, pointing at the vast suspended black lake.

"If you think it's odd to find that here, imagine what it looked like hanging in the middle of space," Eden replied.

"That doesn't sound possible," the Doctor said. "I'm no expert on esoteric interstellar phenomena, but surely that is an artificial construct."

"It is anomalous space," Eden said, "in a highly localized area. The normal laws of space and time do not apply to it. The Anschlasom studied it, tested it, did everything they could think of, tried to force it to reveal its mysteries, but had no success. Finally, they gave it a name: *Som*. The best translation would be 'The End.'"

Cambridge and the Doctor exchanged a confused look.

"The end of what?" the Doctor asked.

"Of everything," Eden replied. "They were able to determine that it was expanding slowly, incredibly slowly. Within trillions of years, it would encompass their galaxy, and from there, eventually, the rest of the universe."

"But what *was* it?" Cambridge persisted.

"I have no idea," Eden shrugged, "because they had no idea."

"How did they get here?" the Doctor demanded.

"The Anschlasom were already an ancient civilization when they encountered *Som*. When all else failed, a small group of them, on behalf of all their people, chose to attempt the unthinkable. Rather than simply allow it to run its course, they decided to battle it. They used power sources so massive we don't even have theoretical constructs for them yet and accomplished nothing. Finally, they decided to try and enter it." Eden gestured to the vast series of carvings that illuminated the ceiling of the cavern. "It's difficult to really say what they found inside it. Every individual who experienced it saw and felt something quite different. But all of them left their impressions here. It was like some sort of communal dream. Some of what they saw was beautiful and inspiring. What others saw threw them into the depths of despair and madness. None of them knew how long they journeyed through it. Eventually, they passed again into normal space, crashing here on this planet, billions of years from their own past."

Both the Doctor and Cambridge stared transfixed at the ceiling for some time. Eden took a moment to refresh her tea, fearing that if she looked up, the indelible impressions of the images above would again overwhelm her.

"And . . . that's it?" the Doctor finally asked.

"You need more?" Eden asked, dumbfounded.

"I think what we're both wondering is how this amazing and thoroughly intriguing archeological wonder is connected to you," Cambridge clarified. "I could spend my next ten lifetimes down here studying all of this. As it stands, I don't expect to sleep at all until *Achilles* returns."

"Returns?" Eden asked, suddenly concerned.

"It was called in to support *Voyager,*" Cambridge replied.

"Why?"

"I don't know," the counselor admitted.

Eden turned to the Doctor. After an uncomfortable moment he added, "There was a lot going on. I honestly didn't think to ask."

Eden looked between them, aghast.

"Oh, for pity's sake, Afsarah," Cambridge said, "you had left the ship without advising anyone. We didn't have time for an in-depth briefing. We found your life signs, grabbed our things, and hopped on the transporter pad."

Eden sighed deeply. "Sorry."

After a moment, the captain said, "To answer your question, I honestly don't know what, if anything, this has to do with me or why I feel connected to it. But I believe my uncles knew," she added. "The more I think about the places we went together, I'm struck by the similarities in context if not in content to this find."

"Was all of this for nothing?" the Doctor demanded.

"I'm not one of them, or their descendant," Eden stated.

"But . . . ?" Cambridge asked, sensing her confusion.

"But somehow they are part of me," she admitted.

Chapter Fourteen

ACHILLES

Commander Tillum Drafar met Seven of Nine and Chakotay in *Achilles'* main transporter room. Having successfully escaped the Tarkons, the ships were carrying out repairs. They were a thousand light-years from their previous position, and far from any known interstellar phenomena that might trouble them. Within a few hours, both ships would be ready to set course for the rendezvous point with the rest of the fleet, arriving several days ahead of schedule.

Seven knew that Chakotay was as curious as she was about

Riley and her people. Drafar had advised them that they were grateful, extremely cooperative, and that Doctor Frazier was quite anxious to meet with Chakotay.

"What have you learned, Captain?" Chakotay asked the moment they stepped down from the pad.

"Doctor Frazier and her people are not what I expected, considering your last encounter with them," Drafar replied as he ushered them into the hall and led them toward the turbolift. A cargo bay had been made over to tend to the medical and physical well-being of their guests.

"In what way?" Seven asked.

"I was prepared for, and advised my security staff to expect, a small Borg collective."

At this, Seven rolled her eyes. Drafar was too tall to notice.

"They no longer function as a collective?" Chakotay asked.

"No," Drafar confirmed. "Although their concern for and protectiveness of one another is what you might expect from any group forced to survive while in hiding from the Tarkons."

Before they reached the doors to the cargo bay, Drafar explained, "Ten security officers are maintaining a presence in the room, though they are doing their best to remain inconspicuous. We have provided our guests with food, clothing, and facilities to refresh themselves. Many have already fallen asleep. But Doctor Frazier is waiting to speak with you."

"Thank you," Chakotay replied.

"Please contact me if there is anything you need, and, Captain, the *Achilles* needs to return to the Mikhal Outpost as soon as possible. Whatever arrangements you intend to make for the ultimate disposition of these people need to be done quickly. This can only be a temporary solution."

"Of course," Chakotay agreed.

Drafar nodded and strode away. Seven met Chakotay's eyes. He had but to reach his hand to the door's security panel to gain entrance, but something stopped him.

"You just went to great lengths to save these people," Seven reminded him.

"I know," he said, dropping his head with a sigh.

"Whatever they once were," she added, "they are individuals once again."

"And all alone out here," Chakotay said.

"Do you still bear a grudge against them?" Seven asked.

Chakotay shook his head. "No. But I can't say I really trust them, either."

"A wise precaution," Seven agreed.

The cargo bay's lights were dimmed, and it took a few moments for Seven's eyes to adjust as they entered. Five long rows of cots had been set up, with ample space between them to accommodate the small cases of personal items that had been provided for each of the refugees.

Seven could vaguely make out several figures roving through the darkness. Before she and Chakotay could go any farther, a slight woman with short, grayish yellow hair and piercing blue eyes approached them with a wide and welcoming smile.

"Commander Chakotay," she said warmly, "and Seven of Nine. It's nice to meet you in person at last."

"Doctor Frazier," Seven replied coolly.

Riley Frazier seemed eager to close the distance between herself and Chakotay with some physical gesture of greeting, but his professional demeanor clearly kept her at bay.

"Actually, it's 'captain,' now," he advised her.

Confused consternation passed across her face as Riley considered the possible explanations for his new rank. Finally she asked, "Captain Janeway?"

Chakotay's jaw tensed as he replied, "She was killed in the line of duty a little over a year ago."

Riley's sympathy seemed genuine as she responded, "I'm so sorry to hear that. I know how important she was to you. You still haven't gotten home?"

Chakotay was clearly uncomfortable with the personal nature of their exchange.

"*Voyager* reached the Alpha Quadrant," Seven advised Riley, "over three years ago. We have returned as part of a fleet exploring the Delta Quadrant and attempting to learn the fate of any former Borg."

Riley's eyes met Seven's with the same warmth she had exuded toward Chakotay. Seven found it mildly disconcerting, but part of her understood the connection that now bound them. "There is a great deal you need to know," Riley said, accepting that her emotional response to this meeting was not shared by the Starfleet officers. "Would you like to take a seat?" She gestured to a small area where a few chairs had been arranged. "I know it's not much, but compared to the way we've lived for the past several months, it's like the lap of luxury."

"Of course." Chakotay finally nodded and moved to accept her offer.

Once they had settled themselves, Seven noticed the sleeping figures arrayed nearby. The privation they had endured while in hiding had clearly taken a toll. An unpleasant odor emanated from many of the small piles of tattered rags beside the cots. Seven wondered that they had not been immediately reclaimed, but quickly reconsidered. When one has had nothing, every single scrap was treated like a treasure and would be difficult to part with.

Speaking with considerable restraint, Chakotay said, "The last time we spoke, your people had reestablished your link."

Riley nodded, her face hardening. "We did, and though I apologize for the way we forced your assistance, I cannot regret the outcome."

"And what was the outcome?" Chakotay asked, clenching his jaw.

"The new link functioned exactly as we had anticipated. Once we were again joined, the conflicts ceased. Over the next few years, we established a new and vastly superior means of coexisting on the planet."

"Superior?" Chakotay said, with an uncharacteristically judgmental tone.

Riley held up her palm in acquiescence. "A poor choice of words. I apologize. But compared to what our life had become, it was certainly preferable."

"How did the collective function without a queen?" Seven asked.

"It was challenging to adapt at first," Riley allowed, "and none of us were eager to impose our will upon the others. Initially we focused more on maintaining a sense of harmony. Gradually, people began to find their way toward a means of contributing to the good of the whole that interested them, and eventually several small hierarchies developed, for directing work or acquiring resources. It was similar to our former structure, Seven of Nine," she added with enough emphasis to communicate that she was not eager to engage in a discussion of the varying hues of pots and kettles.

"So it was paradise?" Chakotay asked, skeptical.

Riley smiled wanly. "No," she admitted, "that came later." She exchanged a knowing glance with Seven.

"How?" Chakotay asked.

"Our society was functional and secure. Everyone received according to their needs and contributed according to their abilities. Over time, there were urges toward more individual means of relation and expression, and where they could be, they were accommodated."

Seven knew that all manner of odd interpersonal relationships had developed among Borg severed from the hive mind. But she could not imagine how this cooperative had functioned.

"Some began to wonder if the link was still necessary, and we debated the idea with great passion. However, few of us were willing to risk the chaos we had once known . . ." Riley's voice trailed off, as if she were struggling to find words for her next thoughts.

"And then?" Chakotay prodded gently.

Riley looked to Seven. "You must know."

"I know what I experienced, Doctor," Seven said. "But I would very much like to hear your version."

Riley nodded and clasped her hands before her. "And then, on an otherwise normal day, everything changed. Our link was suddenly absorbed by—no, lost in—something much greater. At first it was terrifying. I remember thinking that somehow the Borg had found us again. I didn't know what else it could be. We were seventy-nine thousand eight hundred and ninety-one minds, and a moment later, we were millions."

"Billions," Seven corrected her gently.

"But through the chaos, there was a . . . light. I don't know what else to call it. We were welcomed into a new existence, and it was immediately clear that in that place, we would once again be ourselves, and so much more." Turning to Seven, she asked, "Is that what it was like for you?"

"In some ways," Seven acknowledged. "Frankly, I do not remember . . . much."

There was a long pause, during which Riley seemed to search Seven's face with a hungry curiosity. "How could you bear to refuse it?"

Seven felt warm tears rising to her eyes, and slowly she reached out for Riley's hands. Her eyes were glistening, as well, as she accepted Seven's hand. "My individuality had become more important to me than the perfection the Caeliar were offering," Seven replied.

Riley nodded and squeezed Seven's hands. After a moment, Seven pulled back. The feeling of shared loss was almost overwhelming. Seven had not known until this moment how much it would mean to her for another being to have shared her experience with compassion and absolute understanding.

"Why did you refuse it, Riley?" Chakotay interjected softly.

She tore her eyes from Seven's to stare at him in wonder. "I would think that was obvious."

Seven looked at the cots and noted the size of some of the sleepers, as well as the accommodations where several were sharing cots.

"You had children?" Seven whispered in awe.

Riley smiled with joy. "I was trying to put it delicately before, but, yes, we did."

" 'Individual means of relation and expression'?" Chakotay asked with a smile.

"It wasn't anticipated," Riley went on, "but not long after the link was stabilized, many of our more organic urges returned. There seemed to be no reason at the time to try and repress them. We were a collective, but we were not Borg. All of us wanted to explore what we could make of this new life."

Understanding dawned, giving Seven a deeper appreciation for what Riley and the others had sacrificed. "The children had never been Borg," she said softly.

"They couldn't join the gestalt," Riley said, nodding. "We couldn't leave them behind."

"Did you . . . ?" Chakotay began.

"No," Riley replied. "But once I knew that some would remain, I just couldn't . . ." She was unable now to hold back her tears.

Finally, Chakotay moved toward her and gently placed comforting hands on her shoulders. When Riley had collected herself, she continued, "We were left in peace for less than a month, then the Tarkons arrived and began depositing hopeless refugees on our world. We retreated into a series of underground bunkers we'd created during the troubled years and long since abandoned. We scraped by, making runs to the surface to steal food and water. And then, yesterday, you arrived." After a long pause she added, "This should have been the first thing I said: thank you, so very much. You've saved us. *Again.* I don't know how much longer we could have survived."

Chakotay nodded and replied sincerely, "You are most welcome."

Riley smiled, and this time her smile was returned in full force. "Can you ever forgive me?" she asked quietly.

"I understand," Chakotay replied. Riley nodded in acceptance. "You should get some rest now. I'll be back in the morning. We need to discuss our next move."

"Move?" Riley asked.

"Our fleet is going to remain in the Delta Quadrant for the next few years," he offered. "But from time to time, some of our ships may return to the Alpha Quadrant." Riley clearly wondered how this was possible, but held her peace. "This ship isn't designed to accommodate you, but I believe we could make arrangements for you on *Voyager* for the short term. Before I heard your story, I was considering spreading you around the fleet until other arrangements could be made, but not now." He added, "It might be close quarters, but if you're willing, we'll make it work. As soon as possible, we can return you to the Federation, where I'm certain a permanent solution can be found."

"I wonder if I might trespass a little further on your kindness?"

"How so?" the captain asked.

"Those of us who were once Borg were all transformed by our experience of the Caeliar. We still don't understand it, but we remain connected through something the Caeliar left with us."

"They're called catoms," Seven answered her unspoken question. "They facilitated your communication with me."

"That was the oddest thing," Riley said. "I sensed you and I knew I had to speak with you. I didn't actually know how I reached you, but something in me knew I could."

"Your Borg implants were replaced by a very advanced form of programmable matter. If your case is like mine, and I suspect it is, these catoms are meant to sustain the functions formerly performed by your implants, though they present other unique opportunities."

"I would appreciate it if you would share with us whatever you have learned about them."

"Of course," Seven replied readily, earning her a quick glance of disapproval from Chakotay.

"The thing is," Riley went on, unaware of the brief flash of tension, "we haven't given up on our determination to create a new life for ourselves. I believe we can still do that here. We don't need to return to the Federation."

"We could start looking for a new planet for you to colonize," Chakotay offered.

"I know of one, quite a ways from here, and not likely to be troubled by the Tarkons for a long while. If your ship has journeyed this far into the Delta Quadrant from the Sol system, I can't imagine that it would take you more than a few days off course."

"Where?" Chakotay asked, puzzled.

"Arehaz," Riley replied.

Chakotay looked to Seven to see if the name meant anything to her.

"The planet where the Borg originated," she answered.

Chapter Fifteen

Q CONTINUUM

Q laughed. "A third option?"

Kathryn Janeway didn't share in his amusement. As she weighed both of the impossible alternatives now before her, she decided that nothing in the vast array of experiences she brought to this moment had in any way prepared her to confront them. Countless times, when Kathryn had lived, she had spared little time and energy on choices that had better than average chances of ending her life. Often they were made in the heat of battle, where time and energy were at a premium, but the utter recklessness with which she had lived was now incomprehensible to her. Less dangerous but no less significant decisions had been made through rigorous application of reason and logic, weighing pros and cons, risks and rewards, the potential for joy and pain. But looking back, these choices had, as often as not, ended in ways she could not have foreseen.

That was *life,* part of her counseled.

At every turn, guided by her heart and mind, Kathryn Janeway had made the best possible decision she could with the information at her disposal, certain that if it proved wrong, she would find a way, in time, to make it right.

But *this* was not life. She no longer had a heart or mind to help her wrestle through the dilemma. Q had done his best to explain the nature of her existence. She was all that she was or ever would be. She was pure consciousness, no longer bound by the mundane realities of corporeal existence. She had briefly tasted the life of a Q and had been humbled by its magnificence. Now, she was expected to decide rationally whether some greater unknown, and possibly unknowable, power held her in its hand. Was it guiding her toward the ultimate fate of all mortal life? Was the inner certainty that she *must* leave well enough alone, rather than return to her former existence, where every moment would be fraught with danger, doubt, and pain, correct? Yes, life contained its fair share of joys great and small, obstacles conquered, passions shared, companionship and love. But Kathryn could not lie to herself and pretend that the good outweighed the bad. Increasingly as she had aged, Kathryn had felt that her moments of pure, unadulterated happiness were few and further between.

Was that her fault? Had she consciously, or subconsciously, sought out life's challenges out of a need to constantly prove herself? Now, she was forced to acknowledge that she had been driven by the fear that if she did not continue to push herself, she would find herself alone with only her regrets for company.

There was no easy answer here. Either choice, to release control to the will of the multiverse, or reassert her fragile illusion of control upon the multiverse's vast and incomprehensible designs, was terrifying. Kathryn knew that if she chose the second, she would immediately be thrust into a new crisis that now frightened her as much as it did Q.

Her mind and heart, or whatever now stood in their former places, were equally divided.

Do I have a third option?

Suddenly Kathryn remembered standing in da Vinci's cluttered studio, staring into a blazing fire and finding in its depths an alternative choice.

No, she thought, brushing quickly past her fateful decision to form an alliance with the Borg. That had been a tactic, and its greatest virtue lay in the fact that it had never before been tried.

She needed something more than an idea with potential.

Willing herself to stillness, Kathryn sought the eye of the storm, the calm center she had occasionally accessed in times of need. It had never disappointed her.

Another memory surfaced, gently rising through her awareness, and she grasped for it, desperate that it not slip away. She sat in a small room with three aged people, two crotchety men and a woman, who had either represented or somehow actually been the ancestral spirits of the Nekisti monks. Kes, a girl she had loved and nurtured, was near death. Kathryn had undertaken a sort of spirit quest in order to gain the scientific data she required to save Kes's life. The "ancestral spirits" had counseled her to repeat the action that had injured Kes in the first place, to carry her into an energy field that would likely kill both of them. Her only choice seemed to be to let go the science, logic, and reason, and embrace something she'd rarely used: faith.

Following their counsel, Kathryn had survived and Kes had been saved. For several blissful hours after, she had lived in a transformed state where possibilities beyond anything she had ever imagined seemed more concrete than any reality.

Faith.

Her soul.

They had always been there, underpinning what she believed were more useful to her: reason and passion. But, however briefly, Kathryn had touched something infinitely deeper. That short exposure had left her adrift but more firmly anchored to herself.

She had never shared with anyone the absolute devastation she had felt when a scientific explanation had been discovered to explain the "miracle." Had she spent more time in the company of her soul prior to this experience, she would not have been as quick to return to business as usual.

Kathryn did not need to locate her soul within her. This ineffable thing was now the sum total of her reality.

It was all that had been left to her.

And more than enough.

Kathryn Janeway laughed.

"You're right," she said through her mirth.

"About what?" Q asked gently.

"I don't need another option."

"Then you've made your decision?"

Kathryn searched for any hint of inner conflict and found none. She now understood that both of her choices were nothing more than potential paths. One promised immediate bliss, or at least release; the other, more of what she already knew. But the first would always be there for her. The second was a one-time-only proposition.

And this knowledge silenced the doubts that had plagued her from the moment she found herself in the Continuum.

"I will go back," she said. "I don't know if I will succeed or fail, but I find the need to try outweighs the desire to absolve myself of any responsibility."

Q didn't have to express his relief or his gratitude. It rolled through her in a warm wave that buoyed her certainty.

"So, how do we do this?" Kathryn asked, more than ready to get under way.

"It's really very simple," Q replied.

Really?

"Your physical form has been scattered into so many particles of dust, an unfortunate by-product of the manner of your death."

He spoke of it as if it were nothing. Having embraced her decision, Kathryn was now faced with the task of returning her attention to the last moments of her life, and as she did so, the horrors they contained crept toward her.

"But their current arrangement is of no significance. Were your body still intact, it would be easy enough to focus your attention upon it and you would find, as others have, that you could descend back into it with no difficulty. You'll have to work a little harder, but I assure you, it can be done. You must not doubt this for a moment."

"You're saying I need faith?" she asked, teasing him.

"If it helps," Q replied. "More than that, you need to

concentrate. The entire cosmos, every atom that exists, is now visible to you. Allow yourself to see them for what they are, and soon enough you will find those that once belonged to you."

"And once I've found them?" she asked warily.

"They are yours to do with as you will," he said. "Order them to organize themselves as they once were and actually tend to want to be, and they will not refuse you."

After a long moment, during which Kathryn memorized the steps he had prescribed and imagined that she could and would complete them, she was ready.

"Okay," she said.

"You can do this," Q assured her.

"I know."

"I'll be right here," he promised. "If you lose your way . . ."

"I won't," she assured him.

It began as an opening, an expansion. Once the complexity of the multiverse yawned before her, it was tempting to explore, but fear kept her priorities in order.

Kathryn dared not wander too long within the brilliance, the infinite cascading interplay of energy and matter. This was a Q's birthright, not hers. She was working with borrowed knowledge, and, conscious of its limitations, she strove only to do as she had been told.

With no voice, she called to those tiny pieces of light that had once belonged to her. She willed them to return to her. She created an imaginary mirror in which she could view her progress, and projected upon it her best recollection of her former physical being.

Soon enough, in bits and pieces, her call was answered. She refused to allow the fragmentary nature of the experience to dissuade her. Patiently, one atom at a time, Kathryn sifted the sands and accepted, grain by grain, what was rightfully hers.

Turning to her mirror, a sudden chill gripped her. The image that was coalescing, despite her best efforts, was not the one she expected. It was the last form her atoms had known. Cells, tissues, organs, bones, blood, and flesh were re-forming themselves, but not into Kathryn Janeway as she knew herself to be. With them came black motes and their hellish inorganic spawn.

A monster opened its eyes and snarled at her in triumph.

For the first time since she had begun, Kathryn faltered.

No, she wailed, just as she had for the unendurable days she had spent trapped by the Borg cube that had transformed her into its queen.

It's all right, Aunt Kathy. The Borg have no power over you now. They are gone.

Kathryn didn't understand. She tried to refuse the return of the violent and corrupting atoms that formed the nanoprobes that had stripped her essence from her body, but against her will, they continued to join their kindred.

Drowning in a sea of agonized voices, those that had begged her to bring order to their chaos, Kathryn felt herself slipping away as the monster gloried in its resurrection.

No, an infinitely more powerful presence sliced through the chaos.

Grateful for the abrupt silence it brought, Kathryn didn't question it.

I've failed, she thought. But it didn't matter. A power from beyond had compelled her obedience, and this time she would not, *could not* refuse it.

You are not Kathryn Janeway, the presence made it known, and as it did so, the snarl of victory upon the face in the mirror was replaced by stunned awe.

Only now did Kathryn realize that the voice commanding her was not her own, nor was it Q's. It came from beyond her, reassured her, warmed her, and, filled with compassion, refocused her will.

Then, as if it were speaking to each of her individual atoms, it gently encouraged them. *You were created of love and light. You are more powerful in your perfect form than any that was forced upon you. See yourselves as you ought to be, not as you became.*

Kathryn searched the mirror again, and slowly, the terrifying technology that had been grafted onto her body fell away, piece by piece, and disintegrated into oblivion.

Hope replaced fear. Light subsumed darkness. Strength, born of the power of this presence, mingled with Kathryn's own determination and reordered the last of her mangled body and soul, realigning them into all that she had once been.

What she would now be was once again an open question.

With a howl of painful awakening, Kathryn felt herself once again inside her body. She allowed the cry to shudder through her until air forced its way into her lungs and a cleansing breath washed away the last of the agony of rebirth.

She was pleasantly warm. The breeze carried the sweet fragrance of new life. A soft buzzing stirred around her.

Opening her eyes, Kathryn found herself standing in a gently rolling meadow in a patch of tall grass dotted with wild flowers.

Q stood next to her, less dazzling than she had recently seen him, but still solid and comforting. He stared at her with admiration, and then his eyes moved beyond hers to a point over her right shoulder as he said, "Thank you."

I didn't do it for you, a voice—*the* voice—replied.

Kathryn turned to see who, or what, had brought her through the journey safe to shore.

At first, it was difficult to make out the form beneath the glare of pure white light that surrounded it. However, it soon resolved into a simpler, though no less beautiful, shape.

"Kes," Kathryn could barely whisper.

The smile she had thought never to see again, a revelation of inner joy so complete as to be almost painful to see, lit Kes's face.

"Hello, Kathryn," Kes said.

Words could wait. The two were drawn into each other's arms. Where once Kathryn had embraced a delicate child in the body of a young woman, now she received the tenderness of a mother's love from a spirit grown unimaginably old.

The tears filling Kathryn's eyes were beyond gratitude. Those that fell from Kes's were absolution.

Chapter Sixteen

MIKHAL OUTPOST

Afsarah Eden was dreaming.

As weariness of body and spirit claimed her, the Doctor had insisted she try to rest. She remembered settling herself beneath the blanket and rearranging the jacket that served as a pillow.

The next thing Eden knew, she was flying. She'd experienced many flying dreams and reveled in the feeling of freedom. This time she had risen to the ceiling of the cavern and hovered there, lingering over the tumultuous images representing the Anschlasom's experience of what lay beyond *Som*.

Most of the images carved into the walls were easy to read. The intentions of the artists and their personal experiences were crystal clear to Eden. So personal were the communications contained in them, it was like reading someone's private logs.

The engravings on the ceiling were different. Eden could not tell what the artists were attempting to depict; the ceiling roiled with disquieting images, as if the artists couldn't bear to recall what they had experienced as they had passed through the darkness.

A powerful radiance distracted her. Turning, she located the source: the tiny pinpoint of white that lay in the center of the suspended black surface embedded in the far wall.

She floated toward it, watching in wonder as the light expanded, throwing bright ripples over the infinite blackness, as if she were witnessing shockwaves following a massive explosion. The light was so intense it should have been painful, but it wasn't. Eden stared into it, losing herself in it. Then slowly, shadowy figures rose from the depths.

The brightness dimmed, allowing the forms to settle, and with a gasp, Eden recognized them: Tallar and Jobin in the cockpit of the vessel that for years had been her home.

They're so young, was her first rational thought beyond the sheer joy of seeing them so clearly again.

The long white ponytail at the base of Jobin's neck was a shocking black, and his face was unlined. He wore a flannel shirt, one she remembered well, and he was gesturing animatedly as he argued with Tallar. His hazel eyes were alert with the thrill of discovery.

This struck Eden as odd. Jobin had always been the more even-keeled of the pair. It was touching to see his vigorous youth, as well as the unusually calm, gentle Tallar, who was clearly urging caution.

Tallar was younger too, but his deep ebony skin had never seemed to age in the way Jobin's had. His scalp was shaved, and his beard was neatly trimmed. He was an intense and elegant man, and Eden had always found him beautiful, though that wasn't normally a word she associated with masculine attractiveness, and had never really applied to any man save Tallar.

He wore a soft gray shirt, and over it an intricately woven, bright multihued vest. Eden suddenly remembered a favorite and well-worn stuffed bear she had loved to tatters dressed in a smaller version of this vest and was moved that Tallar had cut apart his own clothing to fashion a toy for her.

She strained to discern their words, but could not. Both were discussing something that, from their gestures, was just outside their ship. At times, each pointed to different streams of data on the main console's display, and Eden struggled to focus her attention, past her beloved uncles, to the display.

Soon enough, the odd readings were magnified.

That's impossible, Eden thought.

The display showed a highly localized fragment of anomalous space, no more than a few meters at its widest point, and irregularly shaped. Apart from the fact of its presence, they knew nothing about it. It seemed impervious to all of their sensor scans.

Eden's heart began to race. This was exactly what the Anschlasom had seen at the far end of the universe, though they had encountered a much larger fragment of it. She searched her new memories for those of the first of the ancients to see *Som* and the little scientific data they had been able to coax from it. Their readings were the mathematical equivalent of Jobin and Tallar's.

She quickly looked back at her uncles. Time had passed. Tallar's head bore the stubble of inattention and Jobin's light blue T-shirt was a rumpled mess. Jobin was seated, but Tallar had moved to their small vessel's deflector control panel at the rear of the cockpit. Instantly, she understood.

Tell me you didn't, she pleaded. But of course they had.

The curiosity the phenomenon had provoked in the Anschlasom was mirrored in her uncles' determined faces. Eden had no idea how long they had studied the anomaly, but she knew beyond a shadow of a doubt what they intended to do.

With shared readiness, they released all the energy their small vessel could muster into the solid beam. Once it was spent, Eden heaved a sigh of relief as the readings showed no alterations.

She silently celebrated their disappointment until Tallar placed a firm hand on Jobin's shoulder. Nodding silently, Jobin set course directly into the heart of the anomaly.

The vision began to distort. When it resumed, she was no longer in the ship. Instead, Eden found herself in a vast and beautiful landscape.

She rested beneath a lush tangle of tree branches, their leaves colored the deep reds, oranges, and ocher that heralded the changing of the seasons. Overripe, round golden fruit clung desperately to their stems. A damp blanket of dew-kissed grass carpeted the ground beneath her. Similar trees dotted the garden, and several clumps of large-leafed plants burst forth from the ground. Eden struggled to remember where this garden had been. She was certain she had seen it before with her uncles, but was unable to bring a specific time to her mind.

From behind her, Tallar and Jobin appeared. Tallar's eyes were filled with wonder. Jobin seemed more intent on searching for some means of escape. They wandered in different directions, Tallar calling and gesticulating over a particular unique plant while Jobin lifted his eyes to the sky above with great concern.

Finally, Tallar approached Eden. His eyes seemed to glow, and she realized they were actually reflecting the light of the tree above her. *No,* she corrected herself; *the fruit.* The most puzzling thing was that while Tallar's expression held respectful awe, he did not recognize her.

Jobin came to Tallar's side and likewise gazed up at Eden. Tallar reached up to touch her face and Jobin quickly placed a hand of warning on his arm. They argued briefly, and Jobin relented.

Again, Tallar reached up, and the moment Eden felt his fingers meet her flesh, searing, white-hot agony shot through her. The pain left no room for anything. Her entire existence telescoped down to a single focus where all she knew was pain.

In her dream, Eden began to scream.

The Doctor had decided to spend whatever time they had left in the cavern—a few hours to a day, depending upon *Achilles*—taking scans of as much of the site as he could. Counselor Cambridge had worked with him for a while, but ultimately agreed that he, too, must rest. He settled himself near the captain and drifted into restless sleep.

The Doctor had set his medical tricorder to continuous subatomic scans of Captain Eden. It rested on a stone near her, and the alerts had been set to the lowest volume to avoid disturbing her while she slept. The recent scans he had taken read close to normal, unlike the ones taken when they had initially discovered her in the cavern. He would study them more closely when he could access his own lab, or sickbay aboard *Achilles*. He honestly didn't expect her to erupt into a glowing ball of energy, as Kes once had, but in his experience, nothing could be ruled out.

Several meters into one of the nearest tunnels that radiated from the main cavern, he discovered a series of wide cells. He presumed these were individual storage or perhaps living areas for the former inhabitants, though all of them were empty. The tricorder hummed and blipped as he slowly ran it over the walls. So monotonous had his motions been that he didn't hear the first alarm from his medical tricorder.

He ran back to the main cavern, where he saw Cambridge, snoring obnoxiously. His tricorder was exactly where he had left it and was now emitting low beeps.

Captain Eden was gone.

The Doctor did a quick visual check of the cavern, but she wasn't there. He then grabbed his medical tricorder and used it to home in on her location.

He roused Cambridge.

"Wha . . . what?" the counselor snorted as he was startled into consciousness.

"We have a problem," the Doctor replied.

Cambridge quickly sat up, rubbing his eyes. "Another one?"

Without words, the Doctor directed Cambridge's eyes to the captain's location, and as soon as the counselor saw her, he clambered to his feet.

Eden floated twenty meters above the floor, facing the center of the black surface at the rear of the cavern.

"Well, that's not good," Cambridge offered.

They had almost reached a spot directly beneath her when a series of whimpers escaped her lips, followed by a shrill, terrifying scream that was magnified in its intensity as it echoed throughout the cavern.

"Can you get to her?" Cambridge demanded of the Doctor through the deafening cacophony.

This had not immediately occurred to the Doctor, but he quickly realized that he could.

With a brisk nod, he passed his tricorder to Cambridge and began retuning the photonic generators in his mobile emitter.

"What was that you were saying yesterday about speed in emergency situations?" Cambridge shouted nervously over the din.

"Oh, shut up!" the Doctor snapped back as he completed the necessary calculations.

A split second later, he found himself floating beside Eden.

QUIRINAL

Captain Regina Farkas had rather enjoyed the last few weeks. *Quirinal's* exploration of several sectors near the heart of one of the largest known areas of Borg space had yielded no evidence of the Borg or the Caeliar. In addition, the crew had charted dozens of previously unknown planetary systems and several interesting stellar formations.

Esquiline, Hawking, and *Curie* had all reported similar results. The ships had convened, at Farkas's recommendation, to compare notes, once all of them had reached points near enough for their long-range communications arrays to manage a real-time conversation.

Captain Parimon Dasht, of the *Esquiline,* seemed annoyed by their lack of significant discoveries. The youngest of the four, he was a third-generation Starfleet captain, eager to leave his own mark. It comforted Farkas that a cool and steady head tempered his enthusiasm.

The Vulcan captain of the *Hawking,* Bal Itak, was well into his second century of life. As best Farkas could tell, still waters had never run so deep. Itak seemed neither shaken nor stirred by the serenity his vessel had enjoyed during their explorations, and probably would have taken three more years of the same.

Xin Chan, captain of the other dedicated science vessel, the *Curie,* was a decade younger than Farkas's seventy-two years. He was taking his findings in convivial stride. Of the four, he was the only one to have made contact with another space-faring species in the last few weeks.

"Did you point out to them that dumping several kilotons of toxic waste into the area would have dramatic effects upon local space and ultimately impact the nearest planets?" Dasht asked, as if personally affronted at such reckless behavior by a warp-capable species.

Farkas thought she detected a subtle smirk from Chan as he replied, *"The Malons don't seem to harbor any doubts or misgivings about their actions, Captain. As long as their own people can continue down their obviously unsustainable path, they're willing to pollute as much of the rest of space as necessary to facilitate their lifestyle."*

"If the rest of former Borg territory is as empty as the sectors we scanned, the long-term damage of the Malons' actions might be mitigated somewhat by the sheer size of space now available to absorb their illogical activities," Itak suggested.

"Captain Thoreck was inordinately pleased to have discovered his new dumping ground. I sensed that his only cause for alarm was that we might actually try to prevent his scheduled waste release." Chan went on, *"Or notify one of his competitors about the new unspoiled dumping ground now available to them."*

"Disgusting," Dasht said.

"I was given to understand that the Malons' past interactions with Voyager *were the only source of distress on Thoreck's part,"* Chan added.

Farkas nodded. "Based on my reading, Captain Janeway did all she could to prevent the Malons' activities where possible. She offered them several technological solutions which would make dumping unnecessary."

"Thereby rendering inert a large and profitable segment of their economy," Itak noted.

"Pity our mission parameters don't provide us with the same latitude," Dasht scoffed. *"At the very least it might have been interesting to cause sufficient damage to their propulsion systems to make it difficult for them to escape the effects of their reckless behavior."*

"Don't think it didn't cross my mind," Chan replied. *"But as you well know, intervention is not our purpose here."*

"And rightly so," Farkas interjected, rather enjoying the look of shock her words elicited from Captain Dasht.

"Surely you don't approve of the Malons'—" he began.

"Of course not, Parimon," she replied curtly. "None of us do. But there are limits to what we can and should do in this quadrant.

We're not here to coerce or conquer. We're here to explore and to learn and, when possible, to offer any assistance we can that might enable species like the Malons to make better choices."

Dasht had the good sense to appear moderately chastened.

"The Malons' choices, while incomprehensible to us, are a reflection of their current level of cultural and sociological development. I'm more than willing to petition Command for the authority to invest more time and resources to enable them to restructure their industrial systems and capacities with an eye toward eliminating the creation of toxic waste. But I don't think any of us are kidding ourselves when we acknowledge that such fundamental changes cannot be imposed on another society. They have to want it for themselves as much as we want it for them, and until that time comes, our resources are more valuably deployed elsewhere."

"So they are free to damage as much of space as they can access while we hide behind our self-imposed limitations?" Dasht asked.

"Yes." Farkas smiled. "That's the tricky thing about freedom. And we're not hiding. We're offering them an opportunity to develop beyond their current foolishness. Should they fail to see the futility of their present course, I have no doubt time will force them to see it. The Malon men and women who risk their lives daily to enable this short-sighted ridiculousness are their best hope for change. Their actions might be lucrative, but only because of the hazards imposed on people like Thoreck and his crew. History has taught us that no society built upon the exploitation of any of its individuals can long endure. We just have to hope they come to understand that sooner rather than later."

"Well said, Captain," Chan replied.

"And on that happy note," Dasht interjected bitterly, *"I'm going to sign off."*

"Somewhere you have to be, Captain?" Farkas asked congenially.

"My astrometrics department has reported an unusual discovery, and we're about to alter course to investigate. It won't delay our rendezvous with the rest of you in a few days," he replied.

Farkas's and Chan's eyes widened simultaneously. Itak might have been as intrigued, but as he was the most-Vulcan Vulcan Farkas had ever met, it was impossible to tell.

"How unusual?" Chan asked casually.

With a faint, roguish smile, Dasht replied, *"Well, that's hard to say until we get a little closer."*

Farkas met Dasht's smile with one of her own and said, "You know, Parimon, we've seen all there is to see in our assigned sectors. If you pass along those coordinates, we could combine our efforts."

Dasht's smile widened. *"I'm sure it's nothing."*

Farkas was now equally sure it wasn't.

Chan broke in, *"I'm sure my crew would benefit from the exercise. After our frustrating experience with the Malons, an unusual spatial anomaly would refocus their energy in a more productive direction."*

Dasht now stared at each of his fellow captains with a gleam of mischief in his eyes. *"And fine as your crew is, Xin,"* he replied, *"I'm sure mine will make short work of it."*

After a brief pause, Itak surprised the hell out of Farkas by asking, *"Would you care to place a small wager on that, Captain?"*

Chapter Seventeen

VOYAGER

B'Elanna Torres sat at the edge of the sandbox, watching her daughter intently. The holodeck program currently running had been B'Elanna's creation, a large play-structure complete with swings, slides, bridges, ladders, monkey bars, and plenty of small tubes and bouncers where Miral could freely exercise the new physical skills she seemed to be developing daily. A soft, pliable synthetic flooring ran beneath most of the structure to cushion any falls, and a large sand pit ran along one entire side to accommodate her daughter's endless fascination with digging, molding, and subsequently destroying with great glee whatever she had fashioned. B'Elanna had replicated several sturdy buckets, shovels, spades, and toys with gear-like wheels that turned one another when Miral poured sand through the cones at the top.

Beyond the play structure were several acres of soft grass and climbing trees. With its perpetually warm spring-like climate, the park had become one of B'Elanna's favorite places to retreat with Miral for the last few hours of the day before bedtime. But Miral had never seemed to enjoy her little haven as much as she did today.

Once aboard *Voyager*, Seven had suggested to Riley that her people should avail themselves of the holodeck, if only to escape the confines of the cargo bay they now called home. The entire crew had offered to double up to provide space for the new arrivals, particularly the small families. But Riley had demurred, indicating that for the time being, the group would prefer to lodge together. Given all they had been through, it was too difficult to imagine living any other way.

Seven had specifically suggested B'Elanna's park simulation for the children. By mid-afternoon of the next day several families had ventured out to the holodeck.

Most of the parents arrived in a state of numb wonder and B'Elanna's heart had broken on their behalf. She could not help but imagine herself in their circumstances: forced to take refuge in darkened caves, forgoing their own needs so that their children could have whatever meager scraps of food they could steal, and with no way to fight those who had stolen their planet or hope of surviving if they tried to assert their rightful claim.

During the years she had spent apart from Tom, she had often felt herself unduly burdened. There had been dark days during *Voyager*'s first trip through the Delta Quadrant when she doubted that they would survive, let alone make it home. Her time with the Maquis had certainly come with its fair share of sacrifices. Not that long ago, when Miral had been kidnapped, she had endured horrifying days not knowing if her daughter was alive or dead. But all this she had survived with warm clothing on her back and a full belly. The thought of watching her child suffer as these parents had seen their own children suffer filled B'Elanna with a terrible despair.

The children, however, were a case study in resilience. Although they were understandably shy, particularly around B'Elanna and Miral at first, they showed none of their parents' reluctance to make the most of the new opportunity for fun that was before them. The six oldest of the thirteen children, ranging in age from two to four, needed little coaxing from their parents to begin exploring the structure's many thrilling devices. The others were still infants or barely walking, but with their parents' help also gamboled about or found nice spots in the shade to crawl around on the grass.

But the real revelation, to B'Elanna, was Miral. She smiled as she watched her daughter settle herself next to a scrawny boy named Shon and begin working on a sand castle. In her three-plus years of life, Miral had had no playmates. Shon and his companions had no sense of personal property and quickly surrendered any toy Miral might decide she wanted. But once B'Elanna had explained "sharing" to her, Miral quickly decided she wanted Shon and the others to enjoy her toys as much as she did. Despite the age differences, she was soon engaging with all of her new friends, laughing, chasing, and digging with gusto, until the holodeck could easily have been mistaken for any park on any planet filled with happy children.

B'Elanna had never doubted that *Voyager* was the best and safest place for her daughter to grow up. But until this moment it had not crossed her mind how important for Miral it was to interact with other children. Yes, B'Elanna could create a bevy of holographic playmates, but even the most intricately programmed ones could never compare to a living one.

There were no other children in the fleet. The other parents had left their children behind. As Miral played with unfettered joy, B'Elanna couldn't help but think that her choices, while driven by a desire to protect Miral, might ultimately prove insufficient to her needs.

Captain Chakotay entered the bridge from his ready room.

"Standard orbit established around Arehaz," reported Commander Paris.

When Riley had first suggested their destination, Chakotay found himself wondering if the place was a myth. However they had originated, the Borg had evolved in a manner that made basing their civilization around any single planet irrelevant. Wherever the queen was at any given time would have become the center of their society.

Part of the knowledge Riley had gained from the Caeliar, subsequently confirmed by Seven, was the location of the planet where the Borg had first been formed. Thousands of years earlier, Arehaz had been a fairly standard Class-M world, home to a species known as the Kindir. The original inhabitants had all endured the crudest form of assimilation by the early Borg, or died trying to prevent it. Once the Borg achieved the ability to travel through space, they had stripped Arehaz of all of its resources, departed, and never looked back.

Seven and Riley were in astrometrics, conducting detailed scans of the planet. Chakotay expected to find a lifeless world, even in the wake of the Caeliar transformation. He had suggested this as delicately as possible to Riley, who clearly had pinned all of her hopes on a world she had never seen but to which she already felt connected. Chakotay doubted anything would be left on Arehaz that Riley's people could use to build a new society. At first glance, his fears appeared to be well founded.

Tom's gaze was fixed on the main viewscreen as Chakotay took the seat beside him. Though much of the planet was shrouded in heavy cloud cover, the few visible wide swaths of darkness were as depressing a sight as any Chakotay had ever seen. After a moment Tom said softly, "We can't just leave them here."

"It's not up to us," Chakotay replied.

"But the . . ." Tom began.

"Children?" Chakotay finished for him.

Tom nodded slowly. Of all the changes wrought in Lieutenant Commander Thomas Eugene Paris over the last few years—the newfound discipline and sense of decorum, the aptitude for command, and the seriousness with which he applied himself to all of his duties—the most striking was his deep and abiding love for his daughter. During their lengthy exploration of the Yaris Nebula, Tom and Chakotay had found themselves with many uneventful hours to fill and Tom's favorite subject of conversation had invariably been Miral. Chakotay had heard that once you brought a child into your life, your worldview altered to include a greater sensitivity to the needs of all children. Chakotay had always felt a similar proprietary regard for his crew. What he now saw through Tom's eyes was the way in which it became impossible for a parent to see anyone else's child in need and not imagine their own in the same situation. Survival instincts might drive one to protect their own child above all others, but parents found themselves in a much larger universe where, in some ways, every child became their responsibility.

"I'm not going to abandon them on a world that cannot sustain them. Riley is a passionate and determined individual, but she's not stupid. She'll see reason," Chakotay said.

Tom turned to look at him. "I hope you're right."

"*Captain Chakotay, please report to astrometrics,*" Seven called out over the comm system.

"On my way," Chakotay replied, adding, "Paris, you have the bridge."

Given what he'd seen of the planet so far, Chakotay was surprised when he entered the astrometrics lab to see Riley greet him with unbridled happiness. Seven's eyes, as well, held surprised satisfaction. Unsure of the source of their enthusiasm, Chakotay quickly said, "Report."

"It's more than I dared hope for," Riley said, turning her eyes toward the massive image of the planet on the lab's huge display.

Chakotay looked to Seven, who quickly called up a smaller view of one of the land masses. Beside it, a series of geological and environmental statistics were listed. The first reading that caught his eye was the unmistakable presence of clean water.

"Where is this?" he asked.

"A region of approximately ten thousand square kilometers near the equator," Seven replied. While the image on the screen wasn't going to win a spot in any interstellar travel guide, it bore tentative signs of natural life, fertile soil, and a pleasant climate.

"Did the Borg leave this behind?" Chakotay asked immediately, "or did the planet's ecosystem begin to restore itself after they abandoned it?"

Seven shook her head. "Before the Borg departed the planet, all of its natural resources would have been converted to energy appropriate to their technological needs. The water returned over the last two thousand years, but most of what you see here is what the Caeliar did."

Chakotay looked again at the small patch of land, his curiosity increasing. "But, how?"

Riley smiled shyly. "The Borg did not take everything with them when they left. Their original structures, as well as smaller forms of waste and debris, remained and had begun to disintegrate over time. But the Caeliar didn't simply wave a magic wand and make the Borg and their technology disappear. They *transformed* what was once Borg, replacing inferior technology with their catoms."

"Have you detected signs of catomic activity on the surface?" Chakotay asked. He was concerned that there might be new reasons why Riley and her people should not settle on the planet. The captain wanted to believe that Riley's intentions were pure, but he wasn't sure about leaving her and what had been her "collective" on a planet now infused with technology so advanced that no one in the Federation knew how it worked yet.

"Only its results," Seven assured him. "The catoms now present in my body, and the bodies of Doctor Frazier's people, are limited in their use. They exist to sustain the functions formerly performed by nanoprobes and implants, and although they may heighten some . . . abilities, they cannot be adapted for any other purpose. Likewise, the catoms that have begun to restore this planet were programmed for a single function. Once the planet's natural ecosystem began to assert itself, which appears to have been within weeks of the transformation, the catoms disintegrated, leaving the planet free to evolve on its own again."

Chakotay was stunned. "Is this effect planetwide?"

Seven shrugged. "There are large areas where the planet was stripped so deeply that in the absence of a massive terraforming effort, it will take tens of thousands of years for them to be capable of sustaining life. But, there is more than enough land and water currently available for Doctor Frazier's small group to begin their lives here. We could certainly provide them with the supplies they would need to sustain themselves through several planting seasons, as well as temporary structures that could be reinforced over time." Turning to Riley, she added, "One of our fleet vessels, the *Demeter,* also contains a wide variety of suitable botanical life. I will make a request at the earliest opportunity to Fleet Commander Eden that *Demeter* schedule a detour here in the coming months to check on your progress and to add to your supplies."

Chakotay nodded slowly. To Riley he said, "You're sure this is what you want? It's just habitable down there, and it's still going to be a long walk down a tough road."

Riley nodded, her eyes glistening. "It is. And while I appreciate the offer, I don't want you to feel obligated to do anything more for us. You have given us our lives back, you and the Caeliar. I think it would be an insult to throw away the opportunities now before us."

Chakotay exchanged a brief smile with Seven. "What more is there to say?"

"How about 'welcome home'?" Riley replied.

Chapter Eighteen

ESQUILINE

Captain Parimon Dasht was glad he had taken Captain Itak up on his wager. After arriving first at the coordinates to analyze the "anomaly," he had reluctantly admitted that the sight of it unnerved him. He was now quite grateful that the *Esquiline* was not alone and that four of Starfleet's best science teams were studying it.

Twenty-four hours after their work had begun, Captain Dasht had convened a meeting in his briefing room for his sister ship's captains and their science officers to discuss their progress. He laid out food, as he seriously doubted any of them had taken a break since they had first laid eyes on the thing.

Settling himself at the table, Dasht watched as the captain of the *Quirinal* did likewise. Regina Farkas—a cheery woman with short white hair and a faint scar running along the right side of her face—opened the discussion by asking, "So what the hell is it?" Farkas then quickly added, "And extra points go to anyone who can explain it so I can understand it." Her chief science officer, Lieutenant Hornung, a brunette with light green eyes and ruddy cheeks, grimaced slightly. Nodding toward her, Farkas noted, "Tonil, here, hasn't earned any of those points today."

Lieutenant Lern, *Hawking*'s science officer, said, "It might be easier to begin by discussing what the anomaly is not."

"Sounds promising," Farkas observed.

"It is not normal space," Lern said.

"I'm still with you," Farkas said.

"Nor is it an object occupying normal space," Lern ventured.

Farkas shot her science officer a look that seemed to say, *See, that's not so hard, is it?*

Lieutenant Livermore, who had first detected the anomaly from *Esquiline*'s astrometrics lab, added, "It is not matter, dark matter, a collapsed star, a black hole, or an interdimensional rift. Nor is it a life-form."

"But it is solid," the *Curie*'s Lieutenant Juana pointed out.

"It is not," Hornung contradicted her.

"How would you characterize it?" Lern asked with typical Vulcan restraint.

"It *is* a discrete, highly localized area in which the normal laws of space and time do not appear to apply," Livermore interjected before Hornung had the chance.

At this, Dasht stole a glance at Farkas, whose brow was beginning to furrow. "So, how do the laws of space and time suddenly get suspended?" Farkas asked.

All of the scientists waited expectantly for one of their own to offer a suggestion. Finally, the Vulcan science officer said, "We are, at minimum, seven hours from providing an answer to that question."

"Does it correspond to any other interstellar phenomenon?" Captain Chan asked.

"No, sir," his science officer quickly replied, "at least not to anything in our databases."

"A unique discovery, then," Dasht noted, pleased by the thought.

"That much even I gathered." Farkas smiled. "But how can it be solid and not solid?"

"Quantum scans are inconclusive," Hornung replied. "It acts solid. If a ship were to, say, run into it at impulse speed, it would likely impede our progress, and its presence would make establishing a warp field in its immediate area impossible. But the readings suggest it is more akin to an absence of matter."

Farkas looked as if she dearly wanted to dock points for this, but held her peace.

"The question before us is, to what lengths are we willing to go to learn more about it?" Itak asked ominously.

"Sir?" Lern asked of his captain.

"Further analysis will require us to move beyond passive scans and begin interacting with it, will they not?" Itak said, though Dasht was sure that a scientist with Itak's credentials knew the answer to that question.

"Yes, sir," the Vulcan science officer replied.

"Why is that a problem?" Dasht asked.

"With the limited data available, it is impossible to theorize as to what any action we take, even one we might presume to be safe, might do to the anomaly," Itak clarified.

"You're saying we could break it?" Farkas asked.

"It's not solid," Hornung reminded her.

Farkas then asked, "Is there any chance this thing was created by someone or something?"

"Possible," Itak replied. "But without further study . . ."

Farkas waved him off. "What I'm asking is, if someone or

something put it here on purpose, right smack dab in the middle of nowhere where it's awfully unlikely to be discovered and disturbed, maybe we'd do well to just leave it alone."

"You can't be serious," Dasht exclaimed, certain he was speaking for all of the scientists present.

"I can't?" Farkas asked pointedly. "Look, Parimon, I'm all about discovery. The thrill of it gets me out of my rack every morning. But there are times when our curiosity runs ahead of our capabilities. I just want to make sure this isn't one of those times."

"Something akin to a child coming across a phaser rifle?" Chan asked.

Farkas nodded. "It might get awfully unlucky and accidentally disable the safety."

"There remain numerous noninvasive tests we could run that might shed more light on the anomaly without risk," Hornung offered.

"As long as we're not going to try firing a photon torpedo at it or anything," Farkas said.

"Not unless it fires first," Dasht assured her.

With a deep sigh, Farkas replied, "Well then, why don't we all get back to our respective ships and begin running those extremely safe, noninvasive tests?"

MIKHAL OUTPOST

Hovering next to Eden, the Doctor found himself at a loss as to how best to proceed. Her shrieks had subsided, replaced by several gasps, which slowly gave way to more normal, labored breathing. Basic physical scans were nominal, but the quantum scans were so wildly off baseline, he didn't like to think about what they might portend. The fact that Eden was floating tens of meters above the floor was certainly cause for alarm. His scans detected nothing that might explain it. This meant that getting her down safely could prove challenging.

Toward that end, he asked softly, "Captain Eden? Afsarah, can you hear me?"

Faint murmurs were her only response.

He considered simply sedating her and dealing with the rest once they were at ground level again, then he noted the intense way Eden's eyes were fixed on the center of the black lake. To him, the shiny black surface appeared exactly as it always had. Clearly, she was seeing something that was quite alarming, if only in her mind's eye.

"Tallar?" she whispered so softly, he wasn't sure he had heard her right.

Eden stretched both of her arms forward, as though reaching for something just beyond her grasp, and shouted, "Tallar!"

"Captain Eden," the Doctor called to her more firmly. If this was some sort of waking dream that included sleepflying rather than sleepwalking, it could be dangerous to try and wake her. He slowly raised his hands, preparing to place them around her shoulders for a gentle shake, when she screamed, "Tallar, no!"

He recoiled automatically as her right hand stretched behind her. A loud metallic clank and snap were followed instantaneously by a whizzing sound, and before the Doctor could process what had just happened, a long shaft of metal, similar to the Staff of Ren, was caught in her hand. The Doctor chanced a look down and clearly saw Cambridge bending low and shielding his head with his arms, no doubt worried that other very dangerous objects might soon begin flying through the air.

The Doctor had to find a way to get control of this situation. "Captain," he said again, quite loudly as he placed both hands on the sides of her shoulders.

Eden paid him no heed. Instead, she lifted the staff to shoulder height, reared her arm back, and with grace and precision worthy of a competitive javelin thrower, hurled the shaft through the air.

Its forward end collided with the center of the black surface. A faint and disquieting crunch followed the impact. The Doctor could make out dozens of wide cracks opening in the surface from the center where the staff had struck.

Eden slumped forward. The Doctor grabbed her firmly around her torso and began a gradual descent. She was dead weight, but manageable, and after a few tense moments he once again felt solid ground beneath his feet.

The Doctor laid her gently down as Cambridge rushed to his side.

"Well done," he offered quietly as the Doctor began a new round of scans. "How is she?"

The Doctor simply replied, "Asleep."

Cambridge considered this for a moment, then lifted his eyes to the black surface, where the cracks were continuing to extend. "I suppose it could be worse."

"Really?" the Doctor demanded. "How? No, don't tell me."

A series of high-pitched beeps from their campsite made both of them jump. A smile erupted on Cambridge's face as he said, "Oh, cheer up, Doctor," and hurried back to the source of the signal.

Moments later he returned and hastily began assembling a perimeter of pattern enhancers around them.

"What are you doing?" the Doctor demanded.

"I would think that would be fairly obvious," Cambridge replied. "Here," he added, tossing his tricorder to the Doctor. "I rigged a patch to our comm system yesterday to enhance the signal, on the assumption that the interference from our present location would be tough for the standard setting."

The Doctor stared in amazement at the bright green blinking light that indicated a stable com signal from *Achilles*.

"Whatever is happening to her, I presume you'd rather treat her in sickbay than here?" Cambridge asked.

"Absolutely," the Doctor said, nodding.

Cambridge then keyed a sequence into the tricorder, alerting *Achilles* that they were as ready as they would ever be.

"Energize," Cambridge said with a wink, and the cavern vanished around them.

QUIRINAL

Regina Farkas sat in her ready room, staring out of the large port. The view from her desk, which was parallel to the window, was nice enough. But after returning from *Esquiline,* she'd perched on the long, cushioned bench that ran just below the port, gazing toward a point in space so distant it was impossible for her naked eye to perceive.

Normally, discoveries or tactical situations that disquieted Farkas sent her roaming her ship's halls. She'd always thought best on her feet. Something about this particular anomaly had planted her in the only spot on the ship from which she could enjoy a private, unobstructed, and completely imaginary view of it.

She couldn't place the source of her disquiet. Starfleet regularly stumbled across all manner of interstellar phenomena that could not immediately be identified or catalogued. Farkas was usually content to allow those who had devoted their lives to understanding such things to do their work, and as their captain, she did her best to give them all the resources they required.

This anomaly should be no different.

After the briefing aboard *Esquiline* it was agreed that all four ships were to stay and study it. There was no pressing tactical or logistical reason to cut their explorations short.

The *Quirinal*'s captain continued to check in with her internal early warning system. In the past she had come to recognize a particular tension: years of service had convinced her it was her subconscious letting her know that something was wrong. Farkas had grown accustomed to trusting it, and it rarely let her down.

Right now, that system was eerily silent. Farkas tried to convince herself that this was a good thing. But the longer she stared out the port, the more difficult she found it to shake the completely irrational idea that the darkness out there was somehow darker than usual.

"Nothing to do?" The familiar, rough voice came from behind her.

Turning, the captain found one of her oldest friends and *Quirinal*'s CMO, Doctor El'nor Sal, standing just inside the ready room's door. Farkas replied dryly, "I don't recall giving you permission to enter."

"I did ask," Sal offered, "several times. When you didn't answer,

I had the computer confirm you were in here and that your life signs were normal. Then I hit the door's chime again, and you still didn't answer, so I got worried."

"I could have been in the middle of something indecent."

"In your ready room?"

Farkas smiled faintly at memories from many, many years ago.

"Alone?" Sal added with emphasis.

"Okay, you got me there."

Sal moved toward the bench and sat unceremoniously beside the captain. "How was lunch?"

"As good as replicated sandwiches can be," Farkas replied. "The pickles weren't half bad, though."

"I meant the briefing."

"I know what you meant."

Sal sat back, considering her old friend. "Let me guess. The shiny new space thingie that has every science officer on this ship pulling extra shifts is extra special unusual?" She smiled.

Farkas smiled back. "Pretty much, except for the shiny part."

"You worried?"

Farkas thought about it and shook her head. "No."

"Then what is it?" Sal asked more seriously.

"I think I'm tired," Farkas replied.

Sal remained still, her eyes suggesting she wasn't buying it.

The captain shook her head again. "Or maybe I'm just getting old."

"You're kidding, right?" Sal asked. "A couple of weeks ago you could barely keep your feet on the floor. Your ship almost dug its own grave on an unnamed planet in the middle of nowhere. You were practically killed fighting off an alien invasion. Against all odds we survived, and for weeks you've been running around here with the eagerness of a first-year cadet. But *now* you're tired."

Farkas gently patted Sal's leg. "I know. I'm a puzzle."

"Not usually," Sal corrected her, "at least not to me."

The captain returned her gaze to the window. "What do you see when you look out there?"

Sal's shoulders drooped. "Space." After a long pause she asked, "Why? What do you see?"

"I don't know," Farkas replied. "Usually, I look out there at the stars and I see endless possibilities."

"That sounds about right."

"But today, I just see the darkness in between them."

The doctor considered this, then placed a hand on Farkas's shoulder. "We all have days like that, Regina. Tomorrow, or maybe the day after, you'll start noticing the stars again. And if you don't, we'll figure out why."

Farkas turned back to her with a faint smile of unspoken gratitude. Suddenly, the ship lurched subtly, shooting her instantly to her feet. Before she could tap her combadge, her first officer, Commander Malcolm Roach, called, *"Captain to the bridge."*

Farkas hurried out the door that accessed the bridge and called, "Report," as she moved to the seat Roach had just vacated.

"We're detecting a shift in the configuration of the anomaly," Roach replied.

"On-screen," she ordered.

Within moments a rather mundane view of space was replaced with what looked like an unusually bright light Farkas could have sworn wasn't there earlier. Seconds later, it vanished.

The captain suddenly realized that the thing she'd been struggling with but unable to name for the last few hours hadn't been a sense of danger or fear of the unknown. It was the awful awareness that some things were so unknowable, no fear could do them justice.

"Shields. Red Alert. Ensign Hoch," she called to her flight controller, "put a light-year between us and the anomaly, maximum warp."

"Aye, Captain," Hoch replied.

Farkas counted the seconds with each beat of her heart as she waited for the main viewscreen to show the initial warp field effect of stars stretching out into long white lines. She got to ten and was distracted by a sharp lurch to port, this time strong enough to force her to grab her armrests to maintain an upright position.

"Mister Hoch?" she demanded.

"Unable to establish a warp field, Captain."

"Full impulse then," she ordered. "Farkas to Lieutenant Bryce."

"*Bryce here, Captain,*" replied the young man who had been chief engineer for only a few weeks.

"I need warp speed ten seconds ago."

"*Understood, Captain. But we can't create a stable warp field until we get clear of the anomaly's effects on subspace.*"

"Hoch, do what you can," Farkas ordered.

Five more seconds, and the ship began to shudder and rattle. The inertial dampers cut out, and the ship jerked, pitching her forward. As the dampers cut back in, she barely kept her seat. Her spine crunched as it met the back of her chair at an unsafe velocity.

"What was that?" she demanded.

"The anomaly appears to have shattered, Captain," Hornung reported from the science station.

"I thought we couldn't break it," Farkas whispered. "Non-invasive, perfectly safe tests, my ass," she added under her breath. Then, louder, "Report."

"Multiple fractures have appeared all around us and are continuing to extend beyond our position. Navigating around them at full impulse is not possible. Reducing to half," Hoch said.

"At your discretion," Farkas replied. The captain knew well everyone was sharing the same thought: *Get us out of here.*

"Jepel," she called to her operations officer, "what is the status of our sister ships?"

"*Hawking, Curie,* and *Esquiline* were closer to the anomaly at the moment of . . ." He trailed off, clearly unsure how to describe what he was seeing.

"Of whatever wasn't supposed to happen but somehow did, I know," Farkas replied grimly. *So they're probably worse off than we are.* "Hornung?" she asked.

"We're now reading multiple fractures over a hundred localized event horizons," the science officer said.

"Don't event horizons come with gravimetric distortions?" Farkas asked.

"Yes, Captain," Hornung replied, then added with less confidence, "but these are not normal event horizons, even though that's the best term available to describe the intersection between normal space and the anomaly. What's important right now is that the density of the fractures and their sheer volume make it increasingly likely we will be unable to avoid slipping into one."

"When?" Farkas asked.

"Uncertain," Hornung replied.

"But something we should avoid, if possible, Ensign Hoch," Farkas called to the conn.

"Captain, a fracture is closing on our position," Hornung advised. "We can't outrun it at half impulse."

"How long?" Farkas demanded.

"At current speed, thirty seconds," Hornung replied.

"Send out an emergency hail on our secure frequency. Tell anyone responding to approach our coordinates with extreme caution." Opening her channel ship-wide, Farkas added, "All hands, this is the captain." She suddenly paused, wondering exactly how to describe what was likely about to happen to all of them. She settled for, "Brace for impact."

Chapter Nineteen

Q CONTINUUM

Kathryn Janeway had no idea how long she and Kes held one another, but eventually Kes pulled gently back. Still holding Kathryn by both shoulders, she looked her over from head to toe. A tinge of mischief lighted upon her lips as Kes said, "There. That's better."

Kathryn looked down and realized she was once again clad in the uniform of a Starfleet admiral. It appeared to be a universal law that everyone entered, or reentered, existence naked. The perfectly tailored, form-fitting ensemble had always felt like a second skin covering her body, but now Kathryn became conscious of how severely it restricted her.

Even her skin, she discovered, was taking a little getting used to. Kathryn had faint memories of herself as a young child, coming upon one of her father's discarded uniform jackets. She had pulled it around her, comforted beyond measure by its warmth, but more deeply, by its smell. It was as if she had found a way to wrap herself in her father's love. To stand again in her own body was a similar sensation. It was pleasantly familiar, but like her father's much too large jacket, it was a bit unwieldy. Briefly, she mourned the freedom she had recently known beyond her body. But with each passing second, her new existence became more familiar and real, while her old one slipped into the realm of half-forgotten dreams.

Testing her voice, Kathryn said softly, "How can I ever thank you enough for what you've done?"

"You would have done no less for me, were our situations reversed," Kes assured her.

Kathryn nodded.

"Are you ready, then, Aunt Kathy?" Q asked, stepping closer.

She wasn't. All that she had just experienced would take months, if not years, to process. She knew full well that at least for now, she, Q, and Kes occupied a reality separate from the normal flow of time. Part of her wished to linger here indefinitely, or at least until she felt more prepared to step into the duty she had signed up for when she made this choice.

This is life, the now much more distant voice of her consciousness reminded her.

Forcing herself to set aside her fears, Kathryn asked, "Where exactly am I going?"

"There isn't much beyond this moment that I know anymore," Q replied, slightly chagrined. "But I believe it is the safest point in terms of reducing the impact of your death upon your primary timeline without risking any alterations to the events in which your death was a significant factor."

"I beg your pardon?" Kathryn asked.

"I'm sending you to the point where I believe you are needed most," he simplified.

"You aren't going with her?" Kes asked.

Q shook his head. "Not immediately. There's something else I must know first."

"Amanda?" Kathryn guessed.

"I can only think of one place to look, and if the record exists, it might help both of us better understand whatever this thing is."

"All right." Kathryn nodded.

"But as soon as I can, I'll join you." Turning to Kes, Q said, "If you're not otherwise occupied?"

"I can't," Kes replied. "I must return to Ocampa."

A wide smile creased Kathryn's lips. "You went home?"

Kes nodded. "You wouldn't recognize it. It's so very beautiful."

The thought of Kes returning to her people with her new powers and leading them into a better life than they had known under their Caretaker gave Kathryn a sense of the absolute rightness with which the multiverse sometimes functioned. But this was tempered by the memories of the last time she had actually seen Kes. She was inordinately pleased by the peace and serenity Kes embodied, but wondered at the journey it had taken to bring about this profound change.

Seeming to sense her thoughts, Kes said, "I'm so sorry about that. It wasn't actually me. It was . . . part of me, but not . . ."

"A story for another time?" Kathryn guessed.

"Yes," Kes said, obviously relieved. "She did come home, though, and died there in peace. My son—"

"Your son?" Kathryn gasped.

"Another long story," Q interrupted.

Taking Kes's face in both her hands and lingering briefly over her eyes, Kathryn quickly pulled her again into a brief hug. "Just promise me you'll come back someday and tell me all about it?" she whispered.

"I promise," Kes replied.

Kathryn released her and tugged fitfully on the bottom of her uniform jacket to straighten it. With a wink to Kes, she demanded of Q, "What are we waiting for?"

"I'll see you soon," Q said, and in a flash of white light, the meadow, he, and Kes were gone.

"What have you done?"

"Mother?"

"I give you a centimeter and you take a million light-years?"

"I did what I had to do. And I did it without breaking any of the Continuum's rules."

"Technically, but I don't honestly think—"

"Q!"

"Oh, hello, Father."

"Where is she?"

"Mother's right here."

"You know who I'm talking about. I thought we went over this. Which part of 'we don't bring dead people back to life' were you unclear about?"

"I didn't—"

"You're about to be run out of the Continuum on a rail, son, and having experienced that exquisite pain more than once, I'm here to tell you, you're not going to like it one bit."

"Listen to me. In the first place, I didn't bring Aunt Kathy back to life. She did that on her own. Well, most of the heavy lifting anyway. The rest was accomplished by another interested party."

"You brought Kathryn here!"

"Actually, I did that."

"*Et tu,* my dear wife?"

"And in the second place, I no longer have to explain myself to either of you."

"Quite right. You're a fully grown Q, aren't you? You bend the laws of space and time to suit your whims without a care for the disastrous consequences of your actions."

"I wonder where he gets that from?"

"We're not talking about me right now, dear. We're talking

about our son, who clearly has no idea how excruciating the wrath of the Continuum can be."

"Oh, I think I have a vague notion."

"Tell me, when you offered your godmother the knowledge she required to restore her body, did you bother mentioning to her the fact that a price—one she will no doubt be unwilling to pay—would be exacted for this choice?"

"Um."

"Well?"

"It all happened pretty fast. I might have skipped that part."

"You what?"

"Of course he did. He wasn't thinking about her. He was only thinking about himself."

"And again, I ask, where did he get that from?"

"Stop it, both of you. I know what's at stake here and I fully comprehend the likely ramifications of my actions. Do you honestly think I would have gone this far without good reason? I'm doing what has to be done, and if you don't trust me, then at least believe this: Kathryn Janeway is my last best hope. And yours, too, for that matter."

"We're doomed."

"Be quiet for a minute. Son? Where did he go?"

"Hold that thought, darling. They're coming for us."

"Q!"

Let me do the talking.

With pleasure.

"Q, Q, Q, Q, hello. To what do we owe this honor?"

"Do not presume to toy with this council, Q. You swore to us on your own existence that your son would uphold the values and standards of our continuum."

"I know. And I assure you his misdeeds will be rectified and appropriately punished."

"You understand the consequences, should you fail to mitigate any damage his actions have caused?"

"I do."

"See to it."

"Consider it done."

"Well, that went better than I expected."

"They'll execute him, won't they?"

"Not if I can fix this first."

"How are you going to do that?"

"Please, it's me."

We're doomed.

ACHILLES

. . . vital signs . . . normal . . . quantum scan . . . a few scrapes and bruises . . . perfect health.

"The light," Eden murmured.

Afsarah Eden had no idea how long she had rested in the cool embrace of darkness. As she felt herself returning to consciousness, a warm and acute brightness directly in front of her made it impossible for her to consider opening her eyes.

"Captain?" a low, familiar voice said softly.

"The light," Eden said again, more clearly.

"Of course. My apologies," came the same voice.

The Doctor's, she realized. Within seconds the stark illumination was dimmed.

Tentatively, Eden opened her eyes and was rewarded by a sharp slicing pain running the width of her temples. She raised a hand to put pressure on her forehead to ease its cold fire and as she did so, realized she was lying supine on a biobed in a sickbay she did not recognize.

"Are you in pain?" the Doctor asked.

"My head," Eden replied weakly.

"A moment," the Doctor said and the next thing Eden knew, the cool tip of a hypospray touched her neck and with a light hiss, released its contents. The relief to her throbbing head was instant, if not complete. It did afford her the ability to remove her hand and open her eyes fully.

Hugh Cambridge and the Doctor stood on either side of her, staring intently at her in a way that suggested she might have sprouted a second head or third eye. Behind the Doctor, the CMO of *Achilles,* whose name escaped her at the moment, stood alert, though clearly ceding his authority to the EMH.

Gently, Eden pushed herself up on her elbows, relieved that the pain in her head was now a dull, manageable thudding.

"There's no hurry, Afsarah," Cambridge chided her gently. "You're quite safe."

Ignoring him, Eden shifted her weight to her hands and reached a sitting position, allowing her legs to fall over the side of the biobed. She took a few deep breaths, as much to calm her rising panic as the memories of all she had just witnessed came flooding back as to assure herself that she was physically functional.

Turning her head to the right, the captain said to the *Achilles* CMO, "Doctor Liddy?" unsure of where the name had come from but grateful to have found it.

The doctor moved quickly to stand beside Cambridge and meet her eyes. "Yes, Captain Eden?" he said kindly.

"Are there any critical patients in your sickbay right now?"

"No, Fleet Commander," he replied. "You are our only patient at the moment."

Eden nodded. "Would you and your staff please give us the room?"

Liddy nodded briskly and, calling to the single medic on duty to join him, quickly retreated to his office and sealed the door.

Once they were alone, Cambridge asked, "What happened?"

"How did we get here?" Eden replied.

The Doctor and Cambridge exchanged a wary look, and then the Doctor replied, "There was an incident in the cavern. My readings told me that you were unconscious throughout, but that did not inhibit your . . ." He trailed off, obviously searching for the right words.

"You defied gravity, Afsarah," Cambridge said, cutting to the chase.

"What?"

"I dozed off and the next thing I knew, you were floating twenty meters above the cavern floor. Whatever you saw, it was quite horrifying, if your screams were any indication. Eventually, the Doctor was able to retrieve you. Shortly after that, *Achilles* made orbit, and we requested an immediate transport." After a moment the counselor continued, "We're not sure if the place caused you to manifest this strange ability, or if it was some latent talent that came to you in a moment of need."

"Like the staff," the Doctor added.

Eden raised a trembling hand as a vivid recollection of calling to the rod so like the Staff of Ren and hurling it toward the center of the black surface filled her mind's eye. The Doctor and Cambridge remained silent until she said, "Then it wasn't a dream?"

"What wasn't?" Cambridge pressed.

Eden looked between them, wishing but not daring to refuse them their answers. Not for the first time, she wondered if she'd be better off if she had kept her secrets to herself. But the die was cast, and she had to accept the consequences.

"I saw them. My uncles," she began. "When the Anschlasom made their journey through *Som* they did more than shatter it at the point of entrance. They created multiple instabilities or access points that now exist throughout the universe. Somehow, Tallar and Jobin discovered one before they found me. They studied it, tested it, and eventually, breached it."

"*Som*? What the Anschlasom referred to as 'The End'?" the Doctor asked.

"Is it an alternate dimension?" Cambridge asked hesitantly.

"It's an alternate plane of existence," Eden replied. "It transcends, yet encompasses the entire universe. It truly is *the end*, but it should not have intersected with our reality for countless years to come. It was a mistake." Eden's heart began to burn in her chest at the magnitude of devastation that the ancient explorers and, subsequently, her beloved uncles had unleashed upon normal space and time. The captain began to shake uncontrollably.

"It's all right," the Doctor said in his most soothing voice.

"It isn't!" she retorted sharply. "They had no right, no idea what they were doing." Her teeth chattered as she did her best to continue. Unbidden, warm tears spilled from her eyes, drenching her cheeks.

"Afsarah," Cambridge said, taking both her hands in his, "try to remain calm."

"He's still there!" She needed them to understand her desperation. "I . . . had to . . . try and free him."

"Who?" the Doctor asked.

"Tallar," she sobbed.

Cambridge shook his head slightly, and the Doctor replied with an equally faint nod.

"You need to rest, Captain," the Doctor said calmly, raising a hypospray. "We can talk about this later, when you've had more time—"

"No," she insisted, pushing his arm away. "Don't you think I know how this sounds?"

Eden took several long deep breaths. Although the shaking did not subside completely, she felt able to assert a modicum of control over it.

"All right," Cambridge said, "help us understand. Where did you see your uncles?"

"There isn't time!" Eden insisted, the desperation threatening to overwhelm her again.

Another bright light assaulted her from over Cambridge's shoulder, and the captain raised her hand to shield her eyes from it. Fearing that the past and present were about to lose cohesion again, as they had in her visions, Eden paused before lowering her arm.

However, this time both Cambridge and the Doctor clearly saw it too. Turning simultaneously, their jaws dropped in unison at the sight of the figure now standing where the light had evaporated.

For the first time since she'd awakened, Eden wondered if the last few minutes could have been part of a continuous, longer dream. Nothing else made sense. Her body's shuddering returned with a vengeance as she sat perched on the edge of madness.

"This is my nightmare," she whispered. *It has to be.*

Cambridge raised his hand to his combadge, undoubtedly to call for security, but the figure quite calmly and with absolute authority said, "That's not necessary, Lieutenant."

Finally the Doctor seemed to find his voice. "Admiral Janeway?"

Chapter Twenty

VOYAGER

"She what?" Conlon asked, aghast.

"She insisted I give Shon her toy box and all of the toys in it," B'Elanna replied with quiet pride.

As Tom had already heard this story and felt nothing short of wonder at Miral's concern for the children she had known only for a few days, he took this moment to begin clearing the dinner plates for recycling and ordering up dessert for himself, B'Elanna, and their guests, Harry and Nancy.

"What about *Timmy Targ*," Harry asked dubiously.

"I held that one aside," B'Elanna admitted. "But everything else, including her stuffed Secasian serpent, is gone."

"She loved the little felt eyes right off that serpent," Kim exclaimed.

B'Elanna shrugged. "She wanted them to have her toys. I tried to explain that we could, and did, replicate plenty for all of them, but she kept saying they needed toys that already had love in them."

"She didn't," Nancy said.

"She did."

"You, I understand, but how does this guy," Harry said, gesturing to Tom, "end up with such a sweet kid?"

"You mean one who knows how to share?" Tom asked

good-naturedly as he served each of them dishes of fresh fruit covered with a light *guerno* cream. "It's really pretty amazing when you consider that she hasn't spent much time around other kids."

He caught B'Elanna's faint nod, along with the slight damper this brought to her mood. They had already discussed at some length his wife's new concerns that Miral really needed to interact with other children on a more regular basis and thus far, neither of them had any idea how to remedy this.

"She gets it from both of you," Nancy said, slapping Harry playfully in the shoulder. "Children reflect what they see in their parents and it's only normal that a kid who gets as much love as she does wants other kids to have it as well."

"I don't know," Tom demurred. Turning to Harry he said, "You were an only child and no one is more loving than your folks, but didn't you tell me once about a little girl named Ruri and the shine she took to your favorite talking tea kettle?"

Harry reddened visibly, which had been the point, as B'Elanna teased, "You refused to share your favorite toy with a little girl, Harry?"

"He punched her when she tried to play with it," Tom clarified.

"Never mind that," Nancy scoffed, "you had a talking tea kettle?"

"Tea was a special thing in my family," Harry replied. "And the kettle was a gift from my grandmother. It was actually a small replicator and—"

"Do yourself a favor, Harry," Tom suggested, "and just sit there in your wrongness and be wrong."

"I was five," he insisted.

"Miral isn't even four yet," Nancy reminded him.

"Ruri had her own tea set. She didn't need mine," Harry attempted.

"Harry?"

"Right." He nodded. "I was wrong."

As the chuckling died down, Harry Kim addressed himself to

his dessert to avoid further mortification. Tom couldn't help but marvel at how much he had enjoyed the last few hours. To sit over a delicious meal with friends like this was a pleasure he hadn't been able to savor for what felt like much too long.

"It's still hard to believe we were able to do what we did for Riley and her people," B'Elanna mused.

"Our timing was pretty good," Tom added with a nod. "I don't know how much longer they could have avoided detection by the Tarkons."

"I'm starting to think Seven might have been right all along," Harry offered, obviously pleased that a new subject was at hand.

"About what?" Tom asked.

"Last report in from the rest of the fleet indicated no signs of the Borg or Caeliar anywhere," he replied. "Riley's group was obviously a special case and odds are there might be a few more like them out here somewhere, but it's really starting to look like the Borg are actually gone."

"And not a moment too soon," Nancy added, dropping her spoon and pushing away her unfinished dessert.

Sensing the subtle sea change, Tom asked, "Did *da Vinci* see a lot of action during the invasion?"

Nancy's typically jovial and bright face was already clouded over.

"A bit," she replied tersely.

"Didn't I read a report about you guys single-handedly saving Troyius? Something about making their planet disappear?"

"That was almost a good day," she replied, obviously not interested in elaborating.

Nancy's sudden somber turn brought back vivid memories for Tom of *Voyager*'s particular corner of hell during the invasion, including coming within seconds of ramming a cube head-on. Between Chakotay's near-incapacitating grief, the horror of learning of his father's death, and the carnage at the Azure Nebula, Tom sometimes wondered how he, or anyone else, for that matter, had returned to anything resembling normal life in the succeeding months.

"That's the past," Tom said, hoping to steer the conversation toward a more pleasant path. "A few days ago we saved almost fifty people from certain death and this morning we left them on a new world where they'll have a real chance at watching their children grow up in peace. Not bad for a week's work."

"And with the Borg little more than a memory, I'd say the future for this entire quadrant is looking up," Harry agreed.

"Tom can tell you, I started this week with a sick sense that we were going to find something a lot worse than the Tarkons out here. I don't think I've ever been so happy to be wrong," B'Elanna added. Raising her wineglass she offered a toast. "To the future."

Tom and Harry immediately echoed her sentiment, and soon enough, Nancy did as well, but Tom couldn't help but wonder at her reluctance. She'd always struck him as someone who lived very much in the moment, but he knew all too well that the past could be hard to live with and even harder to put behind you.

Seven of Nine was in the process of recording a lengthy personal log. Many of the insights that helped her process her transformation by the Caeliar had come through her work with Counselor Cambridge. Her initial contact with Riley—in their shared mental landscape of Axion—had been disquieting, but did not approach the trauma of her first visit. Meeting Riley in person and learning of her transformation experiences had brought Seven's own painful memories of that event to the fore. Now, as she searched her feelings, any regrets she harbored about refusing a life among the Caeliar were surprisingly few. This pleased her, and she assumed it would also please Cambridge. Much as she wished to hold on to her anger with him for his insensitivity, Seven believed he had been candid about both his regard for her and his fears about pursuing a romantic relationship. Honesty was a solid place from which to build something deeper. Seven found herself anticipating their next meeting, though she wondered if he would be of more use to her as a counselor than a potential mate.

As Seven struggled to order these thoughts in her personal log, her cabin door chimed. Without bothering to ascertain the identity of her visitor, she called, "Enter."

Chakotay stepped into her quarters, and Seven rose immediately to greet him.

"Captain?"

"As you were," he said, smiling. "I just came by to see how you're doing."

Seven returned his smile and left her workstation, offering him a seat in her quarters' sitting area. The changes wrought in him after Admiral Janeway's death had opened a chasm between them, and every bridge she attempted to build across it was soon set aflame. The lengths to which Chakotay had gone since then to resume their former relationship had comforted her greatly. She knew the captain had paid special attention to her interactions with Riley, and his concern now was what she expected in an old and trusted friend.

"I am well," she confirmed as she took the seat beside him, settling into a relaxed posture that matched his own.

"Did you know what we would find at Arehaz?" Chakotay asked.

"No," Seven assured him. "I imagine it will take us years to determine the full extent of the changes brought about by the Caeliar. But thus far, they appear promising."

"We've all seen so much darkness in the last few years, it's hard to accept that anything good will come from it."

"Do you still harbor doubts about the Caeliar?" she asked, surprised.

"No," Chakotay replied. "I believe what my eyes, and our sensors, are telling us. A part of me just keeps waiting for the other shoe to drop."

Seven nodded. "The Borg left technology on thousands of worlds in this quadrant. If all of them were transformed similarly to Arehaz, it is likely that there will be hundreds of newly inhabitable planets available for colonization."

"Which can only be a good thing, right?" the captain asked, more of himself than her.

"Chakotay?"

"Where there are valuable resources, there are often multiple groups willing to fight over them. I'd hate to see the quadrant devolve into numerous internecine struggles to claim those planets."

"Were you planning to add 'keeping peace in the Delta Quadrant' to our current mission parameters?"

"Not our job, right?"

"No," she confirmed.

"Do you think Riley and those families will be safe there for long?"

"Arehaz is several thousand light-years from the nearest worlds inhabited by warp-capable species. By the time anyone else pushes that far into former Borg space, they will have developed sufficient means to defend themselves."

"Did Riley say that?" Chakotay asked, clearly troubled by the thought.

"She sacrificed perfection to personally ensure the safety of those families. The Tarkons' ability to surprise them and take them by force taught Riley a valuable lesson. They will never again make the mistake of leaving themselves defenseless, though I imagine that for the next several years, their focus will be on creating a sustainable existence. You don't begrudge them the right to defend themselves?"

"Of course not," he said.

"But you still don't trust her?"

"I don't believe she has any aim toward galactic conquest," the captain insisted. "But we've already discovered a few unusual uses for your catoms, and I have no doubts she and her people will explore theirs. . . . I don't know," he added with a shrug. "I guess I have a hard time trusting anyone who could violate me the way she did."

Seven wanted to reach out for his hand, but felt a sudden flush of hesitation. It had long ago been settled between them that their relationship was to be nothing more than friendship. Suddenly, it dawned on her how long it had been since he had shown an interest in any woman other than herself. His reaction to Janeway's death had confirmed her long-held suspicion that his heart had always been hers, although as far as she knew, they had never taken their relationship beyond the platonic level. But her new interest in Cambridge, combined with her and Chakotay's former, more intimate relationship, suddenly made her wary of sending any mixed signals.

"I have decided to change the nature of my relationship with Counselor Cambridge," Seven blurted out, and almost as quickly wished the statement unsaid.

Clearly taken aback, Chakotay's first response was a curious smile. "Okay," he said slowly, as he studied her face more intently.

"I don't know why . . ." she began, then retreated, offering, "Not that it is anything you should be concerned about."

"Seven," he said warmly, "it's all right. I'm glad you feel that you can tell me."

"It is still possible nothing may come of it," she went on, feeling more awkward by the moment.

"Does Hugh know about this decision?" Chakotay asked, his eyes dancing with mischief.

"Yes."

"And I take it he is amenable to the idea."

"I actually came to my decision based on what I sensed was his improper regard."

"Improper?"

"Between a counselor and his patient," she replied.

"I see." Chakotay nodded, still unable to wipe the smile from his face. "Well, that's great, then."

"Do you really believe so?"

Chakotay did her the courtesy of giving the matter a few moments of serious reflection. Finally he said, "Cambridge is unlike anyone I've ever met before, and it took me a long time to really appreciate his complexities and idiosyncrasies. But I like him, and I trust him. I go to him when I need a sounding board. Of course, if things go badly, you're going to put me in the awkward position of wanting to punch my ship's counselor. But it wouldn't be the first time, and it's a choice only *you* can make. If that's what your heart is telling you, you should listen."

Seven nodded, relieved by his candor. She had come to the same conclusion, but it did not alleviate her concerns for Chakotay.

Finally, she took a deep breath and ventured, "And what about you?"

Ever so briefly, a raw and wounded look crossed his face. As quickly as it had flared, it receded beneath the mask of reserved calmness that he had worn since taking command of *Voyager*.

"I'm sorry," she said quickly. "It's not my place—"

"No," Chakotay cut her off gently. "It is. Of course, it is."

"I have caused you pain, and that was not my intention," Seven insisted.

"You haven't," the captain said more intently. "I just don't let myself think about it much."

"Since Kathryn's death?" Seven asked.

He nodded wordlessly.

Conscious of his reluctance, but still curious, Seven asked, "Was the admiral aware of your feelings for her?"

Chakotay nodded, then began softly, "A long time ago, I misunderstood a birthday gift. . . . It led to an awkward moment between us on the holodeck." Seven noted the brief light this remembrance brought to his face as he cleared his throat and continued, "In the end it brought a lot of things that had been unsaid out into the open. At the time, we decided that our duties made it impossible for us to consider a relationship. We both moved on." He paused, and the light slowly left his features. "About a year before she died, we met for dinner at Proxima Station. I was looking forward to catching up. Without duty to divide us, it seemed silly to keep avoiding what we both wanted, and one thing led to another. When Kathryn left, we agreed to meet again when *Voyager* returned from the Yaris Nebula. I waited at a café in Venice for her to arrive. I wanted to make it official and propose. She didn't show up."

An unpleasant heat burned in Seven's chest. Suddenly, the violent shift in Chakotay at Kathryn's death became perfectly clear and took on contours of sadness she could barely fathom. Her eyes glistened. His pain echoed her own grief. Wounds she had long ago thought healed surfaced as fresh and deep as if they had just been cut.

This time, she reached for his hand, and took it between hers. They sat for some time in comfortable silence, until the passage of time allowed for some relief and made speech again possible.

"I still miss her," Seven acknowledged quietly.

"Every day," Chakotay agreed. "I don't honestly expect I'll ever feel that way about anyone else." Giving her hand a gentle squeeze, he added, "But she wouldn't have wanted me to bury my hopes with her. If there is someone else out there for me, I'm sure I'll find her, eventually. Until then, I've got plenty to keep me busy."

Seven had once attempted to end her budding relationship with Chakotay based on the fear of what the loss of love might do to his heart. The Admiral Janeway who had come from the future to bring *Voyager* home had apparently lived that version of reality, and the thought of destroying Chakotay's life had overwhelmed Seven's desire to allow their relationship to develop. Chakotay had argued then that love always came with risks, but they were worth taking. Seven wondered if he would still offer the same counsel.

She wanted to believe that he would, especially when she considered the precarious place her own heart now rested, in the hands of a man she barely knew. But as she searched Chakotay's face for a sign of the hope he professed to feel, Seven found nothing but doubt.

"Captain Chakotay to the bridge. We are receiving an emergency transmission from the Achilles.*"*

"On my way," he replied. Rising, he turned back to her and said, "Like I said, plenty to keep me busy."

Seven smiled faintly as she nodded in farewell.

Once he had left, her thoughts were too focused on what he

had revealed for her to wonder what emergency *Achilles* might have encountered.

Chakotay spent the brief turbolift ride to the bridge clearing his mind. Reliving Kathryn's death had again brought his grief surprisingly close to the surface. He knew better than to deny the pain. Solace would come in time and until it did, it was best to put one foot in front of the other.

Striding briskly onto the bridge, Chakotay turned to Lieutenant Waters, currently manning the ops station, and said, "Go ahead, Lieutenant."

As he sat, the starfield on the main viewscreen was replaced by the harried visage of Commander Tillum Drafar. The transmission was garbled by static.

"*We have retrieved Captain Eden and her team . . . Mikhal Outpost . . . en route to rendezvous with* Quirinal, Esquiline, Hawking . . . Cur . . . *have received emergency distress call from* Quirinal . . . *transmitting new coordinates to you now . . . regroup as soon as possible . . . advised to approach immediate area impulse only . . . les out.*"

"Waters, do you have the new rendezvous coordinates?"

"Yes, sir," she replied.

"Conn, calculate a slipstream jump that will take us to within half a light-year of the coordinates. We'll make our final approach at impulse. Waters, let me know the minute you've got *Quirinal*'s distress call."

"Aye, Captain."

"All hands, this is the captain. We are preparing to execute a slipstream jump to answer a distress call from *Quirinal*. Yellow Alert."

Chakotay settled in to wait. Last he'd heard, *Quirinal* was moving to regroup with *Esquiline* in order to investigate a spatial anomaly. His gut tightened as he wondered how things had gone wrong. The first part of his mission had been a success, tainted only by the engagement forced upon them by the Tarkons. But as the captain had been expecting since returning to the Delta Quadrant, the inevitable other shoe was now on its way down.

Chapter Twenty-one

ACHILLES

Kathryn Janeway wasn't sure what she had been expecting when she left the Q Continuum. Her godson had told her he'd be sending her where she was needed most, and she had assumed that would be to *Voyager*. Her first sight of the room in which she appeared told her she was on a Starfleet vessel. The last she knew, *Voyager* was returning from a deep-space mission and could be near the Sol system. Counselor Cambridge should have been with them. The Doctor was supposed to be working with his creator, Lewis Zimmerman, at Jupiter Station. And Captain Eden rarely left her desk, let alone her office at Starfleet Headquarters.

Where am I?

Eden, who was visibly shaking, pushed herself off the biobed, dismissing Cambridge and the Doctor's attempts to steady her. The captain stepped toward Janeway with the wariness of a hunter approaching a wild animal.

"Who are you?" she demanded.

Really? Janeway wondered. But then, if images of what the Borg had done to her had already been transmitted throughout Starfleet, Eden was right to be on her guard.

As calmly as she could, she said, "I am Admiral Kathryn Janeway."

This elicited a huff of what might have been amusement from Cambridge. He stood with his arms crossed at his chest.

The Doctor immediately grabbed a medical tricorder and directed the device at her.

"I realize you must be surprised to see me here, but I can explain, though I wouldn't mind knowing where *here* is," Kathryn added.

Eden continued to stare at her with something just this side of terror. As the Doctor was checking his scans, Cambridge took the liberty of replying, "We are currently aboard the Federation

Starship Achilles. At this moment we are in the Delta Quadrant, en route to rendezvous with several of the other vessels that comprise our exploratory fleet, of which Captain Eden is the fleet commander."

The counselor paused, perhaps hoping that this would rouse Eden, but when she remained silent, he continued, "And Admiral Janeway died fourteen months ago. While I'll admit the illusion you are creating is compelling, it hardly seems plausible. I don't know who you or what you are, but I'm reasonably certain you are *not* our long-lost admiral."

"She is," the Doctor said quietly, as if he didn't actually believe what his scans were telling him.

At this, Eden's head jerked toward him. "How is that possible?" she demanded.

The Doctor shrugged. "It isn't. But down to the last fragment of genetic material, this woman is Kathryn Janeway."

"You kept her bioscans?" Cambridge asked.

"Many of my former patients' files remain stored in my long-term memory," the Doctor replied.

"And she's alive?" Eden asked.

"And in excellent health." the Doctor nodded, still clearly doubting his scans.

Eden turned back to Janeway, who was still trying to absorb Cambridge's words.

Fourteen months?

Fourteen months!?

And an unpleasant afterthought: *The Delta Quadrant?*

"Can you explain how?" Eden asked, and Kathryn couldn't help but note that Eden refused to address her by name.

"Not all of it," Kathryn replied. "But as to the living part, that was Q's doing, and Kes's."

The Doctor wasn't programmed to cry, but Kathryn saw how much his parameters had expanded as his eyes glistened brightly. He closed the distance between them. "Kes?" he asked in wonder.

Kathryn nodded as she met his look with tears forming in her own eyes. The Doctor steadied himself and said, "On stardate

51514.9, we were alone in the holodeck. You were trying to help me through a particularly difficult time."

"I remember," Kathryn replied. An ethically impossible decision had forced the Doctor's program into a cascade failure. After her initial reprogramming had failed, Janeway offered him friendship, support, and counsel, hoping that he would ultimately make peace with his choice. It had been an arduous but ultimately successful process.

"You were reading a book. Do you remember its title?"

Kathryn smiled. The Doctor was clearly testing her. Fortunately, she knew she would pass. Her former fiancé, Mark, had first introduced her to Dante, but long after their relationship had ended, she had learned to love the ancient poet on his own merits. "*La Vita Nuova*," she replied.

The Doctor then recited a passage Kathryn had found particularly instructive. "In the book which is my memory, on the first page of the chapter that is the day when I first met you appear the words: 'Here begins a new life.'"

"I told you it was relevant," Kathryn nodded as tears began to fall freely from her eyes.

"Kathryn?" the Doctor said, visibly choking on his own emotions, and now obviously quite convinced of her identity.

The admiral didn't know who moved first to close the space between them, but she soon found herself held tightly in his arms.

"Doctor," Cambridge said, interrupting the moment, "are you absolutely certain that this is Kathryn Janeway?"

The Doctor pulled back from the embrace but still held Kathryn at arm's length. His smile was wide and joyful. "I'm not saying I know how this was done. And right now, I don't care. And while I can't speak for the Q, I am certain that if anyone could have saved her, Kes most certainly would have."

Cambridge's confusion shifted to a tentative bemusement, but Captain Eden looked as if she had just been diagnosed with a terminal illness. To her credit, she quickly assumed a professional manner and approached to within a meter of the Doctor and Janeway.

"Welcome aboard, Admiral," she said, extending her hand.

Kathryn accepted it. She knew Eden to be a dedicated, extremely competent officer, and pleasant to work with. The only mark against her was Eden's support of Admiral Willem Batiste's ludicrous proposal to return *Voyager* to the Delta Quadrant to gather further intelligence about the Borg. Sometime in the last fourteen months, Starfleet must have agreed to Batiste's plan. Kathryn was anxious to learn what had brought this about, but was mindful that this was the least of her worries.

"While I was with the Q, I learned of a threat perceived by one of the Continuum's members—my godson, actually."

"Please, tell me—no," the Doctor replied immediately.

"He's matured since the last time you saw him, Doctor," Kathryn assured him. "He shared with me compelling evidence that during *Voyager's* first mission to the Delta Quadrant, the one that took twenty-three years," she continued, hoping that the Doctor would follow; he had lived through the days that saw the arrival of the future Admiral Janeway and her successful efforts to bring *Voyager* home, "we encountered *something* that had a massive effect on the multiverse. By changing *Voyager's* history, that *something* was erased, and the effects rippled out to this point in time. I need to find out what that *something* was and, if possible, determine what woud have been the likely course of action of the *Voyager* of the original timeline. If I cannot, Q's existence may end, and that is something I am not willing to allow."

Now that she'd actually put it into words, Kathryn realized what a tall order she'd undertaken and how many ways she might fail to meet it.

"I grant you, it's a good reason for the Q to have spared your life," Cambridge offered, "but unless they also provided you with a lot more information, I'm not sure how we're going to be able to help you."

"We should alter course to a position where it is possible to speak in real time with Starfleet Command and apprise them of the situation," Eden said hesitantly. "The fleet is set to regroup following several weeks of exploration, and although we do have other pressing priorities at the moment, well, to be honest, I have no idea what Command is going to make of this."

Kathryn nodded as a voice she did not recognize called out over the comm. "*Drafar to sickbay.*"

"Go ahead, Commander," Eden replied.

"*Are you fully recovered, Captain?*" Drafar inquired.

Recovered? Kathryn suddenly remembered that Eden had been on the biobed when she had first appeared.

"I am, Commander," Eden replied.

"*Please report to the bridge. We've just finished long-range scans of our destination.*"

Eden turned to Cambridge, obviously at a loss.

"Before you regained consciousness, Commander Drafar advised us that he had received an emergency distress call from the *Quirinal* and was setting course to intercept."

Eden nodded. "Commander, please forward the data to sickbay. I will evaluate it from here."

There was too long a pause, in Kathryn's opinion, before Drafar said, "*Begging your pardon, Fleet Commander, I would prefer to brief you on the data privately.*"

Concern flashed across Eden's face as she replied, "Understood. I'll be right there."

Kathryn didn't know how much she had missed, but the glances exchanged between Eden, Cambridge, and the Doctor clearly indicated that she had arrived in the middle of what was an incredibly complex situation.

"Gentlemen," Eden said seriously, "we will continue to discuss the other issue as soon as there is time. Until then, I trust I can count on your discretion."

Whatever it is, she doesn't want me to know about it, Kathryn realized.

Eden turned back to Janeway. "While we're gone, Doctor, I'd like you to prepare all possible evidence that this truly is Admiral Janeway. I'm not doubting your word, or your impressions, Admiral, but we all know that many alien species have successfully impersonated Starfleet personnel in the past. Doctor, I think we have to be absolutely certain before news of her presence here is further disseminated."

"Of course," the Doctor replied.

"If the Q are involved," Cambridge added, "I don't think we can rule out that this is some trickery on their part."

For the first time, doubt flittered across the Doctor's face.

"I will submit to any test you require," Kathryn acknowledged. "I agree that before anyone else is advised, you should all be satisfied of the truth of what I have said."

With a brisk nod, Eden left the room.

"Counselor, if you will excuse us?" As Cambridge left the sickbay, the Doctor gestured toward the biobed Eden had recently vacated and said, "I know how you always hated a physical, Admiral, but in this case, I'm afraid I have no choice."

"Of course," Kathryn replied, wondering how she was going to prove who she was if even the Doctor, who knew her so well, was still skeptical.

As she made herself comfortable and the Doctor set to work at the terminal beside the biobed, Kathryn was struck by the fact that the conversation she'd just had would be the first of many difficult ones to come.

Fourteen months? That meant her death had been confirmed and some sort of memorial had been held. As she hurried past this distasteful thought, her heart caught in her chest.

Chakotay.

In a way it was odd that at no time during her interlude with the Q had Kathryn considered how he might be doing. Upon her return, he was the first person she had hoped to see. Her arrival on *Achilles* had forced her to set that aside and focus on the problem before her. She wondered if he had learned of her death before, or after, she had missed their date in Venice. For her, nothing had changed. The love they had finally admitted, and consummated, had left her more at peace than at any other time in her life. Kathryn had half expected that once *Voyager*'s mission to the Yaris Nebula was concluded, one or both of them might resign their commissions in order to be together. In any event, she had been confident they would find a solution, since she was content to realign her priorities to include a more permanent relationship.

Fourteen months . . .

There was no telling what that might mean.

So focused had she been on the larger problem Q had laid before her, she had failed to consider the possibility that—once the matter of confirming her identity was resolved—she would not be able to pick up where she had left off with Chakotay, and all of her other friends and loved ones.

"Did you actually see Kes?" the Doctor asked as he worked, interrupting her musings.

"Yes."

"She is well?"

"She seemed so," Kathryn said. "She was certainly not the same woman who appeared on *Voyager* the last time we saw her. In fact, Kes said as much, though I didn't really understand it."

Nodding, the Doctor raised a smaller scanner to her head and began a slow and methodical evaluation.

"She has a son," Kathryn went on, still warmed by the memory of their brief reunion.

"I know." He smiled. "I was there— Oh." He stopped himself so abruptly that Kathryn turned to him with concern.

"What?"

At this, the Doctor turned away and began to carefully study an image of her brain now visible on the screen.

"Hmm," was his frustrating response.

When he didn't immediately follow that with an explanation, Kathryn said, "Doctor, I know this has been a tough few minutes, but I'd like more than single-syllable responses from you when I ask a question. You're not the only one who is trying to come to grips with this."

"I'm sorry, Admiral," he replied, turning again to face her. "It's just . . . I've discovered something unexpected."

"Unexpected? Is it possible you mean *more* unexpected?"

"Over the years we served together, you sustained several injuries, some small, some large, and one in particular that was cause of significant concern near the end of our fourth year in the Delta Quadrant."

Kathryn searched her memory, but for the life of her, couldn't remember.

"Do you mean at the beginning of our fourth year, when you were forced to place me in a coma?"

"No." He shook his head. "You don't remember because you were never meant to remember. I did not heal these particular injuries. Kes's son, Kol, did. And he warned us that were you to ever come in contact with any information regarding the incident, his work could be undone and the resulting damage would kill you. The ship's logs were purged and the rest of the crew ordered to maintain their silence—an order they all followed most willingly."

"Then why are you telling me about it now?" Kathryn wondered in alarm.

"There was significant scarring of your neural tissues—nothing that would inhibit normal brain functions. That scar tissue, along with any evidence of other past injuries, is no longer present. It seems that when Kes, or the Q, repaired the damage to your body, they improved on the original."

Kathryn smiled in relief. "I think I know how that happened. There was a moment during what I experienced," she said, struggling to explain it clearly, "when Kes intervened, ordering my atoms to revert to their most perfect state. She did this to prevent me from returning in the form in which the Borg left me."

"As always, Kes seems to have exceeded expectations," the Doctor said.

"I'll say."

"I wouldn't," an all too familiar voice said.

Turning abruptly, Kathryn saw Q standing before her.

She was glad to see him. He had been absent from her recent journey, and she still found it hard to shake the idea that he should have been there, that it would have been of interest to him. The stern, angry face he greeted her with made her suddenly regret her enthusiasm.

"Hello, Q," the Doctor greeted him. "I owe you a great debt. What you've done in returning Admiral Janeway to us is a tremendous gift."

"Don't speak," Q ordered him fiercely.

The Doctor tried to reply, but nothing came out. His eyes widened in alarm.

Turning back to Kathryn, Q said, "So, how does it feel to be among the living again, Kathy?"

"You can't possibly be angry with me," she replied, ignoring his question. With Q, it had always been necessary to cut straight to the point.

"I can't?" he replied.

"It was your son who made this possible. You expect me to believe he didn't do it with your blessing?" Kathryn asked, amazed.

"My son is not your concern. He will be dealt with, I assure you."

Ice poured through Kathryn's veins at Q's words. She had seen Q arrogant, playful, dismissive, contemplative, frightened, and frustrated, but she had never seen him angry.

"Your death was what we who actually understand the epic complexities of the cosmos refer to as a 'fixed point in time.'"

"I know," Kathryn replied, crossing her arms defensively. "I saw it, more times than I like to remember."

"You should know that when the multiverse goes out of its way to do anything so thoroughly, it has good reason."

"You son had good reason, too," she argued. "Have you spoken with him about what he's been going through?"

Kathryn seemed to score a point here, as Q's face hardened visibly.

"I won't speak for him, but I will ask you this. Did either of you consider, before you made this disastrous mistake, the likely consequences of your actions?"

"Those remain to be seen," Kathryn argued, pushing herself off the bed to stand before him. If this was going to be a battle, she was damn sure going to meet it on her feet.

"For you, perhaps," Q replied. "But I'm still reeling from the arrogance you've just displayed."

"Then let me get you a mirror," Kathryn shot back.

Q nodded, stung, but went on, "Then you really believe that the multiverse can't continue without you?"

"Of course it can," she said, her anger rising. "This isn't about me."

At this, Q shook his head. "You believe that. But you have no idea what you've done here."

"A sentient being whom I care a great deal about asked me for help. I agreed. That's all."

"No," he corrected her. "You've just trampled all over the laws of space and time *again*," he said with great emphasis. "I know they make you people study temporal mechanics, and I know the greater mysteries are beyond you, but at some point this must stop."

Kathryn suddenly found herself wondering if her new life was going to be considerably shorter than she'd planned.

"For every transgression such as this, there is a price to be paid. The last time you took it upon yourself to alter history—for the mere convenience of getting your motley band of travelers home a little earlier than was fated—the Borg took considerable umbrage. Your destruction of their transwarp hub did not cripple them, as you'd hoped. It pissed them off. They made it their sole mission to wipe humanity from existence. But for a truly alarming confluence of events, the Borg would have succeeded. That cube you so casually decided to study wasn't the worst of it, my dear. A Borg armada followed, and sixty-three billion people lost their lives before the threat was ended."

"What?" Kathryn barely whispered.

"*Returning from the dead?*" Q continued. "I don't even want to know the price the multiverse will extract for this one. You'll want to bear that in mind before you consider wading any more deeply into my son's affairs."

A bright flash heralded his departure before Kathryn could say another word. Suddenly dizzy, she turned and grabbed the side of the biobed for support. The Doctor was soon at her side, gently helping her to sit again.

"Is this true?" she asked, as her heart began to pound and a wave of nausea rolled through her stomach.

"Yes," the Doctor replied gently. "However, I don't believe it's fair to place the blame for what the Borg did on you."

"Sixty-three billion?" The number was too huge to even contemplate.

"Several planets were completely destroyed, and hundreds of vessels," the Doctor admitted, though it clearly pained him to do so. "But that wasn't the whole story. The Borg were actually spawned from another incredibly advanced species, the Caeliar. They intervened and accepted the Borg into their gestalt. The Borg are gone now, Admiral. We've returned here to confirm it, and so far, it seems to be true. You do not bear any responsibility for the Borg's actions, and the ultimate result, despite the unthinkable price, was better than the alternative."

"Better than it taking a few more years for us to get home?"

"Please," the Doctor chided her. "The Borg were coming for the Federation. It was only a matter of time. You know that. Everyone knows that. But because they came when they did, the Caeliar were there to stop them. Ten, twenty, thirty years later, that might not have been the case."

Kathryn knew he was attempting to comfort her. Her hands were ice, and a dull ache thudded with a constant refrain, *sixty-three billion . . . sixty-three billion.*

"Admiral, please," the Doctor said more sternly. "At the very least, we can eliminate the concern that you might be a Q masquerading as Kathryn Janeway."

"That much I already knew," she murmured.

Suddenly, a new thought cut sharply through the miasma. Q was angrier with his son than with her. *Was it possible that her resurrection was the cause of whatever fate awaited his son?* She hated temporal mechanics with a passion, but her brief glimpse of reality, from the Q's vantage point, had opened her mind to the many ways in which cause and effect could transpose with one another.

No, she decided. The darkness she had tasted was something else, something even Q might not yet perceive. It was near at hand, or she wouldn't have been sent back at this precise moment.

What is happening here and now?

Pushing herself off the biobed on trembling legs, Kathryn moved to the Doctor's data terminal. She attempted to call up the display of the emergency transmission the *Achilles* had just received. Naturally, it was classified, but there were ways around that for an admiral. Her personal command codes would already have been deleted, but with a few less orthodox commands, Kathryn soon found what she was looking for.

At first, the image on the screen before her made no sense. The Doctor had moved to stand behind her, and the moment it became clear, he uttered a sharp cry.

"No," he said.

The admiral studied the image for a few more seconds, then said quietly, "Doctor, where is *Voyager*?"

The control Captain Eden had struggled to maintain as she tried to explain her visions to the Doctor and Cambridge had almost slipped through her fingers the moment Kathryn Janeway appeared in sickbay. She had grasped desperately for some elusive hope. It was far more likely this was some alien intervention than the living, breathing Admiral Janeway.

The Doctor's scans, his testing of a deeply personal memory, and everything about the woman had pried that hope from her tentative grasp. The captain made the brief journey to the *Achilles'* bridge in silence. She stepped into Commander Drafar's ready room to study the data.

Eden no longer felt certain she knew where reality ended and her dreams began.

She believed her recurring nightmare had been nothing more than an unpleasant subconscious manifestation of the fear she felt since she had taken command of the fleet. The disquieting senses she had experienced with a few archeological oddities, coupled with her dream, had held ominous portents. But in the light of day, and with Chakotay's help, she had successfully pushed them to the back of her mind.

Even in the aftermath of the Mikhal Outpost discoveries, Eden believed she could find her equilibrium. A thoroughly plausible scientific explanation would be found once the Doctor and Cambridge set to work.

And then, Kathryn Janeway had appeared, as if by magic. Eden now had to accept that forces beyond her control were charting her destiny.

Confirmation of that was now displayed on the small viewscreen in Drafar's ready room.

Four of her vessels, *no, sections of four of her vessels,* hung motionless. Around them, space took on the appearance of broken black ice. The aft section of the *Quirinal,* through its rear cargo bays, was gone. The *Esquiline, Hawking,* and *Curie* had entered the anomaly from a forward angle and most of their saucer sections were nowhere to be seen. The anomaly at the heart of the shattering effect was exactly the same thing the Anschlasom, as well as Tallar and Jobin, had discovered.

Captain Tillum Drafar explained with maddening patience what little he already understood of the situation. The anomaly had expanded and now covered thousands of kilometers. Any approach was extremely hazardous. It was impossible to determine if the lost portions of the ships had been destroyed or had merely vanished into the anomaly. Eden could only remember, with growing sadness, Tallar's face beneath the black lake and her disastrous, compulsive need to free him. She knew she was responsible for the fate of the *Quirinal, Esquiline, Hawking,* and *Curie.*

As Drafar droned on, a single relentless thought tormented her. *What have I done?*

Chapter Twenty-two

QUIRINAL

Captain Regina Farkas hurried against the tide through the halls of Deck 18. Lieutenant Commander Gregor Denisov, her security chief, jogged a few paces ahead, ostensibly to clear her path. She suspected he was under orders from Commander

Roach to prevent her from taking any unnecessary risks once they reached their destination on Deck 16.

"Make a hole, double-quick!" Farkas ordered as she ran, not to get people out of her way, but to instill a sense of urgency as they made their way to the farthest fore section of the ship. Roach and Psilakis were overseeing the evacuation of all areas within half a kilometer of the "barrier." At the same time her officers were coordinating the movement of supplies from the hazardous areas. The crew members she passed were carrying as much as they could.

"Commander Roach, what's our count?" she called out to her first officer over the comm.

"*Confirmed four hundred twenty-three,*" Roach replied. "*But sensors are intermittent near the barrier. We're still working to clear that up.*"

"Understood. Any word yet from the *Esquiline, Hawking,* or *Curie*?"

"*Communications are still down, Captain.*"

"Carry on," Farkas replied grimly.

The captain had come to the Delta Quadrant in command of six hundred eighty-one souls. Sixty-three of them had lost their lives in the Children of the Storm attack and *Quirinal*'s subsequent crash landing.

Thirteen minutes earlier, when her ship had slipped partially into the anomaly, Farkas had potentially lost another one hundred ninety-five.

No.

It was an unacceptable number. Of course, one was equally unacceptable. But she'd be damned if this day ended with triple the body count she'd once thought would be the worst the Delta Quadrant could show her.

"Crewman, I want to see you move!" Farkas barked at an unfortunate young man who'd been catching his breath while leaning against a bulkhead. "You can breathe when you get to cargo bay one," she shouted to his back as he rejoined the jostling throng.

A few paces ahead of her, Denisov was already opening a hatch to the Jefferies tube that ran up to Deck 16. Every other available shaft was being used to bring crew down from the upper levels, but this one had been designated for Farkas's route.

"This way, Captain," the security chief called.

Nodding, she attacked the ladder. As her muscles began to groan after a few meters, she wished she hadn't listened when Doctor Sal had ordered her to take it easy after her brush with death.

Fear steeled her resolve and quickened her pace.

Their sensors had told them that there was a barrier bisecting her ship at a ninety-three-degree angle. It separated normal space from what she hoped had been pulled intact into the anomaly. The barrier ran straight through main engineering.

The nacelles and rear shuttlebays she could live without, at least for the moment. Her engineering staff, particularly Lieutenant Phinnegan Bryce, was another matter.

Phinn had been critical in saving the ship from the Children of the Storm, and his diligence was largely responsible for the *Quirinal*'s speedy rebuild. They had stared down death together once, and the thought that he had been lost to this cursed *thing* galled her.

Farkas had to see for herself what the status of main engineering was, and as she climbed out of the tube onto Deck 16, her breath coming in great heaves, she tried to prepare herself for whatever she was about to find.

ACHILLES

Tillum Drafar stood before his command chair as he received the latest reports. *Achilles* had come to a full stop a third of a light-year from what appeared to be left of four of the fleet's vessels. Captain Eden stood beside him, her arms crossed at her chest and her face a stoic mask. Commander Drafar had briefed her on *Voyager*'s latest actions, their engagement of the Tarkons and the rescue of Riley and her people. He had transmitted several emergency messages to *Voyager*, knowing they would arrive at the new rendezvous coordinates as soon as they were able. Eden had thanked him and settled in his ready room to begin her own analysis of every scrap of data they had received about the anomaly. She had stepped onto the bridge minutes ago at Drafar's request.

"Mapping complete," Rosati advised from ops.

"Are you certain we can move closer without falling into the anomaly?" Drafar asked.

"The distance between the event horizons increases the farther they stretch from the center of the anomaly," Rosati said. "There are a hundred thousand kilometers separating them at the closest location from which we can begin our scans. The shattering effect appears to have ceased, at least locally. If we get closer, that may not be the case."

"Take us in, Ensign Mirren," Drafar ordered, "one-quarter impulse."

Drafar assumed that Eden was as frustrated as he was that they could not obtain sensor readings of the trapped ships' conditions from their current position. They were unable to tell if any of the crews remained alive. The pristine condition of the visible sections of the ships gave him hope that many had been spared, but there was no way to know until they got a closer look.

He turned toward the fleet commander, who had remained silent, her eyes locked on the main viewscreen. Drafar said, "It will take us a minimum of one hour to navigate this region at our current speed. If you would prefer to wait in my ready room or your quarters, I will advise you as soon as our sensors are able to provide any meaningful data."

Eden's wide, cold eyes met his. Though he thought her earlier actions were insupportable, she seemed to be well in command of herself.

"I'll wait in my quarters, thank you, Commander," she said, and left the bridge without a backward glance.

Hugh Cambridge had made himself comfortable on the couch in Afsarah's quarters. The Doctor and Admiral Janeway sat at the room's small table, where she picked at a salad the Doctor had insisted on replicating. A steaming cup of coffee that hadn't left her hand had been refilled twice.

Cambridge had been waiting in Eden's quarters since the Doctor had dismissed him from sickbay to perform his tests. Once completed, the Doctor and admiral had transported directly there to await the arrival of Captain Eden, as neither believed that roaming the halls with the newly resurrected Admiral Janeway was prudent. The medical staff had been grateful to get their sickbay back in order to prepare to receive wounded from the trapped ships. Captain Eden had been advised of their location.

The Doctor had done his best to bring the admiral up to speed on the major events of the last fourteen months. Janeway listened somberly, asking a few pointed questions. The admiral struggled to accept the enormity of what the Borg had wrought in a matter of weeks. She had conceded that, given the circumstances, she could understand why Starfleet had sent *Voyager* and the fleet to the Delta Quadrant. However, Janeway expressed concern about the shortage of resources required for rebuilding efforts in the Federation and whether the fleet might have been put to better use.

Eden entered her quarters, and her guests automatically rose to their feet to greet her.

"Are we there yet?" Cambridge asked lightly.

Eden nodded. "We have thoroughly mapped the area within several million kilometers of the anomaly and are now moving in at low impulse, until we come within optimal sensor range."

"Have sensor capabilities degraded significantly in the last fourteen months?" Janeway asked.

"The anomaly is rendering sensors useless at this distance," Eden replied. "Admiral, the anomaly—"

Janeway held up her hand, explaining, "I used a series of old command overrides to see the long-range data for myself."

"I might find that disturbing if you didn't outrank me, Admiral," Eden observed.

Finally setting her coffee down, Janeway moved to within a few paces of Eden. The differences between them could not have been plainer. Eden stood almost a head taller than the admiral, and her ebony skin was a stark counterpoint to Janeway's fair Irish inheritance. The admiral's long auburn hair had been swept into an efficient roll at the nape of her neck, while Eden's tight curls extended barely an inch above her scalp.

But the similarities in bearing, intensity, and determination made these surface differences insignificant. Both officers had come honestly by the fierceness with which they defended their own. Eden was responsible for the fourteen hundred plus crew aboard the trapped vessels, along with the seven hundred plus who were about to do everything in their power to rescue them. Janeway's command might once have been limited to the crew of *Voyager,* but she was a Starfleet admiral; everyone was "hers" now. Had the circumstances been less dire, Cambridge might have replicated a little popcorn and simply sat back to enjoy the show.

"The information I have from the Q indicates that we have very little time before an event of cataclysmic significance to the entire multiverse. I came back to try and avert it. It's possible that what has happened to the ships is completely unrelated, but given that my source is a member of an omnipotent species that has been around for several billion years, and that I was sent *here* rather than anywhere else, I'm going to go out on a limb and presume that the two are connected. That means I need to know everything you know, as well as any areas where your data may be insufficient. You'll just have to forgive me if professional courtesy takes a back seat to that for a while."

Eden didn't blink. "As the ranking officer present, you would be within your rights to assume command of the fleet."

"I would," Janeway agreed, softening just a hair as she added, "but given my unique position, I don't believe that would serve either of us or the fleet well. Starfleet wouldn't have given you command if you weren't capable of leading this fleet. But, I'm a valuable asset. Why don't we worry about official responsibilities later and work the problem together?"

After a short pause, Eden nodded. "Agreed."

Relaxing visibly, Janeway sighed. "So where are we?"

"The anomaly is one that has never been encountered by Starfleet," Eden replied. "But I believe I know what it is."

At this, Cambridge and the Doctor stepped toward Eden.

"Are you certain?" Cambridge asked.

"Yes," Eden assured him. "It's *Som,* 'The End.' "

"That doesn't sound good," Janeway noted.

"It's not." Eden went on, "I'm also certain that I am the one responsible for trapping the four ships."

The Doctor shook his head, but Cambridge immediately jumped in, saying, "That's not possible, Afsarah."

Janeway's face took on a curious, almost sympathetic expression as she asked, "Why don't you tell me why you believe that to be true?"

Eden stole a glance at Cambridge, who said, "I think the admiral needs to hear the whole story."

"Absolutely," the Doctor agreed.

Gesturing to the dining table, Eden said, "Make yourself comfortable, Admiral. *Voyager* is several hours away and we've got half that time to formulate a rescue plan."

"I think I'm going to need a fresh cup of coffee for this," Janeway said, moving toward the replicator. "Can I get you one, Captain?"

"Tea," Eden replied.

Chapter Twenty-three

VOYAGER

During Ensign Aytar Gwyn's first few months as *Voyager*'s alpha-shift conn officer, Tom Paris felt that she had distinguished herself. The most obvious way was her mastery of slipstream flight. While it might appear that there wasn't much for a flight controller to do when a ship was hurtling through a subspace corridor, monitoring the stability of that corridor was essential. In less than a second, anything could go wrong. The main computer did the endless calculations and was programmed to alert the controller if subspace variances were detected, but Gwyn always seemed to be one or two steps ahead of the computer. She was not technically telepathic, although she was descended from a race of empaths. Tom swore she flew by a sixth sense. Good piloting was instinctual, and Tom could see that Gwyn trusted her instincts.

Less than four minutes before *Voyager* was scheduled to arrive at the coordinates provided by *Achilles,* Gwyn shifted in her chair—well before the alarm indicating possible drive failure— and calmly began entering the commands to disperse the slip-stream corridor.

As she did so, Gwyn reported, "Captain, we can no longer sustain slipstream velocity."

Chakotay immediately set aside his padd and asked, "Can we take the drive off line safely?"

"Yes, sir," Gwyn replied, obviously doing all within her power to accomplish that.

Her next words were less confidence inspiring. "Hang on."

Tom lifted his eyes from his terminal, which had begun display-ing a series of subspace ratios that had to indicate a sensor glitch. On the main viewscreen, the image of the subspace corridor—a tunnel of whirling energies—began to bend inward on itself.

An image of *Voyager* being crushed into dust by a cosmic incinerator flashed instantly through the first officer's mind.

The next moment, Tom was floating, weightless, as the inertial dampers took a fraction of a second longer than normal to com-pensate for the abrupt velocity shift. Thankfully, normal gravity was restored before everyone on the ship was turned into dust. But the pounding that ricocheted up Tom's spine as he slammed down was not one he would soon forget.

The image on the main viewscreen resolved into a calm starfield.

"Well done, Ensign," were Chakotay's first words.

"No problem, Captain," Gwyn replied with enough residual tension to belie her intended lightness.

"Did the drive malfunction?" Chakotay asked.

"No, sir," Gwyn replied confidently. "Subspace did."

"I beg your pardon?" Chakotay demanded.

Turning in her seat, her pale face accentuated by the vivid cerulean shade of her short hair, the ensign said, "I don't understand it either, Captain. But from the readings I'm getting, I'd say somebody in this area has radically altered subspace."

Chakotay turned to his ops officer, Kenth Lasren. "What is our current position, Lieutenant?" he asked.

"We're five light-years from our intended destination," the lieutenant replied.

"Can we make up the distance at warp?" Chakotay asked Gwyn.

She shrugged. "We can try. But it looks like the damage to subspace increases the closer we get to the rendezvous point."

"Engage warp engines at your discretion, Ensign," Chakotay ordered. "Continue at best possible speed."

"Aye, Captain," she replied, and returned her attention to her station.

Chakotay turned to Tom and was about to speak when Lasren said, "Captain, I have an emergency transmission from *Achilles.*"

"On-screen," Chakotay ordered.

"It's a single image, sir," Lasren replied. "Long-range sensor data as *Achilles* approached the rendezvous point. I also have the initial emergency distress calls from *Quirinal.*"

"Let's take a look at the image first," Chakotay ordered.

As soon as it appeared on the screen, Tom's jaw dropped.

After a few moments of silent contemplation, Chakotay, who could probably now guess at the contents of the distress call, rose from his seat and said, "Forward this to astrometrics and ask Seven, Patel, and B'Elanna to meet me there. Commander Paris, the bridge is yours."

Chakotay arrived in astrometrics to find Seven, Lieutenant Devi Patel, and Lieutenant Commander B'Elanna Torres engaged in a heated discussion.

"But that doesn't make sense unless you're willing to ignore the laws of physics," B'Elanna said, clearly frustrated.

Seven's eyes did not leave the disconcerting image on the astro-metrics lab's viewscreen.

"I am ignoring nothing, Commander," Seven replied tersely. "Unless you have a suggestion that incorporates all of the available data—"

Patel cut her off. "There is no way this data is accurate," she insisted.

"Upon what do you base that assertion?" Seven asked, incredulous.

"Maybe the fact that it's completely impossible," B'Elanna said, clearly hoping to gain an advantage through volume.

"Enough," Chakotay ordered. He could well understand their shock and horror, but he needed answers if they were to have the slightest hope of rescuing the trapped ships. When all three had turned to him, still frustrated but finally silent, he said, "Did this fleet just lose over fourteen hundred people?"

Patel responded, "We don't know, Captain."

"What *do* you know? One a time," he cautioned them.

"*Voyager*'s sensors are unable to cut through the interference at this distance to ascertain if there are any survivors," Seven began. "From what we can see of the vessels, there is no reason to believe that personnel who were located in the unaffected areas perished."

"And what is this anomaly?" was Chakotay's next question.

All three exchanged tense looks before B'Elanna decided to take a swing. "We know the four vessels in question came here to study it and likely began doing so more than thirty-six hours before this happened. We have some of their sensor data from just prior to the moment of . . ."

". . . impact," Seven suggested.

"They didn't run into it, Seven," B'Elanna chided her.

"Easy," Chakotay warned.

"The data we have received is . . . I believe it's corrupted, Captain," Patel interjected. "It suggests that while undergoing passive scans, the anomaly shattered from a central point, ripping apart space and subspace in an area that now extends for several million kilometers. The subspace damage extends even farther, but we do not understand why."

"At which point, each of the vessels apparently impacted the nearest of several hundred discrete event horizons," Seven added, almost daring the others to contradict her, "which now separate what we consider normal space from the interior of the anomaly."

"If that much is clear, why are you convinced that the data is flawed in some way?" Chakotay asked his science officer.

"The readings we have are too contradictory to be reliable," Patel replied. "They suggest that the portions of the ships we can no longer see, and everything else beyond the event horizons, does not exist."

"Does not exist in normal space-time, you mean?" Chakotay asked.

"No. Does not exist. Never existed."

"The most likely explanation is that this is an interdimensional rift," Seven offered.

"It could also be the result of some sort of exotic quantum phase shifting," B'Elanna added.

"It's also worth noting we don't know what actually caused the anomaly to alter its previous configuration," Patel added. "I believe that continuing to move toward it could further destabilize it."

"We need to fly carefully?" Chakotay asked.

"Very," Seven agreed.

At the first officer's request, Nancy Conlon reported to the bridge, taking over the main engineering station, as *Voyager* proceeded toward the anomaly. They had cut the distance to the intended coordinates in half, through a brief acceleration to warp five. Maintaining a stable warp field had become impossible and dangerous, and they were continuing on full impulse.

Tom intended to request that astrometrics sensors be reallocated to a real-time, intensely detailed mapping of the area. With new data, they might be able to find a pocket of unaffected space and maneuver in short bursts at warp speeds. If not, they were several days away from their rendezvous point, and he didn't think the *Quirinal, Esquiline, Hawking,* and *Curie* could wait that long.

In the meantime *Voyager's* chief engineer might be able to use the standard sensors to produce similar results. By coordinating directly with the conn, he hoped Conlon could shave at least a day off his current estimates. So far, this arrangement was not going well. He was certain Conlon understood the urgency of the moment, but in Tom's estimation, she was playing it unnecessarily safe.

"Reduce speed to one-quarter impulse," Conlon ordered from her station, and Gwyn released a sigh of frustration as she complied.

Tom glanced back at Harry and offered him a small nod that communicated all that was necessary. He then watched as Harry moved to stand behind Conlon and said quietly, "What are you seeing, Lieutenant?"

Conlon looked up at him, her face flushed and her lips drawn taut. "I'm seeing a whole lot of readings that don't make sense," she replied tersely. "I suggest you let me try to figure them out."

"Anything I can do to help?" Harry asked with appropriate detachment.

"No," she warned.

Tom didn't meet Harry's eyes as he moved back to the tactical station. He didn't need to. Everyone was entitled to a certain amount of shock at what they had just seen, but giving in to it wasn't going to get the job done.

"Lieutenant Conlon, accompany me to the ready room," Tom ordered. "Lieutenant Kim, the bridge is yours. Ensign Gwyn, proceed at best possible speed."

Conlon rose from her station and followed Tom into the captain's sanctuary. The door had barely slid shut when Conlon asked, "What's the problem, Commander?"

"I was about to ask you that, Nancy."

Her face turned a deeper crimson as she said, "There's no problem, sir."

"Nancy?"

Without lowering her defenses, she replied, "Based on what little usable data I can coax from our sensors, we shouldn't even be trying to fly through this."

"It's our duty to make every effort to reach those ships and their crews," Tom reminded her calmly.

Conlon shook her head. "Why don't you just put all of us out of our misery right now and activate the self-destruct? I'm certain that if we get anywhere near those four ships, we're going to join them."

There had been plenty of days during the Borg invasion when Tom had felt the way Conlon did now. Eventually, by working the problem and refusing to look too far into the future, he had found a way through that darkness. Given time, he was sure Conlon would do the same.

"I know it's scary as hell, Nancy," he admitted.

"Scary?" the engineer said, her voice rising. "My . . ." She caught herself and asked through a tightened jaw, "Permission to speak freely, sir?"

"Always," Tom assured her.

There was a long pause as she attempted to collect herself, and finally the lieutenant said, "The people . . . so many people."

"I know," he said, nodding.

"One second they're manning their posts and the next, they no longer exist. How many times do we have to see this before we decide it isn't worth it?" Conlon asked, aghast.

"Right now, there could be hundreds in need of rescue. Don't we owe it to them to try?" he asked gently.

"Of course we do," Conlon said, dropping her face into her hands. "But the harder I try to focus on those sensor scans, the less sense they make. This isn't like me. My instincts are telling us to run, as fast and far from this thing as we possibly can."

Tom took her by the hand and squeezed gently, hoping some of his confidence would reach her.

"They need you, Nancy. They need all of us," he said.

The engineer raised her head and stared into Tom's eyes. Her cheeks were wet and her breath was labored, but she did her best to compose herself.

"I'm going back to the bridge. You take as much time as you need in here." Tom smiled, and then added, "I need you focused only on what is right in front of you. Everything else we deal with later."

"Yes, sir," she replied.

The first officer left her there. It was clear that the constant pressure was close to breaking Conlon.

He was incredibly relieved when a few moments later, Conlon again stepped onto the bridge and got back to work.

Interlude

OMEGA CONTINUUM

"I am Captain Parimon Dasht of the Federation *Starship Esquiline*. My father is Admiral Lukas Dasht. My mother is Selena Royer Dasht. I have three sisters, Merilee, Lilia, and Rowena. Merilee was sealed under the covenants to

"Merilee was sealed under the covenants to (*who*)

"Merilee was sealed to (*I've known him for twenty twenty twenty something years*) Avery!

"Yes, Avery. Merilee and Avery.

"Lilia is (*who is Lilia?*)

"My vessel has been drawn into an anomalous region of (*of what?*) of (*of what?*) of

(*go back*).

"I am Captain Parimon Dasht. (*There is nothing, how is there nothing, I am here so there has to be something*)

"Of the Federation *Starship Esquiline*. My father is (*but there should be something*) Admiral Dasht. My mother (*the light—don't look at it—is blinding*) is Selena. I have three (*I have nothing. I am nothing. There is nothing.*) Where am I?

(*go back*).

"I am Captain Parimon (*how long have I always been always here never here*)

The *Esquiline* (*has never always would have must not be*) here."

"Where?"

"Who?"

"Go back.

"I

"I am Captain (*not here nothing here there is nothing how is it that nothing is so bright?*)

"I am (*no, please, no*) . . ."

"You are Captain Parimon Dasht of the Federation *Starship Esquiline*."

"That's right. That sounds right."

"You are Captain Parimon Dasht. Say it with me, Captain."

"I am Captain Parimon Dasht."

"And I am Captain Bal Itak of the Federation *Science Vessel Hawking*. Captain Chan?"

"I'm here, Itak."

"And is your mind still clear?"

"Yes, thank you."

"Captain Dasht?"

"I am Captain Parimon Dasht."

"Yes, of the Federation *Starship Esquiline*."

"There was an anomaly."

"Yes, and a large portion of your ship is now trapped inside it."

"I have a ship?"

"You are captain of your ship. The Federation—"

"*Starship Esquiline*. Yes. The anomaly. Yes. My father is Admiral Lukas Dasht."

"And who is your mother? Tell me again."

"Selena Royer Dasht."

"And your three sisters?"

"Merilee, Lilia, and Rowena."

"Parimon?"

"How many times have we had this conversation now, Itak?"

"Nineteen."

"Are you the only thing keeping all of us stable right now?"

"The effects of this realm, whatever it is, have confused almost all of us who are now trapped within it. My mental disciplines and those of my fellow Vulcans have made us less susceptible to the effects, so we are each working with as many of our fellows as possible to calm them and focus their thoughts. My priority has been the command staff. You, Captain Parimon Dasht, and Captain Xin Chan. Chan?"

"I'm still here, Itak, reciting regulations whenever I start to slip. A handy suggestion. Thank you."

"Parimon?"

"Yes, I remember now."

"Good. That is good. If you again feel your control slipping, begin with your name and continue with your family. Focus on what you know. Hold on to it with all of your might. The darkness, the light, they are meaningless. They cannot harm you. Ignore them."

"Understood. Thank you, Itak."

"By my estimate we have been trapped in this anomaly . . ."

"Forever?"

"No, Parimon. We have been trapped for less than two hours, although the illusion is powerful."

"The fleet?"

"Good. Yes. We were part of a larger fleet. I have every confidence that soon enough, they will locate us and attempt a rescue."

"They will fail."

"What?"

"Did you hear that?"

"Itak?"

"Bear with me, Parimon and Chan. To whom am I speaking?"

"None of your damn business."

"Please, sir. Identify yourself."

"Go to hell. Or should I say, welcome to it?"

"Either identify yourself or go away. Your anger is useless to our efforts here."

"Tallar. Carson Tallar."

"Are you a crew member on one of our vessels?"

"Not *Curie*."

"Doesn't sound familiar."

"No. I had my own vessel once. A long time ago."

"Was it destroyed?"

"Depends on what you mean by destroyed."

"Was an attempt ever made to rescue you?"

"No."

"Then, begging your pardon, Mister Tallar, how can you be certain that any rescue attempt made by our sister ships will fail?"

"The garden."

"The what?"

"There's a garden here?"

"Please, Parimon."

"Sorry."

"What about the garden, Mister Tallar?"

"Do you see it, Itak?"

"Do you see it, Itak?"

"Do you see it?"

"I do."

"Join me there."

"I will try. Chan?"

"I'll stay with Parimon."

"Parimon?"

"I am Captain Parimon Dasht."

"Xin, we're losing him."

"I'll do what I can."

"That is all that can be expected. I will return shortly."

"Do you really see a garden?"

"Yes. Stay with Parimon. We will surely need him."

"Understood."

"It is illogical to accept that this garden has always been here but I am only now aware of it. How is it that I can only see it now?"

"Because it is my garden. Given enough time, the stronger minds among you would have selected an appropriate frame of reference, one meaningful to you, and allowed it to bring certainty to your new existence."

"Fascinating. Is there a reason you have chosen such a chaotic and clearly damaged mental landscape in which to exist, Mister Tallar?"

"Until you and your ships entered the Continuum, it was different. Not this. That orchard hung with glorious, luminous fruit. The grass was soft and the smell of lavender was everywhere."

"How could something that happened on a physical plane damage your personal mental landscape?"

"It's all one and the same here, Itak."

"I see. I would apologize if we had done this to you intentionally."

"You damn well should. How did you get here? Did you find the patch?"

"The patch?"

"It would have registered on your sensors as a unique anomaly beyond which normal space and time appear not to exist."

"You had a similar experience."

"Many years ago."

"Did you come to the patch from normal space-time?"

"We were in the Beta Quadrant, not far from the Lantaru sector."

"We were in the Delta Quadrant. How many of these patches are there?"

"Obviously at least two."

"Were you a member of Starfleet?"

"Once, a very long time ago. But by the time my husband and I came to study the patch, we had both resigned."

"And your studies brought you here?"

"Yes. Twice."

"Twice. Then you did escape once?"

"Yes, but that was under unique circumstances. It won't happen again."

"And why did you return to this anomaly?"

"I had to."

"Why?"

"At the time, I believed there was only one such anomaly and I needed to close it, to seal it off from normal space-time forever."

"I see."

"Do you?"

"I believe so."

"You couldn't."

"I am a Vulcan. You have opened your mind to me in a way I am beginning to believe would be impossible in any other realm."

"Continuum."

"Continuum. I hear your words and see your wrecked garden, but I also see and hear that which you would rather hide from me."

"The Continuum is speaking to you?"

"Yes."

"And it is telling you about me?"

"No, you are doing that, Mister Tallar. The Continuum is telling me the rest. First, you came out of curiosity. The second time you came back to save her."

"I did."

"But there were two of you?"

"Jobin remains on the other side."

"He is still alive."

"He is."

"He is waiting."

"He's stubborn that way."

"You cannot escape now."

"No."

"Nor can we."

"No. But there's more. Has the Continuum told you the rest?"

"There is . . . I cannot . . ."

"You can. Accept it."

"We must not escape?"

"That is correct. You must not. To attempt to do so would . . ."

". . . further widen the anomaly and its intersections with normal space-time."

"Yes."

"It may already be too late."

"Yes."

"We must act to prevent that."

"You can't."

"Nonetheless, an effort must be made."

"First, you need to get your people to calm the hell down."

"Their terror is adding to the chaos of the Continuum?"

"Do you feel it?"

"The Continuum feeds on it."

"It can't help it. It *is* chaos. Searching for its own perfect order."

"And when it finds that perfect order?"

"Yes."

Omega.

Yes.

Chapter Twenty-four

ACHILLES

Kathryn Janeway rose from the table and crossed to the single
port in Eden's quarters. Her naked eye could not perceive the
massive contortions rippling through space and subspace,
but the occasional abrupt shift in the ship's motion assured her of
what her eyes could not.

She'd been alive again for only a few hours, but her body was
suddenly longing for a good sleep.

You can sleep when you're dead.

The next time you're dead.

Probably.

Mentally shaking herself, the admiral struggled to wrap her
brain around everything Eden had told her.

The first part of the story—Eden's life with her uncles and the many years during which she had lived with terrible uncertainty—had been provocative and a little sad. Eden's reactions to the Mikhal artifact and the Staff of Ren had been intriguing. The Doctor's review of his analysis of Eden's genome had taken Kathryn from intrigued to concerned. Their discoveries on the Mikhal Outpost were intellectually thrilling and tragic. Then Eden's story had veered into the realm of visions and dreams, which Kathryn found herself doubting. The admiral turned her attention to sorting through the puzzle pieces now laid out before her.

The most difficult to place was Eden's absolute certainty that when, in her dream, she had broken the representation of the anomaly the Anschlasom had discovered, she had also damaged the anomaly that the fleet had been studying, and this caused the ships to be trapped between two realities. Cambridge and the Doctor had valiantly tried to convince Eden that this was impossible. Their concerns seemed to be for her mental health, and given all they had just witnessed, that was understandable. Kathryn's questions were scientific: What was that damned anomaly? Could it be related to the darkness that was tormenting Q?

Turning back to Eden, who was pacing beside the table, Kathryn asked, "Forget what is possible and what isn't. What is your best guess as to how you are connected to this anomaly?"

Eden stopped and pulled herself to her full height. "Tallar and Jobin may not have known that they were seeking the Anschlasom, but I believe in my heart that all of those planets we searched when I was a child were failed attempts to find the location where the race that first disturbed *Som* finally came to rest."

"So, before you were born or—my apologies—created, they found evidence in or near Federation space of an anomaly similar to the one we have here. That sent them searching for the people who unintentionally created the anomaly?" Kathryn asked warily. Honestly, it was a huge leap to ponder, let alone accept, but then, she didn't know these men the way Eden did.

"Yes," Eden agreed. "They entered the anomaly and experienced it as a beautiful garden. From there, they went in search of those who had been there first."

"Which would suggest that if our ships have now accessed the anomaly, in the same way your uncles once did, there must be a way to free them. Your uncles obviously escaped and somewhere along the way encountered you. If they found a way out, the trapped vessels will too."

Cambridge interrupted the admiral. "Afsarah, you said that when you saw your uncles in the garden, when they reached for that glowing fruit on the tree, there was intense physical pain. That was *your* pain, wasn't it?"

Eden's brow furrowed as she tried to recapture the memory precisely. "It was. But it couldn't have been my pain. It must have been theirs. That light Tallar touched was a power, an essence of some kind, and whatever it communicated to him, I felt as extreme pain. If that is where he got his knowledge of the Anschlasom, even a fragment of it, I can assure you it would have been painful. Even I struggled with it in the cavern, learning their truth piece by piece."

"But the next thing you saw, if I'm following you," Cambridge went on, "was Tallar's face. You said he was still trapped there and that his sadness and desperation were what drove you to try and free him."

"Yes," Eden acknowledged.

"Well, both can't be true," Kathryn decided. "If they entered the anomaly, as you saw, and left, Tallar is not still trapped there. And if he is, they never left, which means they never found you. I'm inclined to accept the possibility that they did enter it once and escaped. I believe the last thing you saw, the image of Tallar you tried to save in a metaphorical fashion, was part of something else, something you have yet to fully understand."

"You might be right." Cambridge nodded. "Or you might be erring on the side of hope."

"I'd rather err on the side of hope, Counselor," Kathryn replied. "Working from there," she went on, "how do you fit into this, Captain? If your uncles discovered the anomaly before you were born, and spent the majority of their lives, once they found you, searching for the Anschlasom, it might be that you are actually connected to the Anschlasom. You might have been another piece of the puzzle for them. You seemed to believe that they were using you and your unique abilities to help them in their work. You also said that the Anschlasom's journey through the anomaly the first time impacted normal space in many places throughout the universe. You could be descended from that ancient race."

"No, she couldn't," the Doctor finally piped up, and all eyes immediately turned to him.

"Why not?" Cambridge asked with a trace of disappointment.

"You saw the images of the Anschlasom in the cavern, Counselor," the Doctor went on. "They weren't humanoid, let alone human."

"Or *perfectly* human," Eden added, taking no joy in the description.

"And you're all missing the most logical correlation of all of these events," the Doctor said.

"Which is?" Kathryn asked.

"Tallar and Jobin found and entered the anomaly, escaped, then found Captain Eden at some later point—or created her at some later point, for all we know, as a tool to aid them in their search. After they left her on Earth, they went back to the anomaly, where Tallar became trapped."

The admiral sighed, realizing in frustration that this could also make sense.

Turning to Eden, the Doctor said, "The pain you felt could have been theirs alone. Your sense of connection to the Anschlasom might simply be transference of the deep love you feel for your uncles."

"So, you believe she is not connected in any way to the people who left the artifacts?" Cambridge asked, aghast.

"Only through Tallar and Jobin"—the Doctor shrugged—"or through some sort of programming written into her DNA."

Cambridge looked at Eden. "They needed a different kind of human to help them find this race, so they made one and encoded a drive to find them into her DNA?"

At this, Eden raised her hands. "Tallar was a brilliant geneticist, but he could never have created me.

"And they didn't use me," she went on. "They loved me. They cherished me. My contributions to their efforts were minimal at best. If they had been capable of anything as deviant and horrifying as creating a human from whole cloth to serve their needs, they would never have abandoned me until their search was complete, would they?"

"No," Kathryn agreed. She didn't doubt that humans were capable of sinking to the depths the Doctor had suggested. History was littered with many who had done worse. But this description did not track with Eden's memories of her uncles.

A chime at the door preceded a call from Commander Drafar.

"*Fleet Commander?*"

"Yes," Eden said.

"*May I come in?*"

Eden paused, looking directly at Kathryn, who was certain they were sharing the same thought: *He knows.*

"Enter," Eden said decisively, and moments later, he did so.

"Fleet Commander," Drafar began as he stopped just inside her quarters. Kathryn could have sworn she glimpsed a few security officers behind him when the door had hissed shut. Turning to face Kathryn, he went on, "We seem to have an intruder aboard whom you have chosen to harbor, rather than alerting me to her presence."

"As is my prerogative," Eden replied.

"Certainly," the commander said, without agreeing. Kathryn could understand his frustration, but this was one of those situations when rank had privileges. "Had you not been displaying behavior which, to my mind, bordered on unstable previous to this, I would have been content to allow the matter to drop."

"Unstable?" Cambridge asked incredulously.

"After boarding this ship, you required it to take you to a location of no tactical significance to our current mission, you refused to advise me of your reasons, and you then proceeded to leave this vessel without following the standard protocol of telling anyone where you were going or when you intended to return. Shortly after you returned, you requested that the sick-bay be cleared. Almost immediately thereafter, another human was somehow transported into the sickbay without activating any of our internal alarms or setting off an intruder alert. For the last several hours, that individual has been in continuous contact with you. You failed to advise me. Only our most recent standard internal sensor sweep revealed the presence of this intruder."

"We're not plotting a mutiny, if that's what you're worried about," Cambridge quipped.

"Forgive me, Counselor, but my understanding of the events surrounding the departure of Admiral Batiste from this fleet, and Fleet Commander Eden's previous relationship to him, as well as the extraordinary series of events I have just related, make it impossible for me to exclude any conceivable explanation for Captain Eden's actions."

"I'm sorry, Tillum," Eden said honestly. "But the simple fact of the matter is that there isn't anything in the rule books to cover this."

He seemed surprised by her words, but remained hesitant to give her the benefit of the doubt.

"Commander Tillum Drafar, meet Vice Admiral Kathryn Janeway," Eden said.

With her most deferential smile, Kathryn stepped forward at this and offered Drafar her hand. He did not immediately accept it.

"The recently deceased Admiral Kathryn Janeway?" he asked.

"Yes." Kathryn nodded. "It's a pleasure, Commander," she said, wondering how far professional courtesy was going to get her with this one.

Drafar turned to the Doctor. "Assuming your ethical sub-routines have not been tampered with in any way, which is also not outside the realm of possibility, have you confirmed this, Doctor?"

"I have," he sighed, "and will gladly forward my report to you for further study."

"Please do so at once," Drafar replied.

"As to the rest, Commander," Eden continued, "although my actions may seem inexplicable, that is not your concern. If a time should come when I feel it is appropriate or necessary to provide you with further details, I will do so. Until then, Admiral Janeway's presence here is classified. Please advise any of your crew members who have seen your internal sensor scans of this." As if that should settle it, Eden continued, "What is our current status?"

Kathryn smiled faintly. Despite the magnitude of the issues before her, Eden remained calm and in control. It shouldn't have been surprising, but was definitely reassuring and obviously had the intended effect on Drafar.

"We have reached sensor range of the trapped ships and ascertained that over seven hundred remain alive in the visible areas of the vessels. My people are currently working on rescue scenarios."

Eden looked as if someone had just punched her in the stomach. "That's less than half of the total crew complement of those four ships," she said softly.

"The greatest losses were sustained by *Esquiline, Hawking,* and *Curie,* which appeared to have entered the anomaly in a head-on orientation. *Quirinal*'s losses are significantly less, as they apparently had turned to run before they were pulled in. Their nacelles and rear shuttle and cargo areas are lost, but the areas of heaviest crew concentration remain intact."

Eden nodded somberly, saying, "Thank you, Commander."

"We must find a way to get them off those ships," he replied. "It appears that the ships are moving further into their respective fissures. *Hawking*'s case is the most urgent. Communication, to date, is not possible through the numerous forms of interference being generated, though we are also working to rectify that. Our scans show that all remaining personnel seem to be located in the areas of their ships that are farthest from the boundaries separating normal space from the anomaly. It seems likely that their commanders know what is happening and are doing what they can to see to the safety of their remaining crew members."

"What about transporters?" Kathryn asked automatically.

Eden turned to her sharply, and Kathryn shrugged it off.

"Transporters are functional, but not optimal," Drafar reported. "Apart from the interference, which could easily disrupt any beam-out, there is the matter of where to safely house more than six hundred additional people on a ship currently manned at capacity. Our resources are vast, but not infinite."

"That won't be a problem," Kathryn corrected him.

Eden beat Drafar to the punch by asking, "How so?"

"Several years ago, *Voyager* traveled through an area of space controlled by an extremely inhospitable species known as the Devore," Kathryn began.

Eden's eyes widened and a smile creased her lips.

"The telepathic refugees?" Eden asked.

Kathryn nodded, pleased that Eden's knowledge of her ship's previous exploits appeared to be at her fingertips.

"But can our transporter buffers hold that number of people safely, let alone run the necessary continuous reintegration protocols?" Eden asked.

"I don't know," Kathryn replied honestly. "I've been away for a while and haven't seen this ship's specs."

"Commander, alert your technicians to prioritize optimizing your transporters to receive all of the survivors," Eden ordered. "Your second priority is the comm system. We need to alert the crews, in advance, of our rescue efforts, but even if we can't, we will proceed."

Drafar's mind was clearly racing with possibilities, and to his credit, he understood Eden's idea without further explanation. "You intend to transport the officers directly into the buffers and leave them there?"

"Correct." Eden nodded. "And we need to get as many as we can with every single transport."

At this, Drafar smiled. "I believe a number of modifications

Fleet Chief Torres just made to our industrial transporters will aid us toward that end. If you will excuse me, I will begin the necessary preparations."

QUIRINAL

Regina Farkas felt relief as she came to main engineering and saw several of her crew scurrying about just outside the open doors. They were running cable to numerous control interfaces that were in the process of being activated outside of their normal housings within engineering.

"Just do the best you can," Lieutenant Bryce's assured voice rang out over the din of the hurried activities as he peeked his head out the door to check the status of his engineers.

"Lieutenant," Farkas called crisply. The engineer looked her way with bright eyes and an impish flicker of a smile.

"Good to see you, Captain. I figured you'd be down here when you didn't hear from us. We've been doing what we can to restore communications with the bridge, but it's proving to be quite a challenge." He gestured to the melee around him. "The interference from the barrier is scrambling everything. I'm trying to salvage what we can for as long as we can."

"Excellent work," Farkas replied. "How far into engineering does the barrier reach?"

"Not far, yet," Bryce replied, "but it's creeping forward with every passing hour. By my calculations we have less than twenty hours before it hits the core and we lose engineering . . ."

". . . and the ship," Farkas noted.

"Probably," Bryce agreed.

"Is there any way to halt its progress?" Farkas asked.

"None that I've found so far," Bryce replied. "We're still working on it. Since we don't know what triggered the anomaly's fracture in the first place, my number one priority is that I don't do anything to increase its rate of destabilization."

"Do you know what it is and when we can began to study it?"

"No," Bryce admitted. "But it is a hell of a thing to behold."

Farkas shivered involuntarily at this. "Let's take a look then."

"Captain?" Denisov said sharply.

"Don't worry, Gregor," Farkas attempted to calm the security officer. "I'm not going to get too close. I just want to see it."

"Is it safe for the captain to approach?" Denisov demanded of Bryce.

"My people have been working within ten meters of it, and they seem no worse for wear," Bryce replied.

"Did you lose anyone in the impact?" the captain asked.

Bryce nodded, and the boyish charm drained from his face. "Costa, Miller, and Fredericks," he replied. "They were stationed at the aft control panels. It all happened so fast, they probably didn't know which way to run."

"Then engines are still intact?"

"For now." Bryce nodded. "But without the nacelles, which were almost completely lost, they're not much use to us."

"Understood," Farkas said and, turning to Denisov, added, "You're welcome to join us."

"Where you go, I go, Captain," Denisov replied.

"Bryce," Farkas said, gesturing for him to lead the way.

As they entered main engineering, the din of the hallway gave way to silence. Only a few engineers remained inside, working quickly and quietly. From time to time, one of those remaining at their stations would throw a furtive glance over one shoulder, as if expecting to be attacked from behind. As Farkas got her first look at the barrier, she understood their discomfort.

It appeared that the rear of engineering, several meters beyond the central slipstream drive assembly and warp core, was a work in progress. Everything visible was complete and functioning, but it was as if a thick black curtain had been dropped vertically from the overhead to the deck at the far end, creating the illusion that the rest of engineering had yet to be constructed.

The effect was both mesmerizing and ominous. Farkas found it difficult to tear her eyes away from the emptiness. It was so terrifying she felt it could engulf her. She found herself taking short, rapid breaths.

Bryce soon spoke up. "It's weird, isn't it?"

"That's one word for it," Farkas agreed.

"It's doing a hell of a job on our sensors, but for the life of me I can't tell you how or why. All the readings we *can* get say there is nothing there."

"Is it solid?" Farkas asked semi-seriously.

"I don't know," Bryce replied. "I didn't think touching it would be a good idea."

"Any readings from the ship beyond it?" Farkas asked. She had nursed the hope that here at ground zero, she might get some data.

"No," Bryce replied, "but it's hard to believe it's not still there."

"Or we wouldn't still be here?" Farkas asked.

"That's my thinking," Bryce agreed.

"Captain Farkas?" a harried young ensign called from the doorway.

"What is it, Ensign?" she asked.

"We've established a communications relay to the bridge, and Commander Roach wishes to speak with you."

Farkas started to tap her combadge but realized immediately that it wasn't working down here. Hurrying toward the door, she was led to a small screen angled against a bulkhead with several coils of ODN running from its back. Several rows of text were displayed on the screen, ending with the words, *"Please advise when you are ready to proceed."*

"*Text?*" Farkas asked.

"It's the best we can do, Captain," the ensign replied. "I'll be happy to relay your side of the conversation."

"Good work, Ensign." Nodding gratefully, Farkas said, "Go ahead, Commander."

After a few moments, her first officer's reply began to appear on the screen. The ensign read it to her dutifully. *"We have received an answer to our distress call from* Achilles. *Incoming message is text only. They advise us to prepare for transport."*

The ensign looked to the captain with visible relief, awaiting her response.

Farkas ordered, "Acknowledge it. Alert all personnel in safe locations to remain where they are. Advise all others to proceed to the nearest safety zones."

Turning to Bryce, she added, "That includes you and your team, Lieutenant." He started to refuse, but the captain raised a hand to silence him. "No buts, Lieutenant. The thirty seconds I just spent looking into that thing was more than enough to convince me that we're not going to beat it, and we're sure as hell not going to join it. If we're going to learn about that thing, it will be from a ship that is intact."

"Understood, Captain," Bryce replied, though his disappointment was obvious.

"Good man." Farkas smiled. "I'll see you aboard *Achilles*. We'll figure out our next move from there."

HAWKING

Lieutenant Vorik stared at the display panel, suppressing a feeling of relief that washed through him at the message from *Achilles*. The blue glow of *Hawking*'s warp core was the only illumination in main engineering. As he was the only one on duty, there was no one present to witness an emotional lapse. He knew the thirty-two other Vulcans still alive aboard the *Hawking* would sense his loss of control, and as the senior officer and new commander of the ship, he refused to allow that.

The *Hawking*'s entrance into the anomaly had swallowed almost the entire ship, apart from engineering and some of the lower shuttle and cargo spaces. Vorik had worked diligently to assess the damage and see to the crew's safety. All command controls had been routed to his station in engineering, where he did all he could to protect the warp core. The rest of the crew had been evacuated to the cargo bay. A secondary control interface had been established in the event Vorik's was lost.

During the last two hours the *Hawking* had slipped 9.2 meters farther into the void. Vorik estimated that the inky blackness consuming his ship was thirty-eight minutes from contact with the warp core. He presumed that at that point, the ship would be immediately destroyed.

The Vulcan had erected a level-ten force field around the core, but given that the anomaly had digested the ship's much more powerful shields, he didn't expect it to hold. Vorik knew that his only chance for continued existence lay in rescue by one of the other fleet vessels. What readings he could get indicated that the *Esquiline, Quirinal,* and *Curie* were all trapped, although not as deeply as the *Hawking*. His hopes were pinned on the *Achilles* or *Voyager,* who would no doubt respond to their distress calls.

With icy but calm fingers, he immediately forwarded the message from *Achilles* to the crew in the cargo bay. The Vulcan replied to the *Achilles* that the *Hawking* crew awaited immediate transport.

Taking control of his emotions, Vorik waited for *Achilles*. He looked forward to the opportunity to reflect with his entire consciousness upon the loss of Captain Itak. His mentor, along with more than half of the crew, had been lost upon impact with the anomaly. Vorik intended to make it a personal priority to honor the dead.

Just as soon as he had seen to the safety of the living.

ACHILLES

Afsarah Eden wondered when, exactly, she had become so effective at compartmentalizing her life. The captain knew she had taken great leaps forward in this regard when her marriage had collapsed. But, she secretly suspected that it had begun the moment she had left the company of her uncles.

The captain stood waiting in the largest cargo bay on the *Achilles*. Commander Drafar and his four senior transport officers were working to acquire a stable lock on the crews of the four vessels. A smattering of crew members hurried back and forth, making necessary adjustments to the transporter systems on the fly. For now, Eden had set aside the fact that she had learned her very existence was a mystery surrounded by a puzzle encased in an enigma. She refused to examine Kathryn Janeway's resurrection and the admiral's news of a potential universal catastrophe that still needed averting. Eden was concentrating only on the task at hand. There was a chance that the seven hundred sixteen lives could be saved; *that* was the only thing she would allow herself to think about.

Commander Drafar had immediately seen the potential in Admiral Janeway's suggested use of the transporters and set to work modifying the transport protocols. He had personally overseen the modifications to the transport buffers, where the patterns of those they saved would be stored indefinitely. It would be necessary to begin to rematerialize them at regular intervals in order to maintain the stability of their patterns until permanent living arrangements could be made. It was still an open question as to how long more than seven hundred patterns could be safely stored, but less than half an hour after Janeway's suggestion, Drafar had confirmed that he was ready to begin the transports.

"With your permission, Fleet Commander, we will begin with the crew members aboard *Curie*," he said, once all was in readiness.

"Do it," Eden replied. She believed that the *Curie* had been selected because at thirty-one, this was the smallest group they would attempt to transport at one time. Minimal communications had been established with the four ships, and all had indicated they stood ready for transport at *Achilles'* discretion.

Eden watched as Drafar rechecked his controls, for what she hoped was the last time, and with a sharp inhale said, "Lieutenant Cates, is our transporter lock on *Curie*'s survivors stable?"

"Yes, sir."

"Initiate transport."

Eden felt the moment should have been accompanied by the sound of rising strings and percussion. Instead, a high beep was followed by a shrill ascending whine.

"Watch the annular confinement, Lieutenant," Drafar barked as Cates worked his console with great deliberation.

"Aye, sir," Cates replied.

Eden watched as the signal widened briefly and quickly snapped back into the optimal zone.

A few moments of silence, and Cates said calmly, "Transport successful."

Eden allowed herself a small internal celebration before asking, "Are their patterns stable within the buffers?"

"Yes, sir," Drafar replied.

"Keep going," Eden ordered.

"Ensign Chase, is your lock on *Hawking*'s survivors stable?" Drafar inquired tonelessly.

"Aye, Captain."

"Initiate transport."

The operation was midway through completion when an alarm suddenly blared from Chase's panel.

"What's that?" Eden demanded as both Chase's and Drafar's fingers quickened their pace at their respective controls.

The *Achilles* captain was the first to report: "The *Hawking* is slipping farther into the anomaly. We are attempting to compensate."

Eden wanted to order him to hurry, but refrained, knowing that he was doing all he could. A few tense seconds later, the confinement beam controls stabilized and the deed was done. Before Eden could ask the question, Drafar said, "Confirm your count, Ensign Chase."

Chase's fingers finally began to shake as he replied, "Twenty, sir. We only got twenty."

"There were thirty-three signals aboard *Hawking*?" Eden asked.

"Yes," Drafar replied, his voice thick and heavy. "The twenty we did recover are safely stored. *Hawking* has now slipped completely into the anomaly," he added.

Another ship lost, Eden's conscience reminded her. Her heart began to pound at this unthinkable new reality, but she refused to give her grave disappointment any rein.

"*Esquiline* is next," she said evenly. "Let's get to it."

Drafar nodded.

Five minutes later, and with no further complications, the

one hundred fifty-nine of *Esquiline*'s crew and the four hundred ninety-three of *Quirinal*'s were safely transported and stored.

"Well done," Drafar congratulated his staff, before moving on to the next phase of the operation. "Lieutenant Cates, prepare to initiate materialization of the first ten signals retrieved from *Curie* for stabilization."

"Belay that," Eden said quickly, then added, "Commander Drafar, a word?"

He stared down at her with a glare that could have melted tritanium, but followed her from the transporter controls and stood at attention.

"Before we began, *Voyager* was detected on long-range sensors," Eden said with more confidence than she felt.

"They were," Drafar replied.

"Make best possible speed to intercept them. As soon as they are within communications range, alert Captain Chakotay that we have recovered all of the crew aboard those four ships, and to expect transport of four directly to my quarters."

Commander Drafar was attempting to maintain his composure, but his bafflement at her priorities was clear.

"Once that is done, you will move *Achilles* beyond the effects of the anomaly, engage your slipstream engines, and set course for the Alpha Quadrant. As soon as you are in range, you will provide a full report to Starfleet Command of the fleet's condition, which I have prepared, and await their orders for the stored personnel."

Drafar's confusion passed, as her intentions became clear to him.

"Maintaining the stability of the seven hundred and three patterns you are storing is my highest priority. Right now, *Achilles* is in harm's way and I am unwilling to risk a single additional life lost to this madness. Your buffers will remain stable for the time it will take to complete the transfer of personnel to *Voyager*. Once you are again in open space you will begin the materialization rotations, and you will execute them continuously until Starfleet Command provides you with a means to off-load your new passengers."

"And once we have returned to the Alpha Quadrant?" Drafar asked, this time more gently.

"Await further instructions," Eden replied. "I don't know how this is going to end, but by the time you could return to us, I'm willing to bet your assistance will no longer be required. The fleet has lost two, and now possibly five, of our original complement. I am certain Command will want to weigh in on our mission in the Delta Quadrant once this situation is resolved."

"What of the *Galen* and *Demeter*?" Drafar asked.

"That's my concern, Commander. Get the twelve hundred lives now in your hands safely home."

"Aye, sir." Drafar nodded solemnly.

Eden nodded briskly, then turned to leave him to it. Before she had taken two steps, Drafar said, "Fleet Commander?"

"Yes?"

"May the stars guide you in peace."

Eden didn't recognize the saying, but assumed it was a Lendrin benediction. It communicated fully his understanding of the peril she was now facing, and his sincere hope that she would succeed in her efforts. Whatever doubts he might still harbor about her orders, she knew he understood how she felt toward her people and the lengths she would go to to ensure their safety.

"And you as well," Eden replied.

Interlude

OMEGA CONTINUUM

"How many do you consider stable, Itak?"

"Seven hundred eighty-five of our people are now one with the Continuum. Of those, three hundred ninety-one are still cognizant of who they are and what has happened. They confront their new reality with courage and grace, including you, Xin."

"And the others?"

"Our efforts continue."

"If what you've just said is true, it may not matter."

"Preserving the dignity of every mind is a duty we will not shirk, whatever the conclusion."

"Do you believe this man Tallar?"

"Deception is not possible here. His mental fortitude in the face of Omega is astonishing. It is born of his devotion to those he considers his family. I have seen what his garden once was. But I have also listened closely to Omega."

"I still don't understand. How can this be Omega? Starfleet knows Omega. Its destructive capabilities are massive, but nothing on the order you are suggesting."

"Starfleet knows Omega's shadow, a synthetic particle whose power dwarfs any known energy source. This place is the continuum of pure Omega. It is the truth that lies beyond the theoretical particle. It is no coincidence that the area of destabilization through which Tallar entered Omega lies in our Beta Quadrant, near the Lantaru sector."

"If we do nothing, Omega will continue to expand into normal space-time, eventually destroying all of it?"

"This is Omega's nature. It is the predetermined end toward which the universe irrevocably moves. The Omega Continuum is in its infancy, and were it not for our intrusion would still be countless centuries from its release and the concurrent destruction and rebirth of a new universe. The weak point we unintentionally exploited has altered Omega's timetable. Unless we act, and quite soon, to seal this area of destabilization, Omega will continue to expand, and what should have existed for trillions of years will be extinguished within a relative blink."

"Why didn't Tallar's breach have the same effect upon Omega?"

"The mass and energy we have brought into the Continuum is an ocean compared to Tallar's drop of water. His actions have undoubtedly hastened the universe's end, but not by a statistically significant margin. The same cannot be said of our vessels and their crews."

"Couldn't all of us join Tallar in the garden? Destroying our ships is possible, clearly necessary. But must we sacrifice our lives as well?"

"I cannot make this decision for you, Xin. You are the keeper of your own life and the lives of your crew. However, to spare the rest of the universe, I will not hesitate to do what must be done."

"And Captain Dasht?"

"Despite my best efforts, I cannot focus his concentration sufficiently for him to comprehend the magnitude of this decision. His chief engineer, Lieutenant Derek Waverly, retains his faculties, and the decision for the *Esquiline* will be his."

"There is a young ensign aboard *Quirinal,* Sadie Johns. I found her once, and though she is terrified, the ensign has mastered her fear and could act for her ship."

"I would suggest you, I, Waverly, and Johns meet again with Tallar in his garden."

"For your plan to succeed, Tallar would also have to destroy his vessel."

"Yes."

"Do you believe he will do so?"

"He understands what is at stake and would not, I believe, willingly risk the lives of every creature in the known universe to continue the life he has come to despise."

"We are also deciding for those who are still on board our ships in normal space-time? They will have no say in our choice."

"My ship, the *Hawking,* was pulled completely into Omega. Thirty-three of my crew were not on board during the shift."

"You believe they were rescued by the rest of the fleet?"

"That would be the logical assumption."

"Very well. I will find Ensign Johns."

"And I will locate Lieutenant Waverly."

"And how do I find the garden?"

"Decide it is there, and it will be."

"Itak?"

"Yes, Xin."

"How did we get here? What brought Omega into normal space in the first place?"

"I do not know, nor does Tallar. It is a question that has plagued him for most of his life. For him it remains unanswered, and when he ceases to exist it will surely be his most poignant regret."

"Just decide? Decide the garden is there?"

"And it will be."

Chapter Twenty-five

VOYAGER

Captain Chakotay paced the floor of his ready room like a caged tiger. For more than thirty-six hours the image of *Quirinal, Esquiline, Hawking,* and *Curie* hanging fragmented, trapped in space, had not left his mind's eye. Unable to form a stable warp field or use maximum impulse for more than a few minutes, *Voyager* clawed its way to the site in maddeningly small increments. Constant course corrections were needed. The entire senior staff was showing the strain. Everyone had maintained their professionalism despite the burden they all carried. Hundreds of lives depended upon their ability to safely and quickly mount a rescue.

Desperate to do *some*thing, Chakotay had instructed Seven and Patel to focus their efforts on a thorough analysis of the anomaly. Their latest report enumerated in stuporous detail all of the possibilities they had eliminated from consideration of what the anomaly was, but it contained nothing that might be helpful in restoring the trapped ships to normal space. *The anomaly be damned.* All Chakotay cared about was rescuing those ships.

The *Achilles* had reached the trapped vessels, rescued the crews who had remained in normal space, and had reversed course to intercept *Voyager*. Chakotay hoped that they might already have discovered something his staff had failed to coax from the extremely limited data available. Surely, their next move was to mount a joint rescue mission to restore the ships to normal space.

"Donner to Captain Chakotay."

"Go ahead," Chakotay replied to his senior transport officer.

"Captain Eden and her party are in her quarters. The fleet commander has asked that you join them there immediately."

"Acknowledged," Chakotay replied, hurrying to the door and passing swiftly through the bridge.

"When was the last time you left your post?" the familiar, yet unexpected voice of Cambridge demanded of Seven. The answer was thirty-seven hours, twenty-nine minutes, and eight seconds, but the frustration Seven felt, coupled with her ongoing struggle to remain focused while her body was screaming for rest, left her unwilling to grant the counselor anything.

"Why are you here?" she asked instead, without even turning to greet him. While she awaited his response, she continued to review the latest sensor reports of new fractures to the anomaly and map their likely event horizons through the region of space which *Voyager* had most recently traveled. "Surely someone somewhere requires your attention," she added, in case he was about to decide to be intentionally obtuse.

"I missed you too," Cambridge replied, stepping beside her and placing a hand on the console she was operating as near hers as he dared.

At this, Seven did turn to glance at him. She had observed him in numerous states of being in the few months they had worked together. The most common was the maddening and often condescending composure in which he spent the majority of his conscious hours. She had seen that composure strained when he lost himself in a particularly challenging problem, his petulance in performing tasks he felt were beneath him, and his impatience when he felt others were performing beneath their own capabilities.

But only once had she witnessed actual wonder from him,

and though she might now never tell him, that moment had been pivotal in her decision to risk a more intimate relationship with him. It had actually taken place in this room, the first time they had discovered the creature who later came to be identified as the "mother" of the Children of the Storm. In witnessing the birth of dozens of new thoughts from the entity, and Seven's struggle to describe it, she had caught a glimpse of a capacity for genuine astonishment in him. That brief sense of what truly lay beneath his carefully crafted façade had intrigued Seven and left her determined to explore its depth and breadth.

As she looked at him now, she was surprised to see that same oddly charming openness clear in his eyes.

"Has the universe done something in the last few days you weren't expecting?" she asked.

"Apart from opening itself up and swallowing half our fleet?" he asked, without a trace of flippancy, then added, "Actually it has, but you wouldn't believe me if I told you."

Seven considered for a moment whether or not the magnitude of this tragedy might have unlocked his soft center, but quickly dismissed the notion. The carnage before them was massive, but nothing compared to what the Federation had suffered only a few months earlier.

"What is it?" Seven asked, now favoring him with her full attention, her scans forgotten for the first time in more than a day.

Cambridge's eyes left hers and gently moved over the rest of her face, as if he were trying to memorize it. As they did, a faint smile teased the corners of his mouth.

"You've stood here without rest or sustenance ever since you first learned of this tragedy, haven't you?" he asked, with something approaching reverence.

"You already know the answer to that," Seven replied. "Have you come to chastise me for not taking better care of myself when hundreds of our fellow officers require the best efforts I can possibly give them?"

"No," he said, shaking his head slowly. "I've come because I couldn't bear to allow another moment to pass without seeing you again. And because I wanted to be sure I wasn't wrong about something while I still have the chance."

"Explain."

Cambridge's smile widened. "I can't believe I missed it, but until now, I did. Of course it's your fault. With so many fascinating topics to explore, we've still missed one of the most significant."

Seven's deep sigh was enough to force him to clarify without being asked.

"You're so like her."

"Who?" Seven demanded.

Cambridge didn't answer. Instead, he cupped her chin in his right hand and drew her close. Despite the fact that Seven still had no idea who he was talking about, she stopped caring the moment their lips touched. The split second they parted, however, the brief spell was broken and the weight of the duty she had momentarily abandoned returned with crushing force.

"It is inappropriate for us to engage in personal recreation while . . ." she began until he raised a gentle hand to stop her.

"You're right, of course," he nodded. "I'll leave you to it," he added and turned to go. "I'll be back shortly."

Only once the doors had slid shut behind him did she realize that he had never answered her question. This was difficult to set aside, but after a few moments, she managed to return her full concentration to her scans.

As soon as the turbolift halted on Deck 3, Chakotay moved double-quick to Captain Eden's quarters. His slowed his pace when he saw Eden and the Doctor waiting for him in the corridor. That was puzzling, but the looks on their faces as he approached only added to the mystery.

"Captain?" he asked.

"Chakotay." Eden nodded stiffly.

When she offered no explanation, he asked, "Are we holding briefings in the halls now?"

"No," Eden replied. He could see the weight of the disaster written on her face, along with something else. *Fear, perhaps?*

"Then, shall we?" Chakotay asked as he moved toward the door.

"Forgive me," Eden replied, holding up a firm hand to halt his progress. "As you know, the *Achilles* was able to retrieve almost all of the crew aboard the *Quirinal, Esquiline, Hawking,* and *Curie* that were unaffected by their vessels' entry into the anomaly. They were able to do so by storing the patterns of those they rescued in their transport buffers. I have ordered them to set course for the Alpha Quadrant to preserve those lives, since none of our remaining vessels can, even temporarily, quarter that many people."

This struck Chakotay with the force of a blow, but he nodded, quickly deciding that he would probably have reached the same conclusion.

"Our next priority is to prevent further spread of the anomaly's destructive potential and, if possible, to rescue our ships."

Chakotay might have reversed the order of those two agenda items, but was otherwise in complete agreement.

"Right now, I need you to meet with the individual who is waiting for you in my quarters. In one hour, I expect both of you to join the senior staff in the briefing room, where we will discuss how to proceed."

As Cambridge was not standing in the hall, Chakotay assumed the counselor had something to discuss with him privately, but this odd protocol in arranging a meeting was unnerving. Chakotay was further disconcerted when the Doctor said, quite seriously, "I'll be waiting right here in case you need me."

"Has something happened to Hugh?" Chakotay asked.

"He's fine," Eden replied. "I'll see you in an hour."

Chakotay nodded and stepped forward, activating the door's floor sensor. Whatever Cambridge had to tell him, Chakotay hoped it would justify both Captain Eden's and the Doctor's odd behavior.

In the few minutes Kathryn Janeway had been pacing the unfathomably large quarters reserved for the fleet commander, she had found it impossible to find a comfortable place to sit and await Chakotay's arrival. That a suite of rooms created for any single officer on a ship *Voyager*'s size would have consisted of this much square footage was ridiculous. That it contained not a single comfortable chair bordered on criminal.

She was nervous. There was no getting around it. The Doctor told her what he knew of Chakotay's reaction to her death, and his recitation had troubled her deeply. On the one hand, she would have been hurt had her passing not been met with grief. But that anything could have brought about such a radical shift in Chakotay's temperament, especially at a time when Starfleet's needs were so great, mystified her. Despite the Doctor's assurances that Chakotay had recently recovered his equilibrium and mended fences with all of their closest friends, Kathryn had no idea what to expect from him now, or *who* was about to walk through that door.

Since the moment she had returned, Kathryn had been impatient to see Chakotay. Now, she wished she could postpone this meeting until the crisis she had come to avert had passed. There was so much to do, and so little time in which to do it. But before their work could begin, Chakotay, along with the rest of his senior staff, must learn the truth. She hoped they would greet this new reality with the same relief and joy the Doctor had expressed. Why she suddenly doubted that this would be the case, she couldn't say.

So focused was she on Chakotay's imminent arrival, Kathryn missed the bright flash of light that accompanied Q's return. She had been standing, facing a large wooden desk, her hands resting on its edge, attempting to collect her thoughts. When she lifted her eyes, Q was seated opposite her in the desk's high-backed leather chair, his arms behind his head and his feet crossed on the desktop.

"So, Kathy," he asked without a hint of warmth, "how's coming back to life treating you?"

Immediately, Kathryn stepped back, as if to ward off an attack, but Q seemed to consider her patiently, almost compassionately.

"Leave. Now," she ordered, unable to deal with whatever fresh hell he was about to unleash upon her.

He responded by dropping his feet and leaning forward, planting his elbows on the desk and resting his face in his hands. "Don't say I didn't warn you."

"Warn me? About what?"

Q snapped his fingers, and instantly the view of stars that had filled the ports behind him was replaced by the sight of three of the fleet's ships hanging dead in space. She briefly worried that he had moved *Voyager* to make his point, but the absence of the vibration of the impulse engines beneath her feet dispelled the illusion. He was tormenting her, but not placing the ship in immediate danger.

Once this was settled in her mind, she considered the point of his little display.

"You think *this* is my fault?" she asked incredulously.

"There's always a price," he reminded her.

Kathryn wanted to turn away, to run from the possibility that her choice might have caused this catastrophe. Instead, she remained resolutely still and said, "That may be, but *this* is more likely a symptom of the problem your son has asked me to help him solve than any sort of cosmic retribution."

Q shrugged as if he might actually agree with her. At his nonchalance, a new and truly horrible thought crossed Kathryn's mind. "Come to think of it," she went on, "this whole thing practically reeks of your particular brand of meddling. A completely inexplicable anomaly appears and nearly swallows four of our vessels whole? Tell me you didn't arrange all of this as some sort of ridiculous demonstration just to prove your perverted point."

"Is it always about you, Kathy?" Q asked, unmoved by her suggestion.

The glare she directed at him might have obliterated any lesser being on the spot.

Sitting back, Q allowed, "I'll admit, this does bear the faint fragrance of omnipotent action, but not ours."

"Do you know what this thing is?" Kathryn demanded.

"Haven't a clue."

"Would you tell me if you did?"

"I would," Q replied, and much as she hated to admit it, she believed him.

"Space, subspace, and, for all we know, time itself have been ripped to shreds around this place and you're not even a little curious about what's happened here?" Kathryn asked in disbelief.

"I've got a lot on my mind right now," he said, his tone a bit sharper.

"So you just came here to, what, gloat?" she asked.

"No," Q said. Snapping his fingers, in a flash he was standing beside her. "I came here to find out what you and my son think you're doing."

At this, Kathryn smiled. "You can't find him."

"I haven't found him yet," he corrected her.

"And you think *I* know where he is?"

"If anyone does," Q acknowledged, with evident reluctance.

"Sorry." She shrugged, crossing her arms. "But I'm curious, how often do the Q ask a mere mortal for assistance with anything?"

"More often than you might imagine, Kathy," Q replied, softening somewhat.

"Well, my dance card is pretty full right now, so if you aren't here to help me, then just move along," Kathryn insisted.

"As soon as you tell me why my son saw fit to risk his very existence in order to bring you back from the dead. His mother has a sense of why," he went on, "but her understanding is woefully inadequate."

Kathryn sighed. She honestly didn't know if including Q when his son was determined to avoid his father's interference would help or hinder. Still, she was willing to risk it if it brought them closer to the answers they required. "He didn't tell me where he was going, but it had something to do with the Q formerly known as Amanda Rogers."

"What are you talking about? Amanda who?"

"This is part of the problem," Kathryn continued. "Something quite dramatic in the nature of your Continuum, of the entire multiverse, has changed. Q believes it happened as a result of the alteration of the timeline that brought *Voyager* back from the Delta Quadrant earlier than was originally the case. One of the changes has to do with a Q who was born of two of your people who had forsaken the Continuum, to live as humans. Amanda had become quite close to your son, but as of quite recently, apparently no longer exists."

"That's preposterous," Q said dismissively.

"That a Q could cease to exist?"

"That any Q would forsake the Continuum to become human."

"Okay," Kathryn replied, shaking her head. "If *that's* really your primary concern, I honestly can't help you."

"I know who they were, the ingrates," Q acknowledged. "But they never had a child." He mused, "He'd be looking for concrete evidence of her existence."

"And how it ties in to the issue of his sense that very soon, he, too, might cease to exist." Kathryn revealed, "He's certain that whatever is causing this is tied to something my ship discovered in the Delta Quadrant—the first time we were here—and something we didn't discover when our journey was cut short. An anomaly that could swallow a starship, let alone four, could be a likely candidate, which is why anything you can tell me about what's happened—" She was interrupted by the sound of the door behind her hissing open.

Kathryn turned automatically to see Chakotay step into the dimly lit room. He stared first at her, then at Q, then turned back to her in utter shock.

Before she could say anything, Q's voice came from behind her. "Impossible as it might be to imagine at such a moment, there's actually someplace more important I have to be right now."

Kathryn assumed that the faint flash of light reflected in Chakotay's eyes heralded Q's departure. For her part, she could not tear hers away from Chakotay's face.

Chapter Twenty-six

VOYAGER

Chakotay took in the scene before him: Kathryn and Q standing in front of Afsarah's desk. His mind remained stubbornly frozen, absolutely unable to accept what he was seeing. Kathryn looked almost exactly as she had the last time he'd seen her, wearing her admiral's uniform, her hair pulled into a slightly disheveled bun. The look on her face was filled with fear tinged with joyful hope, and her eyes greedily searched his for recognition and acceptance.

The first emotion to surface as his brain sluggishly worked to make sense of this scene was white-hot anger. Q said something Chakotay didn't really hear over the white noise filling his head, and then vanished. This thing that had assumed Kathryn's form stepped tentatively forward. It might have said his name, but the rage pouring through him halted her.

"Q!" Chakotay bellowed. "Show yourself again, you coward!"

A faint utterance from this "thing" barely registered. "I know you're still here! How dare you! How . . . ?" he roared, momentarily unable to find words for the depth of Q's cruelty in bringing this "thing" before him. When his outrage failed to humiliate Q into returning, he tried another tack. "I used to think that even the Q had some standards of decency! But this . . . ? What sort of beast are you?"

"Chakotay!" the "thing" commanded him. It held up both hands before him, palms out in a universally recognized gesture of surrender, and again began to creep slowly toward him.

He flinched, backing up a few paces as it continued to stalk him.

"Stay the hell away from me," he spat harshly. "I don't know what you are or why you're doing this, but . . ."

"Chakotay, it's me."

"Shut up!" he shouted, his anger only fueled by the "thing's" attempt to placate him. "Kathryn Janeway is dead. Whatever you are, you aren't . . ." but further words were consumed by the grief still raw at the center of his being, now forcing its way through his righteous fury.

"Please," she begged, as her eyes began to glisten.

Feeling his gorge rise and unable to continue to look at the thing who was so like and yet could not be his beloved Kathryn, he turned to leave the room. Eden and the Doctor might still be outside, and . . .

"I'll be waiting right here in case you need me," the Doctor had said.

A tinny buzz was now added to the cacophony in Chakotay's head as a wave of dizziness threatened to take his feet out from under him.

They knew. Both of them knew whom he was about to face when he entered this room, and neither of them had been the least bit disturbed by her presence.

Which meant what?

If he could only breathe, he might be able to sort out their impossible acceptance of the thing pretending to be Kathryn. Obviously she had deceived them.

Turning back he saw her, no longer attempting to approach him. She simply stood alone in the center of the room, her hands at her sides and her face unutterably sad. There had been precious few moments between them when he had seen her so emotionally vulnerable. Those he had were cherished memories he had buried deep within his heart. He had learned long ago that he must not dwell on those memories, the ones he prized the most. Perhaps someday, when his grief was bearable, when the permanent hole her absence had left in his heart . . .

But seeing her like this, so small, so tired, and so very alone . . . Every instinct in his body demanded that he go to her and take her in his arms.

Only the awful truth that this must be some sort of illusion kept him rooted to the floor.

She shook her head slowly back and forth, sniffled softly, and gently wiped a tear from her cheek as she struggled to pull herself upright and square her shoulders.

Every gesture was hers. But more than that, every emotion communicated so clearly through them was also *hers*. Countless alien artifices might result in a fair imitation of her body, but surely not her soul.

The anger drained from Chakotay, leaving him incredibly cold. This feeling, too, was frighteningly familiar. He had walked for so long between pain and ice, in the months immediately following her death. He had struggled valiantly to move beyond them. It was exhausting to find himself here again, and more than anything, he wished for a dark place in which to breathe and be still.

She seemed to follow his thoughts, but the hope he had first seen on her face had evaporated. Finally she said simply, "I'm sorry. I'm so very sorry."

For pretending to be the woman I loved most in the universe? For destroying the fragile peace I've worked so hard to find? For insulting the memory of one of the finest officers ever to wear the uniform?

"For what?" he forced through his lips.

"For dying," she replied. "I told you once what grief did to me when I lost my father and Justin. I didn't think you believed me then. How could you? You'd never experienced anything like it. But I guess I was right."

"Right?" he asked even as the memory of the night she had first shared her grief with him sliced through his heart, rending it anew.

"For two people responsible for so many lives, love is too much to risk."

It was a stunning pronouncement, but again, *so like her*. He found it impossible to understand the feeling washing through him, that something incredibly precious might have just slipped through his fingers.

Kathryn? he thought, but didn't dare speak her name.

"When Q—the son, not the father," she explained, "told me he would return me to the place I was needed most, I assumed he meant just shortly after the Borg cube that . . . assimilated me was destroyed."

The difficulty with which she spoke the word "assimilated" set his heart pounding hard in his chest.

"The Doctor was good enough to fill me in on the last fourteen months. Frankly, I'm amazed any of you are still standing, given what you had to face. My death was surely the least of it."

"Your death . . ." he began, but couldn't complete the thought. A hope was suddenly raging in his mind between the impossibility that somehow Kathryn had returned and the irrefutable evidence of every word she spoke.

"And given what we're facing now, coming back from the dead is almost equally insignificant," she added bitterly.

"Kathryn?" he finally said aloud, but just as soon wished he hadn't. *Because to believe it was possible . . .*

"I don't know how to convince you. The Doctor has done all the tests. Maybe you'll believe him." She shrugged as a deep sigh escaped her lips.

Chakotay's heart began to burn with a force he had forgotten, a tense energy binding him to her that had never wavered in intensity, no matter how far they drifted apart. Without consciously wanting to, Chakotay began to move cautiously toward her. Each step gave rise to the fear that if he got too close, she would disappear.

"Q's son?" he asked.

She held her ground as she continued. "Just before I boarded that damned cube, his mother . . . Remember her?"

Chakotay nodded, still moving forward.

"She appeared in my quarters, warning me that if I did what I had come to do, I would surely die. Of course I didn't believe her. She was a Q, and as best I could tell had never liked me much anyway." A momentary spasm of pain flashed over her face. "After it was all over, I was with her again. She told me I was dead, but that death didn't mean anything where I was going. And then I was in the Continuum. Q, the son, was waiting for me. Something terrible is happening to him, and it very well could be my fault. I had to help if I could."

"Q brought you back from the dead?" Chakotay asked, still not daring to believe it.

"He showed me how to do it myself. Turns out, there is a great deal more between heaven and earth than any of us have ever dreamed. It was touch and go for a bit, but then Kes showed up and somehow . . ."

"Kes?"

She nodded as fresh tears welled in her eyes. "I guess it was foolish of me to think that it would be as easy for you to accept all of this as it was for me. Maybe you had to be there."

Finally, Chakotay stood directly in front of her. The warmth of her body, the fragrance he had actually forgotten, the warm tears streaking down her face, all threatened to shatter his heart.

This time, she took a small step back. Only the huge desk behind her prevented further retreat.

"Don't," she said softly.

Every nerve ending in Chakotay's body was suddenly quite painfully alive.

"Kathryn." His eyes blurred with tears.

"I swear to you, Chakotay, if I'd known, I would never have risked hurting you the way I did. We would have gone on as we always had and then, when . . ."

"No," he said, raising shaking hands and grasping her firmly by both arms. "It wasn't your fault. You were just doing what you always did, trying to protect all of us."

"But—"

"No," he said again, pulling her toward him. For a moment, she tried to hold herself back, but he refused to allow it. In the space of a breath, their bodies met in a tight embrace. She buried her head in his chest, as the rest of her shuddered. He was shaking as his hands pressed her close, then began to run over her entire back, consoling her even as they assured him of her warm and very real presence.

Chakotay bent low to press his cheek to hers, and through mingled tears their lips found one another's. For the next several moments, he knew nothing but the familiar sweetness of her breath and their mutual physical hunger. When she finally pulled her face away just far enough to search his eyes, he saw that her fear had vanished.

Together they moved to a nearby long sofa, their arms wrapped around each other in silent wonder. They sat and continued to stare at each other, in a precious stolen moment of pure happiness. Finally, Kathryn said, "You do realize that the universe is tearing itself to shreds around us?"

I don't care, he thought, until reality reared its ugly head and he remembered how much he actually did.

Nodding slightly, he began, "We have—"

"—work to do," she finished for him.

It didn't matter. Nothing mattered. Kathryn was alive.

Anything was possible.

Seven continued to apply herself to the newest sensor readings, which indicated that the anomaly's effects on local space were increasing, without providing any insight into how to impede or reverse its spread. Apart from the portions of the ships that had not been completely consumed, every other particle of matter or energy that intersected with the anomaly appeared to cease to exist. It was not destroyed or converted. By some unknown mechanism, it appeared the anomaly rendered every portion of space it moved through somehow absent. Seven had initially believed that whatever had fractured the anomaly had opened up a new realm into normal space-time. However, the lack of significant gravimetric distortions and radiation readings that were indicative of the interplay between two such radically different states of being were not present. She could not account for why this was so. She had begun to believe, without understanding how it was possible, that the anomaly was not releasing itself into normal space; it was, more accurately, erasing it.

It was a relief when she heard the doors to the astrometrics lab open. Half-hoping that Cambridge had returned, she was surprised to see Chakotay and the Doctor enter, side by side. Both of them wore expressions of mingled expectancy and relief that puzzled her. She wondered if someone might have discovered a solution that had thus far eluded her.

"Captain?" she asked immediately.

Chakotay's eyes met hers, and in them she saw something radiating so forcefully, she was tempted to step back. The possibility of alien possession crossed her mind, so great was the change in his demeanor since their last briefing. Frankly, she hadn't seen Chakotay so positive in months. He looked ready to present her with a gift, and barely able to contain himself.

The Doctor's face held the same excited expectation. Briefly, she wondered if she might be dreaming. Since the Caeliar transformation, her body actually required sleep rather than regeneration, and in the last few days, had been pushed beyond its limits. It was possible she had nodded off at her post, though she certainly felt awake.

"What has happened?" she asked.

"You won't believe it—" Chakotay began.

"Which is why we wanted to assure you that what you are about to see has been thoroughly verified by every test at my disposal and that both of us are convinced of its absolute veracity," the Doctor finished.

"What am I about to see?" Seven inquired.

"Admiral?" Chakotay called to the door, and it opened again.

As soon as Admiral Janeway entered, Seven's knees gave way. Both Chakotay and the Doctor took firm hold of her arms to steady her.

"Hello, Seven," the admiral greeted her with a warm and radiant smile.

Seven held on to Chakotay and the Doctor as she looked between them for confirmation. Clearly sensing her confusion, Janeway stepped into the room and the door closed behind her. She waited patiently for Seven to collect herself.

"I don't understand," Seven said.

"The Q intervened at the last possible moment before my death," Janeway advised her simply.

"When?" Seven asked, even more confused.

"After the cube was destroyed, but before my consciousness was permanently lost," Janeway clarified. "I grant you, a more timely return would have been optimal, but I'm just grateful they did what they did."

Seven's breath began to come in quick, short spasms. She wanted to believe what she was seeing, but nothing in her past experiences had prepared her to confront the wild range of emotions now roaring through her. Disbelief warred with impossible relief, and anger was intertwined with overwhelming happiness.

"It's all right, Seven," the Doctor said in his most soothing voice.

"I know it's hard to believe," Chakotay added.

"No," Seven said, pulling free of both of them and retreating to the far side of her console. She raised her hand to tap her combadge, but even as it chirped, the doors opened and Cambridge entered.

Seven looked to him immediately, desperately seeking confirmation that she had not gone insane in the last sixty seconds.

Casting a withering glance toward Chakotay, the Doctor, and Janeway, he said, "You can imagine my surprise when I asked the computer to locate you three, and found you en route to astrometrics. In your anxiousness to share the news of our fair admiral's resurrection, did any of you consider the shock your revelation is bound to inspire, even in the strongest among you?" He then crossed to Seven and took both her hands in his, squeezing them tightly. "Listen to me," the counselor commanded, "you have not taken leave of your senses. You are well aware of the capabilities of the species known as the Q. You have my word, and that of your friends, that the impossible has come to pass. We are *not* sharing some mass delusion. It will take some time to process, but you should begin at once. Sadly, nothing else about our unfortunate and rather desperate circumstances has been altered, and the sooner you accept this, the sooner we can all return our attention to preventing our imminent demises."

His bluntness had its typical calming effect upon Seven. As she nodded, he added, "I have to believe that the Q's intervention on the part of Admiral Janeway is the exception rather than the rule. If any of us are to survive the mess in which we now find ourselves, we're going to need you at your best."

At this, Seven actually smiled.

"Deep breath," Cambridge suggested.

She complied, then looked past him to stare at Admiral Janeway, who seemed not at all insulted by Seven's initial reaction.

"Gentlemen," the admiral said simply, "would you give us a moment, please?"

"Certainly," Chakotay replied.

Cambridge hesitated, waiting for Seven's response.

"It's all right," she assured him.

With a nod, he followed Chakotay and the Doctor out. Seven suspected neither of them had heard the last from him on their method of relating this extraordinary information.

The moment they had left, Seven turned her full attention to Admiral Janeway and felt her face flushing in embarrassment. "Please forgive me," she said. "The shock I experienced should not be taken as indication that I am not very happy to see you again, Admiral."

Janeway shook her head, dismissing the apology. "In a few minutes, we will join the rest of the senior staff. I'm sure all of them will have a similar reaction, and will want to hear as many details as there is time for me to provide. But before then, I wanted to speak with you."

"Why?" Seven asked automatically. She knew, of course, that her past relationship with Janeway had been unique, but it still felt odd to be singled out.

A faint smile of embarrassment now rose to Janeway's face. "To thank you," she replied.

Try as she might, Seven could not imagine what she might have done to deserve the admiral's thanks.

"For what?" she asked softly.

"For saving me," Janeway said simply.

"I thought you said the Q did that," Seven said, confused.

"I meant from the Borg."

Suddenly Seven found herself reliving in vivid detail the last moments she had shared with Kathryn Janeway. Between the grief that followed so quickly after her death and the Caeliar transformation soon thereafter, Seven had managed to bury the intensity of that moment, when she merged with an ancient alien technology and used it to bridge the barriers the Borg had erected between herself and what was left of the admiral after her assimilation. So painful was the memory that Seven was grateful that it had faded from her consciousness.

Janeway stepped closer, asking, "What I experienced, is that what assimilation was like for you?"

Seven wished she didn't understand the question, but she did.

"No," she replied. "I was assimilated at such a young age. There was no resistance. I was consumed completely and entered wholly into the hive mind."

"How did you know I would still be there?"

Seven considered the question seriously. "I suppose I didn't." Struggling to be precise, she said, "But in order for our plan to succeed, I *needed* you to still be there. And I *wanted* you to be there. I intended to bring you back myself. I knew that the Borg might assimilate your body, but they could never take all of you." Seven's heart began to burn as she recalled the chaos of the battle with the evolved Borg cube, and the times since then when she had wondered if she had done all she could for Janeway. "I failed you," she finally admitted.

"No," Janeway said, closing the distance between them. "I was trapped there, hiding in some small part of my own mind as soon as the assimilation was complete. It took a time for me to understand what had happened, and all my strength to continue to resist while that . . ." Her voice trailed off as the intensity of her memories threatened to overwhelm her.

"It wasn't you," Seven assured her.

"I know," Janeway said, though she clearly did not entirely believe it. "And I also know that without you, the cube would have absorbed the Earth. I know I could not have held out much longer. I would have been lost forever to that monster. But you found me," she insisted. "You kept all that was left of me intact. When it was done, the Q took my consciousness to their continuum. But there would have been no consciousness to take if you hadn't reached it first."

Seven stood stiffly, attempting to accept the admiral's gratitude, but found it difficult to let go of her regret.

Janeway had stopped short of physical contact when Seven had begun to retreat. The intimacy Seven had shared with her, in what she had believed had been the admiral's last moments of life, had been powerful, and like most intimate encounters, left an awkward vulnerability between them in the light of day. Finally Seven said, "You fought not once, but many times, to free me from the Borg. You gave me back my individuality and since then I have come to treasure it, even above perfection. To have attempted less for you would have been unimaginable."

Janeway nodded, accepting Seven's words.

Seven was tempted to close the distance between them with some gesture. A handshake seemed too impersonal; a hug, strangely forward. Kathryn Janeway had always held a place of maternal dominance for Seven, but without the physical bonding that traditionally accompanied the mother/daughter dynamic. The range of physical expressions familiar to them was rather limited. Seven found that the professional distance with which they had begun their relationship many years ago was the only option that offered any sense of ease. The time Seven had spent with her aunt on Earth had opened her to a wide range of expressions of familial love; Irene had never hesitated to greet Seven with a firm hug, and they often parted with a kiss on the cheek. In a few extreme moments, Janeway and Seven had expressed their mutual regard in similar gestures, but something Seven could not name, let alone explain, kept her rooted to the deck, several paces from the admiral.

Attempting to move beyond this uncomfortable revelation, Seven asked, "Was there a particular reason the Q spared you? I know that in your previous dealings with them you formed a personal relationship with Q, but this does seem extreme, even for them."

"I am almost certain it is related to what happened to those four vessels and, quite likely, to Captain Eden."

"Explain," Seven requested.

A smile from Janeway assured Seven that for better and worse, they had just managed to bridge the distance between them. Were it not for the lingering pain of her absence, it might have been as if the last fourteen months had never happened.

Half an hour later, Kathryn Janeway found herself in a modified version of *Voyager*'s briefing room. She liked the changes, but its capacity to hold twenty made the seven people assembled there seem like a very small group. There, the admiral had greeted Tom Paris, B'Elanna Torres, and Harry Kim. Chakotay, Seven, and the Doctor stood by as they took turns expressing their astonished relief in repeated warm embraces and joyful tears.

Once the pleasantries were over, Janeway asked the group to focus their attention on the matter at hand. In the next few minutes, Captain Eden and Counselor Cambridge would join them. Janeway had suggested—Chakotay had agreed—that only these officers would be apprised of her return for the time being. Until the immediate crisis was resolved, the rest of the fleet could wait to be informed. The admiral would work with Eden while Chakotay managed his crew, implementing their joint recommendations.

Harry Kim gave voice to what might have been a mutual assumption. "You're the ranking officer, Admiral. Shouldn't you assume command of the fleet?"

Janeway was surprised at how easy it was for her to dismiss

the notion. "At the moment, I am not your commanding officer and may well never be again. Captain Eden commands this fleet, and Captain Chakotay this vessel. Both of them have my full confidence and support. I am here because the Q who became my godson believes that the crisis we face now, we confronted once before and managed to overcome it. I intend to focus my activities solely on understanding the nature of this anomaly. More than seven hundred of our fellow officers might be lost, but I'm not willing to accept that. Three of our ships are now trapped, and a fourth was fully absorbed. I want those four ships back, with every single person now considered missing in action. I want whatever this thing is to return to wherever it came from, so that it can no longer threaten the safety of this universe. I no longer know the crew aboard *Voyager* as well as I once did. But I know all of you as well as I know myself. We're a family and we've faced worse together.

"Later, when Command can be formally apprised of the change in our circumstances, they will determine our next course of action. Until then, I expect each of you to continue to serve your designated commanding officers with the same loyalty and passion you once served me. Is that understood?"

Nods all around the table confirmed that it was.

"Good," she said, clasping her hands before her and resting them on the table. "Let's get to work."

Chapter Twenty-seven

VOYAGER

Captain Afsarah Eden sat at the head of the oblong conference table. To her right sat Admiral Janeway; to her left, Captain Chakotay. Beyond them, Paris, Torres, Seven, Cambridge, Kim, and the Doctor were assembled. Although they gave Eden their full and respectful attention, she was cognizant of a shift in the energy of the room. The fate of the trapped ships and the threat posed by the continuing expansion of the anomaly was foremost in everyone's minds, but beneath their tense focus was a new, underlying, almost communal positive will. Eden had always privately believed that many of the extraordinary things the *Voyager* crew had accomplished in the Delta Quadrant had been the result of luck, and an absolute, somewhat reckless determination to wrestle success from the hands of anyone who dared to deny it to them. She knew this crew, and she knew their strengths. To see them in the presence of Kathryn Janeway was to understand exactly how, through some mysterious alchemy born of her particular command style, she focused her people's strengths, while taking the option of failure off the table.

Grateful for this fierce determination, Eden couldn't help but envy their confidence, and the woman whose mere existence upheld it.

"How can we be certain that the anomaly is the same one your uncles encountered, Captain?" B'Elanna asked, after Eden had summarized her discoveries at the Mikhal Outpost and the events that had led her there.

Eden knew it would be a stumbling block for the scientists in the room to accept what she said on faith alone.

"I saw the sensor readings Tallar and Jobin took in their first encounter with the anomaly they discovered in the Beta Quadrant. There is no doubt in my mind that their readings correlate precisely with ours."

"Yes, but you saw this in a dream?" B'Elanna prodded.

"The captain's perceptions may not conform to any experience of reality of which you are aware," Cambridge interrupted, clearly offended on Eden's behalf. "But allow me to assure you that I have witnessed her unique capabilities on several occasions. Everything she is telling you is accurate."

"As have I," the Doctor added.

"It's all right," Eden offered. "I understand this is difficult for you to accept."

"I've had my own experience with the truths dreams can hold," B'Elanna said, softening a bit. "I'm not saying it isn't possible. It's just a little convenient that the same time you were discovering the history of this ancient extragalactic race, four of our ships discover evidence of the Anschlasom's actions tens of thousands of light-years from your location."

"Does it matter?" Kim asked. "Whether the Anschlasom caused the anomaly or not, it's here, and we have to figure out how to get our ships out of it."

"Knowing that there are multiple potential access points to this realm throughout our universe does impact our understanding of its nature," Seven replied. "Were it a discrete anomaly, we would make certain generalized assumptions. However, knowing that it extends from here to the Beta Quadrant, and possibly to the very edge of the universe, is significant in deciding on a course of action."

"Agreed," Janeway said briskly. "It is my understanding, and please correct me if I'm wrong," she added with a deferential nod to Eden, "that you believe this realm underpins the entire multiverse."

Eden nodded. "That is what the Anschlasom believed, and given their location when they pulled it into normal space-time, I'm inclined to agree."

"And Q believes that *Voyager* actually encountered this anomaly in the timeline where it took us twenty-three years to get home?" Chakotay asked.

"My godson, yes." Janeway nodded.

"Can we call him something else?" Paris interrupted. "Just for the sake of clarity?"

"How about Junior?" the Doctor offered. Seeing Janeway's withering look, he said, "Well, isn't that what his own father called him?"

"Fine," Janeway allowed, though obviously with regret, "*Junior's* existence prior to the choices made by myself and my future self at the transwarp hub was exactly that of every other Q. When we were together in the Continuum, I experienced this, so I'm not just taking his word for it. After we altered the time-line—for worse, it seems—a rather massive shift occurred across all existing timelines. At that point, Junior ceased to be able to access any point in the future beyond our present day. I've gone back through what little I recall of what my future counterpart told me of her experiences in the Delta Quadrant, and one thing bothers me."

"What was that?" Chakotay asked.

"She spoke of an encounter during which Seven would be killed. If I'm remembering correctly, the timing of that encounter correlates almost exactly with where we are now."

"I don't understand," Paris was the first to admit.

"If we had stayed on our course, and never encountered the future Admiral Janeway, it would be now that we would be facing whatever it was that took Seven's life," Janeway clarified.

"And why does that matter?" Eden inquired, genuinely curious.

"Because I can count on one hand the types of missions I would have considered important enough to have risked my crew's lives," Janeway replied firmly. "Facing the possible end of all space-time is right at the top of that very short list."

Cambridge, who was seated beside Seven, connected the dots. "You believe there is some conscious external force ordering events such that regardless of our actions, across all timelines, *Voyager,* or perhaps just you, Admiral, are fated to confront this anomaly at this precise moment?"

"I'm not sure I would go that far," Janeway admitted, "but I'm also not ruling it out. This *is* the point in time where Junior's existence hangs in the balance. If there is a bigger problem out there that could account for it, I don't want to know about it."

"Why don't the rest of the Q know about it?" Kim piped up. "Don't they claim to be omniscient? And if it might cost a Q his life, shouldn't they be taking an interest?"

"That is honestly one of the most disturbing parts of all of this," Janeway replied. "They *should* know. If any of us were in their position, I believe we would be marshaling whatever forces we command to counter the effects of this thing. That only Junior seems to be aware of it suggests it may be beyond the rest of the Q Continuum."

"I don't like the sound of that," Chakotay acknowledged.

"Nor do I," Janeway agreed. "My godson is a unique individual. He is the only Q ever created by two Q. The only other Q not created at the dawn of time was born of two Q who had become human. There was doubt among the Q that this offspring would even have the Q's powers.

"While aiding Junior in his investigation, she apparently disappeared, and now he is the only member of the Continuum who is aware that she ever existed."

"So we're facing something that appears to have the potential to destroy not only the lives of every being now in existence, but also the lives of at least two theoretically immortal beings," Cambridge said. "And you and this Junior are convinced that another version of *Voyager* encountered the same problem and somehow eliminated this threat?"

"We're pretty good," Chakotay offered semi-seriously.

"We are," Janeway agreed, matching his tone. "But my guess is that whatever we confronted as a single vessel far from home probably wasn't quite as extensive as the anomaly now before us. My question is," and at this she turned directly to Seven and B'Elanna, "if we had come across this anomaly in the same form our other fleet vessels first discovered it, what do you think we would have done?"

"Noted it in our logs and steered clear of it?" Paris suggested wryly.

"Ha," Kim scoffed. "Not likely."

Seven and B'Elanna turned to face one another and for a moment, Eden almost felt they were discussing the question telepathically. Finally, Seven said, "While it is difficult to believe, especially now that we have seen its destructive potential, we might have merely scanned it, and concluded it was unique."

"You would have thrown every exotic particle field its way to see what stuck," B'Elanna chided her.

"Probably," Seven agreed, "but our fellow ships didn't get that far before the anomaly altered its configuration."

"We would likely have sent a probe in," Janeway suggested.

"If it had reacted to the probe in the same manner it did with the ships, we might have recognized it as an unstable rift in the fabric of space-time," Seven stated.

"Would you have tried to close it?" Eden asked.

Considering this, Janeway admitted, "Probably. We would have done everything in our power to eliminate the threat it poses to surrounding space."

"How?" Eden asked.

"I don't know," Janeway replied. "But we need an answer to that question, because I don't believe anything else will restore stability to the multiverse."

After a short pause B'Elanna said, "I need a closer look. All we've been able to discover is what the anomaly *isn't*. We need to know *exactly* what it is."

"I agree," Eden said. "The Anschlasom believed it was the absolute end of all existence. None of us know how the universe will end. It's a question the best minds in the Federation still ponder. There are many divergent theories, but most agree that the universe is in a state of constant expansion that will eventually result in a redistribution of energy, matter, and gravitational forces that will give rise to either extremely high or low temperatures. However, the Anschlasom discovered another outcome. What if we accept that they were right?"

"Go on," Janeway encouraged.

"If the universe cannot expand indefinitely," Eden began, "then at some point gravity can stop the expansion of the universe, and begin to contract it. The Anschlasom might well have been the first sentient race to encounter that effect."

Here, Seven of Nine shook her head. "Very few notable scientists still give credence to the theory of a closed universe. Our understanding of the existence of multiple universes suggests that even if some of them were effectively closed, others remain open and expand indefinitely."

"You said," Janeway interjected, "that the Anschlasom didn't discover the anomaly, that they brought it into our reality."

"What are you getting at, Admiral?" B'Elanna asked.

Janeway sighed. "It's difficult to describe, but while I was within the Q Continuum, I felt connected to every facet of the multiverse. My sense was that their continuum somehow runs throughout everything that is, existing in all places simultaneously."

"Do you believe that the Anschlasom somehow brought part of that Q Continuum into normal space?" Eden asked.

"If they did, I can't imagine that the Q wouldn't know about it," Janeway replied thoughtfully. "But who's to say that the Q Continuum is the only realm that has this property? There could be another."

"There could be countless others," Cambridge noted.

"The only time we entered the Q Continuum was with the assistance of Junior's mother, through a supernova created by their ongoing conflict," Kim interjected. "If the Anschlasom had technology capable of creating interstellar events of that magnitude, they could theoretically have created an entry point."

"So it's like the Q Continuum, but not the Q Continuum," Paris ventured.

"We need to test this theory," Seven said. "We need to conduct further studies from the nearest safe access point to the anomaly."

"We can't get much closer than we are right now," Chakotay warned.

"We could transport to one of the trapped ships," Eden offered. "A barrier exists on each ship dividing normal space from the anomaly, and the side in normal space remains habitable."

"I'll go," B'Elanna volunteered.

"And I will accompany you," Eden stated.

Cambridge sighed quietly. As he met Eden's eyes, she saw his resigned concern. "With your permission, Captain?" he asked.

"I'm fine, Counselor," she said curtly.

"I never said you weren't," he replied. "But we know that this anomaly has unusual effects on you, and given that, I think we should err on the side of caution."

Eden turned to Janeway. "It's your call, Captain," the admiral said.

"Very well." Eden nodded. "Commander Torres, Counselor Cambridge, and I will board the *Quirinal*, as it is the most intact vessel. Seven, brief Patel and Conlon on our new premise. Captain Chakotay, keep *Voyager* out of harm's way."

"Understood," Chakotay replied.

"Dismissed," Eden said, bringing the briefing to a close.

As everyone rose to return to their posts, Kathryn was conscious of a few pangs of regret. Restricting her access to the rest of the crew was appropriate for the time being, but it also meant the assistance she could offer was limited. She had been relieved that her unexpected return had not thrown those closest to her into chaos and privately reminded herself how many times they had embraced the fact that "weird" was part of their job. But she was concerned by the one significant fact Captain Eden had chosen to withhold.

"Fleet Commander?" she said before Eden had left the table.

"Yes, Admiral?" Eden replied evenly. Chakotay and Cambridge slowed their exits.

Looking at Chakotay and the counselor with a gaze that made it plain they were being dismissed, Kathryn said, "A word?"

"Of course." Eden nodded, standing up straighter.

As soon as they were alone Kathryn said, "I'm curious about something."

"The floor is yours, Admiral."

"Was there any particular reason why you did not include in your report your sense that the action you took in the cavern, shattering the representation of *Som,* was the catalyst for what we now see in the anomaly?"

Eden looked away, clearly giving the matter serious consideration. When she turned back, Kathryn saw regret in Eden's eyes. "I do not think it is essential to their efforts," she replied. "Cambridge and the Doctor are convinced that was an emotional response on my part. There seems to be no scientific evidence to support the proposition."

"But you still believe it to be true?" Kathryn pushed gently.

"I know it to be true," Eden said flatly, then added, "and I also know it makes no difference now. We are where we are. My course of action will be no different whether I bear responsibility or not."

"They wouldn't blame you, Captain," Kathryn observed.

"The assignment of blame is inconsequential to the work ahead of us," Eden said. "More likely, they would take it as evidence that I had been mentally damaged by my recent experiences. My effectiveness as their commander would most certainly be compromised."

"Do you believe yourself to be mentally damaged by what has transpired?" Kathryn asked, consciously choosing to echo Eden's description.

"If I did, I would immediately turn command of what remains of the fleet over to Captain Chakotay," Eden replied without missing a beat. "Ever since I first saw the artifact on the Mikhal Outpost, I knew that a force, beyond what I would consider rational, was working to bring me to this moment. I've known my entire life that I was different. All that we have learned so far has only confirmed that belief. The deeper . . . *knowing* that I have been able to access, since I was a young girl, usually results in a feeling of peace and certainty. I trust it. I don't understand what this means, but I'm not wallowing, and I'm not unbalanced. Whether I broke this thing or not, possibly condemning over seven hundred to death, doesn't matter. What does is that I intend to fix it."

"Fair enough," Kathryn said, nodding.

"I've asked Commander Paris to provide you with quarters. Is there anything else you require?" Eden asked.

"No," Kathryn assured her. "I'd like to spend some time with the Doctor, reviewing his medical findings, as well as everything in our databases regarding your uncles' actions while they were in Starfleet."

"There's nothing there," Eden cautioned her. "I've read the reports so many times since I discovered them, I've committed them to memory."

"Fresh eyes can't hurt," Kathryn suggested.

"I suppose not," Eden allowed. "Is there something in particular you are looking for?"

The admiral shrugged. In truth, she wanted to feel like she was doing *something* to help. But she could not shake the sense that Eden's true connection, as well as her uncles', to the anomaly had yet to be discovered. "It is your prerogative to share as much of the information with your crew as you see fit," Kathryn began. "But I hope you will continue to be completely honest with me."

"You can count on it, Admiral," Eden replied.

A moment of tense silence hung between them before Kathryn ventured, "I've been where you are, Captain Eden. I know what it is to make choices that result in unthinkable and painful consequences. Even now, I don't know how I'm going to live with some of my regrets going forward, but I do know that guilt and doubt lead nowhere productive. You aren't alone in this."

Eden rose and nodded. "I appreciate the sentiment, Admiral, but the truth is I've been alone since the day my uncles left me on Earth. It's not unfamiliar territory to me, or to you, I suspect. We form connections with one another, we create ties, and we share experiences that bind us, but there are precious few relationships that go deep enough to allow us to truly be known by one another. You have that with these people. I hoped to create it myself as time went on."

"You still can," Kathryn tried to assure her.

"Perhaps," Eden allowed. "I'll report back to you as soon as I return from *Quirinal*."

Kathryn nodded. As Eden left, the weight resting on her shoulders was evident. Kathryn wanted to lighten Eden's load, but she knew all too well that both circumstance and position meant she could not. She had her own responsibilities to consider, including her godson's expectations. Like Eden, she wondered if she might be forced to shoulder them alone.

Harry Kim found Nancy Conlon and Devi Patel in Holodeck 2 running a simulation to test the potential effectiveness of *Voyager*'s tractor beams on the *Quirinal*, the ship that had lost the least of its mass to the anomaly. It was a good choice, though the smaller *Curie* might have been easier. They were in a holographic reconstruction of *Voyager*'s engineering section, where Conlon was overseeing power distribution while manning the tractor controls. Patel was busy measuring the impact on the *Quirinal* and the anomaly. A scaled-down holo of the *Quirinal* showed where the tractor beams were being applied.

Harry waited patiently for them to complete the simulation. After a tense minute, during which Patel suggested several variations, Conlon finally ordered, "Computer, freeze simulation."

"Are you sure we can't route this through the deflector dish?" Patel asked in obvious frustration as she crossed to Conlon. Neither had registered Harry's entrance.

"Maybe." Conlon, who appeared to be thoroughly exhausted, nodded. "I'd like to avoid that if possible. This way, we might lose our target, but we're a lot less likely to lose *Voyager*."

Patel rubbed her eyes with both hands, as if willing them to see something she was missing. When she removed them, she saw Harry and immediately straightened her posture.

Taking this as his cue, he stepped forward, saying, "How's it going?"

"Great," Conlon replied sarcastically.

"I take it our tractor beam doesn't have the power to pull the ships free?" Harry asked.

"It doesn't appear to," Conlon said.

"And every time the ship moves a hair, the computer indicates additional points of fracture within the anomaly," Patel added.

Harry nodded, then said, "Seven is working on a new theory in astrometrics. She'd like both of you to join her there."

Patel started for the lab, but Conlon caught Harry's eye and said, "Go ahead. I'll be there in a minute."

Once they were alone, the engineer said, "You know, I really like you, Harry, but I don't have time for this right now. You could have advised us of our new orders over the comm. Or Seven could have, for that matter. You came down here to check on me."

"True," he acknowledged. "How are you holding up?"

"Great," she said with forced cheer.

"Okay," Harry replied, unwilling to push too far. "I just want you to know," he added, "I am worried about you, and if you want to talk, I'm here."

"Thanks," Conlon said, and started for the door.

"Nancy?" he called.

She stopped, but didn't turn around.

"Never mind," he decided. The truth was, in the last hour, his life had changed dramatically. Their mission had been complicated by Admiral Janeway's news, but her presence had sparked something in him he hadn't felt since her death. It wasn't that she was an all-knowing, all-powerful savior who had swooped in at the last minute to rescue them. Harry had no doubts that whatever was to come, they'd all be working awfully hard to rescue themselves. But in a universe where so much had been taken from him in the last few years, to have Kathryn Janeway brought back gave him a renewed sense of faith he hadn't dusted off in a long time. He couldn't share this with Nancy, nor did he think the news would have had the same effect on her that it had on him.

He expected the engineer to continue walking, but Conlon turned, and her eyes when they met his were colder than any he'd ever seen staring out of her normally open, bright face.

"On our way to Troyius, *da Vinci* came across a convoy of Elasian ships. Might have been every single ship they had that was warp capable. They were fleeing the Borg, who were supposed to be hours away. We were still working the bugs out of a phase-shifting matrix we thought we could use to hide both of the inhabited planets in the system. Troyius was to be our first effort." Her eyes began to glisten as she continued, "But the Borg showed up a little early. We were in range of Troyius, although we could have come to the aid of the Elasian convoy. We couldn't, however, save both. So we chose the planet. The matrix worked. We made Troyius seem to disappear, and the Borg moved on. But they made short work of the convoy on their way out of the system. It was only after the fact, as we were going over our scans, that we realized that the Elasians had packed as many children on those vessels as they could hold. The Elasians sent their future out on those ships, hoping against hope it would survive. Eight hundred thousand children gone in the blink of an eye. Those children were helpless, defenseless. We could have saved them. And we didn't."

Harry stepped closer, but she raised a hand to stop him.

"I haven't let myself think about it in months. Saving a planet of billions was probably the right choice. But I've never seen that many children die. I've never seen that many people die. I never thought I would see anything like that ever again."

"It was an impossible choice, Nancy," he said softly.

"Yes." She nodded. "And I kept thinking it was one I'd never have to face again. What were the odds that there was something worse out there than the Borg? But I've realized in the last couple of days that there doesn't have to be. More than seven hundred people were lost on those four ships to an interstellar anomaly."

"Not yet," he interjected.

"Unless we can work another miracle, they are," she corrected him. "And I seem to be fresh out of them."

"It's not over, and we might just surprise you," he added.

"It's over for me," Conlon replied.

"What do you mean?"

"I mean I'm going to do everything I can until this crisis has passed to prove myself wrong, but when this mission is over, I'm requesting transfer back to the Alpha Quadrant."

"The end of our three-year mission?" Harry asked.

"No. The end of this rescue mission. I just can't wrap my brain around this much loss again. It's paralyzing. I'm a damned fine engineer, but I'm no good to anyone like this."

In his own recent struggles, Harry had almost come to the same conclusion. He didn't like her choice, but he knew he had to respect it.

"I understand," Harry finally said. Then, he remembered just how much she had come to mean to him in a few short months.

"Good," she replied.

Before she could again turn to leave, however, Harry added, "But I also disagree."

At her puzzled and somewhat surprised reaction, he continued, "If you're looking for a safe place to come to terms with all of this, you're not going to find it in the Alpha Quadrant either. I've traveled from one end of this galaxy to the other, and I'm here to tell you, there is no shortage of terrible, unthinkable stuff going on. Put two sentient beings in a room together and eventually they'll find something to disagree about. Add warp technology and advanced weapons to the equation—"

"I hope you're not trying to make me feel better," Conlon interjected, "because you really suck at it."

Harry stepped closer and continued, "But that's not all there is to life. You can't fix everything. Hell, you can't fix most of what's wrong. But you can try. And it's in the trying that you learn who you are. You decide, in every single moment you draw breath, the quality of your life, how much you're going to contribute, and how much happiness you're going to create in the face of the darkness. And even a universe as frightening as this one finds ways to surprise you.

"I hope you will stay and discover that with us . . . with me."

Conlon's eyes softened. "Okay, that last part sucked a little less."

Tom Paris found his wife standing at the entrance to their bedroom. Miral had fallen asleep in the middle of their bed, curled on her side, her breath slow and regular. Kula, their holographic nanny, stood in patient vigil by the bedside.

He came quietly up behind B'Elanna and felt her start as he wrapped both his arms about her waist. She relaxed, resting the back of her head against his chest. They stood there for a few moments before he bent low and whispered in her ear, "Did you have to volunteer to board the *Quirinal?*"

"Pretty dumb, huh?" she replied softly.

"Just promise me you'll be careful."

At this, she turned and took him in a full, tight embrace.

When they parted, she looked up to him, her eyes filled with the fear he'd seen too often in the last few days.

"We're going to get through this," he reassured her.

After a moment she led him into the living area, still holding tightly to both of his hands.

"Do you really believe it's her?" she asked.

Tom thought for a moment, then said, "Admiral Janeway?"

"Q brought her back from the dead?" B'Elanna went on. "That seems awfully convenient, doesn't it?"

He shrugged. "You're not happy?"

"I'm thrilled," B'Elanna insisted. "I mean, it's great, right? She brought us home safe after seven years here. She'll do it again, won't she?"

"In the first place, the captain . . . admiral may have led us home, but we all did our part. Except you. If I recall, you were goldbricking your way through the last several hours we spent in the Delta Quadrant."

"You mean when I was giving birth to our child?"

"Excuses, excuses," he teased. "The Doctor has run every conceivable scan on her. If she's not the real thing, she's the best imitation ever, and I'll take that in a pinch."

"It's just so . . ."

"So what?"

"So much," B'Elanna finally gasped. "What if she is Q?" she added.

"The only thing better than the actual Kathryn Janeway on our side right now would be Kathryn Janeway with the powers of the Q."

"Am I just being stupid?"

"No. You're on overload. Three days ago, you were figuring out how to reprogram the transporters to save a bunch of folks trapped underground in the middle of a firefight. We barely have time for a nice dinner before you're faced with trying to rescue half the fleet from something we've never seen before. *And* the admiral returns from the dead to tell us the situation is worse than we already thought. If it had been anyone else, Chakotay would have told her to take a number and he'd deal with her once we figure out how we're going to survive this crisis."

"Chakotay was practically levitating in his chair." B'Elanna half smiled.

"Can you blame him? In his place I'd have been doing the same," Tom admitted.

"Part of me just wants to accept it, to say, Great, you're back. You figure this out," B'Elanna admitted, her weariness showing.

"You can't un-ring a bell, B'Elanna," he said seriously. "We've all gotten used to a universe without her, and we do things for ourselves that we once looked to her for. Having her back is a good thing. Of that, I'm certain. But things can never be the way they were before she died, and maybe that's for the best."

"Shouldn't I at least be a little relieved?"

"You're not going to rest easy until this whole mess is behind us."

"I just feel sick. Why can't we just take Miral, pack our shuttle, and get out of here before . . . I don't care where we go. New Talax? Anywhere but the epicenter of the end of the universe."

Tom smiled. "In the first place, our shuttle is aboard the *Achilles,* which is on its way back to the Alpha Quadrant. And in the second, you know damn well why."

"What if we were wrong to run here in the first place? Yes, the Warriors of Gre'thor were a threat, but threats don't seem to be in short supply here."

"I'm not going to waste a second wishing we'd done things differently. And not for nothing, the day we found you out here, Captain Eden would have been well within her rights to cut all three of us loose to the tender mercies of the Delta Quadrant. Every single person in this fleet, even our closest friends, who we lied to repeatedly, have taken us in and continue to protect us on a daily basis. If we turn our backs on them now, when they need the best we have to give, who are we? What are we teaching Miral?"

"That's why I volunteered to board *Quirinal,*" B'Elanna said, nodding slightly.

"I'm sure Eden is waiting for you in the transporter room. Watch your back. I don't think we've heard half of what she really knows about this anomaly so do me a favor and find us an answer."

"Aye, sir."

Chapter Twenty-eight

VOYAGER

"So let me get this straight," Lieutenant Patel said. Her red-rimmed eyes were a testament to hours of lost sleep and of staring at displays. "This anomaly is a weak point in the fabric of space-time between the known universe and some realm that runs throughout all of the multiverse without intersecting it?"

"Isn't that just an alternate dimension?" Lieutenant Conlon asked.

"No," Seven replied patiently. Prior to their arrival in astrometrics, she had run several analyses, beginning from her new premise, and was quite pleased with the results. "An alternate dimension would be inextricably linked to our own."

"And this one isn't?" the science officer asked.

"If what Captain Eden has told us is correct, it was never meant to be," Seven replied.

"And what is the nature of this particular realm?" the chief engineer pressed Seven, trying to understand.

"The nature?"

"Is it a good witch or a bad witch?" Conlon asked.

Seven stared at her as if she had completely taken leave of her senses.

"It's a really old story, Seven," Conlon sighed. "Never mind. You said this realm could share properties with the Q Continuum. That place is the home of we don't know how many incredibly powerful sentient beings whose intentions toward us have usually been dubious at best. Are there life-forms running around in this new realm too, and are they likely to take kindly to whatever we're about to do to it?"

"We do not possess sufficient data to answer that question with any degree of certainty. But, the fact is that these weaknesses have existed between our universe and this realm for thousands of years. And the experiences of the one sentient race of which we are aware as they journeyed through it suggest that it is uninhabited at the present time."

"Except for our people," Patel added quietly.

"That is the hope," Seven agreed.

"Hang on," Conlon said, stepping up to the panel beside Seven and beginning to run her own series of calculations.

"Lieutenant?" Seven inquired.

"I just want to see something," Conlon replied, continuing to work.

After a few moments, a new image appeared on the wide display of the astrometrics lab. At the base of the screen was a small red area that roughly conformed to the present position of the anomaly. Sharp red lines dispersed in every direction from a central point, with small white dots representing the position of the three trapped ships.

"Come on," Conlon hissed under her breath.

"What are you attempting to do?" Seven began, but her breath caught as a few moments later, a second bright red patch appeared several meters from the first. A third, fourth, fifth, and sixth soon joined it.

Conlon smiled faintly. "I'm not a witch at all. I'm the biggest antenna you ever saw."

"What is she talking about?" Patel asked. "Is that the Gamma Quadrant?"

Seven studied the engineer's calculations. "You have directed our subspace sensors into the anomaly." The admiration was clear in her tone.

"Not exactly," Conlon replied. "We're still a little far out for that to work. However, the *Quirinal* is on the front lines. I'm using what's left of their sensor grid, and slaving it to ours."

"And this display represents the entire galaxy?" Patel asked, awed.

"By looking through the anomaly, rather than around it, we get a very clear picture of the weak points in our galaxy," Conlon said. "I bet we could expand the search, but for now, it's not really necessary."

Seven was now working with intensity at Conlon's side. Patel had grabbed an adjacent station, and was also attempting to build upon Conlon's work. "Every scan we've run so far tells us that nothing beyond the anomaly's boundaries has ever existed. That somehow the anomaly erases matter and energy. It *should* have affected the portions of the vessels still in normal space. The fact that it didn't means that the rest of the ships are still there," Patel said, her hands working the controls.

"Which I surmised given the fact that the ancient race who broke this thing in the first place actually survived a journey through it," Conlon stated.

"If *Quirinal*'s comm system can be properly modified, similar to your subspace scan," Patel picked up, "we might be able to transmit a signal to our people."

"Yes," Conlon agreed, "and if we can talk to them, we might be able to coordinate our efforts to free them."

A few moments of silence passed as the three women worked. Finally, Seven activated the comm channel and was rewarded with a harsh burst of static.

"Keep at it, Seven," Conlon encouraged her.

The crackling diminished and finally a single high-pitched whine against a background of white noise filled the lab.

"This is *Voyager* to any member of the Federation fleet who is receiving this signal. Please conform your signal to these parameters and respond."

She repeated her request five times before she was rewarded by a sharp blurt of static.

"Who is it?" Conlon asked.

"A moment, please," Seven replied evenly.

Patel walked from her station and joined the others standing before the main panel. "You've got them?"

"I appear to have someone," Seven replied. She then repeated her original request followed by, "Please identify yourself."

". . . give me . . . minute . . . Federation . . . Voyager? Voyager, can you hear me?"

All three turned briefly to share genuine smiles of excitement. Seven said again, "Please identify yourself."

"Miles Jobin," came a gravelly voice, much more clearly this time. *"Where are you people?"*

"We are in the Delta Quadrant," Seven replied. Conlon called up crew manifests for each of the four trapped ships to do a quick search for his name.

"He's not there," Conlon said, obviously confused.

"The Delta Quadrant? Since when is the Federation sending ships to the Delta Quadrant?" Jobin replied.

"He's not there because he is not one of our crew members," Seven said, faintly, her eyes widening.

"Who is he?"

"I believe he is one of Captain Eden's uncles," Seven replied. "Mister Jobin, please keep this channel open as long as possible." Turning, she activated the shipwide comm. "Captain Chakotay, report to astrometrics immediately."

QUIRINAL

Walking through a starship hanging dead in space was not one of B'Elanna Torres's favorite exercises. In the hours since the rescue of most of her crew, the *Quirinal* had slipped almost a meter farther into the anomaly. As she walked through the halls of Deck 16, the corridor's internal illumination system flickered randomly, giving the ship the feel of a haunted house. Fluctuations in the internal gravity exacerbated the ever-present nausea in her gut, making it awfully difficult to keep putting one foot in front of the other.

After installing a set of pattern enhancers as close to the engineering section as they dared, the three had made their way toward main engineering. As they neared the entrance, the lights flickered on several data interface panels amid a tangle of ODN cables heaped in the hall outside the doors. B'Elanna took a moment to mourn the Herculean effort she had undertaken, just a few weeks earlier, to rebuild *Quirinal*.

"What happened here?" Cambridge asked with an uncharacteristic tinge of fear in his voice. B'Elanna was pleased to see that there were things that breached even *his* formidable wall of wry composure.

"Could this have happened when they entered the anomaly?" Eden added.

B'Elanna shook her head. "No, sir. I'm guessing they were concerned about continuing to work in main engineering and were trying to restore as many systems as possible remotely. We need to get in there and see what happened."

"After you." Cambridge smirked.

"No." Eden stepped forward. "I'll go first. Both of you, a few paces behind."

B'Elanna fell in line behind the captain. Her heart quickened the moment she entered the bay and saw the barrier: a dense, inky blackness cut through a space she knew as well as her own quarters. It took her a few seconds to remember to breathe.

"Hello, there," Cambridge said softly behind her.

Eden's eyes never left the thing, as she lifted her head and scanned every visible inch of the nothingness.

Not wanting to remain there one second longer than necessary, B'Elanna quickly set the portable scanner she had brought along on the deck and began to activate its components. Once she had established baseline functions, she then worked quickly to see if her portable system could still interface with *Quirinal*'s own sensor grid.

Captain Eden walked slowly beside the barrier, altering her course only when the central warp and slipstream assembly forced her to veer way around them. Cambridge moved to her side, and B'Elanna was conscious of an exchange of quiet words between them. So focused was she on her own efforts, however, B'Elanna did not bother to try and make out their conversation.

After granting Afsarah a few minutes of silent contemplation, Cambridge forced his own suffocating fear of the barrier aside and stepped toward her. Standing within meters of it was almost more than he could bear. Only the terror of admitting to Seven that his courage had failed him kept him in motion until he reached the captain's side.

"Well?" he asked.

"My feet are still on the deck, as you can see," she replied.

"Is it telling you anything?"

She shook her head slowly.

Cambridge took out a medical tricorder, set to read the captain's continuing quantum state, and stepped back. He knew that if the display bars shifted from a bright green to an orange-ish hue, there would be cause for alarm. Leaving it active, he dropped it into his pocket. The captain had moved to a position near the bulkhead and remained quite still as she peered upward.

"What is it?" he asked softly.

Her brow, furrowed in intense concentration, suggested she was seeing more than the uncomfortable darkness.

"Itak?" she whispered.

"You see Captain Itak?" Cambridge asked, wondering if she could hear him.

"And Chan."

So at least part of her is still here, Cambridge thought with relief.

"And I think that's Waverly."

"Who the hell is Waverly?"

"*Esquiline*'s chief engineer."

"Anyone else?"

"There's a young woman. I don't recognize her."

"Where are they?"

Her breath grew more rapid as Eden replied, "The garden, or what's left of it."

Cambridge placed a gentle hand on her arm. "Stay with me, Afsarah," he commanded her softly.

"Where is he? He should be there."

"Who?"

"Tallar."

"Your uncle is not there?"

"He must be, but I can't—"

At that moment, the tricorder in his pocket began to emit a low alarm.

"Afsarah, listen to me. I want you to step back for a moment." When she did not immediately comply, he said more firmly, "Captain Eden, listen to me. Look at me."

"Captain, Counselor," Commander Torres called from behind them.

"What is it?" Cambridge asked without daring to tear his eyes away from Eden.

"I've got a stable comlink with *Voyager*. Captain Chakotay is advising that Captain Eden needs to transport back immediately."

Cambridge shook his head. "Have you finished your work, Commander?"

"No. I'll stay," she replied.

"Not alone," he decided. "And the fleet commander is not yet ready to leave, either. Tell Chakotay we need a few more minutes."

"Understood."

As ship's counselor he could declare Eden unfit and relieve her of command, but he knew that whatever was happening to her could be crucial in resolving the situation. Against every instinct for self-preservation he possessed, Cambridge stood in front of Eden and asked, "Captain, do you hear me?"

OMEGA CONTINUUM

"Then we are all agreed?"

"Yes, Itak."

"Yes, Captain."

"Yes, sir."

"Where is Tallar? Shouldn't he be here, Itak?"

"He is nearby."

"Where?"

"I cannot see him, but I sense him. He is reluctant."

"Then shouldn't we reconsider?"

"No, Ensign Johns, I do not believe so. He understands what is at stake here. He will join our efforts."

"And if he doesn't?"

"Patience, Xin."

"I'm still not exactly sure how we're going to manage this."

"In much the same manner as you managed to arrive in this garden, Lieutenant Waverly."

"And you're sure that what we do here will have an effect on the portions of our ships that still remain outside Omega?"

"Our vessels remain intact. When we act as one to destroy the sections we are able to access, the unaffected sections may be cast adrift, but without anything to anchor them, they will quickly decompress and be destroyed."

"When do we do this?"

"When we are all ready."

"And Tallar?"

"I believe he is coming now."

VOYAGER

Less than a minute after receiving Conlon's summons, Chakotay entered astrometrics.

"Lieutenants Conlon and Patel, I'm ordering both of you off duty for the next four hours."

"Captain," they both began to protest.

"I'd give you eight if I could, but as it stands, I need you refreshed, if not well rested."

Although their disappointment was clear, they nodded dutifully and departed. Chakotay then tapped his combadge and said, "Chakotay to Paris. Initiate transport."

"Aye, Captain," Paris replied, and seconds later, Admiral Janeway appeared in a cascade of particles and light.

"What do you have?" she asked immediately.

"I believe the individual on the other end of this signal is Miles Jobin, Captain Eden's uncle," Seven replied.

Janeway nodded. Turning to Chakotay, she said, "Is Captain Eden on her way?"

Chakotay shook his head. "We've established contact with B'Elanna, but she indicated they're not ready to return."

"I don't think she'd want to miss this, do you?"

"I can't exactly order her back," offered Chakotay.

For a moment Chakotay watched Janeway wrestle with the idea that she could, but clearly wouldn't. Nodding briskly, the admiral stepped aside to allow Chakotay to take her place. He turned to Seven. Wordlessly, Seven reopened the channel and signaled Chakotay to proceed.

"This is Captain Chakotay of the Federation *Starship Voyager.* I understand you are Miles Jobin. Is that correct?"

"Yes, Captain," the gruff voice replied. Seven couldn't help but note a tone of dismay that had crept into the man's voice.

"Are you related in any way to Afsarah Eden?"

"Is my daughter there?" Jobin demanded. Clearly the possibility had never crossed his mind. *"Is she safe?"*

"Captain Eden is commanding a fleet of vessels here in the Delta Quadrant," Chakotay replied. "But she is not presently aboard our ship. She will join us as soon as she is able. What is your present location, Mister Jobin?"

"Same place I've been for the last forty years. The Beta Quadrant, just outside the Lantaru sector."

"And how did you come to be there?"

"None of your damn business," Jobin replied. *"Where's my daughter?"*

Janeway exchanged a glance with Chakotay as he replied, "Several of our vessels have become partially trapped inside what we believe is a breach into normal space-time of a discrete realm. Captain Eden is presently on one of those ships, attempting to gather information about the boundary that separates that realm—"

"*Hell and damnation, get her out of there right now!*"

"We have a transporter lock on her as we speak, and I can assure you she's quite safe."

"*None of you is safe. If she passes through that barrier, it's all over. She doesn't know it and that's my fault. But you can't let her anywhere near it. Do you hear me?*"

"Why not?" Chakotay demanded.

Jobin paused, and his voice was thick with emotion when he continued. "*It's my fault. I should have told her before we ever left her on Earth. But Tallar swore we'd be back. He swore to me on her life.*"

Chakotay's voice took on a more compassionate tone. "I believe you had nothing but the best of intentions for her. She knows she is connected in some way to this anomaly and will gladly risk her own life to find out the truth. If you know that truth, Mister Jobin, and if you love her, you need to tell me what it is. I want to help both of you, but I can't unless you tell me everything you know about this anomaly."

"*You swear you'll keep her safe?*"

"I do," Chakotay replied as a faint shudder ran through his body.

"*I used to be in Starfleet, you know. I found the damn thing in the first place. I was a green ensign running gamma-shift sensor sweeps. The first time I saw it I figured it was a glitch. I took the readings to Captain Leeds and he agreed. But I knew there was more to it. It was a gut thing, you know. Anyway, Tallar and I were never cut out for the service. Neither one of us could stomach the chain of command. After our enlistments ended, we resigned, and the first place we decided to explore was my foolishness.*"

"Jobin's Folly," Chakotay said softly, but loud enough for him to hear.

"*She figured that out, did she? Of course she did. Afsarah was smarter than both of us combined, and that's saying something.*"

"The anomaly you discovered was a highly localized area

where the normal laws of space-time were suspended," Chakotay urged him on.

"Try 'negated,'" Jobin huffed. *"The damn thing could eat space-time itself. Nothing that went in should ever have come out. But it's not just nothing. It's a living nothing."*

"I'm sorry?" Chakotay asked, clearly confused. "Are you saying there is some sentience to it?"

"Not life as we know it. But it lives to destroy. Once it knew we were out there, I think it got curious, or lonely."

"Captain Eden believes that another race, an ancient species, pulled this realm into ours. They traveled through it thousands of years ago."

"Afsarah found them too? Damn it all! That's my girl."

"She found the remains of their civilization," Chakotay clarified.

"Then she knows more than I do," Jobin insisted.

"No, she doesn't," Chakotay corrected him. "She knows their story, but she doesn't know her own. Where did she come from, Mister Jobin?"

A long pause from the other side forced Chakotay to look to Seven.

"The channel remains operative, Captain," Seven said evenly.

"Mister Jobin?"

OMEGA CONTINUUM

"Get out of here, all of you!"

"Please, Mister Tallar, control yourself."

"This is my garden and I want all of you the hell out of it now!"

"Xin, Waverly, Johns, remain where you are."

"Yes, Captain Itak."

"Yes."

"Aye, sir."

"Mister Tallar, you know as well as the rest of us that Omega's progress into our universe will continue unless we remove all of the matter and energy we have brought here."

"I know. And I don't care."

"Yes, you do."

"I don't. I was fine until you showed up. You made it worse. You can fix that. But leave me alone."

"Do you believe your daughter would concur with your present choice?"

"Leave her out of this."

"Sadly, I cannot. She is my commanding officer and a model of Starfleet's ideals. If confronted with this reality, she would surely make the same choice we have. It is a necessary sacrifice, to ensure the survival of countless other life-forms."

"That's only because I let you bastards educate her. I should never have let her go!"

"You wanted to save her."

"Yes."

"You have the power to do so right now."

"You don't understand."

"Tell me what it is that I do not understand."

"She'll come anyway. And if I'm not here when she does . . ."

"If we are successful, our actions here will seal this area of Omega. She will not be able to access the continuum from her present location."

"You think that will stop her? You don't know her very well, do you?"

"I know that she will see that her highest duty is the preservation of life, even at the loss of her own."

"Of course she will. But she doesn't understand that it's not that simple. Omega must be returned to its original orientation. If any portion of it remains accessible through the multiverse, the threat still exists. Afsarah is the only one who can right the wrongs I've done. But I won't stand for it. This isn't her fault."

"It isn't yours, either. You did not call Omega into our multiverse."

"And I never found the monsters who did. I never figured out what they did to break it in the first place. If I had . . ."

"Your regrets are understandable, but they are no longer of consequence. The immediate threat must be dealt with."

"Then go."

"Without your cooperation, our sacrifice will be meaningless."

"I just can't. Not yet."

"You want her to return. You want to explain. But only by eliminating any cause for her to return can you hope to spare her. You must join our efforts. . . . Mister Tallar?"

"I can't believe it's come to this. It wasn't supposed to be this way."

"No. None of us are responsible for the present circumstance. That does not change the only course open to us."

"No, it doesn't."

"Then you will join us?"

"Forgive me, Jobin. I'm so very sorry."

"Mister Tallar?"

"Let's get on with it before I change my mind."

QUIRINAL

"Damn it, Afsarah, talk to me!"

Cambridge was within a hair's breadth of grabbing his commanding officer and shaking her senseless when she said softly, "Tallar?"

Eden stepped around the counselor and closer to the barrier. This time, Cambridge didn't hesitate. Grabbing her firmly around the waist, he said, "Do you see Tallar?"

"Tallar, please," Eden pleaded as fresh tears flowed over her cheeks. "Hear me."

Cambridge wondered if this was possible.

The captain stood in silence, straining against him, but he held her firmly in place. Finally, she relaxed and quite abruptly turned. The expression on her face clearly communicated how inappropriate she considered his actions.

"Afsarah?"

"Yes, Counselor," Eden replied, hurriedly wiping her cheeks with the back of her hand.

At this he released her and asked, "What did you see?"

"They were all standing in the garden, speaking to one another. I couldn't hear what they were saying, but Waverly and the ensign were clearly frightened. And Tallar was furious."

"Then what happened?"

The captain turned back to the barrier, as if it might hold further answers for her. "I don't know. They all vanished."

"Well, at least we've been able to confirm part of our theory. Somehow, your uncle did return to the anomaly from another access point."

Eden grew still again, her gaze drawn into the darkness. "I don't like this," she said softly. "Something's wrong."

VOYAGER

"Mister Jobin," Chakotay called again.

"I'm still here," he finally replied. *"I'll tell you what I saw. You won't believe it, but that's not my problem. When you see Afsarah again,* promise *me you'll tell her it wasn't her fault. It was ours."*

"You have my word."

"The first time we entered this . . . thing, I thought we were goners. We'd tried everything else, and Tallar had a feeling it would work. I'd have done anything for him. Gone anywhere. I guess I did.

"One minute we were on our ship with our course plotted. The next, we were standing in this garden. It was like nothing you've ever seen. The grass was too green, even the dirt was vibrant . . . the trees were drooping under the weight of this luminous fruit. It felt like the beginning. It was all so new and fresh. We didn't belong there. No one did.

"But Tallar was like a kid, romping around, smelling everything. 'Wasn't it beautiful? Didn't he tell me?' And all I could think was, Get me the hell out of here. *Every moment we spent in the garden, I felt like my mind was about to pull itself apart. But Tallar took my hand and led me. As long as I could feel him, I could hold on.*

"*Right in the middle of the garden, there was this tree. The fruit was bigger, more beautiful, more tempting than the rest. Tallar reached for one. I tried to tell him no, but I could never tell him anything.*

"*He touched it. It fell to the ground, and then I knew I was losing my mind. It got brighter and then it vanished. But it hadn't. It had transformed. It was her . . . Afsarah. She was a baby, so small, so perfect. She looked just like Tallar, except for her being a girl. The little girl he always wanted.*

"*I don't know how long we stood there, a second or a day or a year. Afsarah grew and grew. I was terrified. Tallar was in love. Finally she stood up. Now, she was three, maybe four. She looked right into his eyes and reached up for him. He was gone. Hell, so was I. She was the most beautiful thing I'd ever seen.*

"*He picked her up and held her close. I grabbed both of them and wished with everything I had that we could all just get out of there.*

"*The next thing I knew, we were all back on our ship. Afsarah was there with us.*

"*But Tallar was never the same. He said the garden had told him its secrets. He said Afsarah got us out because I wanted it so badly. He said the garden needed her back, but he was never going to let her go. We both wanted a child so much, but I never seriously considered the possibility that it could happen. We could have applied for an adoption—lots of children needed good homes. But we didn't have a home. We had a ship and a longing to explore. It was no life for a child, and we weren't going to be able to convince anyone otherwise. But that thing answered our prayers. It gave her to us. I named her, you know. The crown of paradise.*"

"Afsarah Eden," Chakotay murmured.

"*It was easy to run. Tallar said someone had been there before us. He thought we could find them. Maybe they knew a way we could keep her with us. We looked and looked. We followed every path Tallar could think of. And she seemed like any other child. We knew she wasn't, but we didn't know how different she was until she got a little older. Afsarah was always quick, smart, she remembered everything you told her. We discovered that she knew stuff we didn't. Tallar said the garden knew everything. It knew the history of the entire universe.*

It watched all of space-time, it remembered all the things we forgot of our pasts. But it knew because it was the end. It had already seen everything. And Afsarah was the garden, brought to life.

"*We knew it was always hanging over us. The longer we were away, the more she grew, and we knew it would call to her. We knew we had to find a way to close it, so she could never go back. We didn't dare tell her the truth. We left her on Earth, told her it was time for her to get a proper education. We went back with a better ship, determined to do whatever it took to seal that thing off forever.*

"*I sent messages to her from time to time, just so she wouldn't worry. I told her we were heading to the Gamma Quadrant. I figured if she ever went looking for us, she'd end up as far away from our actual position as possible. I guess I—*"

The connection was abruptly terminated as *Voyager* lurched beneath Chakotay's feet.

"Seven," Chakotay demanded.

Seven's hands furiously worked the control panel. "We've lost him. Attempting to restore the signal."

"*Bridge to Captain Chakotay,*" came Paris's harried voice.

"Go ahead, Tom."

"*The anomaly is splintering again. We need to move.*"

Chakotay turned to Janeway. "If Seven gets Jobin back, keep him talking."

QUIRINAL

Eden stood before the barrier, willing it to show her what she wanted to see. All the while, a roar in her head demanded that she run.

She couldn't.

He's there.

Tallar! Tallar! It's me. See me.

See me.

A bright light assaulted her. It illuminated the hulls of five ships. Eden's heart caught in her throat as she recognized the smallest of the five.

Tallar, no.

He was there because his ship was there, trapped like the others.

In a blinding flash, the *Hawking* was engulfed in roiling flames.

From behind her, B'Elanna's voice called urgently, "Captain! Counselor!"

"What is it?" Cambridge asked.

"We're leaving. Now!"

Cambridge grabbed both of Eden's hands. "You heard the fleet chief. Come on."

Tallar!

And then his face was there before her. The rest had vanished. All she saw, all she knew, was her father.

Desperately she reached for him.

Don't! she pleaded.

And this time, she knew he heard her. His own hand reached for hers, and the agony of his torment became hers.

Her fingers had barely grazed the barrier when Cambridge roughly pulled her from behind, lifting her off her feet, propelling her out of engineering and toward the waiting transporter pattern enhancers.

Eden no longer needed to see the barrier to know what was happening. The *Esquiline, Curie,* and *Quirinal* were following *Hawking*'s lead. One by one, each of the vessels exploded in her mind.

Only Tallar's face remained, poised on the precipice between life and death.

VOYAGER

"Have we got the away team?" Chakotay demanded of Lasren. He was seated in his command chair, holding tight to the armrests. Ensign Gwyn was doing her best to maneuver around the new fractures that were opening from within the anomaly.

"Transport complete," the operations officer advised. "They're back."

"Aytar, get us clear of the new fractures, best possible speed," ordered Chakotay.

Gwyn didn't reply, so intent was she on making sure *Voyager* didn't slip into a small slice of oblivion.

"Ensign Gwyn," came Kim's voice from tactical, "a new fracture is opening, dead ahead."

"Got it," she replied through gritted teeth.

Chakotay experienced a momentary sense of free fall before the inertial dampers cut in. The ensign had forced the bow down, clearly intending to pass under the new obstacle. Checking the subspace scans for himself, Chakotay knew it was the best maneuver possible, but it probably had only a fifty-fifty chance of success.

They were less than a thousand kilometers from it when the blackness was consumed by a light so bright it looked like a star had just gone supernova. Chakotay had to raise a hand to shield his eyes. This time, *Voyager* wasn't going to beat the odds.

As suddenly as the light had appeared, it vanished. Darkness yawned before them. He felt an uncertain jolt as the ship came to a halt.

"Ensign Gwyn, what are you doing?" he asked.

She sat at the conn, holding to the front of it with both her hands, her breath coming in short bursts.

"It's gone, Captain," Kim reported.

"What?" Chakotay asked, checking his own readings. And sure enough, the fracture had vanished as abruptly as it had appeared.

"Let's keep moving," Chakotay ordered, thankful of the reprieve the universe had granted him. "Helm, continue on a trajectory away from the anomaly. Full impulse."

Kim reported, "No, Captain, not just the nearest fracture. The entire anomaly has vanished."

"I don't think so," Lasren countered from ops.

"Lieutenant?" Kim asked.

"Check sensor grid sixty-three delta, the anomaly's original position," Lasren suggested to Kim.

"What do we have?" Chakotay asked.

After a moment spent checking their readings, Kim nodded to Lasren.

"The anomaly has not disappeared," Larsen reported. "It has resumed its original configuration. The fractures that captured our ships are gone, and it is reduced to a hundred thousandth of its former size."

"What's the status of our ships?" Tom asked.

Lasren shook his head. "They're gone too, sir."

Chapter Twenty-nine

ERIS

Q sat cross-legged on the floor of the vault. The prism rested dull and lifeless in his palm. As he began to consider all it had shown him, he rolled it back and forth between his hands.

His biggest regret was not forcing Amanda to bring him here when she'd first spoken of it. He could have saved her.

Might have, he corrected himself.

Or he might have just delayed the inevitable by a few precious days.

His father should have been here by now. It couldn't have taken this long for him to figure out where his son would have gone.

Or maybe he just doesn't care.

That thought should have made him angry. Instead, it left him cold.

"So, you found it," his father's voice murmured from the shadows.

There were so many questions Q wanted to ask his father now. Only one really mattered.

Why didn't you tell me?

His father emerged from the shadows, masquerading in the human form Q had always believed was his favorite, though he would never admit it. He wore a simple black tunic over gray pants. He paused a few feet from him and knelt on one knee, his hands hanging low and loosely clasped before him.

"Why didn't I tell you about the prism? It's an amusement, nothing more. And I did tell you about most of the better ones."

"Don't," Q commanded.

"Why didn't I tell you how your godmother's death became a fixed point in time?"

"You had to know I'd find out on my own."

"I honestly didn't. Most of your life you've run from one diversion to the next, pleading innocence, adolescence, the right to follow in my footsteps—whatever you could come up with to excuse your poor judgment. How was I to know that you'd suddenly develop a conscience when I wasn't looking?"

"It wasn't my conscience that led me here, Father."

"Then what was it?"

"Fear."

At this his father was taken aback. "You're a Q. You have nothing to fear."

"Not even the wrath of the Continuum?"

"They'll come around. They always do."

"*Always*. That's funny." Q grimaced.

"Your mother told me you've been having difficulty moving beyond this point in time."

"Do you know why?"

His father's face registered a brief struggle. To his credit—and his son's surprise—the truth won out. "Yes."

"And all this time . . ."

"All this time," his father interrupted harshly, "I've been looking for a solution."

Q searched his father's face. "I don't believe you."

"Son?"

Q rose and began to pace the floor of the vault. "There's only one solution, and you forced me to find it, rather than simply preventing Aunt Kathy's death in the first place."

Q rose, accepting the criticism with uncharacteristic grace. "Is that what you truly believe, even now?"

"You allowed Amanda to go searching for an answer that ended her existence," Q said, his voice rising.

"A price I was only too willing to pay."

"How could you?"

In a flash, Q stood directly before him and grabbed his upper arms. "How could I not? You're my son."

"Then why haven't you helped me?"

Q dropped his hands and shook his head slowly. "Your godmother is not the solution. If I thought for a moment she was, I'd have brought her to the Continuum before she ever learned about that stupid cube. I'd have opened the entire cosmos to her fragile consciousness while offering her intravenous coffee to sustain her."

"But you know as well as I do that she fought the darkness once and beat it."

"As soon as we're done here I'm going straight to your teachers and demanding that they completely revise their curriculum. How they passed you in spite of your incomprehension of the most rudimentary principles of your Q-ness, let alone the inverse relations of cause and effect when temporal matrices have been corrupted, is a crime beyond my ability to adequately express."

Snapping his fingers, his father drew the prism from his hand and set it spinning in midair. Moments later, the image of Kathryn Janeway and her crew working to destroy the anomaly they had discovered in the Delta Quadrant during their first mission played out. Having already watched it hundreds of times, Q felt that, dramatic as events were, they had lost their potency.

"What's wrong with this picture, son?" his father demanded.

"A human found an answer you couldn't?" Q replied petulantly.

"Look again."

Q did so, but whatever his father was getting at eluded him.

After a few moments of silence his father said, "Did you by any chance attempt to enter this timestream?"

"Yes."

"And did you succeed?"

"No."

"And why do you suppose that was?"

"Because the timeline no longer exists. Once Admiral and Captain Janeway altered history, it collapsed."

"Wrong."

Q felt suddenly dizzy and longed to release himself from his human body. Beneath his father's withering gaze, he held his form.

"You can't enter this timestream and neither can I, because Kathy's solution was criminally shortsighted—not unlike several other choices she's made and for which, thanks to you, I might have the opportunity to take her to task. The actions she took here, and the actions you would have her take again, erased the entire Q Continuum from existence."

Q felt his entire body shudder violently.

"That's impossible."

"It took me by surprise as well. This is one of many reasons it pays to study carefully the actions of these lesser beings. From time to time they stumble across things they cannot be expected to comprehend, and even with the best of intentions they create absolute chaos. I'm not just trying to save them from themselves, I'm trying to save all of us from their ignorance."

"How does closing a spatial anomaly erase the Q Continuum?" Q demanded.

"This isn't just any anomaly, son."

"Yes, thank you. That much I already know."

"Anything that occurs within this continuum, much like actions in our own, has the potential to affect the entire history of the multiverse. Do or undo something here, and it is as if the action was taken at the dawn of time."

"So Aunt Kathy closed this continuum and by doing so, altered history . . ."

". . . from the beginning," his father finished for him. "The physics underlying her solution is within her grasp, and you have brought her back to repeat this unacceptable action. Thankfully, I'll be able to prevent that from occurring. But had you listened to me in the first place—"

"You didn't tell me anything but 'no.' You could have brought me here and shown me the consequences."

"I shouldn't have to. I'm your father; you should have taken me at my word."

"Allowing Aunt Kathy to die had nothing to do with the end of the Borg?"

"We'll never know, but play this timeline a few hundred years further into the future and you'll see that if she had *not* altered time to bring her people home several years early, the Borg would have continued their normal, and quite predictable, path of assimilation until eventually they would have reached the Federation with such overwhelming force that it would have fallen in a day. The rest of the galaxy would have followed soon after. I suppose I should thank 'Kathy' for sparing us the incredible tedium of a galaxy filled with Borg, but you'll forgive me if I can't muster the enthusiasm, since none of us would have been around to be bored senseless by it."

Q sighed. "So Aunt Kathy can't help us."

"No. Which is why I told you to leave it alone."

"And you can't either."

"Oh, ye of little faith." His father smiled. "I know already what can't be done. I'm still working on what can."

"Is the rest of the Continuum working with you?"

"No," he admitted ruefully.

"Why not?"

"It's a collective blind spot among them. As soon as I understood that, I knew they'd be useless to me."

"They can't see it?"

"No."

"But you can? How?"

"Because you're my son. Everything that concerns you is of paramount concern to me. And if you'd just left well enough alone, and trusted me, you'd never have known, either."

"Losing my ability to travel into the future made that impossible."

"It's temporary, I assure you."

"How can you be sure?"

"Because the multiverse has our back on this one, even if the Continuum doesn't."

Q suddenly saw a new section of the puzzle quite clearly. "The multiverse wants this continuum returned to its original orientation from which it cannot impact the events of space-time."

"That's right. At least not for a very, very, very long time."

"Aunt Kathy accomplished this once, but when she failed to do it again, the multiverse began ordering events so that someone else would."

"Excellent."

"And that someone is?"

"Me."

"Then you plan to confront Eden?"

The light fell from his father's face.

"I beg your pardon?"

"Eden, the commander of the *Voyager* fleet."

"Who?"

"Father?" Q said, aghast.

Q again set the prism spinning. At his direction it began to show the entire history of the fleet's interactions with the anomaly. As soon as the *Achilles* entered the area, the prism showed a room where a Lendrin male and Afsarah Eden stood staring at a display panel.

His father froze the frame and stared at it for a long time.

"How did I miss that?" he finally said softly.

How did he miss that? The terror that had momentarily begun to abate roared through Q with a deafening force.

"Possibly because this is the only timeline in which Eden exists," Q suggested.

"What?" his father gasped.

"I assumed that meant Eden was one of us, as she is clearly unbounded by time just as we are."

"There are countless individuals who exist in only one time-line," his father corrected him.

"At the epicenter of a convergence containing the possibility of eradicating the multiverse?"

"You might have something there," his father grudgingly allowed. "Where did she come from?"

"She isn't a Q?"

"No."

Suddenly the darkness roared back, threatening to engulf him.

"Father, listen to me," Q said quickly. "Whatever you are planning to do, don't. Just leave it alone."

"Son, please."

"No. You say all of this could have been avoided if I had trusted you. Now I'm asking you to trust me."

"I do," his father said kindly. "But you are out of your depth here. You've barely begun your life as a Q. I've been doing this for billions of years."

"I know. But this isn't your fight."

"Of course it is. Now go to Septurnal Prime. Your mother is worried sick. I suggested she go there and allow the astral eddies to calm her nerves. I'll join you both there shortly."

"But, Father—" Q pleaded.

"No buts. And if you attempt to come within a million light-years of that ship, you can rest assured I will stop you."

With a wink, his father snapped his fingers and disappeared. The theatrical and completely unnecessary flourish was actually touching. No Q actually required a physical gesture to accomplish anything. That his father continued to do so for effect brought a fresh torment to Q's being.

Once he had understood at least part of his godmother's inter-actions with the anomaly, and watched from afar as Aunt Kathy worked with Afsarah Eden to unravel its mysteries, he'd begun to accept how all of this must end. He'd believed that his father would know too, and that he'd never had any intention of trying to change it. This conversation, while incredibly instructive, only confirmed his initial suspicions. That his father might actually

THE ETERNAL TIDE • 299

care was something—though now, Q found himself wishing that his father didn't.

Either way, there was but one path before him. The only problem was that now he wasn't sure he had the courage to walk it.

Chapter Thirty

VOYAGER

"No," Kathryn Janeway said softly as her legs lost their strength, and she availed herself of the nearest chair to avoid landing on the deck in her quarters.

"We've reviewed the sensor logs," Chakotay said calmly. "We were trying to evade a new series of fractures, but we now have definitive evidence that the three ships remaining in normal space have been destroyed."

Seven hundred and eighty-five people.

Sixty-three billion people.

When does this madness end?

"Seven has reviewed the logs and believes that the entire event was instigated by the individuals within the anomaly," Chakotay added.

"How could she know that?"

"We don't have clear readings of what was going on inside, but there is no evidence that anything changed, prior to the event, in the portions of the ships we could scan. One moment, everything was status quo; the next, our ships break off at the barrier and implode. Within seconds, the anomaly expanded briefly to absorb their destruction, then reverted to its original state."

"Seven thinks . . ." Kathryn stammered, struggling to wrap her brain around it, ". . . that seven hundred eighty-five people intentionally destroyed their ships, presumably ending their lives? For what conceivable purpose?"

"To seal Omega."

The admiral looked up sharply to see that Captain Eden had

entered her quarters without bothering to ask. Or maybe she had not heard it.

"Omega?"

"The Omega Continuum," Eden clarified.

Kathryn was glad she was already seated because an entire continuum composed of the most destructive particle known to the Federation was the only thing she could imagine that would make this situation worse.

"We almost didn't get your team out . . ." Chakotay began.

"I apologize, Chakotay," Eden said, quite contrite. "But I was able to gather a great deal of information we needed."

"Where are B'Elanna and Hugh?" he asked.

"Commander Torres is briefing Seven. Cambridge is meeting with the Doctor, undoubtedly to review the subatomic scans he took of me during our time aboard *Quirinal*."

"Could we go back a minute?" Kathryn asked. Finding her feet, she stood and confronted Eden. "The Omega Continuum?"

"Don't you think we should brief the captain first on our conversation with Mister Jobin?"

Before Kathryn could object, Eden raised a hand and said, "That won't be necessary."

"Why not?" Kathryn asked.

"Just before we moved to the transport site, I made brief physical contact with the barrier."

And it didn't kill you? the admiral thought.

"No, it didn't," Eden replied to Kathryn's unspoken thought. "It provided me with a full understanding of how we got here and what exactly we are facing."

"It's Omega?" Chakotay asked.

Eden smiled bitterly. "The particle the Borg thought of as perfection and the Caeliar managed to domesticate as a power source is a pale reflection of true Omega. They were synthetic particles, corrupted by the boronite used to create them. The Omega Continuum is a discrete region underpinning the entire multiverse, composed entirely of pure Omega. It contains the destructive force required to end the multiverse, once it has run its course, and at the same time give rise to the *next* multiverse. It is an integral part of the eternal cycle of birth, life, and death."

"Is it anything like the Q Continuum?" Kathryn asked.

Eden nodded. "They exist to balance one another."

Chakotay shook his head. "How?"

"The Q Continuum contains the ultimate creative power of the multiverse. Omega is the ultimate destructive force," Eden explained. "Both release their power slowly over vast expanses of time and in precise relation to one another until the multiverse has run its course, a process that normally takes much longer than any of us could imagine."

Kathryn began to pace restlessly. The name and size of the problem sounded about right. The thought that there might be a solution within the grasp of any mortal was a little harder to believe.

"The story Jobin told you was true," Eden went on. "I was born of the Omega Continuum. As it evolves throughout the trillions of years of the life of the multiverse, it remembers and records the history of the multiverse. My unique ability to 'know' things is a gift of my heritage. My human mind can contain only a small fragment of it, but all of it is available to me when my quantum state begins to align with its true nature."

"Then you already know what happened to your uncles?" asked Kathryn.

Eden fought back the tears rising in her eyes, and when she had regained control said, "They went back to the portion of the Omega Continuum present in the Beta Quadrant—where they first entered. They believed they could seal Omega off from normal space, thus making it unnecessary for me to return. They wanted my life to be as normal as possible and as long as possible. They had no idea there were multiple access points running throughout the entire multiverse, or that their actions would be futile."

"Why did our people sacrifice themselves?" Chakotay demanded.

"Once they entered Omega, they understood that any mass or

energy brought within its boundaries accelerates Omega's natural progression. The fractures they fell into were a result of my connection to Omega, but once they were created, the only way for the people in Omega to close them was to destroy themselves and their ships. Otherwise, the lifespan of the multiverse would have been shortened to a matter of months, perhaps a few weeks at most."

"Why didn't it work?" Chakotay asked. "The ships are gone, but the anomaly is still there, albeit quite smaller."

Afsarah Eden turned away and could not meet his stern gaze as she replied. "Tallar remains within Omega," she said softly. "In order to close the access points here and in the Beta Quadrant, Tallar would have had to make the same sacrifice our people did. In the end, he was unable to do his part." When she turned back, her face was streaked with tears, "Tallar wanted me to know all of Omega's secrets, all that he had kept from me. And he couldn't bear to take Jobin's life along with his own. He waited too long to follow our people's lead."

Chakotay's face hardened. Kathryn was sure she had never seen him so thoroughly disgusted.

"Don't judge him too harshly," Kathryn counseled.

"It's hard not to," Chakotay replied, "considering the opportunity he just wasted."

"The actions of our crews have temporarily stabilized the anomaly here," Eden said, knowing it was faint comfort. "They have bought us the time we will need to prevent Omega's spread, and the end of the multiverse. Even if Tallar had joined them, the threat would still exist. When the Anschlasom first breached and corrupted Omega, they left ruptures in multiple places. Those ruptures would have remained, and many of them are outside the range of any Starfleet vessels. We could not have solved this problem alone from here."

"We did it once," the admiral replied.

"Perhaps," Eden allowed.

"We did," Kathryn insisted. "Otherwise I wouldn't be here now."

Clearly choosing her next words carefully, Eden said, "The

only thing that will completely seal the Omega Continuum and end its threat to every sentient being in the multiverse is for me to return to the Continuum. Tallar thought he had created me, and in some ways he did. I was made from him, but not to answer his prayers. I was created to restore the balance that had been corrupted by the Anschlasom."

"The Anschlasom wreaked their havoc thousands of years ago," Kathryn said. "You've been around for what, fifty years? Why did the Omega Continuum take so long to try to restore the balance?"

"Everything that happens within Omega effectively happens at the beginning of time. What the Anschlasom did ten thousand years ago they did at the dawn of time. What Jobin and Tallar did allowed Omega to self-correct when all other possibilities for such a correction had been removed."

"You mean when my future self and I altered the timeline."

Eden nodded. "My life was designed by a presence of complete knowing."

"It put you where you would be needed at the right time?" Chakotay asked.

"Because we weren't going to be," Kathryn said somberly. "If I never alter time, Jobin never discovers the anomaly, because it doesn't exist, and you are never created."

"I despise temporal mechanics," Chakotay sighed.

"It's more than that," Kathryn said softly to herself.

"What?" Chakotay asked.

"*I* wasn't going to be here," the admiral replied, as she watched her own death replayed countless times in a loop running continuously in her mind. "I didn't want *Voyager* to return to the Delta Quadrant. I would have risked, I *did* risk, everything to prevent that from happening. Had I survived, even after the Borg were defeated, I would have argued against the fleet's mission. However, had I not prevailed, I would have led the mission. Chakotay would still have been *Voyager*'s captain, and *you*," Kathryn said, indicating Eden, "would have had no reason to be here."

"I don't see the significance," Chakotay admitted.

"My death became what the Q refer to as a fixed point in time. I'm not supposed to be here. The multiverse didn't want me here."

"But you are here," Chakotay insisted.

As Kathryn forcibly willed the recurring images of her death to stop, the voice that commanded her to move on and ignore Q's request sounded again.

This isn't right.

"I don't think I should be," Kathryn admitted softly.

Chakotay stepped in front of her and took her hands. "I do," he said firmly. "I don't know what you saw, or felt, or learned from the Q. You said that the first time you encountered this thing, you managed to contain it. That's why Junior wanted you here, so you could figure out how to do it again. If that goes against the will of the universe or the multiverse or whatever allowed you to die, along with the sixty-three billion the Borg annihilated on their way to perfection, I don't care."

"This isn't your fault, Admiral," Eden insisted. "Any more than it is mine. You're the one who said guilt was a waste of time."

"That was before I knew just how much of it I'd be asked to swallow," Kathryn replied bitterly.

"Do you have to enter the Omega Continuum?" Chakotay asked of Eden, hoping to turn the conversation toward more constructive ends.

Kathryn marveled silently at his newfound strength. She'd always known he possessed the heart of a warrior, but she felt considerably less composed than he appeared to be at the moment. It was an unusual place in which to find herself.

"Our people just made the ultimate sacrifice." He paused before adding with great compassion, "Are you ready to do the same?"

Kathryn studied Eden, and where she hoped to see resolve, she saw only despair.

"I'm afraid it's not that simple," a new voice replied in her stead.

Kathryn turned to see Q standing beside her.

• • •

When B'Elanna Torres rushed into astrometrics, Seven of Nine wasn't there. Ensign Rosio advised her that Seven had returned to her quarters.

Frustrated, B'Elanna retraced her steps to the turbolift, and was soon standing outside Seven's door. She pressed the door chime several times before it opened. However, Seven was not on the other side.

"Seven?" B'Elanna called out into the darkened living area.

A few moments later, Seven stepped out of the doorway that led to her bedroom, moisture still clinging to her cheeks. B'Elanna stepped toward her. "Are you all right?" she asked.

Seven did not look well. The flesh beneath her eyes was puffy and darkened, in stark contrast to the pale skin of her face. Several wisps of long blond hair had fallen free, and there was a definite slouch to her shoulders.

Seven took a deep breath and said, "I am fine. I was just on my way back to astrometrics."

"Seven, when was the last time you slept?"

"Fifty-three hours ago," she replied.

B'Elanna's eyes widened. "Is that a new personal best for you?"

Seven's head cocked to the right, an old tic, and she asked, "Explain."

"You're not Borg anymore. And whatever the Caeliar left you, it clearly can't replace sleep."

"None of us have had adequate time to rest since this tragedy began to unfold," Seven replied.

"No, and it's not over yet," B'Elanna agreed. Crossing to Seven's replicator, she added, "I need you in top form. Two *raktajinos*, hot," she ordered.

As soon as they materialized, B'Elanna crossed back to Seven. "A much needed 'fresher break will only get you so far. Drink up."

"I'd rather not," Seven replied.

"Want me to make it an order?"

Seven's eyes hardened. "Do you need to be reminded that I do not serve aboard this vessel in an official capacity? While I am willing to observe the chain of command, I am not actually obligated to follow your or anyone else's orders when they violate my personal ethics."

"You have a moral issue with Klingon coffee?"

"It is disgusting."

"It will clear your head quicker than a nap," B'Elanna snapped, offended on behalf of her favorite stimulant.

Seven considered the cup B'Elanna held before her. When she still hesitated, B'Elanna added more gently, "I know it must pain you to admit that you are now as frail as the rest of us mortals, but trust me. I know how you feel right now. Infants come into this world knowing how to suck, cry, poop, and deny their caregivers sleep. Five days after Miral was born I hadn't slept for more than an hour. Then my body simply shut down, and *this*"—she lifted Seven's cup—"was the only thing that allowed me to survive it. Grieve the fragile human condition later, hold your nose, and drink."

Seven's face softened, and she accepted the cup. After several dutiful sips, something rebelled, and she only held it down by holding her free hand to her mouth to keep it closed.

B'Elanna watched this with repressed glee, and once the grimace of distaste had left Seven's face asked, "Now how do you feel?"

Seven seriously considered the question and replied, "Better."

"Right. Now look at this," B'Elanna ordered, sipping from her own cup as she called up a display on Seven's personal workstation. B'Elanna then pulled out the chair and gestured for Seven to sit. Once Seven was settled in, she surprised B'Elanna by drinking again. The engineer smiled to herself, but said nothing as the last scan of the barrier she had taken while aboard Quirinal appeared on the screen.

Seven studied the readings. "Are these from *Quirinal*?"

"Right before we transported out."

"How were you able to retrieve information from beyond the barrier?"

"You mean from something that does not exist?"

"Yes."

"I set the sensors on a wide, rotating harmonic, and at the last second, this is what I got."

Seven's respiration increased. B'Elanna worried that the caffeine rushing through a virgin nervous system might have done more harm than good.

"To be honest," B'Elanna confessed, "I'm not sure it was anything I did. Captain Eden was engaging the barrier in some way. I think she was talking to it. Now I'm wondering if she might have weakened—"

"It doesn't matter how you received this data," Seven cut her off. "If it is accurate—"

"—we're in big trouble," B'Elanna finished for her.

Seven's breathing calmed. "No. *This* we can fix."

Chakotay stepped back automatically, dropping Kathryn's hand. He watched her struggle with the same instinct. Then he cheered internally when she pulled herself upright and squared her shoulders to face Q.

"So *now* you know what this anomaly is?" Janeway asked cynically.

Q dismissed the question with a wave of his hand. From the moment he had materialized, it seemed he had eyes only for Captain Eden. She returned his penetrating gaze with cold eyes and a stoic mask.

"I always knew, Kathy," he said briskly. "The longer you didn't, the better for all of us."

Chakotay found himself torn. Q had never appeared without Chakotay experiencing a deep, primal need to punch the unnatural being squarely in the gut. The Continuum had made Janeway's resurrection possible. That was not enough, however, for him to forgive the disdain Q had just displayed for her.

"If you don't have anything pertinent to add to this discussion, Q, then get out," Chakotay warned him.

"Be silent, tattooed boy," Q replied ominously. "You couldn't act on the many dark fantasies of retribution you are currently entertaining even if you wanted to, so I suggest you stand there like the lump of useless wood I've always thought you to be and listen carefully to your betters."

Janeway quickly pressed her foot next to his. Chakotay accepted her request that he do as Q had "asked," even as he continued to seethe. *Sticks and stones,* he reminded himself while forcing his breath to slow down.

"Why can't Captain Eden reenter Omega now?" Janeway asked evenly.

"Because she doesn't actually possess the power required to perform her noble little display of self-immolation," Q replied.

"The power?" the admiral asked.

"Were she to return to Omega now, as she is, she would only seal this particular rupture. And while she was busy trying to convince her ne'er-do-well father to forgive himself for allowing his curiosity to bring eternity to its knees, Omega would continue to intrude upon the multiverse, hastening its demise. We wouldn't be talking about the days your latest display of cosmic ignorance has left you—it would be a matter of years at best. Omega has tasted its appetizers and won't be denied the main course now."

"Is he telling the truth?" Chakotay asked Eden. She did not reply, but appeared to swallow a lump that had formed in her throat.

Q stepped closer to Eden, and for a moment the captain feared for her life. Given Eden's dual nature, Chakotay wondered if even Q had the power to end her existence.

"I am, I assure you," Q replied for her.

"Then how?" Janeway demanded.

"How can she promise to end this threat completely?" Q smiled without a hint of amusement. "Easy. The power she requires does exist. It resides within the Q Continuum. In fact, it *is* the Q Continuum—that which was created to balance the Omega Continuum."

"In order to close Omega, she must destroy the Q?" Janeway asked, aghast.

The look in Q's eyes dared Eden to contradict him.

She met his challenge, replying evenly, "Yes."

Chapter Thirty-one

SAN FRANCISCO, EARTH
STARFLEET ACADEMY

The new term of his last year at the Academy was just under way, and Icheb was already wondering if he was going to survive it. Before he began his studies at the Academy, he'd believed that the years he had spent aboard *Voyager* would have prepared him to face anything the school could throw at him. However, the Academy made the most hectic days aboard *Voyager* appear positively boring.

Naomi Wildman was only a plebe, but she was feeling the strain. They'd met after dinner for study time and commiseration. She had managed to pull three of the toughest instructors and was seriously entertaining a plan to leave the Academy and enroll in one of France's culinary institutions. While she didn't think her parents would approve, she was certain she'd have her godfather Neelix's blessing.

Icheb had counseled her to stick it out for a few more weeks. She had agreed, but the gentle sloping of her shoulders as she'd left his quarters had tugged at his heart. Immediately, Icheb had composed a quick communiqué, asking her to meet him for breakfast prior to morning PT. He had promised Seven to keep an eye on Naomi. He hadn't seen Naomi often since they'd returned to Earth, and most of his memories of her had been as a girl. Since they'd met infrequently, he'd been surprised by her physical development, but she was still so very young. Icheb knew his childhood had been far from ideal, but he wondered if he had ever been so innocent.

He had just finished his note to Naomi when a completely unexpected and almost unrecognizable voice said softly, "Don't worry about Naomi. She'll come around."

Icheb turned to see Q seated on his rack, his hands resting on his knees. He had matured considerably since the last time they'd met. *He could be in his thirties,* Icheb thought with a pang of envy. However, there were still faint traces of the callous young man Icheb had once had the fortune, or misfortune, to know.

"Q?"

"Hi, Icheb," Q replied with a genuine if muted smile.

Icheb rose, feeling incredibly awkward, but pleased that Q had not called him by the least favorite nickname he'd ever acquired: Itchy.

"Why are you here?" Icheb asked.

Q studied his knees for what felt like a very long time.

"Has something happened?" Icheb persisted.

"It's odd, isn't it?" Q finally said.

"What's odd?"

Finally Q looked up at him, and the sadness Icheb saw in his eyes was intensely disconcerting.

"I haven't been alive much longer than you have, but in that time I've traveled through the multiverse, met and interacted with countless beings, many of them beyond your comprehension, and in all that time, I only made one friend."

"Who?" Icheb asked, curious.

"You, you idiot." Q smirked.

Much as Icheb wanted to be flattered by this, his few interactions with the Q made that difficult for him.

"Come on," Icheb demurred.

"There was one other, a female Q, Amanda, who thought she was human for most of her life. But she's gone now."

"She left the Continuum?" Icheb asked, wondering if he'd received this late-night visit for relationship advice. If that was where Q was going with this, he might have chosen a better confidant. A few of his classmates had turned Icheb's head over the years, but nothing resembling a real relationship had developed.

"She died, trying to help me," Q replied.

Icheb swallowed the lump that immediately formed in his throat at this revelation.

"I'm so sorry," he said truthfully.

Q nodded. "Thank you."

Icheb moved to sit next to Q on his rack. He had no idea how one might comfort a Q, but as he had appeared to him in human form, Icheb acted as if he were talking to a friend.

"I didn't think the Q could die," he said, hoping to draw Q out. It was clear that he needed to talk.

"They can, under very rare circumstances," Q admitted.

"I know how awful you must feel," Icheb said. "A number of the older cadets I knew were killed during the Borg invasion. Admiral Janeway's death . . ."

Q turned to look at him, the faintest of smiles hovering on his lips. Then he sighed and looked away again.

"Can I ask you something?" Q said without meeting Icheb's eyes.

"Sure."

"Did your parents love you?"

Icheb didn't have to think very hard to answer this. "No."

Q faced him, surprised. "How is that possible? If you aren't every parent's dream of a perfect son, no one is."

"They never took the time to see that," Icheb replied, refusing to allow the anger he still felt toward his parents to surface. "They created me to save their people from the Borg. They might have loved me for that, but never just for me."

A sad smile crossed Q's lips. "Seems I came to the right place," he said softly. "No wonder we're friends."

Icheb wanted to ask what he meant.

"I need your help."

"What can I do?" Icheb asked, though part of him wondered how *he* could help a Q.

"I have a choice to make," Q replied, "something I have to do, but I honestly don't know if I have it in me."

Icheb considered his words, and then decided to treat this like a scientific problem. "What is the choice?"

"I have to kill someone."

Icheb rose involuntarily.

"Don't worry, it's not you," Q said.

"I should hope not."

Q rose and crossed to Icheb's small desk. He placed both hands on the back of the chair and continued, "I've never killed, on purpose anyway. And I find, now, that the thought is incredibly troubling."

"It should be," Icheb said, aghast. He took a deep breath and slowly explained, "I realize you have been raised to think of all life-forms that are not Q as beneath you, but they are not. There are very few instances where ending anyone's life can be considered morally justified."

"I know," Q said, bowing his head.

"There must be another option."

"There is," Q said, finally turning to face him. "I could allow the entire multiverse to be destroyed."

"The needs of the many versus the needs of the few?" Icheb asked.

"Or one." Q nodded.

"Has this individual committed a crime?"

Q smiled again. "Many," he admitted, "though none that warrants death."

"But if you do not kill . . . whoever," Icheb found it difficult to believe, "life as it now exists across all space-time will end?"

"Yes."

Icheb sat back down. "Is there someone else you can ask?"

" 'If this cup may not pass away from me, except I drink it . . .' " Q said softly.

"What is that?" Icheb asked.

"Nothing," he replied. "I know what I have to do. And somehow, I guess I'll find the strength to do it."

Icheb nodded slowly, dreading either outcome.

"I'm sorry," he finally said. "I don't think I've been much help to you. Is there anything I can do?"

Q's eyes met his, and though his face was that of a grown man, his gaze was that of a very frightened child.

"Would you come with me? Just . . . for a little while?"

Icheb was stunned. He had two quizzes in the morning, or if Q was telling the truth, maybe nobody did.

"I don't want to be alone right now," Q pleaded.

Icheb rose on trembling legs. "Of course."

"Thank you," Q replied with a tight smile.

Icheb asked, "Where, exactly, are we going?"

"This part you may like," Q replied enigmatically.

VOYAGER

Hugh Cambridge had reported to the sickbay and happily turned his medical tricorder over to the Doctor. The sickbay was otherwise unoccupied for the evening, and Cambridge considered retreating to his quarters. He paused when he heard the Doctor call over the comm to Seven.

"*Go ahead, Doctor,*" came her quick response.

"I need you to report to sickbay immediately."

"*I will be there as soon as possible, Doctor,*" Seven replied.

"Not to be difficult, Seven, but unless you are trapped under a bulkhead, I really do mean now," the Doctor said.

After a pause, she said, "*Understood.*"

At this, Cambridge seated himself on the nearest biobed.

A few moments later, Seven strode quickly into the sickbay. She paused and looked at Cambridge, who waved in salutation.

The Doctor directed her toward the main data terminal, saying, "Seven, I need you to look at this right away. For the last several days I have been taking scans of Captain Eden's quantum signatures."

"Why?" Seven asked.

"Never mind that," the Doctor persisted. "These were taken less than an hour ago while she was in contact with the barrier between normal space and the anomaly."

Seven studied the scans quietly. She turned to the Doctor and said, "Thank you. This is most helpful. May I take these readings to engineering?"

The Doctor was taken aback. He'd already violated Captain Eden's privacy by sharing the scans with Seven.

"Is that really necessary?"

"I will not disseminate them haphazardly, I assure you," Seven replied, sensing his consternation.

"Then this is really . . ."

"Omega, yes." Seven nodded.

The Doctor bowed his head as Cambridge shot off the biobed as though he'd suffered an electric shock.

"It's *what*?" he demanded.

"I was already aware of the connection between Omega and the anomaly, Counselor," Seven said. "The fact that, in some physical way, the Fleet Commander shares its nature can only aid us in our efforts."

"Our efforts to do what?" Cambridge practically shouted. "Our four ships are gone. What exactly are we trying to save now?"

"The rest of the multiverse," Seven replied evenly.

Cambridge's shoulders fell as he searched for the strength to rally.

"To hell with it," Cambridge decided. Kneeling before her and taking one of her hands in his, he said, "Seven of Nine, I would be honored if you would consider spending the rest of whatever life is left us with me in a very small space."

"How small?" Seven asked as if she were seriously considering the proposal.

"The size of an escape pod," Cambridge replied earnestly.

Seven grasped his hand firmly and lifted him to his feet.

"No," she said.

"Seven, I . . ." he began.

"You have nothing to fear, Counselor," she assured him. "We are working on a solution to close the anomaly once and for all. The research the Doctor has just provided me will be an invaluable asset. This is not the moment to run."

"If it were, would you even realize it?"

"I believe so," Seven said. "You know that I was briefly joined to the Caeliar gestalt. Their work with Omega vastly transcends ours. Although I did not retain every detail of their expertise, I'm quite comfortable with what I do know of the general principles.

I can extrapolate from there a number of useful techniques to make what might seem impossible to you, quite possible."

Cambridge stared at her mutely.

"Deep breath," she encouraged him.

He did as she commanded.

"Go to Captain Eden. I'm certain she will have need of your counsel very soon."

Without another word, Seven turned and left. The Doctor stared open-mouthed at Cambridge, as if he was seeing him for the first time.

"You and Seven?" he asked incredulously.

Cambridge nodded. "I'm afraid so."

Kathryn Janeway's head was spinning. Once she had shared Q's darkness, she'd harbored no illusions that the challenges she had to surmount upon her return would be easy. But blow after successive blow since her arrival had left her near critical mass.

Eden's icy affirmative to her question had assured Kathryn that Eden would do whatever was required to halt the progress of the Omega Continuum. Kathryn had no idea that the Q's sacrifice was needed as well, or how heavily Eden might weigh that factor.

Turning back to Q, Kathryn said, "If Omega is really the threat to your people that it now appears to be, why haven't *they* taken an interest until now? This could explain what's been happening to your son, but all you've done since he first approached me is offer vague and empty threats. Isn't this your battle, Q?"

"Yes," he agreed, "and no."

Kathryn seriously considered punching him.

"The rest of the Continuum are, even now, unaware of this threat."

"How is that possible?" Chakotay asked.

"We all have our blind spots, Chuckles," Q answered with evident regret. "Omega is *the end*. Finis. Game over. Full stop. If you were designing a multiverse to include a species of unlimited power, any force containing the necessary energy to destroy them would have to remain hidden from them. Otherwise, as you rightly imagine, the Q would have intervened long before now. Call it a hazard of omnipotence and eternal life. After a while, you assume there isn't anything out there you can't see. So you don't bother looking for it."

"But you did," Kathryn said.

"Of course I did. My son was suffering. I made it my business to understand why."

"But you didn't help him?"

"I am helping him," Q thundered.

"All right," Kathryn said more gently. "Calm down." When he had obliged her with a nod, the admiral said, "Should I assume you have come here with a solution that does not include the destruction of the Q but will effectively end the threat to the larger multiverse?"

"Of course."

Kathryn sighed in relief.

"What is it?"

"Obviously, she must die," Q said, pointing a finger at Eden.

Chakotay stepped automatically between Q and Eden.

"Unacceptable," Kathryn replied emphatically.

"She shouldn't be here, Kathy," Q said, unable to comprehend her reaction. "She's only lived this long because, like the Omega Continuum, she was effectively hidden from me, until I received confirmation of her existence from another source."

"*But she is here,*" Kathryn replied, unmoved. "And as best I understand it, her death outside the Omega Continuum won't solve anything,"

"Let's find out," Q tossed back lightly.

Seething internally, Kathryn said evenly, "I need a moment with Captain Eden, alone."

"Oh, I'd be more than happy to jot down any last words," Q offered.

The admiral lifted her eyes to Q's, and something in the force of her gaze caused him to flinch.

"A moment, then," Q agreed, and snapped his fingers.

Nothing happened.

"No games, Q, not now," Kathryn said.

He snapped his fingers again, and again, and again. Nothing happened.

Finally, a look of fear, mingled with loathing, fell across Q's face.

"What have you done?" he demanded of Eden.

In response, Afsarah Eden held up her right hand and brushed her thumb lightly against her fingers. A bright white light blossomed between them and remained fixed there as Eden said, "What was once yours is now mine. As it should be. Omega is rising, and it will take what it requires, what you know very well you should never have had in the first place. The balance must be restored."

Very softly, Kathryn asked, "Captain?"

Eden dropped her hand, extinguishing the luminescent display.

"How dare—" Q began.

"Q!"

"What?" Q asked, seemingly more insulted by the interruption than the theft of his powers.

Motioning to the chair beside the room's workstation, Kathryn said, "Take a seat and be quiet."

"I—"

"Take a seat and be quiet," she repeated.

Q looked for a moment between Kathryn, Chakotay, and Eden, and finally, perhaps motivated by his quite vulnerable state, did as she had ordered.

Turning back to Eden, Kathryn said, "Obviously, I would never have allowed him to harm you. But I'm also not going to stand here and watch you commit genocide."

"Admiral," Chakotay began.

"Is there another word for it?" Kathryn demanded. "Why must the Q be destroyed?"

Though Eden's face had betrayed pleasure in bringing down a Q, as she answered the admiral's question her voice was filled with remorse. "The Q, as you have come to know them, should not exist, just as I should not exist. The breach created by the

Anschlasom did more than damage the Omega Continuum. It simultaneously, from the dawn of time, breached Omega's counterbalance. The Q Continuum was granted access to normal space-time. When given rein as your multiverse expanded, the Q Continuum became sentient, and developed into the species you now know as the Q. But this would never have happened had Omega not been damaged. Both forces should have remained potential powers throughout the life of this multiverse. They would have held each other in check, the creative slowly fading as the destructive began to expand. No sentient being existing between them should ever have been cognizant of nor directly affected by either until the end of time. I was brought into existence in *this* reality by Omega in order to correct the imbalance that exists because of the Q's presence here. This is the multiverse's way of correcting the error. It cannot be helped, nor can it be changed."

"But it must be," Kathryn argued. "Yes, you are Omega, but you are also human. You've had over fifty years to live among us. You've dedicated your life to Starfleet's ideals and upheld its principles. You must have come to cherish all life, even annoying omnipotent life. Can you truly accept the thought of becoming an agent—no, a weapon—of mass destruction?"

Eden looked to Chakotay, silently pleading for compassion and understanding.

Chakotay moved slowly toward her. "You know more than our ideals and principles, Afsarah. You know love—what you feel for Tallar and Jobin, what you felt when *Planck* was lost, and her sister ships. Surely you know that this is not the way."

Finally her control broke as Eden struggled with the pure emotional response. "Of course, I do," she cried. "It's horrifying to think that I could, that I *must* do this. But I honestly don't know how to stop it."

A door chime broke the tense silence following her words. Every fragment of her being urged her to yell, *Go away,* but Kathryn knew that no one would be intruding right now without good cause.

"Come in," she called, and the door slid open to allow Counselor Cambridge to enter.

Clearly taking the room's temperature, Cambridge paused, looked at Q, and asked, "So, is this a bad time?"

"What is it, Counselor?" Chakotay demanded.

"Commander Torres and Seven believe they have come up with a solution to our situation. They've asked that you convene for a briefing in Holodeck One. It will require that Lieutenants Conlon and Patel be made aware of the admiral's presence, unless, of course, she'd like to remain here and keep our newest guest company?"

Kathryn turned to Q. "I think you should come too."

"Well, since you asked so nicely," Q replied as he rose from his chair.

Tom Paris watched as Conlon and Patel resumed their work. He was surprised at how easily they had accepted the news that Admiral Janeway had been returned from the dead by the Q Continuum and would be joining them for the briefing. Conlon had said matter-of-factly, "Well, of course, it's *Voyager*," and had returned to running ODN cables.

Tom then moved to stand beside Kim and the Doctor outside the center of the holodeck. A simulation of the anomaly had been created to facilitate Seven and B'Elanna's presentation. Thankfully, they were using only a portion of the holodeck to create their display, so the black walls were still crisscrossed at regular intervals by bright orange lines. As the presentation took place in the void surrounding the anomaly, and what they now understood to exist within it, someone had been thoughtful enough not to create the illusion that they were floating in space.

Lieutenant Conlon, who had never met the admiral, seemed to be doing much better. Devi Patel, who had met Janeway during *Voyager*'s detour to rescue Tom's daughter from the Klingon cult who had kidnapped her, was unsettled, but remained composed. Tom did note that as the admiral entered—accompanied by Captains Eden and Chakotay, and Counselor Cambridge—Patel's face paled.

Tom's followed suit when Q entered the holodeck on Cambridge's heels. Kim instinctively reached for his sidearm, and Tom waited for the requisite sneer and the snapped fingers in response. Instead, Q meekly followed Janeway's orders, moving to stand well clear of the rest of the group. Tom placed a firm hand on Kim's arm and, in a shared glance, ordered him to stand down.

For a few moments, Seven and B'Elanna conferred quietly with Captain Eden. Although she answered them amiably, Tom didn't believe he had ever seen the fleet commander looking so solemn or so deeply wounded.

Finally, Eden stepped back to stand with Admiral Janeway.

"As many of you know by now," Seven began, "the continuum intersecting normal space at our present location contains a pure Omega molecule."

Tom's stomach lurched violently at the revelation. Kim immediately broke out in a cold sweat.

"*A*, as in singular?" Chakotay asked.

"Yes." Seven nodded. "All of the Omega molecules Starfleet has studied or come upon, and the Omega molecules stabilized by the Caeliar, were synthetic versions of Omega. They were extremely powerful, but they did not approach the destructive capability of pure Omega. They are, however, similar in structure. Each synthetic Omega molecule consists of infinite particles that, once stabilized, assume a flawless lattice structure." The holodisplay behind Seven flickered to life, showing countless luminescent particles floating free in a void, then coalescing into a complex and quite beautiful spherical form. "Once stabilized, these molecules are capable of releasing near infinite power, but the energy required to maintain their stability is likewise massive, and ultimately prevents synthetic Omega from becoming a perpetual and self-sustaining power source. Should a stabilized Omega molecule lose its cohesion, it instantaneously releases all of its energy at once, destroying space and subspace."

"Among other things," Q interjected.

"Quite possibly," Seven agreed. Janeway silenced Q with a glare.

"Thanks to Commander Torres's efforts just prior to *Quirinal*'s destruction, we have been given our first glimpse of the pure Omega particles within the Omega Continuum."

Tom met B'Elanna's eyes briefly, and she smiled at him. The image on the holodisplay morphed into the anomaly, where a dazzling array of bright white filaments moved freely through the darkness and B'Elanna picked up where Seven had left off.

"Our theory, which has been confirmed by Captain Eden, is that the infinite particles of pure Omega contained within the Omega Continuum work naturally, over an incredibly long period of time, to find perfect stability. The moment that order is achieved, Omega's power will be released, destroying whatever is left of the multiverse."

"And likely giving rise to the birth of a new one," Patel noted.

"Correct," B'Elanna agreed, "but given the complexity of pure Omega, the process of stabilizing even one molecule should take trillions of years."

"Then how come everything that enters the anomaly is destroyed?" Kim piped up.

"It isn't," B'Elanna replied. "That's one of the issues we've had to resolve." She added, "I'm not saying we know exactly how things work in there, but the evidence suggests that crossing the barrier into the Omega Continuum does not immediately result in destruction. From our side, anything that enters the anomaly appears to have never existed, although, obviously, it does. As best we can tell, Jobin's vessel is trapped in a portion of the anomaly that exists in the Beta Quadrant, and it remains intact after almost forty years. Further, the Anschlasom managed to travel all the way through it."

"Then why didn't our ships?" Kim asked.

"I can only assume it's because their technology was a great deal more powerful than ours," B'Elanna said with a shrug.

"What is relevant here is that the destruction of our ships had to be a result of actions taken by our people," Seven said. "Their decision was likely based on information at their disposal, which we can only guess at."

"If I may?" Q asked.

Stunned, Seven nodded her assent.

"Nothing can be destroyed upon entry into Omega that does not add to its power. But any matter or energy that crosses the barrier, and the Continuum's continued exposure to normal space-time through these ruptures, exponentially increases Omega's rate of stabilization, thereby hastening the *de*stabilization of any adjacent realm; in this case, the fabric of space-time in this particular universe."

"What happens to the matter and energy that enters the Omega Continuum?" Patel hazarded.

"Do you care about the ships?" Q asked. "Or is your concern primarily for the individuals?"

"We know that every life-form who has successfully passed through Omega has returned with its own version of the experience," Seven said. "It seems likely all individuals frame the experience in a manner they can understand."

"Much as they would a visit to the Q Continuum," Q noted with a pointed glance at Janeway.

"Unless they are driven insane by it," Cambridge added.

"The point here," Janeway said, "seems to be that as long as this pure Omega molecule is not yet stabilized, technology and individuals can enter the Continuum and survive."

"Yes, Admiral," Seven replied. "And that will be key to our efforts."

"Our problem," B'Elanna picked up the explanation, "is that every breach of the Omega Continuum, beginning thousands of years ago with the Anschlasom, has hastened Omega's rate of stabilization. If left on its own now, we believe it is days away from reaching perfection, and thereby destroying everything. In order to prevent that, we must seal every single breach that exists simultaneously."

"How many are there?" Tom asked.

"The scans we were able to complete before the *Quirinal* was destroyed showed six definite breaches, but there are likely more," Seven replied. "We were only beginning the process, when we lost access to the scanners that were close enough to the barrier to complete the operation."

"There are thousands," Eden said softly.

"That's what I expected," Seven said.

"Does it matter?" Conlon asked.

"No," Seven went on. "Our task is to interfere with Omega's natural progression of stabilization, to force it back, as close as possible, to the state it would have been at had it never been breached."

"And can we do that?" Kim asked dubiously.

Nancy Conlon smiled and said, "Yep."

The display now showed what appeared to be a Class-7 shuttle moving toward the anomaly and entering it. Seven said, "This is where our previous work with synthetic Omega becomes instructive. In the past, we successfully stabilized and destabilized synthetic Omega particles in a harmonic resonance chamber."

"You're planning to build a chamber big enough to contain a continuum that is the size of the entire multiverse?" Kim asked.

"Don't have to," Conlon replied. "We already have one."

"The Continuum itself," Janeway realized.

Voyager was now added to the display, moving into position close enough to the anomaly to emit a white beam from its deflector dish.

"Our intention is to create the appropriate harmonic resonance at a single point along the boundary of the Continuum, which will then be transmitted automatically throughout the entire Omega Continuum," Seven went on. "There are several waves with the capacity to create the required resonance field. The most stable at our disposal is a phase-shifted soliton pulse."

Conlon picked up the narrative. "The difficulty is that the pulse must be emitted simultaneously from both sides of the barrier. We can program a shuttle to fly into the anomaly, reverse its orientation, and emit the pulse from the interior within a specific time frame. But the corresponding pulse from *Voyager* must intersect the barrier at precisely the same nanosecond."

"Or?" Kim asked.

"It was really nice knowing all of you," Conlon replied.

"The shuttle needs to be piloted," Chakotay said, stepping up to the holodisplay. Tom's heart sank as he realized that for that pilot, this was a one-way mission.

"Yes, Captain," Seven said, nodding.

Clapping broke a moment of solemn silence. Everyone turned to see Q leaning against the wall of the holodeck, applauding.

"Stop it, Q," Janeway ordered curtly.

"I knew it was only a matter of time until the technological solution hit one of you like a ton of bricks. But there are other priorities to be considered," he said condescendingly.

"Is this what we did before?" Janeway asked.

"No. Your previous ham-handed efforts included the use of antichroniton-infused tachyons, and a secondary vessel located just outside the barrier remotely controlled the shuttle. The result was roughly equivalent, and the secondary vessel's pilot," Q said, with a nod to Seven, "did not survive the feedback pulse that catastrophically damaged her tactical panel."

"But this *will* work," Janeway insisted.

"It will restore the balance required. Unfortunately, it remains unacceptable," Q replied.

"Why?" Seven demanded.

"Because it will force Omega and its counterbalance into their original orientations," Eden replied for him. "Nothing that has happened since just prior to the moment when the Anschlasom first breached Omega will ever have occurred."

Tom watched the admiral's mind work the problem until she found a solution he would never have seen coming.

"The Q will never have existed," she finally said.

As Q nodded, Tom found himself wondering briefly why this was the case and, if so, if that would actually be a bad thing.

"No, that's not true," Seven suddenly interjected.

"You're going to argue math with me, Seven?" Q asked.

"Yes," she replied, unfazed. "An antichroniton-infused tachyon pulse would revert Omega to its initial orientation. A soliton pulse will simply halt its progress from this point forward. Omega will be sealed and continue its stabilization at a significantly reduced rate. We may be shaving a few million years off the next several trillion years of life in the multiverse, but there is no way to prevent that now. However, everything that has occurred since the Anschlasom's actions, including any effect upon the Q Continuum and the birth of Captain Eden, will still have happened. We aren't actually altering time here."

"Is that a first for us?" Chakotay asked. The first officer was relieved to see Janeway crack a smile.

Tom watched as Captain Eden's and Q's eyes finally met. It was clear neither trusted the other.

"Seven's right," Eden finally said, without taking her eyes off Q.

"If it works," he countered.

"I'm willing to give it a try," Eden offered.

Q shrugged. "I'm in no position to stop you, am I?"

"Then it's settled," Janeway said.

Eden asked Seven, "How long will it take you to complete the necessary modifications to the shuttle and our deflector array?"

"One hour. We're already under way, Captain," Seven replied.

"Let me know when you're ready." Eden nodded. "I will pilot that shuttle."

"No, sir, you will not," B'Elanna quickly interjected.

Eden's surprise at being so quickly rebuffed was evident. "And why not?"

Seven stepped forward. "According to your quantum scans, every time you near the barrier, or interact with anything remotely connected to it, you increase Omega's rate of stabilization. You are, in fact, the only member of the crew who is *incapable* of performing this task."

"I'll do it," Janeway said with such finality, Tom suspected from the moment the mission parameters had been laid out she had already decided on this course.

"No," Chakotay contradicted the admiral, his tone simple and quiet and resigned.

"Please, don't argue in front of the children," Q quipped. "You know how it upsets them."

"Q," Janeway warned ominously.

"*I'll* do it," Q briskly cut her off. "I'm a good pilot and I stand a better chance than any of you of countering whatever psychological impact Omega may present."

Janeway seemed to seriously consider his offer, but again, Chakotay said, "No."

"Oh, come on," Q urged. "I'm already mortal. What more have I got to lose?"

Chakotay looked between Eden and Janeway as he replied, "I don't trust him."

"In this case, I'm afraid I don't either," Janeway agreed.

"Kathy, how you wound me," Q said theatrically.

"Enough," Chakotay ordered. "B'Elanna, have your team complete the preparations. Tom, get back to the bridge. Fleet Commander, Admiral, and Counselor, my ready room."

It suddenly struck Tom, for the first time in a while, that despite Eden's rank and Janeway's presence, this was Chakotay's ship and he would be giving the orders on this one.

"Aye, sir," Tom said, and turned to go.

"And what about me?" Q asked.

"Have you ever seen the interior of our brig?" Cambridge asked.

"Lieutenant Kim," Chakotay said, "prepare secure quarters for Q and place him there along with ten of your best officers. Q, you should feel free to avail yourself of the replicators, but the interface consoles will be inoperable."

Off Kim's wide-eyed gaze, Chakotay added, "For the moment, he is quite mortal and poses no threat to any of us, beyond his ability to bore us to death."

"Aye, sir." Kim nodded.

"Let's get to it," Chakotay finished.

The brief trip from the holodeck to Chakotay's ready room was mercifully silent. Chakotay could feel Kathryn's frustration roiling off her. Eden and Cambridge walked a few paces behind them, until the doors of the ready room snapped closed.

Janeway, Eden, and Cambridge stood in a semicircle before his desk as Chakotay stepped up to the railing that separated the room's workspace from the small sitting area. Placing his hands on the railing, he first addressed Captain Eden.

"I trust you are confident that what B'Elanna and her team have proposed will work?"

Eden nodded thoughtfully. "It should."

"Do you have any reservations?"

After a moment, the captain replied, "I wish we could alert Jobin. When the anomaly closes, his ship will be destroyed."

Turning to Janeway, Chakotay asked, "Would it be possible for Seven to contact Jobin again?"

"Even if we could, he would have to free his ship from Omega *before* our attempt, and that isn't possible," Eden added.

"Could you do it?" Janeway asked, and Chakotay was reminded that Eden now possessed the powers of a Q.

"Not without risking the instantaneous stabilization of Omega by my proximity to it," Eden replied.

"I'm sorry, Afsarah," Chakotay offered. "He's been trapped between life and death for almost forty years. His wish was that you would survive, and that will be made possible by this choice."

Eden was fighting back tears.

"And that should make me feel better, shouldn't it?" she said softly.

"It will in time," Cambridge assured her.

"Which leaves the issue of the shuttle pilot," Chakotay went on.

"Who is our best pilot, Captain?" Cambridge asked, resuming a detached and thoroughly professional demeanor.

"Tom Paris," Chakotay replied, without hesitation.

Janeway's eyes widened momentarily.

"But he's not going in there," Chakotay said flatly.

"Why not?" Cambridge asked.

"Two reasons . . ." Chakotay replied.

"B'Elanna and Miral," Janeway finished for him.

Chakotay nodded. "Our next best pilot is Ensign Gwyn, and I want her at *Voyager*'s conn in the unlikely event that our efforts fail. She's spent the last few days maneuvering through areas affected by the anomaly. If it shatters again, she's our best hope of keeping the ship safe."

"Which leaves me," Janeway finally said.

"You're a good pilot, Admiral, but you're probably a little rusty these days," Chakotay replied evenly.

"That's not why you're unwilling to accept my offer," Janeway replied.

"It's part of it," Chakotay insisted, "but there's more."

"Such as?"

"You spent the last fourteen months in the Q Continuum and were brought back by Q's son. Even if the rest of them don't know what's at stake, he does, and if there's a chance that what we're about to do might adversely affect him or his people, I'm guessing he'd try to stop you."

"If he has concerns, he'll try to stop any pilot we send in there," Janeway corrected him.

"No one else here owes him as much as you do, Admiral," Cambridge noted.

"I would never place his wishes above the safety of this ship, or the rest of the multiverse," Janeway replied, stung.

"I know you wouldn't," Chakotay said, rising to her defense.

"But even if he doesn't show up, I'm not sure you're mentally prepared to face Omega," Cambridge interjected.

The admiral only stared at the counselor, clearly at a loss.

"Really?" she finally asked.

Cambridge nodded, not in the least disconcerted. "We know that entering the Omega Continuum affects every individual differently. During Afsarah's last contact with the barrier, she witnessed four of our officers conferring with Tallar in a garden. I'm assuming that was the same garden Tallar and Jobin found themselves in when they first entered Omega. This suggests that Captain Itak, Captain Chan, Lieutenant Waverly, and the ensign from the *Quirinal* . . ."

"Sadie Johns," Eden said softly.

". . . had devised a mental framework to confront Omega that was less powerful than Tallar's. His perception became theirs. He's had years to solidify that perception, so it isn't surprising, but whoever goes in there now needs to be ready to meet Omega on his or her own terms, not Tallar's. They must be able to resist the pull of that garden."

"You think Tallar will try and hinder our efforts?" Eden asked.

"He just gave up an opportunity that, to the best of his knowledge, would have ended Omega's threat. He watched over seven hundred of our people sacrifice themselves. I don't think you or anyone else here knows what he's capable of now or how he will respond to another intrusion into his domain."

"I told you," Eden insisted, "Tallar faltered because he sensed my presence."

"So you believe," Cambridge allowed, "but in this instance only, Afsarah, I'm not certain your perception can be trusted. Your connection to Tallar is part of your humanity, and in that arena, I'm afraid you're as blind as the rest of us when the heart asserts itself."

"I still don't understand why you would question my mental fitness," Janeway said pointedly to Cambridge.

"Oh, let's see," Cambridge said, turning to face her. "The last moments of your previous life were spent enduring the violent assault of a Borg cube, which assimilated you, forcing you to kill hundreds of your fellow officers. Your mental resources, while obviously formidable enough to withstand assimilation, cannot have healed from the injuries you sustained at the Borg's hands before you entered the Q Continuum. You then endured what I can only assume was a rather frightening and painful process of rebirth, during which you required the assistance of not one but two extraordinarily powerful beings. Since then, you have careened from one catastrophe to the next. And while you've done so with the grace and single-mindedness of a Valkyrie, my guess is that it will take years of dedicated work on your part to begin to make peace with all you experienced. Sending you into the Omega Continuum would be throwing a lamb to a pack of ravenous wolves."

"I'm no lamb, Counselor," Janeway said.

"Yes, well, my lack of prowess with metaphor aside, my point still stands."

"Which is why I will be piloting that shuttle," Chakotay said.

"No," Janeway said immediately.

"Here we are in agreement, Admiral," Cambridge added. Turning to Chakotay, he said, "Is there a shortage of skilled pilots among our ranks of which I am unaware?"

"None with the experience I believe this mission requires," Chakotay replied.

"What about Seven?" Eden suggested.

Chakotay bowed his head for a moment, struggling with the only other contender for the job worth serious consideration.

"No," he finally said.

After a brief pause, Cambridge said, "Her experience in navigating surreal psychological states over the years might actually be a plus here, and I wouldn't lay odds that anyone, even Tallar, could shake what has been fortified by the Borg and Caeliar."

"Seven is the only individual in existence who is connected to Starfleet and possesses Caeliar technology. She is valuable to the future of the Federation in ways we cannot yet even imagine," Chakotay said.

"Seven's too important to lose, but you aren't, Captain?" Cambridge challenged him.

"There are two command-rank officers in this room, and *Commander* Paris is ready to step up, should the need arise," Chakotay rebuffed him.

"Are you unable, or unwilling, to send one of your people on a suicide mission, sir?" Cambridge asked directly. "Don't they make command candidates pass some absurd test proving their willingness to do just that?"

"They do," Chakotay replied. "It is not the issue here."

"Then what is?"

"I've made my decision." Chakotay was clearly unwilling to answer the question.

"As ship's counselor, do you have any reservations about Captain Chakotay's mental fitness?" Janeway demanded of Cambridge.

"I've watched him spend the last fourteen months wrestling with personal demons that would have left many beyond hope, let alone reason. I've also come to understand the strength his completely irrational, spiritual beliefs provide during intense psychological struggles. He was able to share a vision with Seven of Nine, while she was at her most vulnerable, that brought her back from the brink of madness. He's put his own darkness behind him while leading this crew through some of the most difficult months they've ever faced."

"Hugh," Chakotay interrupted, reddening slightly.

"Captain Chakotay can complete this mission," Cambridge continued, unheeding. "And while you may technically outrank him, Admiral, until your position is once again formally recognized by Starfleet Command and unless his current commanding officer gives orders to the contrary, I'm afraid you have no authority to countermand any choice he might make here."

"That will suffice, Counselor," Chakotay said firmly.

"This is your decision?" Eden asked Chakotay.

"Yes, Captain," Chakotay replied.

Eden crossed to him and stepped up to stand directly in front of him. "You know I'd give anything to take your place."

"I do," he replied, smiling faintly.

"No greater regret," she said solemnly.

Chakotay nodded and briefly took her in his arms in a firm embrace.

When they parted, Eden turned to Janeway, her eyes filled

with sorrow, and nodded briefly. She said, "Counselor, my quarters."

"You'll stop by before you go?" Cambridge asked.

"Nothing synthetic or replicated," Chakotay requested.

"Perish the thought." Cambridge smiled.

With that, they departed, leaving Chakotay alone with Janeway.

The admiral stepped past Chakotay and took a seat on the long bench beneath the windows of the ready room. Silently, he moved to sit beside her, and after a moment, took her hands in his.

"I see you've managed to inspire a truly frightening degree of loyalty in those you command," she observed.

"I watched you do it for seven years," he replied. "Looks like I finally got the hang of it."

"I am wondering, why didn't you replace Counselor Cambridge?"

"He grows on you," Chakotay insisted.

After a brief pause she asked, "Why are you really doing this? What were you unwilling to say in front of them?"

"There's a chance this won't work," he replied simply. "And if we aren't able to contain Omega here, there's only one person in all of creation who should be standing between Eden and the Q. If I thought I was the best person for that job, I'd send you in there without hesitation. Hugh may be right about all you've just been through, but he doesn't know you like I do. And I pity anyone who tried to get in your way."

"Well, that's good to know," she sighed.

"But we are where we are. *This* is the right choice. You didn't come back to throw your life away again as a tactical maneuver. You came back because a member of an omnipotent species decided your presence was absolutely necessary here."

Kathryn did not want to meet his eyes. She was certain that if she did, her resolve would falter, and she might begin to accept his decision.

"We also have to consider the fate of the fleet. I know I would have seen them safely home, and Captain Eden may still. But if I'm leaving the job to anyone without regret or reservation, it's you."

"I love you," she said softly for the first time. It shocked her to realize she had never spoken the words until now.

"I know." He smiled. "And I love you."

"But not enough to stay?"

"Not enough to fail to do my duty." Choosing his words carefully, Chakotay said, "I know that you would do the same in my place."

"I already did, didn't I?"

Chakotay took her fully into his arms.

As fresh tears welled in her eyes and rolled onto his shoulder, Kathryn whispered, "Just tell me you're not doing this because you can't bear to let me do it."

Chakotay pulled back and stared into her eyes for a long time. As he brushed away a tear, he confessed, "Losing you was the worst thing that ever happened to me. I don't want to do it again. As hard as it might be to imagine, I know *you* will survive, just as I did."

"I'm actually not worried about you," she admitted. "I've been where you're going, and my sense was, there is something quite powerful out there waiting for all of us."

"I've never doubted it," he replied with a warm grin.

"Me, on the other hand . . ." she began.

He lifted a hand and placed his fingers gently on her lips to still the thought.

"One breath, one moment, one day at a time."

Kathryn nodded, interlacing her fingers with his.

After a few more stolen moments, Chakotay kissed Kathryn for the last time and rose, saying, "I need to speak to Tom for a few minutes before I go."

She desperately wanted to hold him back, but she knew it would be pointless. Kathryn thought back briefly to her fears of only a day earlier, when she wondered who she would be meeting on her return to *Voyager*. She knew now that her absence and the need to confront her loss had transformed Chakotay, but not into the worst possible version of himself. The fire had tempered him, burning away the impurities and leaving only what was best.

How she would learn to live without him now, she had no idea.

Chapter Thirty-two

VOYAGER

Lieutenant Commander Thomas Paris sat in *Voyager*'s center seat, watching as Captain Chakotay's shuttle streaked toward the anomaly. When Chakotay had informed him of his decision, Tom had wanted to hit something very hard—possibly Chakotay's head to knock some sense into him. As the captain had recounted his reasons, Tom had reluctantly agreed that, given the long odds, there was no one other than himself or Chakotay who should be flying into the Omega Continuum.

Tom had then, of course, offered to take Chakotay's place, and been flatly refused. Whatever fleeting sense of relief he experienced had quickly been overwhelmed by a more powerful sense of impending loss.

Tom had wanted to say so many things. Holding out his hand, he had barely gotten out, "It has been my honor to serve with you, Captain."

Chakotay took his hand before replying, "If you'll permit me the presumption, I've never been more proud of a journey I've witnessed than yours. If anyone had told me the day *Voyager* first set her course back to the Alpha Quadrant that this is where Tom Paris would be now, I wouldn't have believed it."

For a moment, Tom heard his late father, Admiral Owen Paris, speaking through Chakotay. The praise should have lightened his spirit; instead, it added to the burdens he now carried.

As Chakotay's shuttle sped toward the darkness, Tom felt his heart burning in his chest, and he realized what he wanted to say to his captain and his friend, while he still had the chance.

Thank you, Chakotay, for my life and the lives of my wife and daughter.

Kathryn Janeway had chosen to follow the proceedings from astrometrics. Moment by moment, readings from the shuttle would appear on the large viewscreen simultaneously as they were fed to the bridge. Seven and B'Elanna patiently worked the controls before them. Conlon was stationed in engineering, manning the deflector array. Patel was on the bridge to interpret every step for the command staff.

Chakotay's shuttle sped toward the anomaly. Kathryn's heart pounded out each second that passed as she reminded herself to breathe. Until Chakotay was truly gone, it seemed possible to believe that something, *anything* might happen to prevent his actions. Kathryn wondered if her godson might make a last-minute appearance, but felt oddly certain that he wouldn't. She had stopped by Q's quarters, and from the reception she received was certain he expected to join her in observing the mission's progress.

She had refused, but wanted to ask him one question.

"The price you spoke of earlier, the one you were certain I'd be unwilling to pay. *This* was it, wasn't it?" Kathryn had asked.

Q had shrugged. "It's hard to say, until we see how all of this ends."

"You mean you don't know?" she had demanded.

"No, but now that you mention it, I really wish I'd peeked."

The moment Chakotay's shuttle disappeared into the anomaly, Kathryn answered the question for herself as she remembered that it had been her actions, years earlier, that had brought all of them to this moment. Chakotay, Eden, the Q, the Anschlasom, she would someday make time to forgive.

Herself? She doubted it.

"Personal log. To help maintain my focus, I will continue this log as long as I am able. My course is set, and I will enter the Omega

Continuum in forty-three seconds. The shuttle's computer has been programmed to bring the ship about exactly twenty seconds after entry and target the barrier separating Omega from normal space. The phase-shifted soliton pulse will be emitted simultaneously with *Voyager*'s. My task is to make certain that nothing interferes with this process. If the shuttle's operating system is damaged in any way during passage into Omega, I will manually target and emit the pulse.

"Ten seconds to the barrier. Probably not the best time to wonder if this was really the right choice.

"It was.

"No doubts.

"No fears.

"Course is steady. All systems optimal.

"Three seconds.

"Two.

"I . . ."

OMEGA CONTINUUM

". . . inside . . . absolute dark . . . no . . . light . . . everywhere . . . bright . . . no blinding fragments of . . . must be Omega . . . focus . . . confirm shuttle is coming about. Targeting barrier. Chronometer is counting down . . . ninety seconds . . . maybe I didn't have to be here . . . no . . . the garden . . . I see the garden . . . there is no garden . . . what's left of it . . . a horrible storm . . . high winds, trees blown over . . . chaos . . .

"Chronometer still counting down . . . seventy-one seconds . . . target is in range . . . acquiring . . . unable to maintain position . . . the chaos . . . the lights, everywhere, they are pummeling the shuttle, drawn to it . . . no . . . firing on it . . . routing all available power to shields . . . no effect . . . manually overriding . . ."

"Afsarah?"

". . . *there is no* . . . there is a figure in the garden, his arms wrapped around the base of a fallen tree . . ."

"Please . . ."

"... *Tallar* ... I can't help him. Focus. Reacquiring target. Firing maneuvering thrusters to compensate ... direct hit, starboard thrusters ... compensating ... twenty-three seconds ..."

"Afsarah, help me ..."

"... Target locked. Fifteen seconds ... another hit ... compensatingjustholdpositionjustholdpositionholding ..."

"Afsarah!"

"Tallar!"

"Who?"

"Tallar, take my hand. Come with me. Come to my ship. You'll be safe there."

"There is no safety. Not without her."

"Afsarah knows I'm here. She sent me. Take my hand."

"She ... ?"

"Take my hand."

"So ... where are we?"

"On my shuttle. You're safe now.

"... target stable ... eight seconds to pulse ... holding position ..."

"Who are you?"

"Tallar, your daughter is my commanding officer. Together we have discovered a way to seal Omega. Five seconds ..."

"No! You can't! Not without ..."

"Four, three ..."

"Omega won't allow you!"

... *please, gods of my fathers, no* ...

VOYAGER

"*The deflector array is on line. Preparing to emit soliton pulse,*" reported *Voyager*'s chief engineer.

"At your discretion, Lieutenant Conlon," Tom replied. Chakotay had entered the anomaly, and everything was proceeding exactly as planned.

"The anomaly remains stable," Patel reported from the science station.

"Ensign Gwyn?" Tom asked.

"Warp drive is on line and ready to engage. Escape course plotted, Commander."

"Prepare to take us to warp nine on my mark."

"Understood, sir."

"Ten seconds to pulse," Patel called out.

A solid white beam from the main deflector reached the anomaly. For several seconds, nothing happened.

"Patel?" Tom asked.

"Scanning quantum signature. Awaiting confirmation of return pulse."

"Come on, Chakotay," Tom whispered.

"Commander, the anomaly is shifting visibly," Lasren reported from ops.

"How so, Mister Lasren?"

"Detecting fractures opening . . ."

"Conn," Paris ordered, hoping it wouldn't be the last order he gave. The pinpoints of light that had been stable stars a split-second earlier streaked into long white lines as *Voyager*'s warp drive was engaged. Every second that passed was taking *Voyager* to safety.

"Multiple fractures detected, continuing to expand," Lasren reported.

"We're well ahead of them," Kim advised.

Tom leaned forward. "Gywn, status?"

"Maintaining optimal distance. There's a slight drag due to the ruptures in subspace but the drive is stable at warp eight-point-nine."

"Lasren, how long do we have to maintain this speed to clear the fractures?"

"Unable to determine at this time, Commander," the ops officer replied. "The fractures are continuing to expand well beyond the initial area of impact."

A torturous minute passed in silence as Tom willed *Voyager* to go just a little faster to ensure his crew's safety. He asked, "Patel, what happened?"

The science officer cleared her throat and replied, "It appears

Captain Chakotay was unable to fire the pulse from within the Omega Continuum. We did not seal the Continuum. Instead, we have once again created multiple fractures within space and subspace."

"Do we have a visual?"

"On-screen now, sir," Lasren replied.

Tom's breath stilled in his chest as the screen before him displayed hundreds of long black streaks, lit from within by brilliant fragments of white light from what had been a small amorphous black shape. Now it was a thousand times larger. It burned with the brightness of a star about to go supernova.

Damn, he thought with a shudder. Tom knew that Janeway or Chakotay would have found something to say, but his mind was blank. Getting up, the new captain of *Voyager* crossed over to the conn. He laid a firm hand on Gwyn's shoulder.

"Steady as she goes, Ensign."

As Omega split itself open, Afsarah Eden felt herself expanding. Every atom contained within her skin struggled to burst forth. The frail organ tasked with holding them together tightened, then tingled as if it would rupture. She stumbled, reaching toward the main data panel for support.

"Captain Eden!" Janeway's voice called, dissipating the sensation and bringing her back to the present. Eden found herself doubled over, her breath forcing itself through her lungs in great heaves.

Strong arms wrapped around her, and Eden looked up to see Janeway on one side and Seven on the other.

"What's our status?" Janeway was demanding.

Seven responded, "The pulse we emitted did not meet its counterpart upon impact with the barrier."

"Chakotay failed?" Janeway gasped.

"I'm afraid so, Admiral."

Janeway's hands tightened their grip around Eden's arms.

"Omega has fractured, but it appears we were able to establish a warp field in time to escape," Seven added.

A little dizzy but otherwise better, Eden used the arms holding her to stand upright. After what felt like an eternity, her vision cleared and the stricken faces of all those present greeted her.

Although normal seemed like a half-remembered dream, Eden's duty remained clear. Tapping her combadge, she said, "Commander Paris?"

"*Yes, Fleet Commander?*"

"Status?"

"*We're at warp eight-point-seven, evading the edge of the new fractures from Omega.*"

"Maintain course and speed until further advised. Eden out."

Turning to Seven, Eden said, "Is it possible to make another attempt to seal Omega?"

Seven looked to B'Elanna, who shook her head slowly. "Given the volatility of the fractures and the distance we must now maintain from them, no, I'm afraid we cannot."

Captain Eden then turned to Janeway, who clearly struggled to remain calm and focused.

"Other options?" Janeway demanded.

"No, Admiral," B'Elanna replied.

"I want . . ." Janeway began, but seemed to lose her breath as she placed a hand over her stomach. "I want . . . damn it . . ." Stilling her ragged inhalations, she whispered, "One breath, one moment at a time."

The pain Eden had brought to Janeway's existence should have paled in comparison to the devastation of the last few days for which she felt personally responsible. Instead, all that had been lost in her quest to find her truth was now reflected back to her in the face of the woman who had risked everything she was, time and again, to keep those she led safe and the universe around them in one piece.

"I'm so sorry, Admiral," Eden found voice to say.

Janeway nodded and squared her shoulders, saying, "We still have a job to do."

"There is but one course before us now, Admiral. Even you must see that now."

"You're ready to sentence an entire species to death without even trying . . ." Janeway replied, her voice rising. "No," she said, stepping up onto the small platform that was situated just before the room's gigantic viewscreen. She began pacing. "There must be another way. We can keep ahead of the fractures as long as necessary. Given enough time, we *will* find a solution."

Eden hated to contradict her, but she had no choice. "There is no other solution. We had days. Now we have hours. Omega is continuing to expand. I feel it in every breath I take. The fractures now forming are not simply the result of the pulse we fired. Omega is coming for me, and will continue to shatter space and subspace, until I return to it. I can choose to do so without destroying the Q Continuum, but that won't be sufficient . . ."

Janeway interrupted forcefully. "You say this balance must be restored, but in doing so you are condemning *this* universe, the entire multiverse, to a history in which the Q have never existed. I know you don't know them like I do, but I'm here to tell you, even on their worst day, they have done more good than evil."

"Are you certain you're not just speaking from personal experience?" Eden asked evenly.

"I beg your pardon?"

"They saved your life."

"If *my* life were all that was at stake here, I'd go back without a second thought. This isn't about me. It's about you . . . your *humanity*," the admiral insisted. Suddenly everything dropped away and Eden could only hear Janeway. "I was assimilated by the Borg. One moment, I was myself. The next, I was drowning in a sea of minds, all begging for the order only I could bring them. Wave after wave crashed against me, drawing me under. I knew that to listen to them was to cease to be human, to abandon myself and all hope. I could not resist. But even as I was being violated by their technology, as my genetic code was rewritten, I held on to whatever I could. It wasn't enough. I wasn't enough to prevent the horrors they inflicted on those I'd sworn to protect. But what little they left me, I held on to with every fiber of my being, until the moment came when I was given the chance to destroy them."

Suddenly, the admiral was in front of her, staring directly into Eden's eyes. "You must do the same. Omega is rising, but it is not all that there is of you. Let it come, but never forget that you *are* human. The forces of ultimate destruction erred when they chose a human template for you. We don't accept the unacceptable. We don't give up, even when it seems all hope is lost. We fight with our last ounce of strength to resist the tide, never knowing when we will finally overcome, but believing to the end that it is possible."

"The Q are not human," Eden whispered to her.

"No," Janeway agreed. "They are more than human. They are more advanced than any life-form of which I am aware. They are not perfect. *Far* from it. They may toy with humanity, but each time we encounter them, both parties learn something. When you accepted your commission in Starfleet, you swore to uphold its values. It doesn't matter that the Q should never have existed. They do exist. You are duty bound to protect them, like any other life-form, even at the cost of your own life."

Eden bowed her head, wishing with all her might that it was that simple. Omega's darkness yawned before her, but through it, fragments of memories formed in her mind's eye: Jobin's face, bending over her bunk to gently kiss her good night; Tallar sitting beside a pond and telling her she was beautiful; Willem asking her to be his wife; Cambridge listening for hours on end as she poured out her heart's grief; Chakotay accepting her in all her imperfections and challenging her to conquer them.

Omega was strong.

Humanity was stronger.

Turning back to B'Elanna and Seven, Eden ordered, "Start over. Forget what's impossible. Find us what isn't."

"Aye, Captain," both replied in near unison.

"Don't bother," a new voice came over Eden's shoulder. Turning, Eden saw Admiral Janeway standing in the midst of a dozen humanoids, all wearing long crimson robes with high black headpieces. The voice had come from a tall woman who carried herself like a queen. Once Eden's eyes met hers, she spoke again. "The Q have come, and we will not go gently into oblivion."

Chapter Thirty-three

VOYAGER

Kathryn Janeway strode up to the female Q and without hesitation said, "Leave now."

"This is not your battle," the Q replied. As the woman spoke, the words seemed to come from all of the representatives of the Continuum now present. "She is one. We are legion. What she believes she can destroy, we can re-create, atom by atom if necessary. Hers is the power of death, but before death and beyond it, the power of life holds dominion. Nothing can erase what we have built, what we have become through billions of years of existence."

Kathryn looked at Eden, hoping desperately that the Q were speaking the truth.

For a few brief seconds following the appearance of the Q, Afsarah Eden closed her eyes, willing one image to remain at the forefront of her consciousness. It was Chakotay's face, after he had decided to enter Omega, certain that he would die but equally certain the sacrifice was worth it. She counted the days that had passed since she had told him of her history and the day they had sat in *Galen's* sickbay listening to the Doctor's report on her genome. She remembered that during those days, she had felt more alive than at any other time she could remember. For far too long she had shouldered her burdens alone. Chakotay had embraced the mysteries she placed before him, and fearlessly set her upon the path to unlocking them. Even in the face of death, he had not regretted that decision. She had become something unknowable, unthinkable. But he still saw the woman, the officer he had sworn fidelity to, and the human cursed with a destiny none could possibly prepare themselves to meet.

Chakotay had forgiven her in an embrace and that absolution had carried her to this moment. She had lost so many, but she could not, *would not,* sully his sacrifice by failing him. The humanity Janeway had spoken of was real to her because Chakotay had reflected it back to her every moment they had served together. No matter what came, she would hold his face in her mind, his eyes drawing out all that was best and true in her, his heart . . .

Until the eternal tide broke free and dragged her under.

Afsarah Eden stood facing the Q. Seven, B'Elanna, and Cambridge, clearly sensing what was to come, stood near the door to the lab, as far from her as possible.

Kathryn saw the look in Eden's eyes and knew there was nowhere to run.

The sound of a roaring storm filled the lab.

Kathryn shouted to the Q, "You must go! You are giving her the power she requires to destroy you! Leave, now!"

An ancient male next to Kathryn fell to his knees. His body began to morph as if it were losing its molecular cohesion. All around him, the others quickly followed suit. Only the woman, her godson's mother, stood her ground. With agonizing clarity Kathryn realized her power was probably no greater than that of her companions; she resisted because she was fighting for her son's existence as much as her own.

In a bright flash, the female Q disappeared from her side. Kathryn fervently hoped she had heeded her warning, but another flash brought her back into existence a meter from Eden. She stood before her, proud, arrogant, and determined. The rest of the Q collapsed and crumpled onto the deck.

Kathryn searched Eden's eyes to see if she was aware of what she was doing. Where once, dark almond-shaped orbs had hung, now bright white light streamed forth.

Q raised her right arm, holding it straight out before her, and lifted her palm, her fingers wide. For a few seconds it appeared she might prevail, until her elbow bent and she fell to her knees.

"Afsarah Eden!" Kathryn thundered, raging against Omega. "Release them! Release their power! Let them go, that's an order!"

As quickly as the storm had risen, it subsided. The room became eerily silent as all of the Q lay in blood-red heaps on the deck. Eden stood, surrounded by a white aura. Her eyes blazed with the same pure light.

"It is too late," Eden stated.

"You are not Omega," Kathryn replied. "You are Afsarah Eden, the daughter of Jobin and Tallar."

"I am Omega's child," Eden said.

Kathryn's eyes fell to the still tangle of robes at Eden's feet.

Omega's child.

The Q's child.

It was not too late. Suddenly, Kathryn had no doubt whatsoever about how all of this must end.

Before Kathryn could respond, Eden raised her right hand and snapped her fingers.

For what had felt like an eternity, but had, in fact, only been eight minutes, Tom Paris had sat in the bridge's center seat, willing the warp drive to stay on line. It didn't seem to matter how far or how fast they ran, *Voyager*'s new captain knew that this time, Omega would have them. It would ravage every shred of the fabric of space and time that stood between them until it claimed its prize. As Tom searched desperately for options, he prayed for a solution that did not include sacrificing another life to this thing.

The answer to his prayer came in the abrupt eruption of chaos on the bridge as the room was engulfed in several flashes of bright light. Admiral Janeway, Seven, B'Elanna, Counselor Cambridge, and Lieutenant Conlon all appeared on the bridge simultaneously. It was clear from their looks of shock and confusion that none of them had expected this abrupt change of location.

Over a series of confused exclamations, Admiral Janeway lifted her voice and ordered, "Silence, everyone."

No one dared disobey. Gwyn turned her head to see what had happened, but Tom quickly ordered, "Ensign, attend to your station."

She nodded mutely and glued her eyes to the flight control panel.

"Captain Paris, status?" Janeway asked with measured calm.

"We're at warp eight-point-three. The fractures forming behind us are creating a drag on subspace that will destabilize our warp field within the next two hours," he said, matching her tone.

Janeway nodded as she took in the other arrivals. She paused, her brow furrowing over Conlon. "Lieutenant?" she asked.

The engineer shrugged. "Three seconds ago I was monitoring warp power distribution nodes in main engineering."

Janeway quickly said, "Route all engineering controls to the bridge station." Conlon nodded and moved to the console beside Patel. Janeway then addressed Lieutenant Lasren. "Are any personnel left in main engineering?"

Lasren ran a quick scan and shook his head. "No . . . um . . ."

"Admiral Janeway," Tom finished for him.

"Admiral Janeway," Lasren echoed, though he was clearly uneasy.

"What is she doing?" said Cambridge, as he moved to stand beside Janeway.

Rather than answer, the admiral asked Lasren, "There were a dozen members of the Q Continuum in the astrometrics lab a few moments ago. Are they still there?"

Lasren again dutifully ran the requested scan and replied, "No, Admiral. I have a report from Doctor Sharak. He advises that twelve unknown individuals have just appeared unconscious in the sickbay." After a brief pause, he added, "Additional reports coming in from alpha shift advising that they have been transported from their duty stations."

Stepping out of the command well, Janeway strode to Lasren's post. "Step down, Lieutenant," she ordered. "I just need to see something."

As Janeway began to work his panel, Lasren stepped back. His physical proximity to a Starfleet legend who was supposed to be dead was clearly unsettling.

Standing, Tom watched as Janeway worked.

"Every crew member stationed below Deck Eight is no longer there. All of them have been transported to various locations on Decks One through Seven."

"Is she trying to get them to safety?" Cambridge asked.

"Who?" Kim asked.

"Captain Eden," Cambridge replied bitterly.

The reason struck Tom like a physical blow. "Where is Captain Eden now?"

Janeway again looked at the panel and said, "Deck Eight. Battle bridge?"

Tom nodded. "She's going to separate the ship."

Now it was Janeway's turn to stare at him in stunned silence.

"I know Eden has the power of several Q, but can we survive separation?" Janeway asked.

Tom smiled. "The *Intrepid*-class vessels that came after *Voyager* were redesigned to include saucer separation at high impulse. We were retrofitted with the same capability prior to our return to the Delta Quadrant."

Ensign Gwyn, her voice tinted with alarm, said, "The saucer section is not going to be able to outrun these fractures on thrusters, sir. If we separate, we lose warp drive."

"The captain knows that," Janeway replied quickly, stepping down from ops and moving toward Tom. "She said Omega was coming for her. She must believe it's possible for us to get the saucer section to safety, while she takes the drive section back into Omega."

"So there's really nothing to worry about," Cambridge quipped as he sat in the right center chair.

"One thing at a time," Tom ordered. "Ship-wide."

Tom looked to Lasren, who immediately opened a ship-wide channel.

"All hands, this is Captain Paris. Move immediately to secure locations for saucer separation, and let's keep it orderly. Red Alert." He nodded to Lasren to close the channel.

"Lieutenant Lasren?" Janeway asked.

"Yes, Admiral," he replied.

"Initiate a site-to-site transport for Q. He was assigned to secure quarters a while ago. Bring him here now."

"Aye, sir."

The transport complete, Q appeared beside Janeway.

"Let me guess," he began. "It didn't work?"

"Several of your people appeared in astrometrics a few minutes ago. Until that moment, Eden was still determined to find a way to seal Omega without destroying the Q. But when they came . . ." Janeway paused.

Q sighed, lowering his head. "She took their power."

As Janeway nodded, Kim suddenly said, "Captain, long-range scanners detecting several stars going supernova."

"Several?" Tom demanded.

"I've got six, no, eight," Kim corrected himself. "They're not close enough to pose a threat to us, but—"

"The Continuum is burning," Q said solemnly, "*again*. Eden doesn't even have to go there to finish her work."

"It's going to be all right," Janeway assured him.

"For you, maybe," Q replied.

The admiral stepped up to Paris. "Tom, be ready for an abrupt loss of warp power just prior to saucer separation. Do everything you can to keep *Voyager* intact."

"Are you going somewhere?" Tom asked.

"Transport me to the battle bridge," Janeway replied.

"Wait," Q said suddenly.

"You're not coming with me," Janeway said firmly.

"Was my wife among those who came?" Q asked.

"Yes."

"And where is she now?"

"Sickbay."

Q nodded. "She'll be safe there. But I am coming with you."

"You should join her in sickbay," Janeway said.

"No!" Q shouted, his voice ringing out harshly.

"Q," Janeway said calmly, "I know how this ends. You do too. Don't make this any harder on yourself than it has to be."

"You know nothing, Kathryn," Q replied. "I do. I have a plan, and if you care about the fate of the Q, or my son, you will take me with you. At all costs, we must avoid one thing: Eden cannot be allowed to get anywhere near him."

"You underestimate him."

"Never," Q insisted.

"*When* he comes . . ." Janeway began.

"If she obtains his power the way she took ours, it's over."

The admiral studied Q in silence for a moment. "You have a plan?"

"Trust me."

Janeway shook her head, knowing she shouldn't. Finally, she relented, saying, "Initiate transport of myself and Q to the battle bridge."

"Yes, Admiral," Tom replied, nodding to Lasren.

Once Q and Janeway had left the bridge, Conlon asked, "Who were they talking about?"

When no one offered an immediate answer, Cambridge offered, "Her godson, I would imagine."

Seven stepped down into the command well and stood beside Cambridge. He rose and offered her his seat. She demurred, but silently took his hand in hers.

Before resuming his seat, Tom exchanged a look with his wife. No words were necessary. She nodded, and hurried to the turbolift.

Chapter Thirty-four

VOYAGER

Icheb suddenly found himself standing in the middle of a very busy hallway on what appeared to be a starship. Everyone passing him, in both directions, moved double-quick. Every face reflected the same tense concentration as crimson Red Alert lights flashed.

"This way," Q said, directing his steps toward a nearby door.

"Where are we?" Icheb asked, as he hurried to keep up with Q.

"You don't recognize your old home?" Q asked.

"This is *Voyager?*" Icheb demanded, startled. Looking about, he realized that the hall was familiar, but it was reminiscent of many other starships. "We're in the Delta Quadrant?" he continued.

"Your universe is a lot smaller now," Q replied.

"The ship is at Red Alert. What's happening?" Icheb asked as Q reached a door and opened it without asking to enter.

They immediately faced a stern and intimidating Klingon woman holding a *bat'leth* before her. Ignoring her, Q replied, "The short version is, the fleet commander is a hybrid life-form, now bent on destroying the Q Continuum. If she's not very careful, she'll also destroy *Voyager* in the process."

Icheb searched his memory of his letters from Seven. "Captain Eden?"

Q nodded, then addressed the Klingon, "Please stand aside."

Instead the woman raised her *bat'leth,* preparing to strike.

"Computer, end program," Q ordered, but to his surprise, the Klingon remained.

"*You are not authorized to suspend this program,*" the computer advised him.

"Sure I am," Q said wearily, raising a hand, at which the Klingon flashed out of existence.

Q then passed through the darkened quarters toward a bedroom. As Icheb followed he asked, "You've come to kill Captain Eden?"

Q shook his head. "Not exactly."

"Then who?" Icheb said, stopping short as he caught sight of a small figure sleeping soundly in the middle of the room's large bed. "Q, she's just a baby!" Icheb whispered harshly.

Q turned to him in shocked bemusement. "I know," he replied, quietly. He sat on the bed beside the still figure. Icheb moved to stand beside him, and drew in a sharp breath as he realized who the child was: Miral Paris.

Q raised his hand, and Icheb immediately grabbed it. "What are you doing?"

"I'd like to know the same thing," a cold voice came from behind them. Icheb saw B'Elanna holding a phaser aimed squarely at Q. Consternation crossed her face as she recognized Q's companion. "Icheb?" she asked, amazed.

"Hello, Commander," Icheb replied, smiling.

"What the . . . ?" B'Elanna asked, as Q used the momentary distraction to place the hand that Icheb had freed on Miral's forehead. A small flash of white light accompanied the gentle caress.

"Sleep well," Q said softly, then rose to face B'Elanna Torres.

Icheb's heart began to pound furiously. It was impossible to imagine that Q had brought him here to witness the callous murder of a child.

B'Elanna didn't hesitate. Immediately, she rushed to Miral and picked her up in her arms. Icheb's heart stilled, until Miral moved fitfully in the tight embrace, rearranging herself in her mother's arms.

"Q?" B'Elanna said, finally recognizing Icheb's companion.

"It's good to see you again, Commander," Q replied.

"What have you done to her?"

"Being a messiah isn't all it's cracked up to be," Q replied. "I've just spared her that. Unless you object?"

Gratitude mingled with terror and awe shone on B'Elanna's face as she held Miral even tighter. "Of course not."

Q nodded. "Then if you'll excuse me?"

Icheb placed a hand on Q's arm. "It's all right. The next few minutes will be a little rough, but I think I'm ready now," Q said to him.

"I don't understand," Icheb replied.

Q considered him with compassion. "You will," he finally said. "I've wasted a lot of the life that was given to me. That was a mistake. But I didn't want to waste all of it. You came here with me just because I asked. You're a good friend, probably better than I deserved. And if all goes well, this little girl will have an incredibly bright future ahead of her. It's not everything I might have done. But it's something."

Icheb felt the blood draining from his face as he realized whose life Q meant to take.

"Do one more thing for me?" Q asked.

"Anything," Icheb assured him.

"Tell my parents I understand why they did what they did."

"You should tell them yourself," Icheb insisted.

"I just can't."

"You can," Icheb insisted.

"Your parents are here, Q," B'Elanna interrupted.

"Where?" Icheb demanded.

"Your mother is in sickbay," B'Elanna replied. "Your father is with Admiral Janeway and Captain Eden."

"Admiral Janeway?" Icheb asked, stunned.

"There's no time," Q said, shaking his head. "I could send you back, Icheb. You'd still have a few hours to cram before that quiz."

"No," Icheb replied softly. "I'll stay."

Q smiled, relieved, and then nodded his thanks. A bright flash of light heralded his departure. The moment he was gone, Icheb headed for the door.

"Where are you going?" B'Elanna asked.

"Sickbay," Icheb tossed back over his shoulder as he hurried into the hall.

BATTLE BRIDGE, *VOYAGER*

"*Warning, disengage warp engines. Saucer separation not recommended at warp velocity. Warning . . .*"

"Computer, silence audio warning," Eden said.

Alone on the battle bridge, Eden stared at the viewscreen's representation of the starfield ahead. Within the next thirty seconds, she would bring *Voyager* out of warp as the saucer separation sequence engaged.

Her nightmare had begun.

Omega chided Eden for her continuing weakness. What difference did it make if a hundred and forty-seven additional people died now? The blood of hundreds more was already on her hands, and Tallar and Jobin would join the list soon enough. To risk dividing her focus between securing *Voyager*'s crew and returning home was unworthy of her.

But Captain Afsarah Eden was not lost to Omega. She would give herself back to it entirely, bringing with her all the blood it demanded, and increasing the death toll exponentially when the entire Q Continuum was added, but she would not permit those she had sworn to protect to suffer for sins they had not committed.

Once the warp drive was shut down, Omega would quickly overtake the ship, unless she used her borrowed powers to hurl the saucer section clear of its grasp. Eden wasn't certain she would be permitted to do this, but she would try, before allowing herself to vanish forever into oblivion.

Omega promised her release, a permanent end to the unspeakable anguish she had carried—responsibility for the loss of five Starfleet ships and most of their crews, Chakotay's sacrifice, even the theft of the Q's powers. All of it would be added to the mournful song of the cosmos, restored but permanently echoing the pain of all who lived and died within its vast churning maelstrom. Omega had witnessed worse in the past, and would again in days to come. Cold comfort, but solace nonetheless, was the certainty that Eden's final action would be to restore balance to the multiverse and in doing so, trillions of years of existence for those who would otherwise be denied life and the chance to marvel at the universe's harsh wonders.

Her humanity clung desperately to this truth.

The moment had come.

Eden's sight blurred momentarily as a fresh wave of power enveloped her. Now given free rein, Omega was reaching into the Q Continuum, gorging itself on the power that still remained there. The Q still left resisted its intrusion with all their might.

Reaching back to steady herself on the chair behind her, Eden saw a flicker of churning white light.

Kathryn Janeway materialized next to her.

Her nightmares had prepared Eden for this eventuality. That Kathryn Janeway's death would now be added to the long list was cause for further regret, but was not hers to prevent.

"You should not have come," Eden said.

Janeway looked over Eden's shoulder to a point behind her and nodded faintly.

"Get her!" a familiar voice ordered as Q hurled himself over a control panel and came within inches of tackling Eden to the deck. A whisper of intention from Eden reversed Q's momentum, sending him crashing into the battle bridge's rear bulkhead.

Amid his exclamations of pain, Janeway's face hardened. "'Get her'?" she said in disbelief. "*That* was your plan?"

Q moaned softly.

"Tell me you're going to bring the ship out of warp before you do this," Janeway said, now directing her attention entirely at Eden.

In answer, the thrumming beneath her feet was reduced as the warp drive powered down.

"Please, wait," Janeway pleaded, moving to stand directly in front of Eden.

"If you want your people to live . . ." Eden began, but stopped speaking in order to concentrate all her efforts on stilling Omega's progress.

A series of loud clanks marked the initiation of the saucer separation sequence.

"They're not just my people, Afsarah," Janeway insisted. "They are yours too."

Eden couldn't respond. Every ounce of consciousness at her disposal was now focused entirely on Omega. Her concentration was split, seconds later, by the gentle nudge she used to move the saucer section, propelling it forward at warp 8.

Janeway turned away from Eden to watch the saucer section's progress on the viewscreen. Visible fractures, blazing with Omega's unholy light, stretched toward the saucer. Eden ignored them, demanding only one thing.

Faster.

In response, the saucer section careened toward port as a fresh surge of speed took it. Eden ordered the drive section of the ship—all that was left to her to command—to come about and set course into the nearest fracture.

As she had expected, Eden felt Omega's focus on her. In her mind's eye she saw *Voyager*'s saucer continuing forward and allowed herself a moment of relief, knowing they were, at last, safe.

Finally, she turned to face Kathryn Janeway.

"They will survive now."

"I suppose I should thank you for that much."

"It was the least I could do."

"You could do more," Janeway argued.

Afsarah Eden had known Janeway only briefly, but the sliver of her that remained human marveled at the lengths to which this woman would go to make a point.

"What would you ask of me now?" Eden wondered aloud. "It's too late to send you back to *Voyager,* but you had to know that. If your intention is to make me feel worse than I already do, that is beyond even your formidable abilities."

"In the third year of our mission in the Delta Quadrant, we were embroiled in a civil war within the Q Continuum. The war ended when two Q reproduced, creating the first child ever born to the Continuum."

"Your point, Admiral?"

"That child sent me here to prevent his death. I failed him. But I understand now why I was supposed to."

"He will join the others soon enough," Eden said somberly.

"I don't think so," a new voice said from behind both of them.

Eden saw Janeway's resigned yet prideful smile. Turning, she faced another Q.

Sickbay was a mass of confusion as the Tamarian doctor tended to a dozen confused individuals in various states. The Doctor moved among them, attempting to reassure and, where necessary, silence their outbursts.

Immediately upon entering, Icheb found his quarry. In a corner, a strong-featured woman with blazing auburn hair lay on her side on a biobed. Her eyes were open, and the grief carved upon her features was pitiful.

The cadet made his way to her as quickly as possible.

"Excuse me," Icheb said.

The woman did not answer. In fact, she gave no sign whatsoever that she had even registered Icheb's presence.

"I have a message from your son," Icheb said insistently.

With this, her eyes lifted to his.

"What is it?" she demanded.

"He wanted you to know that he understands why you did what you did."

"He came," she said, as a fresh spasm of pain wrenched her face.

"Can you go to him?" Icheb asked.

"I'm mortal now, just like you," she replied.

"He needs you."

"He knew what would happen if he came here," she insisted. "Soon enough, none of us will have ever existed, so we won't regret his choice."

"He said he couldn't face you. I guess he was afraid of what he'd find if he did. But he shouldn't die wondering if you loved him. My parents were monsters. They created me so they could use me to fight their battles for them. They never even thought to ask for my consent, or forgiveness. Is that what you did? Is that all he ever was to you?"

With obvious effort, the woman pushed herself up off the biobed and stood before him. Icheb was momentarily awed.

Icheb was accustomed to seeing the Q work their particular powers in bright flashes of light. This Q threw her head back and uttered a bone-shaking cry that immediately forced every head in the room to turn toward her. When it had ended, her form slowly began to waver before him. The excruciating pain of the effort she was expending was clear, until she was gone.

Chapter Thirty-five

BATTLE BRIDGE, *VOYAGER*

The anguish that Janeway had held at bay since Chakotay had departed *Voyager* threatened to overwhelm her. She had controlled her feelings, knowing that she had to try and reach Eden. As she stared into the face of the young man who had brought her back from the brink of death and was now facing his own with unflinching courage, her resolve began to waver.

The white halo of energy still surrounded Eden, her eyes glowing with an unearthly incandescence. What had once been Afsarah Eden dismissed this Q.

With a very human sigh, Eden raised a hand, presumably to absorb his power. Her hand rose to the level of Q's chest, but her fingers faltered. Her eyes dimmed as she studied his face.

"Turns out, we're both a little different," Q said with self-assurance. "The rest of the Continuum is yours for the taking, but you can't have my power unless I choose to give it to you."

"How?" Eden asked.

"I don't think the Q were ever incapable of procreation, or had forgotten how to do it. I think they were afraid of what they might create. I think on some level they knew that to bring me into existence was to risk their own destruction."

"The Q thought you would turn against them?" Janeway asked in disbelief.

"They've struggled for billions of years with the power that is their birthright. To imagine a being with power that could surpass their own was a risk they were unwilling to contemplate until they thought they had no other choice."

"Then they knew Omega was coming?" Janeway asked her godson.

"No," Q replied. "*That*, they could never have imagined. But I think they had to know on some level that I was necessary, or even my parents wouldn't have dared."

Janeway stepped toward him, struggling to maintain her composure. "Did you know I would fail?"

He appeared stricken by the suggestion. "Of course not," he assured her. "I hoped you had a solution I couldn't see. It was too much to ask of you. I know you've suffered since you came here. I'm truly sorry."

"No, I'm sorry," she whispered.

He looked at her warmly. Smiling grimly, Q said, "It's not everyone who gets to die saving their race, along with the entire multiverse. Apparently, the reason I couldn't see the future beyond this point is because no matter what, I was never going to be a part of it."

"Omega cannot be restored without the power of the entire Continuum," Eden said.

"Wrong," Q replied. "Omega needs me as much as it needs you. What it doesn't need is the rest of the Continuum."

Eden asked again, "How?"

"If I give you what is mine, it will suffice. You can restore to the Q what you have already taken. We will enter Omega together, the multiverse will be healed, and balance will be restored."

At this, Eden asked Janeway, "Do you believe him?"

Janeway nodded. "I do."

Suddenly the deck shifted. Janeway grabbed the back of the nearest chair to stabilize herself. "What's happening?"

"Our motion has stopped," Eden said, cocking her head to the right and listening intently. After a moment, she returned her gaze to Q. "You have done this," she accused him.

"That's right," he replied evenly. "I'm not letting you go back to Omega with the blood of my people on your hands. We'll stay here as long as it takes for you to accept what I'm telling you. But the longer you wait, the further Omega progresses and the greater the odds that it will overtake *Voyager*."

A shadowy form began to solidify behind her godson. Q turned, and was soon standing face to face with his mother.

She took a moment to assure herself that she had survived whatever means she had used to reach the battle bridge. She then moved to embrace her son, but he stepped back.

"Son?" his father murmured as he pulled himself up to stand beside his wife.

"How did you come here?" Q asked of his mother.

She shook her head dismissively. "The power of the Q Continuum is great, but it's not the only source available to us."

"We're not permitted," Q stammered.

"Like that could ever stop your mother," his father chided him. Placing an arm around her and pulling her close, he added, "The Continuum will never forgive you for it, though."

"I don't care," she replied.

"You know, that's what I've always loved about you," his father said, smiling wickedly.

"Yes, well, now that that's settled, I'm afraid this is good-bye," Q interjected.

His father nodded, kissed his wife's cheek with incredible tenderness, and stepped toward his son.

"You're right. It's time," his father said.

Q nodded. "All right then."

"There's just one thing, son."

"What's that?"

"You are not giving your power to that woman," his father said evenly.

"But—"

"You're giving it to me."

"What?" Janeway said, shocked.

"You are right, of course, that yours is probably the only power that can restore the balance and eliminate the necessity of the rest of the Continuum's sacrifice. And you are also right that I knew, as did the rest of the Continuum, that your power would eclipse ours. It's why they were so hard on you, why they tethered you to my apron strings, for as long as they dared. You were created to save the Continuum, but you've already done that. Now, it's my turn. You will give your power to me, and I will go with Eden into

Omega." After a brief silence, his father added, "I'm afraid there's nothing I can do about your future. You won't be a Q any longer. You won't be immortal. I'm sure your mother will do all she can to make the time you have left as magnificent as only she can."

"That's why he couldn't enter the future?" Janeway asked. "Because after this, he would no longer have the ability to do so?"

He nodded without taking his eyes from his son.

Q had listened intently to his father. Once he had finished, Q nodded reverently, saying, "I love you, Father."

His father's chin dropped in a slight nod. "Yes, well . . ." But before he could say anything more, Q reached for him and pulled him into a tight embrace.

Her heart pounding furiously in her chest, Janeway watched for a sign that the power transfer from Q had occurred.

When they parted, Q smiled sadly.

"Son?"

"It's not just the power, Father. You know that. It's also the vessel. I am the only Q in existence capable of containing all that I am, all that she needs," he stated. "It has to be me."

"No," his mother pleaded.

"You can't," his father insisted. With no greater argument at his disposal, he begged, "I love you."

Few moments had passed since Kathryn Janeway had returned when she did not question her choice. No matter how much determined effort she had focused on the task at hand, each step she had taken in her new life had brought loss, pain, and regret. Finally, however, she understood why she had to be here, in this moment.

"Then let him go," she said softly.

"This isn't your concern," Q snapped harshly.

Janeway swallowed hard, then continued, "To ask any parent to suffer the loss of a child is to ask more than any parent can possibly give. But to deny any individual the right to walk the path they have chosen, because we cannot imagine our lives without them, carries a heavy price. You have never known this because you have never faced this choice. You've never had to sacrifice anything, because of your power to alter reality to suit your whims. I understand this truth. We mortals have tried to soften it in platitudes. 'The needs of the many outweigh the needs of the few.' 'Death before dishonor.' In the end, nothing makes it easier to accept. I've given my life once for those I love, and I'm about to do it again. To have made any other choice was to grant fear dominion. Your son is a remarkable individual. Don't ask him to be less than he is. He has made his choice."

"What choice?" Q raged. "If he goes with her, there's no telling what will happen. Maybe he's right. Maybe the multiverse will revert to its previous state. But what if he's wrong? This may be nothing more than a delusion of grandeur."

"He comes by it honestly," Janeway observed.

"Your father is right," Eden interrupted. "If you add your power to the rest of the Q Continuum, Omega will be sealed. But how can you ask me to accept that you alone possess all that I require?"

"Faith," the admiral answered for him. Despite the inhuman aspects of Eden's form, Janeway moved to stand directly before her and stared into her blindingly bright eyes. "Nothing is certain here, but in my heart of hearts, I know he's right. You are both unique, the only individuals of your kind. You've already glimpsed his power. It's preventing you from returning to Omega even now. From the beginning this has been about balance; the child of the Q and the child of Omega are the balance restored."

"I've given this a lot of thought, Afsarah Eden," Q said. "I haven't lived as long as my parents, but I've come to understand this about the multiverse: on its deepest level, it strives for harmony. It's beyond small concerns, but it moves the living on paths that lead to opportunities for renewed balance. It's not personal. It's not an individual consciousness. It is countless parts, in constant motion that over time must ultimately end. But how much time that process takes matters. To end the life of this multiverse prematurely, or to remove from it the creative force of the Q Continuum, is wrong. You must feel that as I do. Neither of us caused this catastrophe. But we are the only ones in existence with the ability to contain the damage. It's why we're here, even though neither your father nor mine would have it be so."

"Afsarah, you don't have to destroy the Q Continuum to solve this," Janeway pleaded.

"What if he's wrong?" Eden asked.

"Then he's wrong." Janeway added, "But this is the only option that does not require you to completely abandon the humanity that was as much a part of your creation as Omega."

"Please," Q asked of Eden.

Eden closed her eyes and bowed her head. The white aura surrounding her blazed, enveloping the entire battle bridge. Janeway automatically raised her hands to shield her eyes. When the moment had passed, Eden stood before them, human once again.

"All is as it was," she said softly to the young Q. Turning to Janeway, she added, "Humanity is a stubborn thing, Kathryn Janeway. It hopes, even when all hope is gone."

"It does," Janeway agreed.

Eden extended her hand to Q.

"Thank you, Aunt Kathy," he said simply. Turning to his parents, he said solemnly, "I want you to remember something. Humanity was part of my creation too. The most important lessons I learned in my life—and many of yours, I imagine, as well—were through them. You won't want to, but I ask that you forgive them."

His mother nodded mutely, but his father's face hardened.

"Father?" Q asked.

"I'll try," he finally replied.

Q nodded, then turned back to Eden and extended his hand.

The instant their hands touched, the battle bridge was bathed in light so harsh, so bright that Janeway felt its heat roaring through her. It no longer mattered that this might be the last moment of her life. She had done what she'd come back to do. It wasn't everything she might have wished for, but it was enough.

In the beginning, there was light, all consuming, followed by darkness so complete, Kathryn Janeway wondered if she, and her godson, might have been wrong after all. But this darkness, unlike the one she had briefly shared with Q, was still warm, as if the radiant light that preceded it could not be erased.

As her eyes began to adjust, the familiar lines of *Voyager*'s battle bridge slowly took shape, and Kathryn realized she was prone on the deck. As she pulled herself up, her eyes were drawn to the main viewscreen.

It was empty but for a few distant pinpoints of light.

The stars.

Kathryn moved to the conn. With leaden fingers, she worked the console and called up the drive section's current position and heading. It confirmed they were still in the same section of calm, open space, and hadn't moved since Eden and Q had departed.

A muffled whimper startled her. At the back of the bridge, Q was holding his wife. Her head was buried in his shoulder and her body was racked with convulsive sobs.

"He did it," Kathryn said softly.

Q's cold, appraising eyes were beyond angry.

"You did this," he said, biting the words out one by one, judging her once and for all.

"You should be proud of him," Kathryn insisted. "If ever there was an example of exemplary Q-ness, this must—"

"Silence," Q castigated her.

At this, his wife raised her head and looked at him in fearful wonder.

"Q," she said, her disappointment evident.

"No," Kathryn said, finally taking hold of her own righteous indignation. In what had felt like a matter of days, she'd endured life, assimilation, death, resurrection, unspeakable loss, and now, to her complete surprise, more life. If there was something else the multiverse had to show her, it could just bring it.

"You know I was right. Don't you dare diminish his sacrifice by pretending there was another choice. Don't . . . you . . . ever . . . dare."

A visible shudder passed over Q.

"You could have stopped him," Kathryn continued. "Your

power was restored before he took her hand. But you didn't, because you knew what had to be."

"He would never have forgiven us," Q's mother acknowledged.

After a long pause, Kathryn asked, "Q?"

"You have made an enemy of me today, Kathryn Janeway," Q replied. "I know you led my son here, and that but for you, he would still be with us."

With that, he snapped his fingers and vanished.

The agony carved into his wife's face seemed to age her, but her eyes held none of her husband's fury. Through her tears, she said, "He'll come around. I'll make him see reason."

Kathryn nodded, absolutely certain that would never happen.

Then she vanished.

Kathryn Janeway was alone.

Duty demanded that she move back to the command chair and hail the saucer section. Something infinitely stronger kept her rooted where she stood. The crisis had passed, but the price of peace had been intolerably high.

The only sensation of which she was now aware was emptiness. Every loss she had ever known had been defined by burning, aching, sickening anguish directly proportional to the amount of love she had felt for what had been lost. But this was something new. There were no tears to be shed, no icy shudders to be stilled. The absence was beyond physical sensation. It was impossible that she could continue to draw breath now that so much of herself was gone.

One breath . . .

No.

. . . one moment . . .

No, please, no.

. . . one day . . .

That Chakotay's counsel should return to her now was no surprise. The sixty-three billion, and the seven hundred eighty-five, Amanda, her godson: these were losses that would haunt her forever . . . but Chakotay.

Chakotay . . .

His loss would remain fresh, would return with crippling force, building in intensity rather than diminishing.

One breath . . .

Kathryn Janeway inhaled.

One moment . . .

With strength that was not her own, Kathryn stepped toward the command chair.

One day at a time.

Accepting the unacceptable, banishing Q's vengeful rage, Kathryn steadied herself and sat in the battle bridge's center seat.

A few more breaths and she would find the additional strength she required to send for the saucer section. But she would allow herself as much time as she wanted now to try and remember what it was like to live as a whole person, rather than one recently excavated.

Her heart was the first casualty to show signs of life. It erupted in her chest, pounding fitfully as a bright flash of light sliced through the dusky shadows directly in front of her.

Q.

She hadn't expected him to return quite so quickly. But maybe it was for the best, if it put an end to this thing she no longer wanted to call living.

A figure stepped out of the shadows.

"Chakotay?" she said with the faintest of breaths.

This isn't real. This isn't happening. This is a test, a punishment, Q's first strike against me.

Chakotay stood stock-still, taking in his surroundings in obvious confusion. His hands rose to his chest as he took a moment to assure himself that he was all there. Finally, his eyes met hers.

"Kathryn?"

At the sound of her name, she rose on unsteady legs.

"I have a message for you, from Q," Chakotay went on.

Absolutely certain she did not want to hear it, she nodded automatically.

His eyes began to glisten. "The son, not the father. He said not to worry about the price for your choice anymore. This one was on him."

In an instant, every cell in Kathryn Janeway's body was pulsing with incoherent energy. Then, she was in Chakotay's arms. She fell into him, unable to repress the sobs that burst forth from the center of her soul.

BETA QUADRANT

Miles Jobin came to consciousness with a sickening lurch. He had fallen asleep, as he often did, in his pilot's chair with his head tipped forward and a shooting pain now rose up the back of his neck.

He began to pull himself upright in his chair, a procedure that these days could take up to five minutes. He began by firmly gripping the armrests, but he was stopped by an unusual sensation. Ignoring the ancient aches in every limb, Jobin pulled himself forward using his console. He blinked several times before assuring himself that what the nav computer indicated was true.

"I'm dreaming," he said aloud.

He had to be.

Nothing else could explain his new coordinates, several hundred kilometers from the fixed point his shuttle had occupied for almost forty years.

"You're not," a familiar voice came from behind him.

"Of course I am," Jobin replied, too weary even for his despair. "Afsarah did it."

In all the times Jobin's subconscious had played with this particular fantasy, he had never heard these words. Swiveling his chair around, he saw Tallar, his shoulders stooped, his hair and beard a tangled gray mass, and his eyes almost vacant.

Jobin was on his feet before his body could protest. He stepped toward Tallar, but stopped short of touching him, certain that when he reached out, the illusion would vanish.

"She came home," Tallar said, as relief, anger, and sadness lit the vacancy behind his eyes.

"Did you see her?" Jobin demanded.

Tallar nodded.

"And what . . . ?"

"She said we had suffered too long. She thanked us for the life we gave her. She swore that it was more than enough. She said she made it possible for her to do what she must. She asked that we remember the love, only the love."

Jobin stepped close enough to Tallar to feel his body's heat. With shaking arms, he reached out, and as soon as his fingers brushed Tallar's arm, he pulled him close.

Tallar stood rigidly, saying, "She forgave us. She forgave us." Again and again.

"Tallar, it's me," Jobin admonished him, and at that, Tallar's frail, painfully thin body relaxed against his.

They stood like that for several minutes, relearning the feeling of touching another body before Jobin asked, "How do we forgive ourselves?"

Chapter Thirty-six

VOYAGER

Captain's Log, Stardate 58696.6

After successful reintegration of the saucer and drive sections of the ship, we remained in the area for forty-seven hours, running continuous scans. No traces of the Omega anomaly were detected. The damage to space and subspace was reversed. Though our losses continue to weigh heavy, it appears that the sacrifice of our former fleet commander, Captain Afsarah Eden, and the young Q had its intended effect. As best we can tell, the Omega Continuum has been permanently sealed. Based upon Admiral Janeway's last conversation with Q and his mate, we believe that their Continuum was also restored to its previous condition.

The *Esquiline, Quirinal, Curie,* and *Hawking,* along with

the seven hundred eighty-five members of Starfleet who entered Omega, have been officially declared missing in action. Once we departed the site of the tragedy, we moved immediately into communications range with Starfleet, using the relays dropped by the *Esquiline* during our transit to the Delta Quadrant. We provided Starfleet Command with a full report of our encounter with the anomaly, as well as the news of Admiral Janeway's return and the unexpected transport of Cadet Icheb to Voyager by Q.

We were advised that the *Achilles* successfully returned to the Alpha Quadrant and that all of the personnel stored in their buffers survived the journey.

While it is hard to argue that the final outcome here was better than we had any right to expect, this entire series of events remains one of the most difficult I or any of my crew have yet endured. An appropriate ceremony honoring those we lost will have to wait until we have regrouped with *Demeter* and *Galen*.

Although Admiral Janeway has had several private discussions with Admiral Montgomery over the last few days, no final orders have yet been issued for her reinstatement. I can't imagine, however, that they would not ask her to assume the duties of fleet commander.

The bigger question seems to be whether or not the fleet, now reduced to three ships, will be allowed to continue exploring the Delta Quadrant. It is my fervent hope that we will. The admiral has spoken of several new significant developments in the political structure of the Federation, most centering on the formation of an alliance known as the Typhon Pact. She seems to believe that we might do more good closer to home, given the ongoing reconstruction efforts and what appears to be a very real new threat.

I could not disagree more strongly, and the admiral has assured me she will make my recommendation clear to Command.

I just can't help but think that, through no lack of effort on our part, we may have given Command all the reason they would need to recall us and abandon continued exploration of this quadrant. Although we've only had a chance to scratch the surface of the new landscape here, our initial work certainly suggests that the Borg and Caeliar are gone. But what of unique situations like Riley and her people? This discovery alone leads me to believe that our mission here has truly just begun.

Personal Log: Although I remain committed to following the orders of my superiors, and concerned that they will respond to these developments with the heads of bureaucrats rather than the hearts of explorers, I hope they will surprise me. Kathryn certainly has. I don't remember her ever hesitating to go boldly forward. I understand her unique perspective, given recent events, and I see her determination not to allow all that has been lost to blind her to the possibilities of *our* future. But I honestly don't know where her heart is. We have spent every available moment together. She even grudgingly agreed to spend some time with Counselor Cambridge. I think he's harder on her than I can be . . . but that's probably for the best. The rest of the fleet has been briefed on her return, and they seem to be taking it in stride. Considering all that has occurred in our first five months in the Delta Quadrant, Kathryn's resurrection is actually one of the least traumatic developments and everyone present who has served with her in the past takes great comfort in her presence.

I'm still not sure what to make of Q's decision to return me to *Voyager*, but I'm willing to accept it as a blessing and move on. To have Kathryn back in my life is the most extraordinary opportunity the fates have ever granted me. I learned how much time I wasted when I lost her. It is a mistake I do not plan to repeat.

Harry Kim hesitated for a few moments outside Nancy Conlon's quarters before activating the chime. The last five days had been a blur of activity. He didn't expect this day to be less hectic, but he wanted to know if Nancy was any closer to a final decision about leaving the fleet. He'd had to twist Tom's arm pretty hard to get him to admit that Conlon had not officially requested a transfer. He was still wondering if this was a good idea when the door slid open, and Conlon nearly ran right into him.

"Oh, I'm sorry," she began, then added, "Hi, Harry."

"Good morning," Kim replied, working hard for the right balance between concerned and cheerful.

"Checking up on me again?" she asked seriously.

"Yeah," he admitted.

Conlon crossed her arms before her and said, "You want to come in for a minute?"

"Yes."

As Nancy ushered him inside, he took a quick inventory of her quarters, and his heart sank as he noted their unruly state. Most of her belongings were strewn about haphazardly, a possible prelude to packing.

She caught his gaze and said immediately, "I guess there's something you should know."

"What's that?" Harry asked, wishing he hadn't.

"I don't really do tidy. My workspace is immaculate. My quarters, not so much."

Harry smiled, relieved.

"How are you holding up?" she asked.

"Me? Oh, you know." He shrugged.

"Harry?"

"It's awful," he finally admitted. The abrupt honesty felt strange but in all the activity since the ship had been restored, he hadn't really had a chance to share with anyone the confused tangle of emotions he was now experiencing. "I mean, we did good, right? The universe, or the multiverse, or whatever is still here. Admiral Janeway came back from the dead. All it cost us was . . ." His voice trailed off.

"Four ships and almost eight hundred people," Nancy finished for him.

"Yeah. Tom and I have been talking about a memorial for them. I'm sure they're doing something back home for the families, but they were all our family too."

Nancy nodded somberly. "I don't think an assembly like we did on Persephone would feel right."

"Too much empty space," Harry agreed. "Tom's thinking about a reception."

"Equally depressing."

"Yeah."

After a long pause, Nancy said, "We're still in range of the comm network, and will be when we return to New Talax. We could set up a real-time link with our people back in the Alpha Quadrant; maybe run a feed to the main cargo bay. It would be close quarters, but we need to reconnect with them, at least for this. We lost too many, but it might help to remember how many were saved."

Harry nodded, liking the idea. "I'll talk to Tom. Thanks."

"Anytime."

"Anytime?" Harry asked.

"Oh," Nancy said, realizing what he was referring to. "Yeah, about that transfer."

"It's okay if you haven't made up your mind. Or even if you have," Harry said quickly.

"Harry, hush," she ordered. "The minute we got the ship back in one piece, I went to Counselor Cambridge."

"Oh?"

"Yeah. We've talked daily since then. And will continue for as long as I need to."

"Then?" Harry dared to hope.

"You were right. Well, he agreed with you."

"About what?"

"There's nowhere to run. Life has its share of truly awful days. It's what you do with the rest of them that makes a difference. I'm going to deal with this now. Here."

Harry smiled in relief.

"I've got one of the best engineers in Starfleet backing me and people who are as resourceful as they come all around me. It's not going to get better than that. But it's something else, too."

"What?" Harry asked.

"Seven hundred and eighty-five of our finest gave up their

lives so we could go on living. I wanted to save them. I wanted it more than I've wanted anything in a long time. But there are days when you get to do the saving, and there are days when you are the one who is saved. To run away now, to let the grief consume me, to waste the chance they gave us—that would be wrong."

Harry nodded. After a brief pause he asked, "Are you heading to the holodeck for your morning workout?"

"No," she replied, "too much to do in engineering. But I'll be there tomorrow."

"You want company?"

"Yes."

"Okay then. It's a date."

"It's exercise, Harry."

"Oh."

"Dinner, my quarters, tonight. *That's* a date."

"Are you going to clean up around here?"

"Nope."

"So you're a love me, love my mess kind of girl?"

Nancy nodded. "The upside for you is that I'm willing to return the favor."

"I'm not . . ." Harry began.

"A mess? Oh, Harry."

"I'm not."

"Maybe not on the outside."

After a long pause, Harry said, "Fair enough. I'll see you tonight."

"Leave, now," Seven ordered.

Hugh Cambridge, who was lying facedown in blissful, semi-conscious contemplation of the previous evening, murmured, "And if I refuse?"

"You will have to explain your unclad presence in my quarters at this early hour to both the Doctor and Icheb, who are due to arrive here in the next five minutes," Seven replied. "And I warn you, they are constitutionally incapable of tardiness."

At this, Hugh rolled over and opened his eyes, staring up at the graceful figure beside the bed, who was a vision of sartorial perfection. The navy blue bodysuit she wore almost made it physically impossible for him to sit up. Seven's perfectly coiffed hair and the combadge affixed firmly to her chest clearly indicated that she was already on duty.

"You really don't want me to leave, do you?" he asked.

"More than you can possibly imagine."

"Seven?" he said, feigning injury.

"You are the one who has spoken quite annoyingly and at length about the necessity for balance in my life."

"I was talking about your human/Borg/Caeliar balance."

"The point remains valid."

"So all play and no work?"

"Is not conducive to a healthy relationship," Seven finished.

Cambridge sat up on his elbows. "I'd say given the amount of work involved in the last few weeks on both our parts, we're overdue for a little more play. We do have five minutes."

"Three," Seven reminded him. "And even you . . ."

"Don't finish that thought," Hugh snapped as the door chimed.

Seven nodded with a clear *I told you so* expression, then left the bedroom, calling out, "Come."

The counselor made a dash to the 'fresher, grabbing his uniform. Looking at the two days of stubble now dotting his chin, he wondered if he should just go ahead and grow another beard, before deciding that Seven would not approve. Much to his dismay, this now mattered to him, but a thorough morning's ablution would have to wait until he reached his own quarters.

Squaring his shoulders and clearing his throat, Cambridge stepped out of the bedroom. Seven, the Doctor, and Icheb were seated at the room's small dining table, sharing freshly replicated fruit and bread.

"Good morning, Doctor, Icheb," Cambridge greeted them.

The Doctor's expression was priceless, simultaneously abashed and insulted on Seven's behalf. Icheb puzzled momentarily over the direction from which Cambridge had emerged, then looked to Seven in admiration.

"Would you care to join us, Counselor?" Seven asked with the clearest possible subtext. *Don't even think about it.*

"Please do," Icheb immediately requested, causing the Doctor's eyes to protrude to the point that they appeared ready to flee their photonic sockets. "I am considering asking the Academy to allow me to complete my final year of studies here on *Voyager*. I would appreciate hearing your thoughts on the matter, Counselor," he added, clearly ignorant of his breakfast companions' desires.

Cambridge looked briefly at Seven, who seemed genuinely torn, and the Doctor, who appeared frozen. While the thought of tweaking the hologram was tempting, part of Cambridge knew that he should respect Seven's wishes. With what he hoped was a convincing air of regret, he said, "I would enjoy speaking with you about that at length, Cadet, but unfortunately, I have a number of appointments scheduled for this morning. Stop by my quarters later, we'll set a time."

"Thank you, Counselor." Icheb smiled, then returned his attention to his orange juice.

As he headed for the door, Cambridge couldn't help but add, "Seven, if you find my jacket, would you just toss it in the recycler for me?"

"Of course," Seven replied, her ire rising.

"Carry on." Cambridge smiled.

"And who's that, honey?"

"Captain Proton!" Miral squealed with delight, raising a small arm skyward in salute of the figure that had just appeared on the screen. Tom Paris had recently instituted a new ritual for those mornings when he had sole custody of his daughter. Pillows and blankets from the bed were pulled onto the living-area floor before his prized antique, replicated television set, and breakfast was served for both of them while Tom introduced his daughter to the exploits of his favorite old heroes.

"And who's that?"

"Chaotica," Miral growled.

"And he is . . . ?"

"A very bad man," Miral said quite seriously.

"That's right."

Eventually they would share the holodeck re-creations Tom had created for these characters. The thought of having Miral as his "Buster Kincaid" filled him with absolute delight. But for now, the much less threatening two-dimensional versions were almost as much fun.

Tom had his back to the sofa, and Miral was snuggled under his right arm, munching absentmindedly on a piece of toast, when B'Elanna entered and stopped, merely shaking her head in mock disappointment.

"Mommy, look!" Miral commanded, pointing to the screen.

"I know, sweetie," B'Elanna replied, trying to meet her enthusiasm. "Tom?"

"I'll be right back," Tom said as he extricated himself. Miral rearranged herself, collapsing onto her tummy and propping her head up on her hands.

Tom then followed B'Elanna into their bedroom. Before she could say anything, he began defensively, "Honey, it's just a little television. And it's totally age-appropriate."

She shot him a look that effectively silenced further attempts at justification.

"Sit down," she said, and he instantly sat beside her on the end of the bed.

"What is it?" he asked, placing an arm around her shoulders. The dark tension that had consumed her since the mission began had yet to really fade. Tom wondered if she had new concerns about what Q had done to Miral. He was committed to believing that Q had altered his daughter's future for the better.

"I picked up the latest communiqués from the Alpha Quadrant," she began, pulling a padd from her jacket pocket. "It's from Kahless."

He took the padd and quickly scanned its contents.

"Is he sure?" Tom asked in disbelief.

"I can't see Kahless sending this if he wasn't. The encryption codes were legitimate."

Tom now shared his wife's shock. "Is this what Junior was talking about?"

"I don't see how," B'Elanna replied. "The confirmation only came in the last few weeks, but this must have happened six months ago."

"The Warriors of Gre'thor are gone," Tom said, trying the thought out aloud.

"They tried to stand against the Borg during the Invasion. I'm not really surprised they came out on the losing end of that one. They may have been lunatics, but they were Klingon lunatics. Nothing would have kept them out of that fight."

"So we could . . ." Tom began as his mind churned with dozens of new possibilities. "We could go back to the Alpha Quadrant now without . . ."

". . . constantly looking over our shoulders? Yes," B'Elanna said.

"Then what did Q do?" Tom asked.

"I'm kind of hoping we won't ever really know," B'Elanna admitted.

Tom took a moment to study his wife, then said, "Shouldn't you be happy about this?"

B'Elanna only sighed heavily.

"No, think about it," Tom told her. "There's a good chance Command is going to cut this mission short, and if they do, we can go home. No more worrying about Miral having a more normal life with other kids around her."

"Yeah, we actually don't have to worry about that either way," she replied flatly.

"Honey?"

She turned to face him, both her lips and eyes hinting at mischief.

"Honey?" he asked again.

"I think that sick feeling I've been having for the last several weeks had less to do with my precognitive abilities than my physical condition."

"Are you . . . ?" Tom asked, beginning to put the pieces together. "Are we?" he corrected himself.

"Going to have another baby," B'Elanna confirmed.

Tom could not repress the wide grin that erupted on his face as he let out a loud yelp of excitement. He then pulled B'Elanna into a fierce embrace, which she met with equal intensity.

"This is going to be great," he whispered.

"If you say so," she replied.

"No," he said, pulling back and taking her face in his hands. "This is going to be beyond great."

"It really is." B'Elanna finally smiled.

Chakotay was about to head to the bridge when the door to his quarters chimed.

"Come in," he said from his desk. Counselor Cambridge entered and ambled toward him in a crisp uniform, more polished in his personal deportment than Chakotay could ever recall. Wondering how much of this might be Seven's influence, but resisting the urge to needle Hugh, he settled for, "Good morning, Counselor."

"Captain." Cambridge nodded.

"Is everything all right?" Chakotay asked.

"You tell me," Cambridge replied.

"I'm not sure what . . ." Chakotay began.

"Oh, I don't know," Cambridge began with feigned nonchalance. "Six days ago you decided to end your life on behalf of your crew, only to have the sweet release of death snatched from your fingers by the Q, and you still haven't told me what Omega was like for you. The woman you have been grieving for for over a year is suddenly back in your daily life, and if my conversations with her are any indication, a little worse for the wear. Our efforts to help our friend discover her true history led to her suffering the torments of the damned before she was forced to sacrifice herself for all our sakes. By the way, if they ever offer you the job of fleet commander, I'd run in the other direction. I'm beginning to think the position is cursed."

Chakotay nodded, then offered, "Coffee?"

"Why not?" Cambridge agreed. Chakotay replicated two fresh cups and offered the counselor the chair before his desk.

"My patient load has quadrupled in the last few days," Cambridge said. "We're not quite meeting Borg invasion statistics in terms of PTSD and grief counseling cases, but I'd say everyone could use a fairly long stretch of routine for a while. Does the Delta Quadrant ever do that?"

"Not so far," Chakotay replied, retaking his chair. "Am I adding you to the list of my senior officers who think we should be heading back to the Alpha Quadrant sooner rather than later?"

"How many officers are on that list now?" Cambridge asked.

"Captain's privilege."

"Well, I'm counseling my patients to suck it up," Cambridge replied, "of course, phrased a little more delicately. There are a handful I'd actually recommend for extended leave, unless you really think we're going home now, in which case I'll save myself the paperwork."

"You'll know when I know." Chakotay shrugged.

After a long, thoughtful pause, Cambridge said, "Your Kathryn is really quite extraordinary. I'm actually pleased events have allowed me to get to know her better now."

"You'll get no argument from me there."

"But I confess, as the only person on board who knew Afsarah well before this mission, I'm still struggling," Cambridge admitted.

"It doesn't seem fair, does it?" Chakotay asked.

"No," Cambridge agreed. "And I'm not one who thinks it really should be or often is. But I truly despise the way the universe used her."

"She earned Kathryn's respect," Chakotay offered. "The admiral told me that in her final moments, Afsarah rejected Omega's demands and embraced her humanity, thereby saving the Q."

"And while that doesn't surprise me a bit, I wonder how

many of us could have done the same in her place," Cambridge replied.

Chakotay sat back, remembering a conversation that had taken place only weeks earlier but now felt like a lifetime ago. "I've always thought the universe puts us where we need to be at any given time."

"You'll forgive me for quibbling with its priorities this once."

"Afsarah was created to repair a damaged multiverse," Chakotay pointed out. "And she did that."

"I guess I wouldn't have minded if she could have found a little happiness before bowing to the will of a god she would never have chosen to serve," Cambridge shot back.

"As would I," Chakotay agreed. "But we don't all get that chance, do we?"

"No."

After a long pause, Cambridge said, "Present company excluded, of course."

Chakotay smiled mirthlessly. "I'm not complaining. But Kathryn and I have never had a chance, until now, to see who we are together as more than fellow officers. I know what I want, and she seems to want the same. But there are old patterns that will be hard to fight, old habits I don't want to see us fall into."

"You have your work cut out for you, my friend."

"And you?" Chakotay asked, unwilling to allow Cambridge any less personal scrutiny than he was dishing out.

"What's the saying? 'When the gods want to punish us, they answer our prayers'?" Cambridge replied seriously.

Chakotay felt his eyebrows rise in surprise. "I thought . . . you and Seven . . ." he began.

"Have completely taken leave of our senses?" Cambridge finished for him.

"If this isn't what you want, Hugh, I forbid you to lead Seven on," Chakotay said, his face falling into hard lines. "You should consider that a direct order."

Cambridge did not wither under his forceful gaze. "Stand down Red Alert, Captain. I'm completely lost to the woman. I

380 ■ KIRSTEN BEYER

just never expected, that is to say . . . to have found immeasurable bliss, right on the heels of such radical chaos, just seems the height of poor taste, doesn't it?"

"Actually it sounds like a pretty normal reaction. Coming that close to death often inspires people to immediately reach for whatever makes them feel most alive. I think Afsarah would have understood," Chakotay said. "I know she would have."

"Do you think when all of this is truly behind us, those who served with her will remember her as a woman, or as the monster who brought us all within a hair's breadth of oblivion?"

"Those of us who knew her will remember the truth," Chakotay replied simply. "She held back the tide that should have swept away all of us."

Cambridge nodded. "That does seem the unfortunate destiny of the only two women who have ever commanded this ship," he observed. "Now I'm wondering if captain of *Voyager* is a significantly safer post than fleet commander."

Taken aback, Chakotay said, "I hadn't really thought of it that way."

"Don't, at least not for too long," Cambridge advised, rising from his seat. "Take comfort in the fact that as a man, your brute strength rivals that of the fairer sex of our species. Of course their capacity to endure is an awe-inspiring thing. It must be hardwired into their DNA, undoubtedly to allow them to survive childbirth and the nurturing of the young. If we weren't built to succumb to them so completely, and didn't require half their genetic code, we'd likely have burned them all as witches long before we had a chance to come to our senses."

"If this is you happy," Chakotay said, also leaving his seat and accompanying Cambridge to the door, "I'm not sure I ever want to see you truly miserable."

"It's a damned thin line, isn't it?" Cambridge asked as the door slid open and they crossed the threshold to whatever the new day held.

Epilogue

"My death was a fixed point in time."

"What does that even mean?"

Kathryn Janeway peered up at Chakotay through the dim light cast by the stars.

They maintained separate quarters, but they had not spent a single night apart since her return. She liked the way Chakotay held her as they slept, or as she struggled against the terrors that now populated her dreams. Usually the wee hours found them as they were now, comfortably intertwined as Kathryn tried to give form to her fears and he patiently beat them back with gentle words and tender caresses.

"It means the multiverse went out of its way to make sure I *wouldn't* be here now," she replied.

"Well, you sure showed the multiverse, didn't you?" Chakotay teased.

Kathryn smiled in spite of herself.

"Think of it this way," he went on. "You alone, among all of us, have a clean slate. No predetermined fate, or destiny, can claim you now. The future is whatever you choose to make of it."

"Can it really be that simple?" she asked.

"I think so."

"Really?"

"Maybe your death became what it was because the multiverse didn't want you here, in which case, I say, the multiverse can go kick rocks. Or maybe your death was its way of throwing up a bright red flag that your godson couldn't miss so that he would respond exactly as he did. I don't know anyone, other than you, who could have helped Afsarah hang on to her humanity. Your experience with the Borg was frighteningly similar to what she was going through. And I don't know anyone else who could have made Q understand why his son's death . . ."

"Maybe," Kathryn cut him off.

"Either way, it's no use trying to second-guess our decisions now. My mother used to say that the gods made the world round so that we could never see too far into our own future."

"You think if I'd seen my death coming I would have made a different choice?"

"No. You did see it coming. The Q showed up and told you exactly what was coming and you still marched right onto that cube to do your duty."

"And you climbed into that shuttle," she said, then added, "Is there something really wrong with us?"

Chakotay laughed lightly. "Not with us, maybe with our choice of professions." After a moment he asked seriously, "Why are you still hesitating to accept Starfleet Command's offer?"

Kathryn turned onto her stomach so that she could look into his eyes. "Because before I put us back essentially where we were, you commanding *Voyager* and me commanding the fleet, I want to make sure I know in my heart it's the right thing to do."

Chakotay's brow furrowed. After a moment he said, "No, that's not it."

"I beg your pardon, it most certainly is."

"No," he insisted. "You know the only way Command is going to allow us to continue our mission in the Delta Quadrant is if you endorse it by agreeing to lead this fleet. You and I are not the problem. We're never going to be the problem. For the first time in your life, you're considering playing it safe. You could send us home in the next few days, and right now, you're wondering why you shouldn't."

"I'm not wondering. You've lost five ships in five months, two fleet commanders, and more than eight hundred fifty officers and crewmen. All this at a time when Starfleet needs every single capable individual working night and day to hold the Federation together with both hands. We can't keep going through ships out here like we used to go through shuttles. Our benomite reserves are back in the Alpha Quadrant with the *Achilles,* and our slipstream drive is the only thing standing between us and another really long trip home. This isn't about a failure of nerve. It's an objective assessment of our current status weighed against the needs of the Federation."

"That's one way to look at it," Chakotay agreed.

"You have another?"

"Our first day back in the Delta Quadrant we rescued B'Elanna and Miral, saving Miral's life in the process. We then encountered a unique collective species with a most unexpected perspective on the Borg. I'm wondering how many other species in a similar position sustained themselves through thousands of years of the march of the Collective through their space. The answer to that isn't in the Alpha Quadrant. We reconfirmed our peaceful intentions toward Species 8472, and they're definitely worth keeping happy and on their side of fluidic space. We helped a collective species come to grips with their true history, but we still don't know how that story is going to end. We've provided New Talax with substantial material aid, enhancing their efforts to maintain a peaceful community. We brought solace to an ancient life-form whose thoughts had become sentient creatures bent on destroying the Borg, and then any complex life-form that approached its territory, teaching them in the process that creation is as worthy a goal as annihilation. We've barely scratched the surface of former Borg territory and while saving a small group of survivors from a hostile force also learned that the Caeliar transformation extended beyond the drones of the Collective. And a few days ago, we kept the universe from ending trillions of years before its time."

"I'm not negating your achievements by looking realistically at the costs associated with them," Kathryn insisted.

"You're thinking like an admiral and not like a starship captain."

"What does that mean?"

"You didn't join Starfleet to maintain the status quo. You joined to explore. The problem with focusing on the whole board is that it forces you to draw lines that don't truly exist. You want us on the front lines of the rebuilding effort. I'm saying the universe we inhabit got bigger over the last ten years. We're the front line now, Kathryn. It's not about the Alpha Quadrant anymore. It's about the galaxy. We can do more good for the Federation out here than we ever could at home by simply acknowledging that we are part of something much bigger than the planets that form our union. We don't get to pretend anymore that the Alpha and Beta Quadrants are the only areas that matter or that can strike at us whenever they please. We must move beyond our desire to live long and safe lives, even in the face of all we've lost, because our mission, our duty, to continually push the boundaries of our knowledge is what makes Starfleet worth serving and the Federation worth sustaining. *This*," he said, taking both her hands in his and squeezing them gently, "is who we are. This is what we do. This is what makes my death, your death, and the deaths of so many we loved worth bearing."

Kathryn lowered her gaze to their tangled hands and tenderly brushed her lips against his fingers. After a few quiet moments she said, "You've resigned from Starfleet not once but twice, and now you're defending its deepest ideals?"

"I see what it is, and what it can be. I'm ready to spend the rest of my life, and to lose it if necessary, making sure it rises to the new challenges now before it. For most of our lives together, we struggled with one impossible task: to get home. What I know now that I didn't know then is that we *are* home."

"I love you," Kathryn said simply.

"I like hearing you say that." Chakotay smiled.

"Good," Kathryn replied, resettling herself beside him, "because if we do this, we do it together."

"Get some sleep," he urged her as he pulled himself up and swung his legs over the side of the bed.

"Where are you going?" she demanded.

"I need to finish a letter."

"Now? To whom?"

"My sister," he replied. "I just realized what I needed to tell her."

"I'm so glad I could be of assistance," Kathryn grumbled.

"Sleep," he ordered her.

"Aye, sir," she replied, then warned, "And if you're not back in this bed in fifteen minutes . . ."

"You'll what?"

"You want to start out your first day under a really cranky new admiral of the fleet?"

"No, ma'am," he assured her.

Certain that the serenity descending on her could exist only where she had made peace with her choice, Kathryn Janeway closed her eyes, and slept.

Acknowledgments

Heather Jarman bears more responsibility than usual this time around, and not just because of her work with many of the characters that appear here or are referenced from her contribution to the *Star Trek: Voyager—String Theory* trilogy. Bringing this story into shape without her patient suggestions would never have happened. Finding the strength to persevere throughout one of the most arduous creative endeavors I have ever attempted is also a testament to the bravery with which she confronts every aspect of her life.

Mark Rademaker was, once again, invaluable and has my sincere gratitude. In addition, Christopher Bennett was his typical generous self with all manner of time travel tech and his creation of the Eridian vault.

I remain grateful as well to have been asked once again to take *Voyager*'s characters a little further on their journey by the good folks at Pocket Books.

The confidence to even attempt this one came largely from my favorite editor of all time, Marco Palmieri. Equally significant was the patient commiseration of my fellow writers, Dayton Ward, Kevin Dilmore, David Mack, and David R. George III, and the former editor of *Star Trek Magazine,* Paul Simpson.

My family and friends continue their support from afar. I've seen too little of all of them this year, and that's not their fault. Maura and Lynne remain my anchors as I seem to move daily through ever-shifting water.

My husband, David, lost me for six months to nights of constant writing. His sacrifices have not gone unnoticed, nor have the love and devotion he continues to lavish upon me. My daughter, Anorah, fills my days with the light that makes the long nights of work bearable.

I cannot help but fear that some will see this story as a failure of nerve, and others, most unwisely, as a vindication of the narrow constraints they would see put upon all Trek literature. Neither is true. This story, as much as those we have told up to this point, required telling. My greatest comfort lies in the fact that ultimately, I was the one chosen to tell it.